Witl

whose many book abethan architecture opened my mind and heart to these wonderful buildings and the people who built them.

Thank you.

From the Ground Up

A Robert Smythson Mystery

Katherine J. Scott

GLB

Glowing Log Books

This is a work of fiction. Characters, places, and events are the product of the author's imagination or are used fictitiously and are not to be construed as real. Any resemblance to events, locales, or organizations, or persons, living or dead, is entirely coincidental.

ISBN-979-8-9911267-1-7 paperback

ISBN-979-8-9911267-0-0 ebook

Library of Congress Control Number: 2024918198

Produced in the United States of America

Glowing Log Books, Austin TX

Contents

Chapter 1

Wiltshire, England
March 1568

Throughout England, wealthy men were building a new kind of house. In this time of peace and prosperity, there was no need for fortification or defense. Instead, they boldly stated their incontrovertible wealth and status through homes that faced outward, with large windows and great chambers and halls in which to entertain. Their ultimate goal: a house worthy of a visit by Her Majesty, Queen Elizabeth, and her court. Stonemason Robert Smythson was on his way to join the workforce at Longleat, where Sir John Thynne was building his legacy, a house that would proclaim his worth for generations to come.

Robert shifted in the saddle, nudging the horse faster. The ninety-mile trip from Caversham, near Reading, to Longleat, in Wiltshire, had been long and lonely. His friend, the Queen's Master

Mason, Humphrey Lovell, had warned him of Sir John Thynne's impatience, and here he was arriving late. If he didn't arrive soon, he might as well turn the horse around and return to Caversham, which wouldn't be the worst thing. His beloved Anne was still there. God's breath, he missed her already. All he had heard of Thynne had done nothing to increase his confidence. Demanding, uncompromising, and driven were some of the nicer words used to describe him. Still, Sir Francis Knollys had been clear: Robert's job as a stonemason at Caversham was over, at least while Knollys, one of Queen Elizabeth's closest advisers, was in the north, dealing with Mary, Queen of Scots.

The lane narrowed; dense growth cut off the early spring sunshine. Robert ducked his head to avoid another wet branch. A chill rushed through him, and he worried about the impression he would make. As he wondered if he would have time to change or at least wipe the worst of the mud away, the view opened, revealing a church and Corsley Manor, both built of brick. Robert slowed and took in the view. Sunshine fought with the clouds for full access to the sky. Birds flitted and swooped, arguing among themselves over the best places to build a nest and fighting for the longest twigs with which to build them.

Corsley Manor was Thynne's temporary home due to the fire that had destroyed Longleat the previous year. As Robert approached the manor, a stone gate caught his attention. He dismounted to get a closer look. Imposing and symmetrical, it did not resemble the building beyond it. Robert ran his hands along the pilasters to either side of the main arch, feeling the quality of the stone. He took in the detail of the entablature and the pediment that stood above the gate. A slight smile crept over his face as he saw the lion carved on the gate. Not shy about proclaiming his worth, was he? With its classical lines and symmetry, it represented the same kind of building he had seen at Somerset House in London. Robert could see the skill level that had made the gate, and his stomach sank. How could he compete with whoever had carved that?

"Who are you?" An old man stepped out from the shadows.

"Robert Smythson, new mason. Here to see Sir John Thynne."

"New mason, huh? Reckon he'll want to see you right away. I'll see your horse gets stabled; you go on to the house."

"Thank you." Robert tried to stamp the mud from his feet before handing the reins to the ancient retainer. "That way?" he asked, gesturing to the main building. "Should I ask for Sir John or someone else?"

"Don't think Cavell is here. Better go straight to Sir John."

Robert turned back to the main building and took a minute to appraise it, as he did to all buildings upon first seeing them. Corsley Manor had two stories plus generous attic gables. In form, it was quite traditional. Then Robert noticed the windows were squared off at their headers instead of the usual arch. A small style adjustment in an otherwise serviceable and pleasant manor house, but one lacking in both size and grandeur for a man of Thynne's stature and reputation.

Moments later, without an opportunity to clean the mud from his clothes and boots, a servant led Robert to Sir John Thynne's business chamber. In a dark-paneled room behind an enormous wooden desk sat Sir John, intently studying an accounts ledger. He was a thick-set man with a long face covered on top by receding dark hair and on the bottom by a full dark beard. His eyes were dark and glowering, covered by heavy brows, and his muscles bulged beneath a worn velvet doublet.

He looked up, flashed a dark glare of disapproval at the interruption, and turned his gaze to the newcomer. "The mason Robert Smythson. You've been expecting him." The servant hastily made the introduction, then fled, leaving Robert hovering in the doorway under Sir John's penetrating gaze.

"Smythson? Thought you'd be bigger. About time you arrived."

"Yes, Sir John." What was he agreeing with? He bowed before stepping forward and handing Sir John the letter of introduction he'd brought from Humphrey Lovell. "Here is the letter confirming the arrangements I believe have been agreed upon."

Sir John took the letter, scanned it quickly, and dropped it into the pile of documents on the desk. "You have driven quite a hard bargain at sixteen pence a day. You better be worth it. I expect a full day every day."

"I . . . trust you won't . . . be disappointed," Robert stammered.

"Not many men would expect such generous treatment. But Lovell, as well as Sir Francis Knollys, have recommended you. I expect you to live up to their recommendations. Get to work quickly. Is your team here yet?" Thynne spat out his sentences in rapid succession without allowing a response. Robert listened in stunned silence. Answers were not expected. Questions were commands with no room for disagreement.

"No, sir. I expect them within a few days, although there may have been some delay." Robert replied carefully, treading lightly between respect and truth. "With the recent rains, the roads are muddy, and the carts have a hard time."

"There is always mud. It should be planned for. No more delays, Smythson. Make haste. I want progress. Get your team settled and working quickly. The masons here are too slow and have no leader. Their work is miserable, not worthy of Longleat. I expect you to get them into shape before your team gets here. Boy!" Thynne yelled past Robert, and the servant reentered. "Send someone down to get Cavell."

"Yes, Sir John," the boy replied, scurrying out.

While Sir John's attention was with the servant, Robert had looked around the room. Paneled walls were covered with maps; scrolls and ledgers were piled on every surface. Near the window, Robert spotted a small wooden model of a compact square building. He moved toward it, transfixed. There, in wood, was what the masons would soon try to achieve in stone and mortar.

"Ah, you've found the model," Thynne said, stepping out from behind his desk. "Longleat. Or what she will be. What do you think?"

Robert walked slowly around the structure, inspecting it from each angle. The future Longleat was there, compact, symmetrical, and imposing. The design was traditional, with gables and turrets, but there was a pleasing emphasis on symmetry and uniformity. Robert was equally moved by the design of the building and the model itself. He had heard that craftsmen in France and Italy often made one, a miniature representation of the structure to be built. "It's amazing. I've heard of these models, but I've never seen one."

"It's the first one of its kind to be made in England," Sir John said, lifting his chin and gesturing toward the model. "I've designed a masterpiece, haven't I?"

Still engrossed in his study, Robert didn't respond. It made so much sense to take this middle step. To see in whole what you were working on in piecemeal long before you had completed it was like getting a glimpse into the future.

"Speechless?" Sir John laughed. "It is impressive, and it's your job to translate this vision into reality."

"Sir John, are the plans for Longleat all yours?" Robert asked. "They are quite complex and involve many specifics that are usually only known to master craftsmen."

"Do you doubt my abilities?" Thynne's eyes narrowed as he fixed his gaze on his new mason. A stillness settled in the room as he waited for Robert's answer to his challenge.

"I believe Humphrey Lowell mentioned he had some hand in the designs."

"Smythson, the plans are mine! Mine alone!" Sir John snapped. "I learned all there is to know about building: masonry, carpentry, and other skills when I oversaw the design and building of Somerset House."

"Yes, Sir John. I understand." Robert understood that the conversation was finished, although he still had his doubts about the origin of the plans.

"Good. I have hired you to execute my plans. There will be no alterations, no modifications without my knowledge and consent. I trust that is clear."

Robert was saved from replying as the door opened and a tall, thin man carrying a brown leather pouch overflowing with sheaves of papers and parchments entered. "Sir John?"

"Cavell, there you are. This is Robert Smythson, the mason. Richard Cavell, my steward. He'll see to what you need. Be quick about it, Cavell. We're already behind schedule."

"Smythson, welcome. We're glad you're here."

"Never mind all that," Sir John cut him off. "Take him away, show him the lodgings and the masons lodge with the tracing room. Make sure he has the plans. After dinner, I'll take him down to Longleat myself and show him what he's to do."

As the two junior men turned to leave, Sir John added, "Does Maynard know of his arrival yet? Probably not too happy to hear that a man of Smythson's promise has come to unseat him." Sir John chuckled to himself. "It won't do him any harm to feel a little pressure. He puffs himself up and struts like a peacock, just because he's French and thinks he's the only one who can translate his precious French designs. Let's see what Smythson can do. No more delays or excuses this time."

Robert followed Richard Cavell to the steward's office, a cramped space with barely enough room for the two men to maneuver and a ceiling so low Cavell had to maintain a hunched position just to fit. Cavell sorted through the stack of papers on his desk, a smaller version of the one in Sir John's chamber, and pulled out some parchments, handing them to Robert. "These are the plans for the new Longleat," he said, clearing a space on a bench and indicating that Robert should sit down before taking a seat himself behind the desk.

Robert studied the plans intensely, the hint of a smile dancing across his face. Looking up, he noticed he was being watched. "I'm sorry. I was being rude. Humphrey Lovell did not have a copy of the plans, so today was the first I've seen of them. That model was impressive."

"That's quite all right. I enjoyed watching your reaction. The model is usually in Thynne's chamber, but it can be moved if you need to study it alongside the drawn plans. Adrian Gaunt, our head joiner, made it. He's also from France," Cavell said.

Robert understood that the "also" referred to Alan Maynard. "May I ask you exactly what the situation is with Alan Maynard?" Robert had heard of Maynard, and his presence in the area was one attraction of coming to Longleat, although Robert did not admit this aloud.

"No doubt you have heard he is a gifted sculptor, and he is." Cavell hesitated, pulling at his scraggly beard. "He can also be hard to work with, proud and arrogant. He frequently clashes with Sir John, and at the moment Maynard is out of favor and working elsewhere. His disgrace—or misfortune—is your gain."

"Excuse me, but does that mean that if Maynard and Sir John mend their differences and he returns, my services won't be needed?" Robert let the plans for the new building slip out of his hands as he thought of all the people he had uprooted based on long-term employment expectations.

"Relax," Cavell said. "I know what you're thinking. You've seen for yourself how impatient Sir John is to make use of your talents. You will be here for quite some time, if your skills live up to what we've been promised." He leaned back and sighed. "I'm going to tell you what Sir John won't. Both Sir Francis Knollys and Humphrey Lovell have told Sir John that you're one of the most talented masons they've ever seen, with the vision and sense of perfectionism that will turn Longleat into the masterpiece Thynne wants. They've also led him to believe he's getting a mason who understands how to work for an important man. I hope you won't let us down. We're counting on you to make good progress and take the pressure off the rest of us."

This description in no way eased Robert's reservations about what he had agreed to, but again Cavell seemed to sense his thoughts and reassured him. "Don't worry. There's enough work to be done at Longleat for two teams of talented masons. Sir John may have thoughts of using you to put pressure on Maynard. Lord knows those two dance around each other like dogs sizing each other up before a fight. I'm caught in the middle, trying to do what's best for Longleat. We plan on having you and Maynard lead separate teams. At least that's the plan after your presence causes Maynard to come crawling back and agree to Thynne's terms simply out of curiosity to see the new competition." Cavell grinned, and Robert thought he was enjoying the prospect. "And then Longleat will have two of the best masons in all of England. She will only benefit from that." He stood up and ushered Robert from the room. "Come, let us eat, and then we can go down to Longleat so you can get your first glimpse of your future."

Once the midday meal, a rushed and crowded affair, was over, Robert followed Sir John and Cavell from Corsley Manor to the building site at Longleat. Although it was only a couple of miles, the lanes looked like those Robert had traveled on for several days, bordered by hedgerows, overlooking fields or woodlands, now and again a house or cottage. Robert tried to remember the way, but the roads all began to look alike. It took most of his concentration to keep up with Sir John, who set a brisk pace.

Eventually, Sir John pulled up and gestured toward a large open space, a shallow valley surrounded by gentle wooded hills. As they approached from the north, Robert shook himself alert. In the middle of the generous plain stood Longleat House, or rather, where it would be. It looked more like a pile of burned-out rubble than a manor house.

"I remember the day I first saw Longleat, surveying the dissolved Carthusian priory along with Edward Seymour, although it was before the old king died and Seymour became Lord Protector of England. It was he who encouraged me to buy Longleat. I built Bedwyn and Somerset House for him and took everything I learned there and applied it here for my benefit. I've been designing and building this magnificent house since 1546. By God, I went to the Tower for that man; he owed me as much. But you see how I not only escaped his fate, but I will outlast his memory as well. The Thynne family will outlast him and outbuild him."

Originally, Thynne had simply modified some of the existing buildings, adding a tower, removing some features and adding others. Thynne's vision of symmetry had begun here. Later, he added a wing of six rooms, expanded the existing hall, and eventually added two more wings, on the east and north sides, to expand the building to a complete square. But in April of 1567, a fire destroyed the entire building, sending the Thynne family back to Corsley Manor and Sir John back to the design phase.

Robert could make out the remains of the old structure. Walls stood at various heights in a rough rectangle, bifurcated by an interior wall, creating a courtyard space. The tops of the walls had all been pulled down, suggesting the fire may have started on an upper story. Or perhaps this was because of the stylistic changes Thynne was now considering.

Robert felt Sir John watching him as they closed in on the building. "There it is. We've cleared most of it. The men have set aside any stone that might be reusable," Sir John said. "What do you think of the site?" Rather than waiting for an answer, Sir John turned his attention to a few men working halfheartedly with shovels. "You there," Sir John yelled at the men. "This is your boss, Smythson, the new mason. He'll soon have you in shape. No more half efforts or I'll dock your pay. Understood?" The men nodded, looked back and forth from Robert to Sir John before resuming their work with renewed vigor.

"You've seen the plans, and you've seen the place. Get those walls started as quickly as possible. Cavell will see to what you need. You'll report to him or directly to me if need be. Understood? And get to the quarry quickly to ensure the stones will be ready. Get to it. Cavell, I want him settled and working by tomorrow. If I'm paying him, he needs to be productive." With those parting words, Sir John turned his horse and rode back toward Corsley Manor.

Once Sir John left and Robert's head stopped spinning from all the conflicting instructions, Robert walked toward the site, imagining what the earlier building had looked like, piecing the shape together from the remains and the lines.

"We've already cleared away quite a lot of the worst of it," Cavell said. "Some of that stone Sir John is hoping to reuse. One thing we're hoping you can do is to determine what is reusable and what isn't. If it were up to him, he would reuse the lot to save money."

"The biggest issue with stone that has been in a fire is discoloration. That's usually noticeable, but not a problem. If that's the case, we can reuse the stone for some internal purposes. More dangerous would be any structural issues." Robert leaned down, picking up a piece of charred stone. The smell of burnt limestone immediately pulled him back in time, to the hissing and sparks of the flames, the heat, the feeling of being trapped. He froze, reliving the feeling of helplessness as he watched the flames engulf the room where his sister was. He dropped the stone, shaking his head to return to the present.

"Are you all right, Robert? You look like you've seen a ghost."

"In some ways, I have. There was a fire in our house when I was a youth. Seeing these remains, well, it's all coming back to me. We lost everything, including my sister." He didn't tell Cavell that it had been his fault his sister had died.

"I'm sorry, Robert. I didn't know. As I said, we were very fortunate. No one was badly injured or killed."

"Lovell mentioned that. I think he wanted to reassure me. It was years ago, but the memory resurfaces sometimes." Robert took several steps away from the rubble and the memories. "What can you tell me about the fire?"

Cavell paused before answering. "Not much. It was last April, almost eleven months ago now. It started in the middle of the night. The family awoke when the smoke got too thick, but by then it was too late to save the place. It burned all day. We had no provisions, no plans in place to put out a fire. Perhaps that's my fault. With Sir John always demanding speed, sometimes those types of things aren't done as well as they should be. Fortunately, no one was hurt, just the building."

"Does anyone know how it started?"

"No."

"Did Sir John not want it investigated? Was it an accident, or could someone have deliberately set it?"

Cavell hesitated, sighing before replying, "There was a general inquiry, but not a full investigation. I assume it was an accident since there was no obvious evidence that it was not."

The two men had been walking the perimeter, now coming to the south wall. Robert picked up a piece of stone lying loose on the ground and held it up to the light. "This was good stone. But it can't be used now, except as filler. I would think Sir John would want to know how the work of so many years was destroyed, wouldn't you?"

"I have learned that it's best not to question Sir John if you want a peaceful life. I think he wants to look forward and not back. As soon as the fire cooled, he gave orders for the clean up to begin and immediately went to work on designs for the replacement. Designs we're hoping you can bring to fruition."

It seemed that Cavell, like Sir John, wanted to look forward and not back, so Robert dropped the subject and continued his study of the site. He studied the plans Cavell had given him, going from plans to site and back. Already, he could see the potential Lovell had promised him. There was something that bothered him, but he couldn't name it. Too much chaos at the site and too much noise in his head. It would come to him. Over the years, he had come to trust his instinct with lines and stones. If something felt off, it usually found its way to the surface of his mind later. In the meantime, the sun was making its way down the sky, and it was time to think about lodging for the night. There would be time enough for the real work to begin tomorrow.

Chapter 2

Robert followed Cavell north to Corsley Heath, a small hamlet between Corsley Manor and Longleat, where many of Longleat's labor force lived in cottages or small houses, some with gardens or a few acres of crops behind. Cavell pointed out workshops used by blacksmiths, carpenters, and the like, and the local alehouse, all surrounding the small village square.

"The few junior masons here are badly in need of leadership, as are the ones out at the quarry. Before the fire, Maynard had already gone with most of his men; others drifted off later, so there are plenty of lodgings available for your team," Cavell said. "And here's the large masons lodge."

Robert walked into a large thatched cottage with a generous loft. "There's another workshop nearer to Longleat, which Maynard and the junior masons used," explained Cavell as Robert walked around the space. "This one is closer to Sir John at Corsley Manor, so perhaps you should use it initially, at least while you are consulting with him frequently."

Robert's heart sank as he looked around the dust and clutter in the masons lodge in the late afternoon light. So many people were depending on him to quickly turn this chaos into order. And chaos it was. There were workbenches in disrepair, so rickety they would never hold up to heavy use. Pieces of stone littered the floor, the finishing half-done. Robert picked up a dusty chisel and tested it. Blunt. He moved on to another, equally blunt, and set it next to the first. "It certainly needs a good cleaning, but I suppose it will do."

Robert climbed the ladder to the loft and was pleasantly surprised by the airiness and light coming into the space. A large section of the room was set up as a tracing floor, where thin coats of plaster were used as a blank canvas to trace large templates. There were several windows in the walls and thatch, letting in good light. "The upper level is much better," he told Cavell. "In fact, if you can have someone bring in a bed, I think I'll use this as my lodging space for now."

"Are you sure?" Cavell asked. "As master mason, you're entitled to a house for yourself. I've got several I can show you."

"No, this is sufficient for now. I want to be close to everything, and I don't want to be fussing with extra land. Perhaps at a later date," Robert's voice trailed off as he wondered if he'd ever get up the nerve to ask Anne to join him.

Together, the two picked small cottages for his team. One would serve the brothers Edward and Valentine Merser, along with Edward's wife and children. Another would do for the three Johns: Hills, King, and Hodgkyns. Once they settled on the lodgings, Cavell led Robert into the local alehouse, the Royal Oak, where Robert had a hasty meal before ending the day.

Cavell had offered him a bed in Corsley Manor, but Robert was anxious for some time alone. Between the traveling and all the new people and places, he wanted some quiet and space to clear his head. Someone had hastily brought in a pallet and torches and swept out the upstairs. Robert thought he would collapse into a deep sleep from exhaustion, but instead he stared at the dark ceiling, playing over the previous day in his mind.

Arriving at Longleat, he had felt ready to meet the new challenges set before him, but the welcome he had received made him unsure. Despite the warnings of Lovell and others, he hadn't been prepared for the cold, brisk manner of Sir John, especially after the warm and easy relationship he had enjoyed with Sir Francis. He pushed away his disappointment, reminding himself that Cavell was more approachable and would be the person he dealt with more frequently. Sir John's steward had an air of long suffering about him, but also a wry humor, which was promising.

Questions circled as his body stopped fighting the exhaustion and fell asleep. Sleep was fitful, full of dreams of Anne. Finally, he got out of bed, walking over to the window and looking up at the sky. He never slept well, and apparently Longleat would be no different. Somewhere to the east, under the same sky, Anne slept. Or he hoped she did. Or was it possible that she too was awake, looking out at the sky and thinking of him?

Anne Palmer, daughter of Edward Palmer, a religious scholar and tutor for Sir Francis's children, had been a member of the Knollys household for several years. Despite having no official position, she was valued as much for her sweet temper and gentle spirit as she was her skill with a needle. She was a particular favorite of Sir Francis's wife, Lady Catherine Knollys. Lady Catherine was not only the Queen's cousin but also served Her Majesty as Chief Lady of the Bedchamber and was often in attendance at court. Anne's father had resisted attempts by Lady Catherine to elevate his daughter at court, preferring that she remain with him. Between their many duties and their affection for both father and daughter, the Knollyses had stopped trying to convince him to see to his daughter's best interests.

Despite his deep feelings for Anne, Robert had been reluctant to pursue this relationship. He was merely a craftsman, while she was the daughter of an educated man and member of a great household. Anne seemed at home in a room hung with tapestries and lined with bookshelves, while he was more accustomed to unfinished buildings, masonry workshops, and quarries. He had previously raised the issue with Anne, but she continually assured him that her father was simply a poor man trying to do the work of the Lord and that she was only a part of the Knollys household out of their affection for her father. She appeared to enjoy spending time with a mason, a man who frequently smelled of sweat and was covered with dust.

He looked down at his hands and remembered one evening when Anne had offered to help Robert with his tools. He had been meeting with Sir Francis at the Knollys family home, Greys Court, and had done some repair work to a damaged gateway while he was there. Anne had visited him and remained once the work was done. Robert had looked down at his heavy tools, covered with dust and chips of stone, and the rags he used to wipe them down. Then he'd looked at her hands, soft, delicate, and small. He had followed his impulse to reach out and take one of her hands. It was as soft as he had imagined. It looked even more delicate lying in his large, dirty hand. The hands of a mason grew older than the man himself. It was impossible to avoid injury when you were learning the craft, and you carried the scars with you always. "No," he had replied. "I don't need you to hurt these beautiful hands. You help me just by giving me your company."

It was true. Time was sweeter when spent with her. Her graceful appearance reminded him of an unblemished piece of marble. Robert thought about the conflict he felt when starting to work on a new flawless piece of stone: excitement and anticipation about what it would become, fearful that he might make a mistake and permanently mar its perfection. Robert understood this conflict and had allowed fear to caution his movements, as he did now with Anne. He enjoyed each moment with her, greedy for more, but cautious lest rushing things would wreck them.

Robert had not asked her to go with him. He had no family left. Not since the fire and his father's accident. He would not, could not, ask her to abandon her father. Now, thinking about the lukewarm reception he had received at Corsley Manor, he understood he had made the right decision. That thought darkened his future more than any promise of building could brighten it. Longleat, as it was now, was not suitable for his precious Anne. There was no comfort, no society worthy of her.

It was more than that; he was unworthy of such a treasure as Anne, regardless of what Longleat might be like. Her position was too high. He had tried, in his awkward way, to say as much, but she had protested.

"Robert, you make me sound like Lady Catherine. I am only a poor man's daughter. I have no position, no rank, no real future."

"No, Anne. Do not say that about yourself. You know Lady Catherine wants to give you a position at court. How could I ask you to give that up to come with me? I can't."

She had gently rested her hand on his arm. "You know I do not care for court. But I cannot leave my father." And he would not ask her to do that. Not after how he had lost his. They had left it at that. An embrace, a lingering of her hand in his, a quick pressing of his lips on her delicate flesh. The memory of it made his heart ache. Perhaps Lovell was right and Longleat would be the start of a brilliant career, one that would enable him to return and claim Anne as his own. Until then, all he could do was adjust to his new environment.

The next day was almost as disappointing as the first. Robert put the junior masons to work cleaning out the masons lodge and tracing room. He watched as they awkwardly shifted things around, not understanding what he wanted. Robert knew that Sir John would not approve; he would see this as wasted time. But Robert was in charge now, and this was his way of establishing authority with the younger masons. The real work could wait until his team arrived. Until then, they would sharpen their tools, organize their workspace, and get to know one another. Robert felt his stress decreasing as they left a workshop Humphrey Lovell would not despair of and found their midday meal delivered as arranged.

They spent the rest of the day visiting the mortar pits, visiting with the other craftsman responsible for other aspects of the construction, and making another visit to Longleat. It was an afternoon of disappointments for Robert, and he tried to hold on to the progress they had made in the morning.

Fortunately, the next day his team arrived. After a happy reunion, moving the equipment, and getting them settled in their lodgings, he explained about the two masons lodges. Robert could not explain exactly why, but he was reluctant to take over the one closest to Longleat. It had been Maynard's headquarters, and Robert felt an uneasiness coming from the younger masons whenever they used it. Since his team would be living in Corsley Heath, Robert decided the lodge there should be their primary one, with the lodge closer to Longleat used only when necessary.

Robert was especially happy to see John Hills. Hills was an older mason, a burly man with a broad face and deep voice. His reddish hair was thinning but still held a curl. He had worked for Sir John when he was much younger. Hills had also been part of the crew at Winchester, where an accident had cost the lives of Robert's father and brother and left Hills with a limp. As Robert had virtually no family left, Hills acted as a close friend and father figure to him.

"I'm glad to have you here, John," Robert said in the evening as the team assembled in the Royal Oak, the new and old craftsmen eyeing each other with a mixture of curiosity and relief. Robert had already picked up on the general feeling of anticipation in the neighborhood. He was the man expected to take charge, meet Sir John's demands, and shelter them from Sir John's wrath.

"How are you finding Thynne?" Hills asked Robert.

"Impatient for progress, demanding."

Hills laughed. "That's Thynne. I believe you're up for the challenge. Do you?"

"I appreciate your faith in me." It was good to spend time with someone who he knew well and knew understood him. Over the years at Caversham, he and Hills had grown to trust and respect one another. Now, sitting in the tavern's corner, Robert felt he could relax for the first time since he had left Knollys's employment. "I'm not sure Sir John understands everything that is involved before we can make visible progress. Things here are a mess, with no one in charge. The stones may be ready, but the state of the mortar pits is appalling. At this time of year, there should be a good supply of finished and aged mortar waiting to be used, prepared in the fall and left to age over the winter. Instead, it's been completely neglected, putting our entire schedule behind. Without it, we can move nothing into place. Sir John won't like that."

"No, he won't. Never mind. We're all here now; things will start to happen. There's one thing I've seen that I don't like."

"Only one?" Robert quipped.

"Well, you said it yourself, the site is a mess, a mixture of damaged and new stone, half-built walls, no organization. But no, I'm not worried about that. We'll soon have it put to rights. What I don't like is your choice of lodging. You were hired as master mason. You should have the nicest house of all the craftsmen; you should not be bunking in a room over the masons lodge. What possessed you to make such a choice?"

Robert shrugged, becoming fascinated with the bottom of his mug, as if he could find the answer there. "Did Anne say anything after I left?"

"Anne Palmer? No, there was no word. I don't think anyone went up to Greys Court after you left. We had enough to worry about packing up our belongings and tools."

Robert tried to hide his disappointment.

"Sorry," Hills said. "Is that what this is about? You should be using your position here to make a home worthy of her, not hiding out licking your wounds."

Robert replied to this advice with a wounded look, revealing that the elder mason had hit his mark. Robert changed the subject, lowering his voice and leaning closer to Hills. "What do you know about a French mason named Alan Maynard?"

"Maynard? Don't think I've met him, but I've heard of him, as I'm sure you have. Brilliant sculptor by reputation. Why?"

"He's done a lot of the work here that was destroyed in the fire. Apparently still lives nearby."

"Have you met him?"

"No, but I've heard he keeps up with the happenings at Longleat. The masons here are reluctant for me to take over his workshop. They act as if he still has some influence here."

"What does Cavell say?"

"Nothing much. It seems unresolved." Robert sighed. "Also, I noticed this afternoon that the rubble seems to be thicker on the north wall."

"The north range was the most recently completed, I think," Hills remarked, filling his mug again from the pitcher of ale.

"There's something off with the angle as well, where the north range meets the east. I've measured it, but it just feels off to me. And the masons want to keep clear of the whole north side, but no one will say why. They've taken down the gables, but I think Sir John is hoping to keep the walls."

"I don't like the idea."

"Nor do I. It will mean further delay, but you know as well as I do that once stone has burned, you don't know the effects of the damage. If Sir John wants to put those banqueting houses on the roof, I think we should pull it down and start again. I'm just not sure how to tell him. Lord's mercy, it's good to have you and the team here."

Over the next couple of days, Robert was busy coordinating the efforts of his team with the junior masons and laborers who were already at Longleat when he had arrived. The younger masons continued preparing the lime mortar while the more experienced men from Robert's team were examining and testing the stones that remained from the fire. Robert's men understood his standards, and it was not surprising that few pieces were good enough to be reused. Some were acceptable for interior pieces that other bricks and stones would cover, but if there was any question about their structural integrity, Robert had them removed. It might cost more to replace, but less than it would to repair or recover from an accident. He knew it would take time for everyone to work together as a cohesive unit and he understood he was being watched and evaluated by everyone. The days were long and exhausting, but the challenge kept him focused.

At night, he stared at the moon from the small window in the tracing room turned bedchamber. He often had trouble sleeping once he had gotten over the initial physical rest his body required. He would awaken in the early morning hours and draw or build in his mind. Once his brain was engaged in a building problem, sleep was over for the night. Robert had asked for and received copies of the plans for the building that had burned. Now, in the dim light of a small fire, he studied the plans he had received from Cavell and the ones he had drawn himself and waited for the sun to come up. Running his fingers through his hair, he leaned over the drawings again and sighed.

Two images rose in Robert's mind: the symmetry and proportion of Somerset House and the wooden model Gaunt had made for Longleat. Before he had come to Longleat, Robert had visited Somerset House with his mentor, Humphrey Lovell. The building was unexpectedly simple. No trace of Gothic ornament, just clean lines and a pleasing flow and balance. The evolution of Sir John's desire for symmetry had started there, and he had brought it to the new Longleat. What made them both so beautiful was the wholeness, the complete unity of the two buildings.

Robert thought about how hard it was to achieve balance and symmetry when you started with something already in existence and added on. The very nature of the many years that Sir John had worked on Longleat meant it had evolved rather than risen as a cohesive whole. How many master masons, each with their own styles, temperaments, attention to quality, had touched the building? The enormity and privilege of what Robert was being asked to do dawned on him.

The conflicting pressures of time versus quality pushed and shoved against each other in the early morning hours, dredging up old memories. Standing as a young apprentice in front of a building where a cornice was about to be attached to an upper story. The angles had been all wrong. His brain had felt fuzzy, off, as he'd stared at the balance of the scaffolding and the heavy piece of stone. He had tried to tell his father something wasn't right, but his father had just dismissed him. "You spend all your time just staring at the stone. You don't hold the chisel with your eyes, son, but with your hands. Get a move on." Robert remembered the sickening feeling in his stomach as he'd watched the scaffolding collapse and his father fall, how his feet had stayed planted, unable to move, his father's last words full of critique and scorn. It made no difference that Robert had been right.

Remembering the balance of Somerset House and comparing it with what he had seen at Longleat, he knew the solution, but he also suspected he knew the reaction to his suggestion. Would being right matter this time? There was no life on the line, just the perfection of a building and a schedule. Robert knew Sir John wanted speed, but would he be willing to sacrifice quality? He could imagine Sir John's frustration at the destruction of all those years of work and planning. It made him understand Sir John's impatience. Understanding helped, but it did not make it easier for Robert to stomach what he was about to suggest.

By midmorning, Robert stood with Cavell near the north wall, struggling to find the courage to speak. He stalled, bringing up the design of the building before making his recommendation. "It's odd that Sir John opted for a full square, not the E shape that is so popular nowadays, is it not?"

"Sir John has no desire to play to the monarch as other men do," replied Cavell. "He had his fill of power years ago. Sir John wasn't always a titled man. He started out as a steward, like me, serving the Duke of Somerset before his disgrace, when his head was still attached," Cavell laughed. "Sir John helped him dissolve the monasteries. He's shrewd and hardworking and expects others to be as well. He worked his way up, taking advantage of every opportunity. But not without cost. During Somerset's fall, Sir

John was imprisoned twice in the Tower. He got as close to the flame as he wanted and got scorched. Now he prefers to remain a safe distance away from the fire of politics and court life." Robert turned the words over in his mind and thought it odd that Cavell would choose a fire metaphor when speaking of Sir John. Was that coincidental, or was there a hidden meaning behind the words?

Now, however, he focused on the problem at hand. "Cavell, I've been thinking . . ."

"Yes?"

"I know Sir John wanted to save as much work as possible from before the fire, but I'm not sure that's the best plan of action. How do you think he would react if I suggested we pull everything down and start afresh?" Robert already knew the answer but asked anyway. This would mean a significant delay. Sir John would not be happy.

Cavell shook his head. "Frankly, I'm not surprised. Longleat has needed someone to oversee the entire process for some time. Maynard, when he was here, was a good sculptor, but he wasn't concerned with the overall process of putting together the house. This is further proof of our need for you. Sir John won't like the delay, but get it done right."

Robert hoped Cavell would volunteer to break the news to Sir John, but Cavell was firm. "This is your job. It's your suggestion; it's for you to take the blame or credit. Besides, it might be difficult for me to explain exactly what needs to be done." Robert knew he was right, but that didn't make the prospect any more pleasant.

Chapter 3

Robert made his way through the narrow and dimly lit passageway to Sir John's business chamber in Corsley Manor, rehearsing what he would say. His palms were sweating, and his hands trembled. He tried to steady himself, telling himself he was right. Did being right matter? Sir John was not the type of man to thank the messenger of bad news. His steps slowed as he heard yelling coming from within.

"I can't get my spring planting done!" an unknown voice bellowed. "There's no labor available. Everyone I've used in the past is over at your precious Longleat, hauling stone."

"It's my fault no one will work for you? Listen to yourself, you old fool!" Sir John replied. Robert could almost picture the sneer on his face.

"I would have thought you would respect the traditions of the community. There has always been an agreement that the neighborhood would share the laborers during times of planting and harvest. Respecting tradition would go a long way to legitimize your presence in the region."

"My presence, as you call it, is plenty legitimate. I've been here for years. Perfectly good money bought this land."

"Bought? You stole it! From its rightful owners: God and the true Church!"

"Watch it, Kington. Words like that can get you into trouble. You never know who's listening."

Kington. Robert thought he remembered Cavell mentioning a man by that name. He was the owner of Cley Hill Farm, Sir John's closest neighbor that wasn't leasing their land from Longleat. Was Kington a papist? Perhaps, although Robert thought he had seen the man at church. Robert knew there were still some followers of the old religion around, their beliefs tolerated as long as their outward behavior conformed.

Robert wondered if he should make his presence known. He coughed loudly and rapped on the door.

"See, someone was listening." Sir John laughed as Robert entered the room. "Oh, it's you, Smythson. Are you going to report our neighbor Kington here to the authorities for being a Catholic sympathizer?"

Robert looked from one to the other. Both men stood, facing one another, Sir John's big desk between them. Despite being close in age, the two men were very different in appearance. While Sir John was well filled out, neatly groomed, and decently dressed, Kington appeared haggard. His long, scraggly beard was streaked with gray. His cheeks were sunken, and a sallow complexion was visible despite the fury now displayed on his face. Sir John's expression appeared equal parts mirth and impatience. Not the mood Robert had hoped to find his employer in. "I . . . hadn't . . . planned on it," Robert stammered. "Wanted to talk to you about the north range," he paused, trying to find his courage, "but if this isn't a good time . . ."

"No, no, something I actually care about. Kington, our business is finished. If you want the men to work for you, try paying them more." Sir John snorted. "I wouldn't get your hopes up. See yourself out. Now, what's this all about, Smythson?"

Kington glared at Sir John, then stormed out, letting the heavy door close with a thud. Robert jumped at the noise. "That encounter didn't seem friendly," Robert observed.

"Kington's never happy. I don't care," Sir John said with a sigh, taking his seat. "He's a local farmer who always has a grievance of some kind or other. Today, he complained about all the traffic driving past his farm, saying the noise of the carts is upsetting his cows' milking. As if I care. You heard him whining about a lack of laborers to help with his farm. Not my problem! Nothing I do is ever good enough for him. He's even pestered me about his daughter marrying my son for several years now. As if I would let my son attach himself to such a nobody, even if he was old enough to marry, which he isn't."

Robert tried to take this in. Or perhaps he was just putting off what he had come to discuss. "If he dislikes you so much, it's odd that he would consider marrying his daughter into your family."

Sir John shot Robert a look, then chuckled. "You're quick to grasp the truth of it. He only complains if he can't weasel his way in. He failed, as usual. The ironic part is that rumor has it she ran off with a mason."

"What? A mason? Who?" If a local landowner's daughter could marry a mason, why not Anne?

"Don't know. Doesn't matter. Someone who left with Maynard. Now, what did you come to see me about?"

It was hard for Robert to leave this topic, but he knew Sir John had moved on. Now was not the time or place to pursue the story of Kington's daughter. He pulled out his drawings and stammered through his thought process.

"Between the delay in the mortar pits and the risk of further damage caused by possible imperfection . . . To pull the existing wall down . . . While it would require extra work . . . We can't add new stone until the mortar has had time to mature . . ."

Sir John listened, watching Robert with a furrowed brow. "Whose fault is it that the mortar isn't ready?"

"I don't know, but it isn't. With no one overseeing the entire process, it wasn't thought of. But why not use the wait to ensure that the building is completely symmetrical and balanced?"

"How do I know this isn't a ploy to get more money from me? To delay, stretch things out, just to add to your own purse?"

"It's not. It's not about money; it's about quality." Robert paused, trying to gather his nerves. "I thought you were after perfection. Let's not reuse any stone that may be damaged." He walked to the model and gestured toward it. "This. And Somerset House. There's an opportunity to do something special with this building. The balance, the symmetry. I can't explain it. I feel it. I sense what you're trying to do when I look at the model and the plans. A restfulness or tranquility. But I don't see it or feel it at the site. Something's off there. The proportions aren't right, and it has something to do with the north range. It's more than just the rubble and chaos. It's more than just damage from the fire. There's something off about the angle. I know it sounds odd to align a wall with the sky or the position of the sun or a tree line, but I feel like it's just off." Robert looked down, then looked at Sir John for the first time. "I want to move it."

Sir John rose to meet Robert, but Robert was in too deep now. He paced in front of Gaunt's model, his passion building his courage. "If you want perfection, a unified whole, a statement and a structure that will remain to proclaim your worth and legacy long after both you and I are gone, then you need to start from the ground up. Clear it all out and start fresh."

Sir John stared at him, anger and amusement jostling for dominance in his eyes. Then he tossed his quill onto the desk, splattering ink, lowered his sizable frame into his chair, threw his head back, and made a sound that might have been a laugh. "There it is! Finally, we see a glimpse of the mason Lovell promised me. Lovell said you would do this. He said you had the best eye and best gut in the business and that you would say things that wouldn't make sense but that I should trust you. Assured me you were the man for the job, someone who cared for perfection as much as I did. So be it. Do it. But mind you, be quick about it! Make haste! I'll need a revised schedule within two days. If I think you're dawdling, you'll hear about it."

"Yes, Sir John, of course." Robert left quickly before Sir John could change his mind.

Robert leaned against the dim passageway wall, giving his heart a chance to slow down and climb down out of his throat and settle into its usual position. He had fully expected Sir John to command him to pack up and leave, taking his crazy ramblings with him, dismissed with a wave of the hand, just as easily and thoughtlessly as Kington had been.

Now it was Robert's turn to laugh as a mixture of relief and disbelief gurgled up inside him. He was unsure what was more astounding: that he had spoken his mind or that Sir John had listened and agreed. He allowed himself to exhale deeply, trying to quiet the trembling he still felt. Then he heard Sir John chuckle behind the heavy oak door and decided he should get away quickly before Sir John reconsidered.

Robert was about to ride through the gate at Corsley Manor when he saw Kington leaning over the gate, studying the stone. Robert dismounted and approached. "I see nothing special about it, other than it being of stone and not brick," Kington said to Robert. "That Maynard fellow worked it. He's supposed to be some kind of genius, but it looks like a gate to me."

"It's to do with the symmetry and also the classic motif," Robert replied. "It's quite remarkable. Robert Smythson, by the way. I don't think we've officially met."

"Henry Kington. You're the new mason, huh?"

"Yes, but please don't hold me responsible for any argument you may have with Sir John. I'm just a hired craftsman trying to earn a living."

Just then a rock came flying from somewhere and landed at their feet. Kington looked around as laughter came from a clump of trees near the church. "Probably some of Thynne's many sons," Kington said. "I swear everything he touches seems to prosper."

More laughter came from the courtyard. Robert and Kington turned to see Lady Thynne, her stomach swollen with child, and two of Sir John's daughters crossing toward the stables. "There isn't much love lost between you and Sir John," Robert observed. Kington grunted. "If that's the case, why did you want your daughter to marry his son?"

"I thought he would want to join his family to one of the oldest in the neighborhood. He's an upstart, making his fortune off the Church. Thought perhaps he would want to make amends. But no." Kington began walking, and Robert joined him, leading his horse quietly, to encourage the man to talk.

"When the fire destroyed Longleat last April, I wished Thynne would give up and leave the area. Perhaps then I could reclaim the land that's rightfully mine. Since then, things have gotten worse, not better. Thynne moved back to Corsley, and the traffic just keeps increasing."

"What's this about your daughter running off with one of Longleat's masons?"

Kington turned down the lane that led to his farm and sighed. "Years ago, when I was first married, I was full of hope. I thought I could enlarge the farm and leave a real legacy to my children. But over the years, only one child appeared, a daughter, Mary. Then my wife died, and Thynne bought up all the surrounding land. He would buy my farm if I would sell it to him, which I won't."

They had almost reached the farm and could see two men slowly working their way down the rows, struggling to dig up the earth. "You see? The only men I can afford to hire are too old for the job, certainly too old for Thynne to hire, which is why they're available and willing. Look! I've been gone for over an hour, and the men have barely moved on from where I left them. And now you're here, and it looks like Thynne is enlarging Longleat, if that model in his chamber is any indication."

Robert didn't know how to respond to any of this. All he wanted to know was if the daughter of a landowner would be a suitable match for a mason. Would it make a difference if the mason was a master mason?

Kington had stopped walking and was gesturing to his house. "It was beautiful once. When I was a boy, it was prosperous and boisterous, the land teeming with life. Now it looks like the forlorn and empty farmhouse it is."

Robert followed his gaze and assessed the house. No work had been done to the stone in many years. Pieces had crumbled off, mortar had chipped away, and the roof could use some work.

"Maybe I should imitate Thynne and hire some masons to fix it up," Kington continued. "How would Thynne like it if I stole his new mason out from under his nose? How much money would I need to offer you?"

Robert froze. "I'm under contract . . . I suppose I could help . . ." His voice drifted off as he saw Kington shake his head.

"It's just a dream. I have no money for such repairs. Well, I suppose we both best get back to work. Goodbye, Master Smythson."

The next day, Richard Cavell joined Robert at Longleat, where Robert was drawing up a schedule and making estimates. "That took some nerve, Robert. Telling Sir John something that will cause a significant delay. In the end, it was your passion that persuaded him. Frankly, I wasn't sure you had it in you."

"Neither did I, Richard. Between you and me, I was shaking. We all want the same thing here: the best Longleat we can build. I just focused on that."

"I think Sir John realizes the courage it took to confront him. You've earned some of his respect. We made the right decision bringing you here."

"After the fire," Robert asked, rolling up the new schedules he had been working on, "did Sir John have anyone come and survey the damage or recommend pieces which could be reused? I don't remember Lovell mentioning it."

"Sir John was impatient, as usual. He spent a day or two trying to decide what to do, then gave orders for the worst of the walls to be torn down. I think Maynard may have come and met with him. It may have been him who convinced him to save the north side."

Robert lowered himself onto a piece of stone, grateful for the break. Then he laughed. Cavell looked at him quizzically. "I just realized what this will mean. Henry Kington was with Sir John yesterday, complaining that Longleat was taking all the laborers in the region. If we are to start over, we'll need an even larger labor force. Now he'll really have something to complain about." Cavell joined him in laughing, both men releasing tension.

"What's Kington's story anyway?" Robert asked once the laughter had stopped. "It sounded like he might be a Catholic recusant?"

"He was, but then weren't we all not too long ago? He might still be, but he attends enough local services to avoid anyone asking too many questions. Mostly, he resents Sir John for his success. I think the Kingtons were connected to the old priory at Longleat, and when Sir John purchased the land and tore down the old buildings and converted others, Kington harbored a grudge he's had a hard time letting go of."

"And the business about his daughter?"

"Yes, that's another sore point between the two." Cavell sighed. "Kington's wife died after only one child, a daughter. Sir John's had not one, but now two rich wives and already has ten children with another on the way. Kington has been after Sir John to marry his oldest son to Kington's daughter, Mary, but Sir John wasn't interested."

"What do you think of such a match?"

"Kington was reaching. His daughter is several years the boy's senior. I think Kington thought it would make sense for Sir John to establish himself in the area by binding his family to one of the neighborhood's more prominent families. But he failed to consider Sir John's past and present connections with powerful people. Just because he spends most of his time here does not mean he isn't well connected. Kington didn't understand. When Sir John's first wife died, Kington even hinted that Sir John marry Mary. He could not understand why Sir John bellowed with laughter at the idea."

Was Robert imagining it, or was there a touch of bitterness in Cavell's voice? "He also said something about the daughter running off with a mason?" Maybe now he would hear the story.

"Yes, or at least that's the rumor. Sometime last year, when many of our masons left, it seems Mary went with one of them. Some lads knew about the affair between the two, but of course her father disapproved. Life has been one bitter disappointment after another for Kington. I feel sorry for him. But he brings some of it on himself, I think. Enough about him. How are we going to proceed?"

"Luckily, the stones for the new walls haven't been laid yet. I'd like to see the entire building go up as a whole. The goal here is a unified building of one cohesive style. The best way to achieve that is to start fresh. We'll start by removing all the rubble on the north side and bring down the walls that are there. All the way down to the foundation. Once we clear things out, we can see what remains at ground level. There's something about the angle that may need to be corrected. Once it's cleared, we'll be able to tell. It will mean pulling the men off the work of the west wing, but I think it's better for the earth that way rather than building up one side before you've touched the other."

"Whatever you say, Robert. You're the expert here."

"Sounds good," Robert replied with relief. The whole encounter had gone better than anticipated. He would have to work hard to encourage the crew to work quickly and efficiently, but it would be worth the delay to have it done right. He relaxed enough to bring up a new subject. "Alan Maynard. Do you think he's responsible for such bad advice? It seems beneath him, if all I've heard is true."

Cavell laughed. "Still worried about him, are you? Let's see. Yes, I do think he could make a mistake of this magnitude, although I stop short of thinking he would do it on purpose. Maynard's a brilliant sculptor. But other than the precision on the piece he's working on, he's not particularly careful about details. He's more self-centered than concerned with the perfection of someone else's house, especially Sir John's."

"Does anyone know where he is? I thought I heard that his wife is still in the area?"

"Yes, he's married. The Maynards rent a house from Sir John in East Woodlands, not too far from Longleat, and she is still there. I'm not exactly sure where Maynard is now, although I've heard rumors. He comes home now and again. I think he likes to monitor what's going on at Longleat. Frankly, I am a bit surprised we haven't seen him since your arrival. I thought the rumors would have flushed him out of hiding by now."

"Would I have met his wife? Does she attend services at Corsley church?"

"Not usually, no. I think they go elsewhere. Not all of Sir John's employees like to see him on Sundays. Many choose to travel a longer distance to avoid him."

Robert laughed. He hadn't been in the area long, but long enough to understand that desire. The conversation was interrupted by rapid hoofbeats, and Robert looked up to see Sir John approaching. Robert's heart raced; he hoped Sir John hadn't had second thoughts.

"Smythson, how are those new schedules coming along? To make it perfect, it will have to be redone. Get it corrected as quickly as possible. I am not a patient man. Make haste."

"No, sir, I mean, yes, sir." Robert was unsure how to respond. "I'll have the men get to work as fast as possible. If this dry weather holds, we should have the foundation finished and the walls well up by midsummer." Sir John paced around the exterior of the building. Robert understood that he was seeing not what was actually there, but the building complete and standing for eternity. He understood because he was doing the same.

Cavell waited a moment and then changed the subject. "Sir John, I've received word that Ned Bright and George Russell have been seen up at Lacock Abbey. There's no word on William Spicer's location, but do you want an arrest made for the other two?"

"No, just keep an eye on them. It's Spicer I'm after. If I take the other two, he'll just go deeper underground. If he thinks they're safe, who knows?" He paused in thought. "Isn't that just like Sharrington, to content himself with second-rate craftsmen. His brother wouldn't have it so. Well, second-rate is good enough for him, I suppose."

"I've also heard that Maynard may be up there as well. Nothing second rate about him, is there?"

Sir John stopped and looked at his steward sharply. "Maynard at Lacock? Well, well. Let him cool his heels there, I suppose. It's as good a place as any for him. He'll be back here as soon as he hears about Smythson." He looked around at his property once more, then rode away.

"What was that all about?" Robert asked Cavell as they watched Sir John leave.

"Nothing to worry about. Some masons ran off without completing the work, and one of them, William Spicer, took some of Sir John's rent money. We've been trying to trace them, without luck until this week."

"I don't understand. How did a mason end up with Sir John's rent money?"

"Spicer's a local boy. He started working for Sir John when he was barely more than an apprentice, and somehow he climbed his way up to the head of things," Cavell answered. "Spicer was a slippery one. He tricked Sir John into naming him as master mason and convinced him to use his designs. And when that wasn't enough for him, he insinuated himself into Sir John's business affairs and became bailiff and rent collector for one of Sir John's other estates."

"What happened to him?" Robert asked.

"No one knows for sure. Spicer's star descended as fast as it ascended. He left in disgrace and scandal, without completing the work we contracted him to do and taking the rent money with him. Sir John was livid but gave up the chase once he realized that to track Spicer down would cost more than he could wrestle out of him if he caught him."

"What about the other two names you mentioned, Bright something?"

"Ned Bright and George Russell. They were a couple of masons who left at the same time Spicer did. No real loss to Longleat. Bright and Russell weren't particularly good masons. That's why

Sir John called them second rate. Come to think of it, I think Ned Bright was the one that Mary Kington ran off with. I wonder if her father would be interested to know he's been seen?"

"They're at Lacock Abbey? I've heard of that."

"Yes, Lacock is some twenty miles north of here. Used to be owned by William Sharrington, a good friend of Sir John's until he died, and his brother, Henry, took over. Now there's not much love lost between them. I've learned it pays to keep abreast of other properties and building projects in the area. So now that you have Sir John's approval, shall we get started with the removal work?"

"Yes, we'll start the additional work as soon as possible. It's a shame it will slow things down, but better to do it now rather than later."

"All I can say, Robert, is that I'm glad you are here."

Chapter 4

ROBERT SAT IN A corner of the Royal Oak at a table with John Hills and one of Longleat's carpenters, Dick Crispin, and his wife, Charlotte. The Crispins were also new to Longleat, and Robert had enjoyed befriending the young couple. Dick was an earnest young man with a deep faith, while his wife had a livelier nature, quick to laugh but also quick to read people and situations. As he watched them share stolen glances, their hands finding reasons to touch one another, Robert felt a longing for that kind of companionship. Perhaps one day he could bring Anne into their circle.

For two days, Robert had worked on the revised plans. On Monday morning, weather permitting, they would start pulling down and removing the north wall and surrounding debris. Tonight, it was time to relax and enjoy some ale, a game of cards, and fellowship. Robert sipped his ale and tried to relax. It gratified him to see the masons he had brought with him begin to bond with the masons already at Longleat. They were teasing the youngest, a shy boy named Fred Horton. Young Fred, as he was called, blushed but took the good-natured ribbing in the spirit it was intended. They were all good lads who worked hard when it was asked of them. They deserved their Saturday evenings, with their Sabbath rest to look forward to tomorrow.

The door opened, and a man and a woman entered. A hush fell over the crowd as the newcomers seemed to take the air out of the warm, dark, convivial chamber. Robert looked on with mild interest. The man stood more than half a foot taller than Robert, with sandy hair and a barrel-shaped chest. His shoulders were broad and bent, telling Robert he was an experienced craftsman. Clutching his arm was a considerably younger woman, well dressed, with a round, pretty face and blond curls escaping from her cap. The couple paused at the door, aware of the attention their entrance had caused. Someone gestured toward Robert's table, and the two approached.

"And which of you is the mason come to unseat me?" the man spoke with a French accent and a raised eyebrow as he surveyed the group.

Robert stood up. "Don't know about replacing you, but I'm Robert Smythson. You must be Alan Maynard." Telling himself he had no reason to feel insecure, he held out his hand and tried to smile confidently as he introduced Hills and the Crispins. The hand that reached back to clasp his was clearly one of an experienced mason. Years of work with stone and tools had built up calloused fingers and a firm grip. Robert was immediately aware of the contrast between the dominating physical presence of Maynard and the delicate, beautiful pieces he created.

"Not much to look at, is he?" Maynard said to the woman.

"Oh, I think he's quite handsome, but I do see what you mean. On the small size for a mason, yes." Her head bobbed up and down, sending the curls swaying.

The Maynards pushed their way onto stools near Robert and his friends, motioning for the occupants to vacate them as he signaled for a fresh jug of ale to be brought. The rest of the occupants of the Royal Oak settled down to watch the interaction, some presumably hoping for a bear-baiting or cockfight.

Robert was used to people underestimating him because of his size. In truth, his compact frame was merely average, not undersized, but people often assumed stonemasons must be large men, like the one facing him. "You should know, Maynard, of all people, that it is not strength but rather precision that makes for beautiful carving."

"Yes, of course. So you are the new mason who comes to us so highly recommended," Maynard said with an appraising gaze. "Sir John expects great things from his new master mason come to replace me."

In a matter of seconds, Maynard had put his finger on the question that had gnawed at Robert for weeks. Was he "master mason" of Longleat? He thought he was, but neither Sir John nor Cavell had used the title officially. What did it mean? There was certainly no one currently on-site who was above him in masonry responsibility, but perhaps Sir John was just waiting for Maynard to return? Aware of Maynard's steady, inquisitive gaze, Robert stumbled out a reply. "Didn't come to replace you. Sir John said you left. I don't have any say in where you work."

"Now," Maynard smirked, "Smythson, is it? I believe you have not traveled to France or to Italy and only know the great works of those countries by drawings, is that not so?"

So this is how it's going to be, Robert thought to himself. "Yes, although we used some Italian plans, Serlio and Palladio, at Caversham."

"For Sir Francis Knollys? I'm surprised he had heard of them."

"Knollys trusted me. I've studied their work, seen their plats." Robert had spent countless hours during his apprenticeship poring over the classical orders of Serlio and the designs of Palladio, both of which filled his mind with balanced, proportional delights. "I believe we can learn from the masters but also create our own

English style." He tried to get his thoughts out, but his words were not as smooth as the thoughts in his head.

"Interesting idea. Tell me, what does Sir John think of your new English style?"

"We, I mean, he," Robert tripped over his words, "we have not discussed it in depth." He had studied the designs for Longleat, and they were good. He had instinctively understood that Sir John was not seeking design input from him, so he had not made any suggestions, although that did not stop him from changing a few things in his own imagination.

"Yes. I can believe that." Maynard laughed. "Let me introduce my wife, Betty," he said, drawing the woman forward. The woman tightened her grip on Maynard as if he would get away and dipped her head in acknowledgment of the others.

Charlotte politely engaged her in conversation. "Have you and Master Maynard been married long? Have you been to France, or did you meet here?"

Betty giggled and fussed with her sleeves. "No, I've not been to France. I caught him right here. Imagine me, just a local farmer's daughter, married to the great Alan Maynard. Well, my friends didn't think it would happen, but I just played it right and got him to marry me before he changed his mind. Now I live in a large house with real glass windows and two girls to help me. Of course, one's my cousin, but that makes it even better."

"Oh, indeed. That sounds comfortable," Charlotte replied, exchanging a smile with her husband. No doubt she would have a laugh about this later.

"I see you haven't taken over my workshop," Maynard asked. "You could have, you know. The work I'm doing now will probably keep me quite busy, and then who knows where I'll be wanted next."

"You have no plans to return to Longleat?"

"Certainly not at the present. I've heard rumors that you are still in the demolition phase. Sir John doesn't need a man of my skill to knock down a wall. Is it true you've convinced Sir John to tear down the north wall? Are you sure that's wise?"

How did Maynard hear that? And what concern was it of his? Robert's head spun. Surely, he didn't need to justify himself to Maynard. "Yes, to achieve the unified building that Sir John desires, it is best to start fresh. The delay will be more than made up for by improving the quality of the building."

"I'm impressed," Maynard replied with a big laugh. "You've got him listening to you already."

"I just want what's best for Longleat."

"Of course," the reply came with a sneer.

Hoping that would end the argument, Robert changed the subject. "I believe you were at Longleat at the time of the fire."

"No, I was not. I had been working there, of course, but Sir John and I had, shall we say, a disagreement, and I left. He begged me to come back after the fire, of course, because he needed me for the design. He likes to say it is his, but no, he did not do that all himself. Even before the fire, Sir John was tinkering with drawings, wanting things redrawn, never satisfied. Sometimes he would change his mind about the design, and entire months' worth of work would be torn down or taken apart and completely redone. Always changes and changes. Never satisfied. And then all of it gone and we start over."

"Do you have any idea what started the fire?" Robert could not let go of this question. Silence had always followed his past attempts to bring it up. No one seemed to want to discuss it. Until now.

"You know what people say about the fire, don't you?" Maynard set his mug on the table and filled it from the jug before leaning back, making sure he had everyone's attention.

"What do people say, Maynard? You know you're dying to tell us," one man replied.

"Some say Sir John started the fire himself." Maynard glanced around him, taking in the size of his audience. "Some believe that Sir John was so unhappy with the design of the building once again that he burned the thing to the ground to have an excuse to start over."

Laughter and scoffing were the only replies he got. "Can you picture him wasting the money to purposely destroy something he'd paid good money to build? Him as tight with his money as he is," John Lewis, Longleat's long time head carpenter, countered.

"There's another possibility as well." Maynard shrugged. "Maybe Sir John burned it down to be rid of any trace of William Spicer, or maybe William Spicer came back to Longleat under cover of darkness and set fire to the building himself." Maynard rubbed his hands together. Robert had the impression that Maynard was enjoying the gossip and a chance to stir up trouble.

"Why would he have done that? Surely, it would have been quite some trouble to travel that entire distance and risk discovery?" John Hills remarked.

"Revenge is a powerful motivator. They say that he wanted to get the last word in his argument with Sir John. Or that he didn't want any building standing that he had contributed to if he wasn't to receive any credit for it."

"What argument?" Valentine Merser, the youngest mason on Robert's team, asked.

"Spicer's the only man I know who has played the game with Sir John and won. Sir John can't stand that he got away with stealing his rent money."

"He stole rent money? Who would dare do that? What game are you talking about?" questioned Valentine, his eyes wide open.

"You know, the game where Sir John tries to get us to do the work he needs without paying us. Spicer got the contract to add the new wings to Longleat and a whole lot more. Not only did Spicer not build the wings, but he got Sir John to name him bailiff for one of his other estates and then stole the rent money."

"You're just jealous, Maynard." John Lewis laughed. "All you know how to do is carve stone. You've no head for business, and Sir John knows it."

Robert got the impression Lewis didn't care much for Maynard and did not hide it.

"Spicer's head for business didn't help him, did it? Sir John chased him off. He can't come back here, or Sir John would have him arrested."

"I hear it didn't hurt him too much," Lewis said. "Apparently, Spicer's career is going quite well in London, and we shall soon see big things from him. Why would he risk his current success for an argument long over?"

Maynard shrugged impatiently. "I don't want to talk any more about Spicer. Who's to say what happened? Perhaps it was just an accident."

"Maybe you are the one who set the fire and are just trying to throw suspicion onto someone else to cover for yourself," Lewis said.

"Why would I do that? Why would I want to destroy my own work?" Maynard shifted his body so that his back was facing Lewis, signaling that the conversation was done. The room was quiet for a while with a few whispered conversations, the younger masons and craftsmen returning to their games of cards and darts.

Maynard rose from his stool. "Come, Betty, it's time we left. So," he turned to Robert, "you'll start pulling the north wall down Monday?"

"If you're so interested," John Hills said, "why don't you come join us?"

"Thank you for the offer. My future lies elsewhere. Within a few months' time, I'll be working for one of the most important men in England," Maynard replied with such a twinkle that Robert wondered if Maynard himself hadn't set the fire, or at least knew more about it than he was saying.

"Good night lads, and good luck." Maynard pulled his wife away from the group and swaggered out of the alehouse, leaving the rest staring at the space he had just vacated.

After saying good night to the Crispins outside their cottage, Robert and John Hills continued toward their own beds. "What do you make of Maynard, John?" Robert asked his friend. "That was odd, him knowing about the demolition of the north range already."

"It's a small community. I think he's greedy. He wants to be part of Longleat without doing the work. I'm sure he has his spies among the craftsmen. One of them must have gotten a message to him, wherever he was. He brags about having more important work to do but clearly cannot seem to stay away. Don't let him bother you."

"I won't. I'm just trying to understand the complicated history of this place. Why do I think I'll have more success here than Spicer or Maynard or any of the others?"

"Because you already have. You've convinced Sir John to listen to your recommendations. Don't belittle yourself. You'll feel better when we get the work going on Monday."

"You're right, as usual. Once we get the whole workforce moving in one direction and start making progress, I'll feel better. Good night, John."

Robert left his friend at the door of his own cottage and made his way toward the masons lodge, where he spent a restless night, dreaming of fire licking the stones he had just set on Longleat and chasing Anne down long stone corridors filled with flames. He was grateful when the sun rose and he could get up and go to church. A peaceful day was what he needed.

Chapter 5

The delicate scent of hawthorn blossoms filled the now familiar lanes as Robert rode from Corsley Heath down to Longleat. The sun was just poking up across the horizon, bringing the promise of warmth to the April chill. It was going to be a long day, but the weather looked like it would cooperate. Robert was hopeful the men could make good progress and ease some of the pressure from Sir John. As he approached the building site, the stones were veiled in a delicate mist, adding a mystical quality at odds with the demolition work to be done. Robert pulled up his horse, pausing to take in the dew-covered grass, the early crocuses, and the overall peace of the morning. Cavell soon joined him, and Robert brought his focus back to work.

"I heard you met Alan Maynard on Saturday," Cavell said.

"Yes." Robert was not surprised the news had reached him. "We had an interesting conversation. He had a theory that William Spicer started the fire at Longleat. Is that possible?"

"Not that old story again. Listen, Robert, don't let Maynard lead you down that road. Spicer would not have come back to Longleat. He's moved on, insinuating himself into someone else's household. I feel I should warn you: Sir John does not like to have the fire discussed, especially any speculation about how it started. I've told you, he wants to look ahead, not back. So on a more current topic, did Maynard indicate that he would be ready to return?"

"No, on the contrary, he was boasting about a new job he was trying to get. Seemed confident about it. For someone of high importance, apparently."

"Oh well, perhaps it's for the best," Cavell concluded as they joined the crowd of laborers and junior masons already gathered.

Nearby stood the assorted picks, axes, and shovels that would be necessary to break up and remove the stone and rubble and various wheelbarrows and carts to haul it away. Robert could hear the men grumbling amongst themselves. "Seems like we're going backward." "I thought you'd come to build a house, not tear it down." "Why do they keep changing their minds?" He understood. It would be hard work for them, and it was seemingly idiotic to tear down a wall just to replace it. Most of these men did not have the age or experience to understand why it was necessary.

"All right, lads. I trust you're all rested and ready. If we all work together, we'll have this done quickly and get back to the main task." He divided them into groups, placing an older, experienced mason with several younger masons and laborers.

A short while later, the only sounds were the clinks of picks against stone, the clunks of stones hitting other stones as they were tossed into the waiting carts, and grunts from the men as they shifted the heavy loads. Robert walked up and down the line, checking the men's positions and giving encouragement. Robert was clearly the head mason on the project, and the head mason was typically the head craftsman of a building project of this magnitude. Even the head carpenter, head joiner, head plasterer, and others would report to him. It was his responsibility to coordinate everyone's activities. If Robert decided that work on the other wings should halt while they tore this one down, then so be it. He did not want to risk shifts in the ground upsetting other stones. The others may not understand his decisions, but they had to abide by them.

Robert spent a few minutes helping the masons move a few pieces near the western corner where a large amount of debris and rock had been pulled down and left. Farther down the line, the joiners were busy erecting some scaffolding so that the upper ranges of stone could be reached. All across the north range, men were working, and Robert was pleased with the way the day was going. As he moved farther down the row, he heard Young Fred let out a large groan. "Do you need help?" he called. As strong as these young men were, some of these pieces required several men to lift or a wedge to help get them out.

"No . . . Wait . . . Master Smythson, there's something here. I don't think it's a stone."

Robert strode back to the western corner while several other masons gathered around, eager to get in the way. "Perhaps it's some treasure the old friars stored here when it was a priory," one of Maynard's masons, Nick Vincent, joked.

"Master Smythson, sir," said Young Fred, moving small pieces out of the way. "I don't know what it is, but it feels large."

"See, I told you it was treasure," repeated Vincent.

"All right, men, enough jokes. You there, help Young Fred with whatever it is." Robert pushed his way in and prodded around where Fred had been working and felt the resistance. It wasn't as hard as a rock, but it was certainly something. As a mason, his hands instinctively understood form, size, and texture. Traveling down the surface of the object, he tried to trace the size of it. The other men watched what he was doing, and when they understood, they joined in. Soon, several men were removing dirt and fragments of rock and mortar away, trying to pry the object loose, while others noticed the commotion and wandered over.

"It's big, whatever it is," Young Fred said.

"I found it first. I claim the treasure," shouted Vincent.

"No, you didn't," another said. "Young Fred did. We all heard him."

"Pipe down, men." Robert tried to maintain control as a crowd gathered. "Whatever it is, if it's valuable, which we have no reason to believe it is, it would belong to Sir John. You all know that. All right, Fred, have you reached an end over there? I think I have. Clear out as much dirt as you can from around the sides. We'll try to lift it up and out so we can take a look."

It took a few more minutes of careful removing of dirt, but they managed to free the object and lay it down on clear ground. It was wrapped in a heavy canvas tarp that had been coated with tree sap or tar, the kind often used in building projects to protect existing pieces of stonework from damage while work was being done nearby. Whatever it was, it hadn't been there since the priory days but may have been left during the construction work.

"Should we try to open up the tarp and see what's in it?" Fred asked.

Robert got a sick feeling in the pit of his stomach. The object was several feet long and about a third as wide. The men had lifted it with relative ease. Whatever this was, he had a premonition it wouldn't be good. "Vincent, fetch me a knife or something sharp. I suspect this tarp may be difficult to cut through."

A moment later, Vincent returned, grumbling, and handed him a blade. Robert made a small incision in the tarp. Another cut and he could lift a piece and peer under. "God's breath! I think it's a body."

He breathed deeply, steadying himself. Everyone was looking to him for leadership, but he had no experience with buried bodies. "Hodgkyns, ride to Corsley and find Sir John. Bring him here as quickly as you can." Robert stood guard in front of the wrapped object while his trusted mason carried out his instructions. The rest of the men stood gossiping in groups. All work had stopped.

Poor Horton, he looked as pale as a ghost. Poor choice of words. The day had started out so well, full of optimism.

Maybe he was wrong. Maybe he had misunderstood what had looked remarkably like fingers. They would open the tarp and find . . . what? Stone fragments? Tools? Animal bones? Anything other than what he feared. He prayed he was wrong, but the sick feeling increased. He would gladly suffer the embarrassment if they could prove him wrong.

Just then, Cavell approached on horseback. "Robert, what's this all about? I saw Hodgkyns on his way up to Corsley, and he said something about a body? He wasn't making any sense, but he was shaken enough to get me moving. What's going on?" Fear and panic showed themselves on the lanky steward's face as he tossed his reins to someone and dismounted.

"Give Cavell some room; get back to work." Robert gave these instructions, knowing there was little chance of them being carried out. In a quieter voice, he said, "The lads are all looking to us to be calm. Hopefully, I am mistaken."

Cavell looked at the old tarp, and all remaining color drained from his face. "Whatever that is, it's not supposed to be there, is it? Why don't you start from the beginning?"

"The men, well, Young Fred over there, were clearing out the pile of rubble there, near the northwest corner, you remember?" Cavell nodded. "Buried within all the stone, he came upon this. We uncovered it as best we could and found this tarp. I'm pretty sure there's a body in there. Look." Robert turned back to the object and made the opening a little bigger. Both men bent to look in, then rose abruptly, gagging. There was no mistaking it. It was a hand, partially decomposed but still recognizable.

"Dear Lord, who could it be? How long has it been there? Lord, preserve us. Sir John is going to be livid." Cavell rocked on his heels, pulling on his beard.

Robert counted the minutes as he imagined how long it would take John Hodgkyns to ride to Corsley, locate Sir John, and return. In the meantime, Robert played out the next logical steps in his mind. Move the body to a safer place and then, if possible, identify it. Following that, notification of next of kin, determining cause of death. One thing was for certain: the body had not wrapped itself in a tarp and put itself there. It was far too early to draw any conclusions, but foul play must have been involved. Deciding that Cavell was in a useless state of shock, Robert sent a few other men to bring a large wheeled cart. Then he shifted everyone farther down the line and tried to get them working again. His attempts were mostly useless; rumors were already flying faster than the dirt should have been.

"A plague upon you!" Sir John yelled at Robert once he was close to being within earshot, as if he were blaming his mason for the discovery. Still believing it was either a joke or some misunderstanding, Sir John did not hide his contempt. "What excuse are you going to bring me next, Smythson? At least this one is original. Get the men back to work and cease from this nonsense."

"Sir John, I swear on the Holy God, what I say is true. Come see for yourself," Robert pleaded, trying to maintain his composure. He could understand Sir John's derision; it was almost impossible to believe. Sir John took his time dismounting, making a show to everyone as to the ludicrousness of the situation, and then ambled over to where Smythson and Cavell stood over a lump on the ground.

"What's all the fuss about? You've dug up a builder's tarp. Surely, that's to be expected. We were still completing the masonry at the time of the fire. Someone left some tools or stones in an old tarp, and it got buried under a pile of rock after the fire. It's nothing to concern me with." Sir John turned to leave, shaking his head in disgust.

Robert knew he needed to stop Sir John from leaving, so he reached out and grabbed him by the arm. "'Tis no pile of rock, I assure you. Come and see." Sir John yanked his arm free and took another step away.

"Sir John," interjected Cavell, still obviously shaken by what he had seen. "Listen to Smythson. You need to see this for yourself."

Sir John looked from his mason to his steward and back. He sighed as if giving in to humor a small child and walked toward the tarp. Robert ushered the other men away and once again enlarged the hole in the tarp, allowing Sir John to see the contents for himself. The older man bent over and peered in. He quickly rose again, a stream of oaths flowing from his mouth. Robert waited for Sir John to calm down, then asked him what they should do.

"It should be obvious! Move the damned body to a place where it can be examined and get the men back to work," Sir John bellowed, throwing his hands up in the air.

"Should we not first investigate the area for other clues?" Robert asked. "What if there are additional bodies or other things—weapons or something like that?"

"No. The most important thing is to get the men back to work. We can't let one body, whoever it is or however long it's been there, slow down progress. Tearing down this wall has delayed us enough. No more excuses! Make haste! Take a few men to help you move the body and send the rest back to work."

Robert was surprised by Sir John's callous attitude, but he obeyed.

Two hours later, Robert, Richard Cavell, Sir John, John Hills, and a few other trustworthy men stood around a large workbench in Maynard's old workshop. It was an odd place to lay out a body, but they needed a large surface where they would not be disturbed, and someone had suggested this. Sir John had stationed a couple of guards outside the door to ensure privacy.

It had been impossible to hide the fact that they were moving a body up from Longleat. The large wheeled cart had trundled its way toward the building site, and several of the men had helped to move the body from the ground to the cart. Young Fred had been standing a few feet off, trying to keep what was left of his breakfast down, with John Hills nearby to steady him. Robert had tried to get the remaining men back to work. Some of them had started enthusiastically removing additional debris, perhaps hoping for another discovery. Others clearly had no stomach for another morbid discovery and milled around uselessly until Sir John's glowering got them moving.

Once the body had been disturbed and lifted out, it began to smell. They wrapped the entire thing in a new tarp as tightly as they could before they laid it in the cart and transported it up to Maynard's empty workshop. Robert had huddled with Cavell, trying to get the steward to recover his equilibrium and take charge. After a few attempts, Cavell pulled himself together enough to suggest Sir John needed a man of medicine to assist him with the investigation. Now they stood waiting for the surgeon to come over from Warminster. The quick peek they had taken assured them, they thought, that it was indeed a person. What awaited them beyond that, no one seemed in a hurry to find out.

"Is there anyone else we should alert or summon?" Cavell asked. "Perhaps a witness would be useful. We do not want to be accused of being too insular, especially as it now appears that foul play was probable."

Just then, the messenger arrived, bringing Roger Williams, the surgeon of Warminster. "Sir John, what is this I hear of a body being discovered?"

"Just that. My men were digging out the last of the debris from the fire and stumbled upon an unmovable object. My man Smythson here," he said, indicating Robert, who acknowledged the reference, "looked in and saw a hand. We've had the body moved in here, but otherwise we haven't disturbed it."

"Well, I don't know what use I'll be to you. I usually see people when they're still alive, but I guess we should look. Has anyone thought of summoning a minister?"

"No, do you think that matters? I don't think last rites would do much good at this point," John Hills said wryly.

"It wouldn't hurt to be on the safe side. Not that I'm superstitious, but having a holy man around while you examine a mysterious body seems like a good idea to me," Williams countered.

"Nonsense," Sir John snapped. "I'm all for religion, but it could take us hours to get Reverend Harrington here. We'll have to proceed without him. The sooner we can wrap this mystery up, the sooner we can get back to building."

"As you like, Sir John. No one has touched or disturbed anything? Good. Let's see what we have. You there, bring in some more lights." The room was quiet for a moment as Williams unwrapped the outer tarp. Robert and Hills helped him, and soon they were standing over the item they had unearthed. The builder's tarp, covered in dirt, had started to break down. The tarps used to protect stonework in progress were tightly woven and often treated with wax or tar, but exposed to elements for any length of time, they would disintegrate. Williams rolled the body over, checking to see where the tarp's seam was. Carefully, he began to lift portions of it off.

Dust, ash, and small pieces of stone fell away, emitting the foul odor of rotting flesh mixed with burnt stone. Without exception, all the men gagged and turned away. Cavell dashed out of the building and vomited. Once the tarp was removed, what emerged was a smallish body, a woman, based on the honey-colored hair and what remained of her clothes. "Oh dear God," Williams said. "Saints preserve us."

"Who is it?" asked Robert, struggling to maintain his composure. The most intact parts of the body were the woman's hair, clothes, and shoes. The rest of the body was in various stages of decomposition, mostly bones with the occasional lump of flesh. Williams covered her with the new tarp to hide both the sight and stench. "Clearly, whoever she was, she has lain in the ground for quite a while," Robert observed aloud, his voice steadying the others in the room and bringing them back to their mission.

"I would say that the body had lain there for many months, perhaps longer," Williams said. "From the smell, I would say she could have been there since the fire. Perhaps she died in the fire? Obviously, a woman, perhaps a girl even. The quality of the hair seems to indicate someone quite young. Were any of the household staff missing after the fire?"

"No, everyone was accounted for," Sir John responded.

"By the looks of her shoes, I would say she had some money and was dressed for a journey of some kind," Robert observed.

"Is there anything buried with her?" Williams felt carefully around and beneath the body but didn't find anything.

John Hills had been quietly observing the scene but now ventured into the conversation. "If she wasn't part of the household, who could she be? People who die in a fire don't usually wrap themselves up neatly in builder's tarps, do they?"

Robert regarded his friend thoughtfully. "Unless she thought the tarp would protect her, and then she fell?"

"I suppose that's possible," Williams chimed in. "But look here. There's a head wound that could result from a fall. I'll have to get a better look."

"Perhaps we'll know more when we know who she is," Robert said. Seeing Cavell in the doorway attempting to compose himself,

Robert called out to him, "It's a young woman, Cavell. Any idea who it could be?"

Cavell took a few steps closer, then covered his mouth again while Williams moved aside for him to see clearly. Struggling to keep his stomach contents down, he gasped, "I think it's Mary Kington."

"Who? Kington's daughter? How did she get there?" Sir John asked.

"Are you all right, Cavell?" Robert asked, noticing that Cavell had turned as pale as a piece of alabaster stone.

"Cavell's as pale as a ghost. No, a corpse. Someone get the man outside. I can't abide weakness." Sir John turned his attention back from his steward to the girl's body. "Looks like the worms have gotten to her, haven't they?"

Williams had been gently examining the body, or what was left of it, and seemed to come to a decision. "Looks like her skull has sustained a blow. If I were to guess, I would say she had had her head bashed in by something small and sharp. I think we're dealing with a murder."

The entire room felt like the air had been sucked out of it. The men looked from one to another and then to Sir John. He would not be happy with this pronouncement. Longleat seemed to be under some kind of curse.

Robert was the first to recover. Turning to Sir John, he said, "I suppose you will have to go tell Kington and have him confirm it's his daughter."

"Me? Why? What a waste of time. No, you're going to do it, Smythson. You're the one who found the body."

"Me? God's breath, Sir John. Are you not the sheriff and the justice of the peace for the county? Does this not fall under your jurisdiction?"

"Are you questioning me? If it is in my jurisdiction, then I'm free to delegate, am I not? I delegate to you. Take Cavell with you, if you think he can stomach it." Sounds of more retching outside made that doubtful.

"Whoever is going to do it should do it quickly. We need to get this girl's body back in the ground, where it belongs," Williams added.

"Agreed," responded Sir John. "Get her identified and buried and get back to the business of building. That's what I'm paying for."

"But, Sir John," Robert began, "if someone killed her and buried her on your land, surely you need to investigate?"

Sir John grunted in response. "Telling me what to do again, Smythson? Why? No one has missed her. Longleat is what matters. Get this cleaned up and the rest of the work done. Make haste! And, Smythson? No more surprises." Sir John called for his horse and rode away, leaving the rest of the group dumbfounded.

Chapter 6

ROBERT AND CAVELL RODE toward Cley Hill Farm. Neither man spoke. Cavell was still green and having trouble maintaining his composure. Robert was full of questions but kept them to himself. If everyone thought Mary had run off with one of the Longleat masons, how did her body end up wrapped in a tarp underneath a pile of rubble at Longleat, and when had it been put there? How had Kington reacted when his daughter disappeared? Had he made no effort to see her? Did she mean so little to him that he could just let her go without attempting to go after her? Or had he resented her choice so much that he was willing to cut her out of his life?

Robert couldn't help but draw comparisons with Anne. One of the first thoughts he'd had after the shock of discovery was how alike the two girls' hair color was. From what he could tell, they were the same general size and build. He imagined his beloved's body exchanged for Mary's, and the bile threatened to rise again.

What if he had convinced her to go with him, how would her father react? More than just a physical resemblance, there was a similarity in the father-daughter nature of both the Kington and Palmer families. But the Palmers had the protection of the influential Knollys family, whereas Kington seemed all alone. Would Robert be happy with Anne if her choice had broken her father's heart? Who was this mason that Mary had supposedly run off with, and where was he now? Was his body lying in another section of the foundation? So many questions and no answers.

"Richard, what do you know about the mason Mary supposedly ran off with?"

"Ned Bright? He left after Spicer did, I think. As I told Sir John, I believe he's at Lacock Abbey now. He's been gone for a year and a half at least; how could he be involved in this? He wasn't a particularly good mason, if that matters."

"I can't see how that would be relevant," replied Robert as they approached the farm and saw Henry Kington in his fields, coaxing a skinny horse down a narrow row. Robert felt a surge of sympathy for the man. Struggling to keep his farm going, at odds with his closest neighbor, and now about to learn that his only daughter had met with a violent end. Robert glanced at Cavell, who looked as down as Robert felt. Kingston looked up at the two men as they approached and stretched his back before walking toward them. Kington's appearance looked, if possible, worse than it had previously. A foul, unwashed odor wafted toward Robert as he braced himself for what was to come.

"Master Kington, a word sir, if you please," Robert said.

"What do you want? What are you doing on my farm at this time of day? Don't you have a building to build?"

Animosity emanated from the man like dust from a mason's bench, Robert thought. If he was this rude and resentful before they had even spoken to him, how would he react to what they had to say?

"Relax, Kington," Cavell warned. "You're going to want to listen to Smythson."

"Is that right? Well, I suppose you better say your piece, young man, and be done with it," he replied, looking warily from one man to the other.

"Master Kington, we are here with news of your daughter, Mary. When did you last see or hear from her?" Robert had dismounted and led his horse closer to Kington. He stayed near the horse's head, running his fingers through the its mane, straightening and smoothing the hairs.

"I don't see what business that is of yours, you impertinent fool."

"Kington," Cavell's voice was soft, but it contained another warning.

"She ran off with one of Thynne's masons, you know that, Cavell. Why? Is she back?"

"Not exactly." Robert looked from one man to the other. There seemed to be a deeper relationship between the two than their geographic proximity would explain.

"Are you just going to stand there playing with your horse's hair, or are you going to tell me what's going on?"

"Sir, we have found your daughter. I mean," Robert hesitated, "we believe we found her body. I'm sorry, sir, but it appears Mary is dead."

"What?" Kington grew still, the belligerence knocked out of him. His body slumped forward, and Cavell moved quickly to catch him before he fell.

"Let's get him into the house," Robert said, leading the horses to a nearby tree and tying them before assisting Cavell to half guide, half carry Kington toward his house. It was a large two-story thatched farmhouse. From the outside, it looked comfortable, if a bit run-down, but as they opened the door, a foul stench greeted them. The door resisted as Robert pushed it against an obstacle to make an opening wide enough to allow the men to enter. Furniture, jugs, equipment of all kinds filled every inch of space. It was hard to maneuver, but Robert and Cavell stepped carefully and led Kington to an empty chair by an empty fireplace and carefully settled him in.

The two men looked around, taking in the sight. The room was dimly lit and would have been cramped even if it had been empty. Cavell picked his way through the clutter and found a jug of ale that still had some in it. He sniffed it. "It's not fresh, but it will do," he said, wiping out a nearby tankard and filling it. "Henry, pull yourself together and drink this."

Kington obeyed, draining the tankard and blinking to refocus his eyes. Seeing Cavell, he rose from the seat. "You're involved in this somehow; I know you are."

"Relax, Master Kington," Robert said gently, motioning to Cavell to refill the tankard. It would at least remove him from Kington's reach. "You've had a shock. Drink up and then tell us when you last saw your daughter."

Henry Kington sank back into the chair, defeated. He looked from one man to the other and sighed. "It's been about a year. She ran off with that mason, Ned something. For weeks and months before that, he was all she talked about. I tried to get her away from him, but she would have none of it. Finally, she ran off with him. Left me a letter and went. I still have the letter somewhere."

"You didn't go after her? You've had no communication from her or from Ned since she left?"

"What happened? What are you not telling me?"

"I think you should come with us. We have been cleaning out the last of the debris remaining from the fire, and we found a body buried there." Robert paused, allowing the older man time to digest this. After glancing at Cavell for approval, he continued, "Cavell thinks it's Mary."

"Where? When? I don't understand."

"At Longleat. Near one of the old walls. We need you to come see it—her, I mean. If it's her, well then, I don't think she ever went off with Ned. That would be my guess." Robert felt he was making a muddle of this.

"Let's take this a step at a time," Cavell interjected. "Henry, come with us and see if you agree with me. We should warn you that seeing her will be quite a shock. She's . . . well, she's been dead for quite some time.

Again, they paused while Kingston absorbed all they had said. Robert was anxious to leave the farmhouse as the clutter and stench were threatening to overwhelm him. He stood motionless, trying not to breathe in any more of the stale air than was necessary. Finally, Cavell extended his hand and asked Mary's father if he felt fit enough to ride.

A short while later, the three men stood outside the masons' workshop. Despite their earlier efforts, the smell of death and decomposition had seeped out. "Kington, I need to warn you that this won't be easy. She's been dead a while," Robert put his hand on the man's shoulder to steady him and guide him toward the door.

"How do you know it's her?" Kington asked.

"We don't for sure. Cavell recognized her hair color, and we're hoping you can confirm her identity. Please, I know this isn't easy, but it is necessary."

The three went inside, passing the guard Sir John had begrudgingly left there, and approached the body. It was still wrapped as much as possible in a new tarp. Robert began to lift the tarp away, enough for Kington to get a look. Kington was looking around the workshop, anywhere, everywhere, except at the body.

"Master Kington, sir. We need you to look and tell us if this is Mary," Cavell encouraged him. Robert continued to lift the tarp up, revealing the length of the body, the gown, and shoes.

"Yes, that's her." Kington swiveled his head away and ran for the entrance. Robert replaced the tarp and followed him out.

"Are you sure?"

"You think I don't know my own daughter?"

"Well, under the circumstances . . ." Robert let his sentence drift off.

"Those are—were—her shoes. Her gown. Yes, I'm sure." Kington began pacing back and forth in front of the workshop, his color rising. "All this time, I let myself believe she was with that Bright fellow, that she was happy. And all that time . . ." Kington took a couple of steps toward the workshop, then backed away again. "My poor angel, my poor, sweet angel. How could this have happened to you?" He dropped to his knees and sobbed, huge racking waves of grief. The two men stood quietly by, allowing the man his dignity.

It didn't take long for the initial grief to turn to anger. Kington got to his feet and resumed pacing. "This is Thynne's doing," his voice raised and pace quickened. "It's his fault. He did this! Where is he?"

"Now, Kington, I know you've had a shock, but we don't know how Mary's body came to be here. Sir John was just as surprised as you were."

"Are you defending him?"

"Kington," Cavell interrupted. "Smythson's just saying that we don't know. There's no reason to believe that Sir John was involved. Perhaps it was an accident?"

Robert shot Cavell a look. Bodies didn't accidently get hit in the head and carefully wrapped up in tarps. They had already established that. But Cavell's words had calmed Kington down, and he had stopped pacing.

"What about you, Cavell? Did you have a hand in this?"

"Of course not, Kington. You know I would never have hurt Mary."

Kington gave Cavell a hard look. "Sir John. Where is he? By God, he'll answer for this."

"He's likely back up at Corsley Manor," Cavell said. Turning to Robert, he continued, "Given everything, I think Kington has the right to talk to Sir John, don't you?"

"I suppose so. Don't think it will help much, but Sir John is the man in charge. I'll go with him."

"No, I'll take him. You stay here at Longleat and try to get everyone back to work. Sir John will be easier to deal with if I can tell him that work has resumed and you're overseeing it."

"You're probably right." Robert watched as Cavell led the distraught father away, then turned his attention back to the building site.

That evening, Robert sat staring into the fire, a tankard of ale in his hand, a bowl of mutton stew growing cold on the table near him. He could only imagine the scene that had transpired at Corsley Manor. Lost in thought while the other patrons of the Royal Oak gave him a wide berth, Robert barely noticed Richard Cavell's entrance. He didn't even look up when Cavell walked to his small table.

"That was a rough day," Cavell said as Robert finally registered his presence. The tall man folded himself in two on the stool next to Robert and signaled the barmaid to bring him some ale.

"How did things go at the manor?"

"About as bad as you'd imagine. Both Kington and Sir John bellowing away at each other, past grievances rehashed, blame bandied about. Finally, Sir John had Kington thrown out and removed from the premises. There's bad blood between the two, and today's discovery only made it worse."

"I don't understand why Kington seemed to think you were involved. Is there something between the two of you I don't know?"

Cavell swallowed his ale and looked off into the distance. When he spoke, his tone was flat and distant. "It seems so long ago now. There was a time when I was quite fond of Mary Kington. I even made her an offer of marriage, but her father rejected it. Didn't think I was good enough for her, he said. He was holding out for a higher match. He wanted Mary to marry into Sir John's family, not to his steward. Mary didn't seem disappointed, so perhaps it was for the best."

"I'm sorry," Robert said kindly. "How did you feel when Mary started up with the mason?"

"By then, I was resigned to my fate. I suppose I just wanted her to be happy. I certainly didn't want her to end up like this."

"No one wants anyone to end up like that. What happens next?"

"Mary's body will get a proper burial. Sir John wants the lads to hurry up with the work. And you probably need to visit the quarry and make sure everything is going smoothly there."

Robert turned to the steward. "I meant about the investigation. Surely, there will be an investigation, an inquiry into her death. Who would be in charge of that? It appears she was murdered. We can't just bury her and go on like nothing happened."

Cavell sighed. "That would be up to Sir John and Kington, I suppose. I wouldn't hold your breath waiting for those two to work together."

Chapter 7

SEVERAL DAYS WENT BY, and other than gossip among the laborers, no action was taken to investigate Mary's death. Her body, or what was left of it, was hastily buried at Corsley Church next to Corsley Manor. Few people attended the service. Robert and Cavell were present; Sir John was absent. One person was heard whispering that this was the closest Henry Kington could get his daughter to the Thynne family, but Kington himself was too despondent to react.

Robert continued to be troubled by the young woman's death. The image of her decomposing body came unbidden whenever he closed his eyes. Sometimes it was lying in the ground, at other times laid out on the slab table in the masons' workshop. When he slept, the body got up and walked toward him, arms outstretched. Sometimes the dead girl's face transformed into Anne's face; sometimes it was unrecognizable. Either way, it haunted him waking and sleeping.

What troubled him most was why it was not having the same effect on others. No one seemed concerned that they had unearthed the body of a young woman at Longleat. It was treated as an inconvenience more than anything else, especially by Sir John. When

Robert tried to pursue the topic, Sir John changed the subject and talked about getting the building project back on schedule.

An uneasy feeling tugged at Robert's conscience. It was the same with the fire. A blaze had destroyed the work of many years, and no one was concerned with how it started. If foul play was suspected, as it was with Mary Kington's death, should not the guilty parties pay for their crimes? Robert kept waiting for an investigation to be started, but nearly a week went by with nothing.

On Sunday, Robert walked to Cley Hill Farm after church, from which he'd noticed Henry Kington was absent. Robert told himself this was a social visit, but it was more than that. His heart ached for the man's loss, but he also was hungry for answers. How could a young woman go missing and turn up dead more than a year later and no one investigate? He understood that the crime had happened a while ago, but certainly there was no timeline or schedule for outrage and grief.

When Kington cracked the door open, Robert assured him it was merely a social call. "I wanted to check on you. With the shock you have had, I thought you might need a friend to talk to."

"And you think you're that friend?"

"To be honest, Master Kington, I don't see too many others knocking on your door. I may be new here, but I understand the pain of losing someone close to you." Kington looked at him for a minute, then opened the door wider and let him in. The room was just as cluttered as before, the stench just as foul. Robert suggested they step outside as the day was pleasant and he would like to see Kington's property.

Kington shrugged but allowed Robert to lead him outside. They walked toward Cley Hill, past the fields, while Robert asked him to tell him about Mary.

Keeping his eyes on the ground, Kington sighed. "She was an angel. My angel. After her mother died, she was all I had."

"Sounds like you two had a close relationship."

"She was a good lass, kindhearted and innocent. Are you musical, Master Smythson?"

"Not particularly, and please call me Robert."

"Well, Mary had the voice of God in her. When she sang, it was a choir of angels. Sent straight down from heaven, she was. Not very strong, though. Frail-like, you know?"

"I do. She sounds like a young lady I have the pleasure to know."

"Like her mother, I suppose. She wasn't made for a hard farm life either. That's one reason I wanted to wed Mary to Sir John or his son, to give her a chance at a softer life. One filled with comfort and ease. Not that any Thynne would be good enough for her, but the farm hasn't been doing well, and she needed the comfort that money can provide."

"The farm seems like a good property. Why hasn't it been doing well?"

"It's the prettiest piece of land hereabouts. Just look at these views and rich fertile land blessed by God." Kington clenched his fists, and Robert could see the blood pulsating in the veins in the older man's neck. "What I don't have is men to work the land. Thynne has seen to that! Hires them all for his precious Longleat." The sneer he gave the last word was obvious. "I can stand here and look out over the rolling hills rich with good soil, able to grow anything. I know Thynne has tried to get my land. His isn't nearly as fertile—mostly woodland, isn't it? Filled with deer and his river is full of trout, but higher land is always better, and Cley Hill farm is loftier than Longleat."

They had reached the summit of Cley Hill, passing many other families and groups enjoying the beautiful Sabbath afternoon. The view of the countryside was beautiful, and Robert could see the woods in the distance. "Has he offered to buy your farm?"

"Not exactly buy, no. He's an outsider, like all those outsiders coming in here to take the land that doesn't belong to them, God's land."

"Do you not mean the Queen's land?"

"Not originally, no. See down there?" Kington pointed toward Longleat. The day was clear enough Robert could just make out the location of the building and its foundations. "All of that was once an Augustinian priory. And before that, it was connected with my family. Then the old King sends Somerset and Thynne with their forceful ways and takes it away from the true Church. Next thing, Thynne figures out how to buy it himself at a mere fraction of its true worth. Robbery and villainy it was, but I won't let him get his hands on this piece of it."

"Unless you had married your daughter to one of his sons or the man himself. Wouldn't the farm be included in the bride's portion? Isn't that usually how land gets transferred?"

"We would have worked something out to my advantage. I wouldn't have let Thynne cheat me."

Robert could feel the anger rising in Kington's voice. "What did Mary think of your plan?"

"It was her nature to be compliant enough, at least until she met that Bright fellow. After that, he was all she could think about."

"Did you know she was planning on running off with Bright?"

Kington looked at Robert askance. He paused before admitting, "I guess it did not come as a complete surprise. She wanted to marry him, but I forbade it. Bright wasn't even a good mason, from what I've heard. He completed his apprenticeship but then failed to advance. His carving, if that is what you call it, wasn't good, and nobody would take him on to train to be a master mason. He went back to the bench. There was no bright future for him, despite his name. No upward movement expected. How could I allow my only child, one who was so far above him in talent and education, to join herself to that kind of future?"

"I can see that it would have been difficult, but to deprive her of happiness seems a little harsh too, does it not?"

"What would you have had me do? You are not a father yourself, are you?"

"No, at least not yet." Robert felt the sting of missing Anne.

"Then you don't know the difficulties of such a choice. I didn't want her to be unhappy, but I thought she would recover, forget him after he left. I didn't think her heart was that touched."

"I'm a bit confused about the timing of all of this. I thought she had gone with him when he left."

"No, he left earlier. One of Thynne's disgraced masons got him employed up at Lacock, or so I heard. I thought that would be the end of it, but I was wrong. Apparently, he was coming back and seeing Mary whenever he could."

"How far away is Lacock?"

"About twenty miles. Should have been far enough, but what is that to a man in love?"

Kington's comment stung Robert. His heart lurched out toward Anne. Of course, she was over twenty miles away. Nevertheless, he could understand the desire and drive that would cause a man to travel to see his beloved.

"I see you understand," Kington said. "There must be someone you would travel a great distance to see."

"Yes," Robert nodded, his gaze lingering over the hills. "There is."

"But not enough to stay behind or bring her with you? I understand you were employed by Sir Francis Knollys, were you not?"

"I was. There were complications. I couldn't . . ." *Separate her from her father,* were the words Robert was going to say. Did that not make Kington's argument valid?

"Well, never mind. Our heart does not always get what it wants. There is more than love that goes into a marriage to make it successful. Tell me, why did you leave Knollys?"

"He was called back to court, for what will probably be a protracted time. He gave up on his building projects for now. Queen's business called him from home."

"Ah yes. I believe she wanted him to deal with Queen Mary's heartbreak in Scotland."

That was an odd turn of phrase, Robert thought. Mary Stuart, the Scottish Queen, had married the man who many believed had killed her previous husband, perhaps with her involvement or consent. She was currently being held prisoner at Lochleven Castle, having been forced to abdicate the throne in favor of her infant son, while her new husband had been driven from the land. Here in Protestant England, Mary was not seen as a tragic figure, but as a troublesome neighbor who had designs on Elizabeth's throne and was the target of many Catholic plots. To publicly proclaim support for Mary was unwise.

"I see you do not agree with my assessment of the fair Queen Mary. Unfortunately, few do."

This conversation was making Robert uncomfortable. He was a true believer of the new faith, believing that man was responsible for his own relationship with God rather than the priest acting as an intermediary. He also believed it to be a private matter, not one to be fought over and politicized. What he wanted was to get back to Mary Kington's death and the lack of investigation. After a pause, during which the two men looked out at the view from the top of Cley Hill, watching families take their Sunday afternoon pleasures, Robert tried again. "Why did you not give them your blessing and be done with it? Give Mary and Bright the farm. Who knows, perhaps he would have been a better farmer than he was a mason. That way, your grandchildren could have inherited the farm you built. Certainly, knowing the farm would continue in your family would have been one consolation?"

Kington was silent for a moment, his gaze fixed on the past. "One can understand yet not accept. She was all I had left in the world. To see her throw herself away on such a worthless man was more than I could bear."

"What will happen to the farm now?"

Kington sighed. "I don't know. I suppose it will be sold when I am gone. Thynne will probably end up with it," he spat with disgust. "Unless God shows me some mercy."

One thought still rankled Robert. "Why did you not look for her?"

"To me, she might as well have been dead. She was supposed to marry Thynne's son, join my family to his. As much as I don't like him, I'm not stupid. I can see the advantages to the match and to the alignment. My daughter and grandchildren would inherit a beautiful and prosperous estate and be local gentry. My lineage should be good enough for Thynne, but he wouldn't hear of it. Mary was pretty, with the voice of an angel. For her to waste it all on someone like Bright, against my wishes . . . What use did I have for her then? Come, let's go back to the house, and I'll show you a painting I had done of her. Besides, I could do with some ale."

A short while later, Robert nearly retched at the clutter and oppressiveness of Kington's home. Only his curiosity and his determination to see Mary's gruesome death solved allowed him to swallow his discomfort. Once Henry had poured two beakers of ale, he motioned for Robert to sit. Robert looked around the crowded space, swatting away some flies and trying to find an empty spot to perch. Kington retreated to the back corner of the room and shuffled through books and papers.

Robert's gaze followed him into the dimly lit corner, where he was startled to see a crucifix. Images of the crucifixion were forbidden under the new laws, and yet here was one out in the open in this man's house. While Robert was still puzzling over what he had seen, Kington returned with a miniature portrait.

Robert dutifully, and with genuine curiosity, looked at the portrait and blanched. His hands shook as Anne gazed up at him from within the frame. Lifting it up to catch the meager light coming from the small window, he realized it was not Anne, but the young woman in the picture bore a remarkable resemblance to her. There was no way to reconcile the portrait with the body he had seen, which was barely a recognizable body. The girl in the portrait was pretty, as her father had said. Her hair was the same honey shade and with the same gentle curls as Anne's. He had noticed that when the body had been uncovered. Now he saw that they both had green eyes set in a delicate face. They were not identical, but close enough to have been made from the same mold.

"She's lovely. I am deeply sorry for your loss. You must miss her a great deal."

"I do. Now even more when I think of the violence she must have experienced at the end. My angel did not deserve that." Kington sighed, lost in the past and full of regret. "Perhaps I would have had to accept that marriage to one of Sir John's sons would not happen, but that is a great deal different from letting her run to a life of poverty and strife with a worthless man."

Robert now came to the real question he had. Seeing Mary's resemblance to Anne, how could it not? Just the thought of someone he loved experiencing a death as Mary had filled him with anger. How could anyone sit by and not pursue justice? "Kington, have you any idea who might have done this?"

Robert watched as Kington got up from his stool and tried to pace in the small space. The man seemed to struggle within himself. "It had to be Ned Bright. When Mary ran off, she left me a letter." He walked back to the same corner from which he had brought the portrait and handed Robert a folded piece of paper.

"Do I have your permission to read it?" Robert asked. At Kington's quick nod, Robert unfolded the letter and read: *Dearest Father, do not seek me. I have gone to be with Ned. We will be married at Lacock. Ned is my choice and my future. Do not come after me. Your loving daughter, Mary.*

Robert folded the letter and returned it. "It sounds as if she went willingly and with thoughts for the future. Why do you think he would hurt her?"

"It had to be Bright. Maybe he changed his mind. Maybe she made him angry somehow. Who else would have cared enough about her to do such a thing?" Robert watched as Kington's fists opened and closed and his lips pursed.

Robert tried to calm him. "It could have been anyone. I do not think someone as deeply in love as you describe Ned to be could have done this. I know I could not." The thought of violence happening to Anne turned his stomach.

"But you do not have the temper Bright did. Ask around. He was known for his quick temper."

No one had volunteered this knowledge of the young mason, Robert thought. But then, there were few left at Longleat from the time before the fire. "When do you think this happened? Did she run away before or after the fire last year?"

"What? Has no one told you? It was on the night of the fire. With the entire neighborhood involved in trying to put out the fire before it spread, she slipped away unseen. That was the last time I saw her."

Robert turned this over in his mind. Could Mary's death be more closely related to the fire than previously thought? Two crimes on the same night could logically be connected, couldn't they? Robert shook his head, the stale air and ale making his head fuzzy. He made his excuses and stood to leave. Kington walked with him outside of the house, and Robert looked at the structure, noticing that the southwest corner stonework was crumbling. "You should get that repaired. It's easier to fix it before it gets too bad rather than waiting for additional damage that can put too much stress on the other walls and even the roof line. If you like, I can send a couple of men over to shore it up for you."

"Mighty obliged, but I'm not sure I can afford to pay them just now. Maybe after the fall harvest, if the weather cooperates this year."

"I wouldn't wait too much longer." Robert said farewell and walked down toward Corsley Heath. He had a lot to think over, more questions than answers. A young lady fell in love with a young man; her father disapproved of the match. There was nothing unusual about that. Was that not the same situation he found himself in? Why the Lord was so unkind to bind unsuitable hearts together, he did not understand. In this case, the girl had run off with the young man, despite her father's wishes. If he returned her affections, which his traveling twenty miles just to see her seemed to show, then what motive could he possibly have? Surely, Kington could see that.

If it were a random crime, if Mary was intercepted on her way to Ned by someone intent on doing the young, attractive girl harm, then why hadn't Ned come in search of her? He either did not expect her to run off with him or had reason to believe the relationship was over. Neither option seemed to make sense. Unless—the thought filled Robert with dread—they were soon to dig up his body as well.

He tried to think of the next logical steps in an investigation. Finding Ned Bright seemed to be at the top of the list. That and to ask the surgeon, Williams, if he had made any more discoveries about Mary's body. It remained curious to him that no one seemed to be concerned with finding answers to how and why the body of a local girl was found lying dead at the bottom of one of Longleat's walls. Could it have been an accident? If she had indeed died during the fire or near the time of the fire, could she have been there trying to help? It all seemed so unlikely.

On the way back home, Robert met Dick and Charlotte Crispin, who invited him to join them for the evening. Soon after, ensconced in their cozy cottage, Robert could not help but compare their living situation with that of Henry Kington. The building was smaller, but in all ways that matter it was superior. Neat, organized, warm, inviting. Charlotte stirred the pottage hanging over the fire, then went to the table to cut thick slabs of bread that would serve to soak up the stew. "It's humble fare, but I trust you'll like it," she said as she served the food.

Dick said a prayer, and the three friends ate in companionable silence for a bit. Robert noticed Charlotte watching him closely as he straightened his trencher, set his cup of ale down in the same spot, and even reached out to adjust something on the table, correcting the angles. He saw the look she exchanged with her husband.

"I know people think it's odd," Robert said. "I can't help it. It's like an itch. Or a twitch I can't get rid of until things are at the proper angle or distance. I've always been this way. Apparently, as a child I would line things up, cheering when I got things perfectly spaced. My parents would laugh indulgently. It was a long time before I realized that other people don't see things the way I do."

"It's what makes you a great mason. I sometimes wish I could do it visually and not have to measure all the time," Dick said.

Robert laughed. "Oh, I still measure. My father would often say something was good enough when it wasn't. He wouldn't take my word for it. We would have a fierce argument until I finally had to measure it to prove it to him. It took a lot of patience to wait until I got something lined up perfectly, patience they didn't always have."

Washing the last of the pottage down with fresh ale, Robert began to tell of his afternoon with Kington. "His house is so chaotic and untidy. Not at all like this place," he said with a smile to Charlotte. "I had a hard time staying inside. Environments I can't control, especially cluttered ones, are stressful. But the man has lost his daughter, so I tried to be understanding." He relayed his conversation about Kington's opinion of Sir John. "What do the carpenters and joiners think about the body being discovered?" he asked Dick.

"Lewis discourages gossip, but it's hard to stop with something of that magnitude. I've heard all kinds of theories."

"Really? What are some of them?"

"Lots of outlandish tales, mostly. That Sir John killed her to punish Kington. That she got in the way of William Spicer setting fire to Longleat. My favorite is that the ghosts of Augustinian priors came and killed her. Nothing to be believed."

"Her father is convinced that Ned Bright killed her."

Dick reached across the table to cut some cheese. "That's the fellow she ran off with? Seems unlikely. Why does Kington think that?"

"There's something about Kington I don't like," Charlotte said. "There's an anger there, a kind of defiance. I don't trust him."

Her husband laid his hand on his wife's arm. "Be kind, Charlotte. The man's lost everything. His wife, now his daughter. His farm is barely surviving. And he's had to sit by and watch Sir John's success. It can't have been easy for him."

Charlotte sighed and squeezed Dick's hand. "That's my dear, always seeing the best in people. You're right, of course." She stood up and began clearing the table, wrapping up what was left of the bread and cheese. "Unless," she paused. "You don't think he set fire to Longleat as a way of getting back at Sir John, do you?"

"He wanted to marry his daughter into the Thynne family. Why would he want to destroy what he wanted to join?" Robert asked. "Oh, enough! I don't want to talk about this anymore. I've had a lovely evening spent in the company of good friends. Why ruin it with this morbid subject?"

"As you wish. We might as well finish up this ale before it gets stale."

Robert laughed. "Excellent notion. I had enough stale ale at Kington's place for one day."

Chapter 8

ROBERT STOOD IN FRONT of Longleat's crumbling walls, surrounded by men shoveling the dark earth at great speed. He too held a shovel and drove it into the soil, pushing it deeper and deeper. "Master Smythson," a voice down the line called. "I've hit something."

"Me too," cried another man, even as Robert's own shovel met resistance. All down the line, men scooped out dirt with their hands or tools, revealing tarps wrapped around large objects. Robert frantically worked on his tarp, desperate to unearth its contents. Moments later, he found the loose edge and lifted it cautiously. That golden hair again, matted with dirt and blood but still beautiful. He turned the body over, and Anne's serene face stared up at him.

Robert awoke with a jerk and dragged himself out of bed. He had been having the same dream for several nights, getting less and less sleep as the week wore on. At the work site, he was jumpy and grumpy, trying to spur the men on, eager to get the rubble cleared and started on the new walls before they found any more tragedies.

He went down to the main chamber, stirring up the banked embers and bringing the small fire to life, using it to light some candles. He dropped his body into a nearby chair and tried to breathe. After a few minutes, he pulled a folded piece of paper from his bag and opened it. If he adjusted the angle here, raised it up just a fraction, would that improve it? He had been working on this design for a chimney piece on and off for months, and he could feel that he was close to getting it right. Now, gazing at the mantel design, he remembered one of his final times with Anne.

Robert had found Anne in one of the smaller corners of the Knollys home, stitching next to a window to catch the failing light. Pausing to watch her before she noticed his presence, his heart had ached at the thought of leaving her. The slim shaft of winter light had fallen on her work, a complex weaving of green vines, much like the tangle of his thoughts. He could not ask her to leave her home, her father, to follow him to an unknown future.

Anne had shifted and noticed Robert, a smile crossing her face. Robert had pulled up a stool and admired her needlepoint while she in turn examined the changes in his chimney piece. Despite their unfamiliarity with each other's media, they could appreciate artistic expression and delight in finding a pleasing shape or line.

"Is it true?" she had asked quietly, returning the drawing and folding her small hands in her lap.

"Is what true?" Robert had replied, noticing the frown clouding her face.

"You'll be leaving?"

"Nothing is definite. I am going to London with Knollys, to visit my old mentor Humphrey Lovell and to talk about . . ." He'd drifted off, unable to continue.

"A new job. I heard Sir Francis talking to my father. He seemed fairly sure he would be leaving for some time and said it wasn't worth keeping the building at Caversham going."

"Nothing is settled. I do not want to—"

"You have to go where there is an opportunity for you. If Sir Francis isn't going to keep you at Caversham, I'm sure he will find a good place for you, yes?"

"Of course, and for my team as well, but . . ." He hadn't been able to finish the thought. Longleat was some eighty or ninety miles away. There would be no visits. Leaving Reading and Caversham would mean leaving Anne. Unless? No, it was hopeless to consider it. He couldn't ask Anne to leave her father, the only home she had ever known. Not for a simple life as a mason's wife.

Now he studied the chimney piece again, and it seemed to ground him in happier times, when young ladies with golden-honey hair were alive and smiling next to him, when the work was simple and unchallenging. He tried to focus on the drawing itself, following the lines up, around, across, enjoying the symmetry and certainty of each element. Then, closing his eyes, his mind walked through a building with each line perfectly proportioned, each angle squared, until he felt his heart rhythm return to normal. A warmth near his hand caused him to open his eyes to find flames licking the paper and consuming his work. Slapping it out with his calloused hands, he tried to save it, but it was no use; too much had been scorched. He tossed the rest into the fire and watched it burn. Perhaps now he had a small taste of what Sir John had felt when Longleat had burned.

Walking to the window to see how close dawn was, Robert came to a decision. A second week had gone by, and Robert still waited for an investigation to be conducted, evidence to be collected, questions to be asked, but nothing happened. It was time to leave Longleat and head to the quarry. He needed a change of scene, and the visit needed to be made. No use putting it off. He would take Young Fred Horton with him. The lad needed a change of scene as well, and Robert liked him. It would be good to see what he made of the quarrying process. Who knew, it could be the beginnings of his master mason training.

The quarry was about twenty miles north of Corsley, and Robert would be gone for several days. He spent the rest of the morning planning with Hills, Cavell, and the team. Then he rode to Corsley Manor to tell Sir John of his decision.

"Good. It's about time you focused on the building," Sir John grunted when Robert told him of his plans. "Don't think I don't know about your digging around in Kington's affairs. I know all about your visit to him last week. I don't pay you to consort with the likes of him! Get up to the quarry and see what's keeping them. Why hasn't the stone been delivered?" Sir John was full of instructions for Robert's quarry visit. Last fall, he had negotiated the purchase of a quarry north of Longleat near Box. It was reputed to be one of the best sources for good quality Bath stone, known for its beauty and durability. They would build this new Longleat with the best stone, even though it meant additional transportation expense.

The next day, Robert and Young Fred rode off north, the weather blissfully cooperating. Birdsong filled the country lanes, the meadows full of late spring wildflowers. Robert could feel the tension melting with each mile farther from Longleat. A glance at Fred told him the young mason felt the same. Within a few miles, Robert had Fred chatting happily about his childhood spent nearby. Robert asked him if he knew Ned Bright, but the subject clearly upset the young man, so he dropped it. They stopped to rest and eat at an alehouse in Bradford on Avon, sitting on the banks of the narrow Avon River while Robert pointed out all the Bath stone in the local buildings.

The uniform gold color and quality of the stone made Robert eager to get to the quarry and begin selecting pieces for Longleat. As they continued to Box, Robert's pulse quickened. Now he would see what Sir John's passion was promising. To work with such fine quality stone, to build something that would outlast them all, that was what Robert was looking forward to. Now he would run his hands along its surface and watch the play of light bounce from it. No more pits and dead bodies. To work with quality stone was the dream of all masons.

Sir John's new quarry was one of several quarry pits in the area supplying Bath stone to builders and masons. Robert inquired and received specific directions from some dirty boys carrying water to the quarrymen. It was not large, but it would meet Longleat's initial needs. As Robert entered, the same lack of organization he had found at Longleat dismayed him. His hopes of quality workmanship combined with quality stone sank, but at least this was a problem he knew how to solve. He asked around for the quarry master and was directed to a large stone house situated several hundred yards from the stone pits.

A young lad answered their knock on the door and called out, "Master Saunders, there's some men here to see you." Robert heard irritable groans from inside before a large man lumbered out into the bright sunshine.

"Who's come to interrupt my afternoon rest?"

"Robert Smythson, Sir John's mason from Longleat, and this is Fred Horton, one of my junior masons. We're here about the stone to be sent down to Longleat."

"Smythson, huh?" The large man looked him over suspiciously. "Reckon I might have heard of ya. Weren't there some masons by that name killed in that accident at Winchester?"

Robert blanched. Would he ever live that down? "Yes, my father and brother were both killed in that accident, along with several other masons."

Saunders rubbed the considerable stubble on his chin and shrugged. "No Maynard this time?"

Robert tried to keep up with the changing of topics. "No, he is no longer working for Sir John. I assume you have instructions from Cavell or perhaps Sir John himself. Horton and myself will require lodging for the next several days, and I'll meet with the team you have here and let them know my requirements."

"Requirements? La, don't ya sound important! Wonder what Sir John makes of that? I trust the work we've been doing here is sufficient. Boy, see about some rooms for these two. Horton can stay with the quarrymen in the cottages, but the high and mighty Master Smythson would probably like to stay in the inn. How does that sound, Master Smythson?"

Robert ignored the air of condescension in the quarry master's tone and nodded his approval. Nothing was going to be easy here, he thought. "We'll get settled, and then I'll meet with the men. First thing tomorrow, I'll get them started on loading up the stone to prepare for transport. I trust you've had them squaring them off satisfactorily."

"Oh aye. Let's hope they're up to Your Lordship's standards."

"Master Saunders, my standards are high because Sir John's standards are high. We are hoping to do some fine quality work at Longleat. I hope you will want to be a part of that. Now please show me to the inn." Robert directed the last command to the young boy, who had been listening and watching the two men spar with great interest.

A few hours later, Robert sat in the common room of the Quarryman's Arms, local alehouse and inn, finishing his meal with a tankard of ale. He had held initial meetings with the quarrymen and inspected the work they were doing. It was sufficient, but more finishing would be required at the building site itself to ensure the stone was properly dressed. Might as well wait until it was there, where men Robert trusted could oversee the work. He felt he was being watched by the few people in the inn and retired early to avoid the inquisitive stares.

The next morning, he gathered the team and began instructions. Samuel Saunders, the quarry master, stood nearby, quietly observing. Robert carefully examined the different piles of rock which had been cut from the quarry bed, and roughly shaped. He asked a few of them to be turned over to inspect each side. An hour into the work, he came upon a stack of particularly fine stone. The color was uniform, the lines clean and smooth. He was marking the stack as ready for shipment when Saunders plodded up, shaking his head. "No, not this stack. Ya can't take that one."

Robert frowned. It was clearly the best stone. "Why not?"

"Oh, I'm afraid that's reserved for another customer. Ya can't have it, much as I'd like ya to take it."

"I don't understand. Sir John owns this quarry. All the stone is his." Robert's frustration was growing. Why couldn't anything ever associated with Longleat go smoothly?

Saunders tilted his head and squinted. "Well, yes, but as quarry manager, I have the power to negotiate with other clients. On Sir John's behalf, of course."

"So with his blessing?"

"Oh yes, of course."

Robert noticed he was being closely watched by several of the men present. He shrugged and moved on to another stack and continued with the work. The same exchange happened twice more during the day. Every time Robert found a quality piece of stone, Saunders claimed he had already promised it to someone else. Robert's anger grew with each refusal, but he held his peace throughout the day.

That evening, having declined Saunders's invitation to dine without regret, Robert took a walk around the quarry. Young Fred was settling in with the quarry masons, and Robert wanted some quiet to think. This business of the best stone being held for someone else seemed suspicious. Would Sir John tolerate that? Saunders said it was with Sir John's blessing, but Robert was doubtful. Perfection was the one thing Sir John valued higher than profit. It made no sense to purchase a quarry and then let the best stone go to someone else. Robert wished he could talk to Cavell to see if it were true.

He was aware all the time he was at Box how close he was to Lacock, and he considered riding over to have a look around. Perhaps he could find Ned Bright and relieve himself of the fears that they would soon unearth his body at Longleat. Robert picked up a small piece of stone, feeling its edges, turning it over in his hand. Each surface seemed to represent another problem he had encountered. Death, delays, demands, and now deceit! He drew back and threw the stone against a tree with as much force as he could muster. The thud it caused as it hit the tree was not nearly as satisfying as he had hoped. He sighed and returned to the inn, knowing he would not go to Lacock. *Deal with the problem at hand before looking for more trouble.*

His nightmares had followed him to Box, this time adding the bulbous face of Saunders to the mix, and Robert had a restless night. In the morning, a gray mist dampened his spirits as well as the earth. He confronted Saunders. "About the stone you've reserved for another customer . . ." Saunders grunted in assent. "Who exactly is that customer, and when was that agreement reached?"

"Are ya questioning me, young man?"

Robert squared his shoulders, trying to look determined. "Yes, I am. I believe Sir John owns this entire quarry, with full and complete rights to any and all stone contained within. If there had been any exceptions, he or Richard Cavell would have told me."

"Oh, ya think so, do ya? Or perhaps ya just want a share of the take?"

"What? No, I . . ." Robert couldn't believe what he was hearing. "Saunders, are you offering me a share in your scheme to cheat Sir John?"

"Just trying to see what kind of man ya are. No harm in that, is there?"

Robert ran his hand through his hair, incredulous at the man's gall.

"Do ya, want in? Ya could make a tidy little profit. Sir John doesn't have to know."

"No! I don't." Robert began pacing. "I am disgusted that you would suggest such a thing. It's dishonest and appalling. Sir John hired me to build him the best possible house, and that means using the best possible stone."

"So ya found your principles, did ya?" Saunders shrugged. "Suit yourself."

"Saunders, whatever side arrangements you have will cease now. All the piles of stone I select will be loaded immediately and readied for transport to Longleat. If you refuse, I will have to report you to Sir John upon my return to Longleat."

"Well, well." Saunders laughed. "The mason's found his backbone. All right, ya can have all the stone." Saunders turned to walk away, shouting to the rest of the men, "Ya heard him, lads, it all goes to Longleat."

Robert was shaking. What the hell had just happened? He was tired of being manipulated and lied to. "Was this some kind of test? Was it Sir John's idea or your own?"

The quarry master turned around, walking back toward Robert. "A little of both," he replied, still laughing. "We wanted to see what kind of man ya were. For a while there, I thought ya were a weak one. Can't have that. No, we can't. But ya might be a gullible one, and that's not so good either, now is it? Probably think ya can just drop a glove and find stone, don't ya?"

Robert was confused by this revelation. And angry. "Sir John told you to test me? I should have expected something like that. But what does dropping a glove have to do with finding stone?"

"Oh, have ya not heard the fable, then? Suppose not, seeing as how ya're not from around here. The legend of this place is that almost a thousand years ago, Saint Aldhelm was riding across this land and threw down his glove. Where it landed, he told his men to dig and they would find great treasure. That's how this great stone was first discovered."

Robert's head was spinning. Saunders was changing directions so quickly Robert felt like a hand drill going round and round. He stood looking at the large man, wondering what he would say next.

"Go on, it's all yours. Get on with it, son." Saunders turned and walked away, leaving behind the sound of his booming laughter as he went.

It was hard to do the work with so many questions looming. Dead bodies, fires, now tests of loyalty and acumen. Robert wasn't sure what Sir John was testing in him; he just knew he was tired of it. He had come to the quarry to get away from Sir John's intensity and demands and had met with a different intensity.

Over the next few days, he tried to put all thoughts of buried bodies and deceitful quarry masters aside and focus on the task at hand. A building the size of the projected Longleat would require an enormous quantity of good quality stone, and Robert thoroughly enjoyed evaluating the different lines that had been brought up and squared off. With every piece, his determination to see the building of Longleat through to the end grew. Robert focused on the work at hand, tried to push other thoughts aside, and stayed out of Saunders's way.

They made plans for the first load of stone to be loaded into carts and driven to Longleat. Robert decided to leave Young Fred at the quarry. The lad seemed happier away from Longleat. Why not give him a bit longer to recover from the shock of discovering Mary's body? Besides, he showed promise at being able to choose good stone from bad. Let him have more experience and time away from the stresses of Longleat and its memories.

If he were honest, Robert was envious of Young Fred. He wouldn't mind some additional time away from the recent events at Longleat. Sir John's refusal to investigate Mary's murder gnawed at him, as did Kington's ambivalence. The logical thing to do was to go to Lacock and see if Ned Bright was there. As Robert mounted his horse for the return trip, he peered eastward and almost galloped off toward Lacock. But the games Saunders had played changed his mind. Who knew what spies Sir John had watching him? Besides, he had questions that could be answered closer to home. With those in mind, he headed south.

Chapter 9

UPON HIS RETURN TO Longleat, Robert rode to Warminster. He got his men started on their work for the day and left. The time at the quarry had reminded him that occasionally he needed a break from Longleat, so he planned on shopping and mingling with people unassociated with Sir John. He wanted to see the surgeon, Roger Williams, for several reasons. One was personal. He was hoping the surgeon could recommend something to help stop the nightmares that hounded him since Mary's body was discovered and let him sleep.

He also wanted to know if Williams had come up with any additional insight into Mary's death. He entered Warminster, the market town nearest to Longleat and felt his heart quicken. His first stop was to William's surgery, where he was fortunate to find the man in. "Well met, Smythson. What can I do for you? Haven't found any more buried bodies you need me to look at, have you?"

Robert's expression reflected the humorlessness he felt, and Williams looked suitably contrite. Robert explained about his disturbing dreams and lack of sleep. The surgeon recommended a tincture of catnip and valerian root, for which Robert gratefully paid. As he tucked it into his bag, he noticed the potent smell.

Williams assured him it would work; despite its strong odor, valerian was effective. Then Robert explained the second part of his errand.

Williams seemed confused. "I gave my full report to Sir John, who promised to relay the information to Mary's father and any other interested parties. Are there still some questions? I thought it was resolved."

"I suppose you could call it my curiosity that won't rest, as well as my body, since I was one of those who discovered her. When I last spoke to Henry Kington, he did not seem to have additional information. I would be surprised if Sir John kept his promise."

"I'm happy to tell you what I told Sir John. As we thought at the time of discovery, I believe the cause of death was a blow to the head. From further examination, I think it came from above, from someone quite tall, or she was in a seated position."

"Any idea what the killer could have used?"

"Well, judging from the size and shape of the injury to the skull, I would say it was a sharp, narrow object of regular proportions, not a rock, for example. Given the location of the body, I would surmise that we're probably looking at one of your masonry tools. Well, not *your* tools, of course, but the tools of the trade." Robert's heart sank; he did not want any mason implicated in the crime.

Williams continued, "Is it usual for the tools to be left at the job site? Or would they be cleaned up?"

"I see what you're asking. Could anyone nearby pick up a mason's hammer and use it, or are we looking specifically for a mason who would have easy access to his own tools? It depends. A well-run job site would not allow tools to be left lying around. However, I do not think Longleat has always been well run. So I really don't know."

"Have you had any success finding the father?"

"Henry Kington? He's at Cley Hill Farm, as usual."

"No, not Mary's father. The father of her baby?"

"What? What baby?" Robert stepped back in surprise.

"You didn't know? I can't be absolutely positive because of the extent of decomposition, but I believe Mary Kington was with child at the time of her death."

"Really? And you think I should have known? I don't think Kington knew. Who did you tell?"

"It was included in my report to Sir John. I suppose he kept that to himself." Williams sighed with the air of a man who was used to having no power.

"Do you think she knew?"

"I would think so. The remains of the unborn child were just recognizable."

"So she was with child." Robert paused, digesting this development. "Probably Ned Bright's, although I suppose there's no way to be sure. Nobody has accused her of anything other than being true to an unsuitable mason, so I think we can safely assume the child was Ned's. Mary's father thinks Ned killed her. If he knew she was carrying his child, do you think he would kill her?"

"Unfortunately, I have known men to do just that."

"Oh dear."

"Yes, in my profession, I see the best of life and the worst of it. But in this case, I don't think so."

"Why do you say that?"

"It's the way her body was wrapped up carefully in the tarp. We know that the fire didn't kill her, but it didn't burn up her body either. The way they took the time to wrap up the body and place it carefully next to the building. It's more of a protection, almost a burial. I think whoever did this to her had a great feeling for her, maybe even loved her."

"I hadn't thought of that," Robert reflected.

"Who is handling the investigation for Sir John?"

Robert laughed ruefully. No one was. Sir John seemed inclined to just bury the girl and move on with the building. If Kington didn't make a fuss, there might not be an investigation. Should he say as much to Williams? He didn't know the man or his relationship with Sir John or anyone else in the area. Instead, he answered vaguely and then changed the subject. "Did Mary ever come to you for medical attention?"

"No, I have had no real dealings with the Kingtons since Mary's mother died. And that was many years ago. Either they are a healthy lot or they seek advice and treatment elsewhere."

"Thank you for your time and the information, Master Williams."

"I wish you luck finding out what happened. May her soul rest in peace."

Robert left the surgery and walked along the narrow town streets, pondering all he had learned. It had been over a month since he had been to a town the size of Warminster, and he explored at his leisure. For once, let the workers at Longleat make progress without him. He took his time walking down the streets, looking at the buildings and indulging in one of his favorite hobbies: redesigning. To one building, he enlarged the windows to allow more light to come in. To another, he widened the angles of the gables. To a third, he extended the side to add symmetry. It always soothed his soul to see new buildings and imagine how he would alter them.

Usually, it was the exterior of a building that caught his interest, but occasionally it was the inside. Suddenly, he caught a glance of some fabric the exact color of Anne's eyes in a shop window, and before he knew it, his feet had carried him into the store.

"Good day, my dear fellow. What can I interest you in? A new pair of hose perhaps," the shopkeeper said, looking Robert up and down with appraisal. "We offer some tailoring if you would like to get a new jerkin made."

"Good day, actually it was that fabric that caught my eye."

"You certainly have good taste. A gift for the mistress, perhaps? I would be happy to make that into a kirtle or perhaps just some sleeves for her."

"Not yet, perhaps one day." Robert grinned. "The fabric is the exact color of her eyes."

"Ah yes. A gift like this could turn hope into reality. How much shall I cut for you?"

Robert laughed, knowing he was being manipulated but willing to go along with the hopeful plan. "I don't think I need the fabric, but do you perhaps have any threads in that color? My . . . She . . ." He hesitated to think how to describe Anne. "She's a gifted needlewoman and would not think it too forward of me to give her some threads."

"Ah yes. I have some silk threads in just that shade. Over here. They're quite fine. Shall I wrap some up for you?"

"Yes. Two lengths, please. And tell me, do you perhaps know of another girl whose eyes matched this color?"

"Ah, you speak of Mary Kington, do you not?" Robert watched as the man selected the threads with a flourish, allowing the color to catch the light. "News travels quickly in these parts. For example, I guess that you are Sir John Thynne's newest mason. Am I correct?"

"You are indeed. The name is Robert Smythson. It is good to meet you." The store was not busy, and the proprietor seemed willing to talk. Why not ask some questions? "Did you know Mary Kington well? What kind of girl was she?"

"I did not know her well, but she came in with her father over the years. A quiet girl, well mannered, compliant, I would say. Running off with a mason would have been the boldest thing she would have ever done. He must have been quite the fellow to get her to go against her father's wishes."

"Why do you say that?"

"Have you met Kington? He was a hard father to live with, I would imagine. Unyielding, often angry. I heard him raise his voice with her more than once. Here you go." The shopkeeper had carefully wrapped the threads while he was talking. As Robert paid him, his gaze was drawn to a display of gloves. His thoughts went back to the story the quarry master had told him. Just throw a glove down on the ground and find treasure, as easy as that, he thought. The shopkeeper followed his gaze. "Can I interest you in some gloves? For yourself or perhaps for your young lady?"

Robert shook his head. "Not this time. But how about this? If she becomes my wife, I promise to bring her here and buy her a pair of gloves."

The shopkeeper smiled. "I'll hold you to that promise," he said. "I look forward to meeting this young lady of yours when you bring her in as your wife."

Robert mirrored his smile as the shopkeeper emphasized the word *when* instead of *if*. "I look forward to that day too, sir. Good day." Robert tucked the silk into his pouch, thinking wistfully of the time he could give it to Anne and make good on the shopkeeper's faith in their future. Truthfully, he wasn't sure it would ever come. He had no plans to return to Reading or to the employment of Sir Francis. How was he to get to her? What was to stop some other young man from making an offer of marriage to her? Perhaps even now Lady Catherine was planning her wedding to someone far more suitable than him.

Without the shopkeeper's friendly chatter, his hopeful mood turned despondent. Finding himself by an alehouse, he went in. A tankard of ale and a bowl of fish stew later, he felt a bit more revived. As he paid, he casually asked the barmaid if there was any news. "Aye, that gentleman there just rode in from Salisbury with news from London. I'm sure he won't mind telling it again, especially if you buy him a drink." Robert took her hint and paid for another pitcher of ale, which he carried to the gentleman's table.

"Sir, I hear you have news. Would you care to share my ale while I share your news?"

"Certainly, good fellow. Yes, big doings up north. The Scots Queen has escaped from her prison and tried to fight the Earl of Moray. Stupid woman. She was defeated, of course, and guess where she went? You will never guess," he said, slapping his knee and liberally pouring Robert's ale into his tankard. "She's crossed the border and come into England. Just a week ago, from what I heard. Thinks our Queen will take her in and help her get her throne back. Not likely. Why would we help a heretic like her?"

Robert immediately thought of his old friend Sir Francis. "What has been the Queen's response?"

"Sent a band of soldiers to greet her and welcomed her straight into Carlisle Castle, where she will stay until Elizabeth decides what to do with her."

"Did you hear anything about the man leading the soldiers? Is it Sir Francis Knollys?

"No, nothing like that has reached my ears. But I can tell you the latest rumors of who will marry the Queen. They say she is considering marriage to a Catholic, if that can be believed. And what would that do to Mary Stuart? I don't think it will happen, but speculation and betting are rampant in London." Robert listened for a few more minutes but heard nothing more of personal interest. He thanked the man and decided it was time to return home.

Retrieving his horse, he rode home with a head full of new knowledge. Mary Stuart was in England. No doubt Sir Francis was involved somehow. Queen Elizabeth trusted him to handle complicated and delicate situations. Robert sighed. All this heartache over religion. And if Catholic Mary Stuart was in England, many would be encouraging her to take over the English throne. Robert shuddered. Did anyone want to go back to the days of Bloody Mary Tudor, where men and women were executed, burned for their faith? Anne had told him how her uncle, Jocelyn Palmer, had been burned at the stake as a Protestant heretic. Her own father had been taken in by Sir Francis Knollys out of affection for her uncle, who had previously been a tutor for the Knollys family. Under Queen Elizabeth, the country had found a sense of calm and peace over the question of religion. Would all of that get stirred up again? Robert knew there were Catholics who would welcome the removal of the Protestant Queen. Was Henry Kington one of them? His mind went to what he had learned about the Kingtons. Henry supposedly had a temper, and Mary Kington had been with child at the time of her death. How did any of that play into her death? As the road from Warminster rounded Cley Hill and approached Corsley Heath, Robert hoped things were calm back at Longleat.

Robert's first stop was Corsley Manor. There was the issue of the stone at the quarry and Saunders's attempts to prevent him from bringing the best to Longleat, and Robert wanted to know if Sir John knew about the scheme. Then Robert needed Sir John to know that he knew Mary Kington had been both pregnant and murdered. How could there not be an investigation? Yet he remembered Sir John's warnings not to interfere. Every time he approached the gabled house and walked under the stone entry arch, his stomach tightened. He felt like a new apprentice bringing what he knew was a flawed piece of work to his master. He tried to stir up his confidence to challenge Sir John with not one, but two serious issues. Instead, the fish stew threatened to come back up.

"Is Sir John available?" he asked the boy lurking outside Sir John's business chamber, waiting to be summoned. Receiving a positive answer, he knocked and entered. Sir John was sitting behind his oversized desk, as usual, reading a letter.

"Smythson? What brings you here? Shouldn't you be supervising the men, or God forbid, helping with some of the work? Did the first load of stone arrive? How does it look?"

"About that stone, Sir John, I . . ." Robert hesitated, "are you aware Sam Saunders, the quarry manager, was trying to cheat you out of the finest stone?"

To Robert's surprise, Sir John dropped the letter he was reading and roared with laughter. "Who do you think put him up to it?" he bellowed. "Saunders is a tricky bastard, but he wouldn't have thought of that plan by himself. I told him to give you a little test, see how you'd respond." Sir John gestured to the letter he had been reading. "Says here it took you a while, but you finally stood up for yourself and Longleat. Smythson, you're going to need to do better than that if you're going to work for me. Time to get demanding, insist on doing what's best for Longleat and damn the rest."

Robert lost his footing and bumped into the paneled wall. It was worse than what he had suspected. It had been a test, but not one of Saunders's invention. How was Robert supposed to work for someone who sent spies and set tests for his employees?

"Now, Smythson, don't get upset. I need to be sure I don't have another Spicer on my hands. I need to make sure you're putting my interests first, not your own. Now why are you here?"

Robert tried to find his balance, both physical and mental. There was still the matter of Mary Kington. "I went to Warminster and spoke with Williams, the surgeon. He had some surprising news about Mary Kington."

"Warminster? Do I pay you to go to Warminster? Sixteen pennies a day for an honest day's work, not to go traipsing off to Warminster for a social call."

"It wasn't a social call. It was to get information about Mary Kington, whose body we discovered at Longleat. Sorting out this mystery is important. We cannot, in good faith, continue the building project until we know what happened to the girl."

During Robert's plea, Sir John's attention was still half-focused on the papers on his desk. Now he fixed Robert with a steady gaze, brows lowered. "Good faith? What has that got to do with anything. What mystery? The girl was killed and dumped. End of story."

Robert recoiled at Sir John's words, feeling like he had been punched in the stomach. He could not believe what he had just heard. Was Sir John incapable of human feeling? "You cannot be serious! The girl was attacked and brutally killed. She could be one of your daughters."

"But she's not, is she? She's a local girl who had acted against her father's wishes. It is Master Kington's business, not mine. He has not been hounding me to investigate, so I won't." Sir John's voice was rising. "And neither will you!"

"God's breath! After what I learned today? Did you know she was with child at the time of her death? How can you let this girl's death go uninvestigated, her killer unknown and unpunished?"

"I may have heard that. Is that supposed to make a difference?"

"I would think so."

"Smythson, I am not paying you to think or to investigate dead bodies. I am paying you to organize my masons and build me a house." Sir John rose to his full height and leaned over the desk. The ermine cape he wore to keep the cold of his chamber away only added to his intimidating bulk. "Lovell led me to believe you would be easy to work with, that you would focus on the building and not cause trouble. Now here you are, clearly causing trouble. Tell me, are you capable of putting aside this girl's death or not?"

Robert wished he could say yes. He wanted to get lost in the stonework, organizing and encouraging the lads, teaching them how to take pride in their work, watching the building rise from the ground, one beautiful piece of stone at a time. He fidgeted, aware of Sir John's dark eyes boring into him. His hands brushed against his doublet and felt the package of threads for Anne. It would be so easy to agree, to build a reputation and savings enough to support her. All he needed to do was lay aside the nagging question of how Mary's body ended up in the Longleat foundations. He swayed with his eyes closed momentarily, Mary's face merging into Anne's, seeing Henry Kington's pain over the loss of his daughter. There was only one possible answer. Sir John's eyes bulged as Robert muttered, "No, sir, I don't think I can."

"If I were you, I would rethink that answer. If you cannot stop these questions and focus on the job at hand, I will find someone who can!"

Robert stared at him. Sir John could not possibly be serious. Robert stood motionless, waiting for Sir John to continue. The two men glared at one another for a moment before Sir John took his seat, picked up a letter, and continued as if the interruption had never happened. Finally, Robert turned and walked out of the room.

Chapter 10

Robert galloped down Deep Lane away from Corsley, tears blinding his eyes. How could a man be so callous? His body shook with fury as he passed the turn for Cley Hill Farm. He should go and talk to Kington, tell him about Mary's pregnancy. He was sure that Sir John hadn't and did not intend to do so. The thought of facing the grieving father, who now had to face the loss of a grandchild as well, was too much, and Robert rode on.

Reaching Corsley Heath, anger still surging through him, he urged his horse onward, not knowing or caring where he was going. He considered stopping at the Royal Oak and drowning his feelings, but the image of questioning faces spurred him away. He continued westward, eventually riding down unfamiliar narrow lanes bordered by spring flowers. The trees in full leaf and the sounds of birdsong soon began to soothe his temper. He slowed the horse down and felt the warmth of the spring afternoon sun. Sir John would probably not pay him for today, and at this point Robert did not care. He was not sure he would be returning to Longleat, so what difference would one day's pay make?

As the trees began to grow thicker, blocking views of the fields, Robert passed a sign for the Woodlands and remembered that

Alan Maynard lived nearby. He was suddenly filled with a longing to see how the former master mason of Longleat lived and speak to him if possible. A short while later, he came to the tiny hamlet of East Woodlands. It was even smaller than Corsley Heath, just a few cottages and two or three small timber-framed houses tucked behind neat rows of shrubbery and surrounded by tall trees.

He tied the horse to a tree and walked down the narrow lane, trying to decide what to do. Here he was, the supposed master mason of the great house at Longleat, living in a single cramped room under a sloped roof, while Maynard lived in one of these homes. A youth stepped out from one of the cottages, a boy with hair so light it was almost white, dressed shabbily. "You there, might you know which of these houses is the Maynards'?" The boy pointed to the largest of the houses, then ran back inside. Robert stood in front of the house, admiring its form: stone on the ground level, a full timber-frame story above, plus attic space, probably a total of at least eight rooms, real glass windows, the garden covered with bluebells, signs of a fine kitchen garden planted to the side, and a small stable behind. How much was the rent on a house like that?

As he stood looking at the house, Betty Maynard came out and called to him. "Robert Smythson? Is that you?"

"Yes, Goodwife Maynard. Well met. Is your husband home, by any chance?"

"No, he's away just now. He will be sorry to miss you. Do you have news of Longleat? Is Alan wanted back?"

"No, nothing like that." Although, he thought to himself, it could be very much like that. Who knew? Within a week or two Maynard could be back in place as master mason and Robert could be looking for work. "I just thought I would come see where he lived and maybe talk if he were home. Sorry to bother you."

"No bother, Master Smythson, no bother. Come in; my maid will get you some ale. We have a fresh batch, and I believe it is quite good."

Robert soon found himself sitting across from Betty Maynard in a comfortable chamber, politely sipping ale. The room was light and airy with a good-sized fireplace and well-made furniture. He made a comment about how comfortable the room was.

"Thank you. I pride myself on the quality of our home. You're not married, are you, Master Smythson?"

"No," he admitted, thinking about coming home to Anne in a place like this, with a maid to help her. If he could get this, perhaps it was worth putting up with Sir John's bellowing. Maybe.

"Well, maybe I could be of help to you in that area. I'm sure I can find you a suitable girl. Let me think."

"Thank you, Mistress Maynard, but that won't be necessary," he replied, blushing.

"Oh, I see you've got someone in mind already. Wonderful. Who is she? Well, you marry her, and I'll find you a home to take her to. Let's see, what would be suitable? I suppose you could have this one once we leave. If you could afford it, that is. Old Thynne isn't generous with his money, is he? I've heard that you're living in quite meager lodgings. I suppose that's all you can afford."

"Actually—"

"Never mind. I'll think of something. Who is the girl? Is she local?"

So many questions. What would happen if Betty Maynard and Sir John ever had a conversation? Robert thought. "No, she's not local. Anne is connected with the Knollys family, for whom I used to work."

"Oh, the Knollys family. I've heard of them. Aren't they connected somehow with Her Majesty?"

"Yes, Sir Francis Knollys's wife, Lady Catherine, is the Queen's cousin. But Anne is a junior member of their household."

Betty gulped her ale a little too quickly and coughed. After the emotional upheaval of the day, he admitted he was amused to see Betty's discomfiture with the idea that the man who had replaced her husband was soon to be married to a girl connected with the Queen herself.

"Well," she sighed after a long pause, "we will soon be moving in exalted circles as well." She tossed her curls and straightened her back. "Alan's designing a great house for someone intimately connected to the Queen. Once he's finished, we'll be off and away, I expect. I've lived here all my life, but soon I will be leaving, on to greener pastures, as it were. Big happenings. Of course, Alan will be glad to leave Longleat in your capable hands. I'm sure you will be able to do what Sir John wants. Always changing his mind. Alan found it quite difficult, but then Alan is so brilliant, isn't he?"

Robert, confused, decided to just nod in agreement. He imagined that Betty could babble all afternoon about her husband, but she surprised him with her next question.

"I'm glad you stopped by today so we could have a private chat. I've been wanting to ask you about Mary Kington. I understand you've been making inquiries about her death?"

"Well, yes, I suppose. Sir John isn't doing anything to solve her murder and doesn't want me to either. In fact, earlier today he made that crystal clear."

"Makes you wonder what he might be hiding or covering up, doesn't it?"

"Yes, exactly. No one seems to want to talk about her. You're one of the first people to ask. Did you know her well?"

"Not well, but yes, I did know her. What have you been able to discover so far?"

"Very little, I'm afraid." Robert wondered if he should divulge the latest news to Betty. It was unusual to have someone want to talk about Mary's death. He decided it wouldn't do any harm. "Although just earlier today I did learn that Mary was with child at the time of her death and that whoever killed her probably cared for her."

Betty's hand fumbled her beaker of ale, sending it crashing to the floor.

"Oh dear, I didn't mean to upset you," Robert said, bending down to retrieve the beaker, which thankfully had not broken on the rush mats.

"No, no, I'm fine. Daisy, bring some rags to mop up the ale I spilled. Clumsy me. And such a waste of fine ale. Master Smythson, can I get you some more?" Betty moved to take his beaker and refilled both from the pitcher, keeping her back to him for several minutes.

A young woman came in and dabbed at the spill, somewhat hopelessly as the rushes had already soaked up the little that had spilled. Robert received his refilled beaker and sipped politely, allowing Betty to regain her composure.

"We assume the father was Ned Bright as everyone has said the two were devoted to one another."

"Oh yes, of course." Betty looked relieved.

"Did you know Ned? You say you've lived here all your life. He was a local boy, I believe."

"Ned? Of course I know him. I've known him since childhood. We both grew up in Frome. We're probably related in some distant manner."

"What was he like?"

Betty covered her mouth with her hands. "Master Smythson, you seem to be speaking of him as if something happened to him. Ned's body's not been found as well?"

"No, no, nothing like that. It's just that . . ." Unsure how to continue, Robert's voice trailed off.

"Oh. I see. Well, everyone knows Ned Bright: the boy with the golden voice and his head in the clouds. He wasn't much good for anything else other than his music. His parents insisted he pick and train for a trade. Said there was no future in music for a boy without looks or charm."

"That's probably true. Shows good sense on their part. And he chose masonry?"

"Yes. He's a good lad. The kind that goes along. Tell him what to do and he does it without question. That is, until he met the Kington girl. A spark kind of woke up in him once he met her."

"I'm afraid I don't understand. If you were all local people, why hadn't they met each other before recently?"

"Mary's father is a strange one. He protected her, didn't let her out much. I think he was afraid of losing her. Then he got the notion of marrying her to one of Sir John's sons and started bringing her around Longleat. That was before the fire, when the Thynnes all lived in the house even while the masons were still working on it. Once Mary heard Ned singing, which he does—or did—while he works, they were brought together like bees to flowers. Heels over head, they were, just like me and Alan."

"Do you know where Ned might be? I'd like to talk to him about Mary's . . . disappearance. See if he knows anything."

"I suppose he's still up at Lacock. Don't see why he wouldn't be there. I'm not sure he'll be able to help. Alan says he's been melancholy of late, doesn't talk much, not working well, not that he ever did. But he used to sing and play all the time. We used to invite him over to entertain our guests. Alan says there's no music left in him. I guess I didn't think about it, but maybe it has something to do with Mary. Do you think so?"

"Most likely. If they were as close as I hear they were."

"Alan says they're not going to finish the new tower for another several months. Hoping to have it done by the end of the summer."

"He's working at Lacock with Ned?"

"Alan? Yes, sometimes. He's overseeing the work while also bidding out for another job, the one I was telling you about. Lacock is just a side project until the big job comes in. You know, when we leave to move to the new job, you should take over our lease here."

Robert could think of nothing he would like better. Then he remembered that he might not have a job at all. Daisy reentered the room, bringing some candles to light against the growing gloom. That reminded Robert that it was getting late. He thanked his hostess for the ale and the information and said his goodbyes.

Later that night, Robert dragged a stool outside the masons lodge and sat watching the stars. A little brown tabby cat who had started visiting him wrapped itself around him for a few minutes before falling asleep at his feet. The evenings were staying lighter longer as May slid towards June. He had a choice to make. Stay at Longleat and drop the investigation? Go to Lacock and find Ned Bright? What would he do then? Had Ned heard about Mary? Could news travel that far that fast? Betty had heard the news, and if Maynard had been home and then gone back to Lacock, certainly he would have told Ned.

He decided to take the questions one at a time. Could he stay at a place where a murder was ignored or uninvestigated? Robert reached down and picked up the cat, settling it on his lap and stroking its fur. "Does Sir John care so little about the lives of those around him that a young pregnant woman could be killed and dumped without so much as an inquiry?" The cat remained silent. "And why isn't Mary's father pushing for this to be investigated? If Kington thinks Ned killed Mary, why not send someone the twenty or so miles north to ask him about it?" The cat purred loudly in response. "I see you agree with me, cat, don't you? Should I go up to Lacock and find out?" Robert considered this question.

There was probably no way to hide a visit from Sir John, who apparently had spies throughout the district. Yet a visit needed to be made.

Robert's thoughts turned to the Maynards. Their behavior surrounding Longleat and the Kingtons seemed odd. Maynard had showed up prior to their removing the north range. Was he protecting it, and if so, was it because of Mary's body? Betty had seemed upset to learn of Mary's pregnancy. Was that related? Could the Maynards have had something to do with Mary's death? Too many questions.

"Nothing more we can do tonight," Robert said, putting the cat down and going inside. He lit the torch and remained in the workshop, looking at the drawings for the new Longleat. It was going to be something special. Large, square, symmetrical, dotted with gables rising to the sky, situated in a beautiful green valley. He wanted to be a part of it. But at what cost? Robert kicked the stool he had dragged in. It fell over, startling the cat, who had followed him inside. He was frustrated and angry. Frustrated with missing Anne, with living above the masons lodge, while just down the road the former master mason of Longleat lived in comfort with his plump, content wife. What was he doing with his life? Taking orders from a grumpy, impatient miser who cared nil for the people under him.

He went upstairs to get ready for bed. As he removed his doublet, the silk threads he had bought for Anne came tumbling out. Had that been today? It seemed almost a lifetime ago. He let the silk slip through his fingers a few times, feeling the smoothness of it, picturing the one for whom he had bought it. Then he reached a decision.

Someone needed to care that this girl with the golden-honey hair and green eyes had been killed and dumped without ceremony into a pit. The first load of stone would be delivered soon from the quarry. The men had been working hard to speed up the mortar production. The next steps would be to finish squaring and polishing the stone to start building the south walls. The work would be simple; nothing that would require his skill or oversight. Perhaps John Hills could oversee the men while Robert traveled to Lacock. If Sir John didn't like it, he could fire Robert, and Robert would deal with that when it came. Until then, he would do his best to investigate.

Chapter 11

The following morning, Robert found himself in Maynard's old workshop, the place where they had laid Mary's body. The structure had not been used since. As he entered, the smell of decay and death wafted toward him, faint but still noticeable, so he left the door open wide to let some air in. He hadn't slept well the night before, Sir John's ultimatum swimming in his head. He wasn't sure why he had come to this workshop, just that he felt this space had something to tell him.

The room was in disarray, items strewn in the corners and on the floor, where they had been hastily thrown when they brought the body in. Robert began to straighten up, his hands unconsciously picking up items that had been knocked over. He covered one of the workbenches with a tarp and began to line up tools on it, instinctively lining them up by size and function.

He was soon interrupted by the arrival of John Hills, who joined Robert in his task. As they worked, Robert filled his sensible friend in on the events of the day before.

"Have you considered why Sir John is so anxious to keep this quiet?" the older mason asked.

"Yes, and Richard Cavell as well. Did you know he once wanted to marry Mary?"

"I'm not surprised. Sounds like it would have been a good match. Her father had other plans?"

"Yes, you've heard that Kington wanted Mary to marry into the Thynne family. There was something odd about Cavell's reaction to finding Mary's body. He was particularly distraught."

"Everyone was distraught. It was both shocking and gruesome." Hills began to sweep the floor while Robert adjusted the tools, straightening the lines, making sure the spaces between individual tools and sets were even.

"No, his reaction was more visceral. As if it were more than just a body. It seemed personal."

"Like he had something to hide?"

Robert looked off into the distance, searching for answers. "Maybe. Although it was Cavell who first identified Mary. No one else seemed to have a clue who she was."

"Are you saying he already knew she was there?"

"What reason would Cavell, or Sir John for that matter, have for killing Mary, assuming they don't want me to investigate because they are somehow involved?"

"Her death could have been accidental, but the placement of her body wrapped in a tarp and carefully set near a burning wall was not."

"Mary's death supposedly occurred the same night as the Longleat fire," Robert observed. "I suppose she could have witnessed someone deliberately setting the fire and been killed to keep her quiet."

"Or the fire was set to cover up the murder," Hills replied.

"And why wasn't the rubble moved from that area last year? Did someone know her body was there and didn't want it disturbed?"

"Possibly. Although they had to know it would be moved eventually. Who made that decision?"

"Sir John, but apparently from Maynard's advice. That's another thing." Robert told Hills about his visit with Betty Maynard the previous day. "She seemed shaken about Mary being with child. Her reaction to the news was too strong for a disinterested party."

"She couldn't possibly be involved, could she?" Hills asked.

"No, I doubt it. But what if she thinks or knows that Maynard is?"

"But why? What possible motive could he have for killing Mary Kington?"

"I don't know, but why did he show up just before we discovered her body? The timing is suspicious." Robert paused; his hands stopped wiping the chisel he held. He gestured to the room. "This whole thing makes me so angry! A young woman was killed, and nobody seems to care!" The desperation bubbled up from within, and he slammed the chisel down on the table with the force of a man used to breaking stone. He looked at the tools now arranged on the bench. There was a hodgepodge of tools, no complete sets. What was he looking for? A complete set, marked by their owners, with one piece conspicuously missing so it was clear what had been used as a weapon?

"And the fact that the young woman in question looks like Anne Palmer has nothing to do with it?" Hills asked. Hills was the one man at Longleat who knew how much Robert loved Anne.

"Yesterday, I stood staring at Maynard's house, wishing it was mine, mine and Anne's. How I envied Maynard at that moment."

"What's stopping you from asking Anne to marry you and bringing her here?"

"Everything. Our unequal social status, uprooting her from everything and everyone she knows, bringing her here to this harsh place where women are killed and dumped, where my employment rests on Sir John's fickleness, his mood of the day. What if I bring her here and he fires all of us? How could I face her then?"

"What's bothering you?"

"This. Mary Kington's death and the fact that no one cares enough about her to find out what happened."

"Then you care." Hills leaned closer to Robert, speaking quietly and calmly.

"What?"

"You solve it. Yes, I know everything Sir John and Cavell told you. But you are master mason here, and it was you who unearthed the body."

"What are you saying?" Over the past few years, Robert had come to trust Hills's opinion and his work with the men. He was even-tempered and reasonable, a decent mason, and a better man. If Hills was giving him advice, Robert knew he should listen.

"Robert," Hills continued with an air of seriousness and purpose that caught Robert's attention. "It's time you stopped acting like a junior mason seeking everyone's approval. You are the master mason of the great house of Longleat. Act like it. Take the job and yourself seriously. If you want to find out who killed her, then do it."

"What about Sir John's threats?"

"Be smart about it. Do your job, but also keep your eyes and ears open. Look, Robert, I don't mean to criticize, but you're not taking your position here seriously. And if you don't, no one else will. Your choice of home reflects your position and status. That's why these landowners are building these houses in the first place. You saw where Maynard lives. If you think all you're worthy of is a loft above the masons lodge, then that's the way people will treat you. You have to demand respect to get respect."

Robert let this seep in. Part of him knew his friend was correct, especially after seeing Maynard's house. If he could just put all this death and plotting behind him. To do that, he felt he needed to solve Mary's murder and said as much to Hills.

"You spoke with Marys' father?" Hills asked. "What did he say?"

"Kington seems convinced Ned Bright is responsible. I admit that for several days I was worried we might dig up Bright's body as well, but it seems he's up at Lacock Abbey, at least according to Betty Maynard."

"Sounds like someone needs to go up and speak to him."

"Yes. You're right. I'm thinking about taking a trip to the quarry and adding a trip to Lacock to my agenda."

"Good. That's what I had in mind. Do the work of a master mason but find ways to get answers while you do it. And, Robert, when are we going to find you a proper house?"

Robert sighed. He knew Hills was right. "I'll deal with my housing choice later. First, I want to solve this murder."

"Good. I'll help however I can."

No opportunity presented itself over the next couple of weeks. Robert was careful to appear compliant, doing the work he was hired to do with no talk of Mary's death. Sir John seemed satisfied that his wishes were being followed. He was preparing for a trip away from Longleat and wanted continual meetings to bark out instructions Robert already knew about or to ask questions Robert had already answered. In the meantime, the building site was finally cleared, the foundations cleaned up and ready to be added on to.

Robert wasn't sure which he hoped would happen first: the arrival of the first load of stone or Sir John's departure. As it happened, they occurred in that order, just one day apart at the end of May. The arrival of the stone created a buzz of excitement throughout the building site. The day was sunny, and the bright light made the stone glimmer and shine. Sir John inspected the first load and grudgingly admitted it was of adequate quality. "It should be; it cost me a fortune!" he added.

"It's well worth the price, Sir John," Robert answered. "This stone will outlast us all."

The two men watched the stone being unloaded and the masons starting on the finishing work. The stone had been squared off at the quarry, but it still required the finer facing and pointing to be done before it could be laid in place. Sir John grunted his approval. "I'm glad to see you're using Maynard's workshop and have ceased all that nonsense about the Kington girl."

Robert swallowed down the retort that sprang to his lips. "Any word about Maynard?"

"No, why?" Sir John looked at him shrewdly. "Have you heard anything?"

"I spoke to Mistress Maynard a few weeks ago. She expects Maynard to be awarded the position of master mason for some new endeavor far away from here. She talked about leaving the area for good, even suggested I take over the lease on their house."

"Did she give any clue as to who the patron was?"

"No, other than that it was someone in a high position, well connected."

"Have you heard anything from Lovell?"

"Nothing," Robert replied.

Sir John stroked his beard thoughtfully. "Humph. I'm leaving tomorrow. Make haste. I'll be gone for several weeks, and I expect to see walls when I return! I'm tired of everyone crammed into Corsley Manor. If we're to get those staircases up before winter, we need walls. Cavell will be sending me regular updates. Progress, Smythson! I expect progress!"

Sir John walked away, and Robert exhaled thankfully. He was ready to enjoy a few weeks at Longleat without the owner breathing down his neck.

Chapter 12

THE WIND KICKED UP and sprayed mist in his face, making Robert's travel difficult. Before leaving, he and Hills had agreed that if anyone asked, Robert had decided to make a trip to the quarry. It took the better part of the morning to get to Lacock, resting briefly in the village of Melksham before continuing.

As Robert rode through the small villages that dotted the route, he allowed his thoughts to wander toward his future. He considered Hills's advice and his own gloomy attitude. He had seen for himself the building projects undertaken in London. Maynard was bidding on another large project. Why was Robert so afraid of losing his spot at Longleat? If Sir John fired him for investigating Mary's death, he would get another job. With these thoughts, he bolstered his courage and spurred his horse on.

Once at Lacock, he found a stable for his horse and continued on foot. He walked down the narrow streets of the kind of village that sprang up near any large house, whether it were an abbey or a manor house. Much like Corsley Heath, Lacock seemed to contain a collection of small stone houses and cottages dotted along narrow lanes. There were the necessary support buildings of a smithy, alehouse, bakehouse, church, and the like. It looked like a prosperous village, a nice place to live. Between raindrops, Robert spotted an inn called Sign of the Angel. Kington had called Mary his angel, so perhaps this was a good omen. Deciding he might as well enjoy the perks of Sir John's salary while it lasted, he booked a small private room for a couple of nights. Then he ordered some ale and found a seat by the fire in the common room and dried off.

Like most small villages, everyone in Lacock knew each other. Strangers attracted attention, and Robert was no exception. He took advantage of the stares and asked for directions to Lacock Abbey. Fortunately, the serving wench was talkative and happy to provide more information. "Oh, it's easy to find. Just go down Church Street, take a right onto East Street, and then a left onto High Street. Of course, 'tis an abbey no more. It's the home of the Sharingtons now."

"I understand there's still some work going on there."

"Would you be looking for a job, then? Are you a craftsman? A joiner or blacksmith, perhaps?"

Robert laughed. She was a pleasant lass, and it felt good to relax and converse with a pretty girl. "Neither. I'm a stonemason, but I'm not looking for work. I'm looking for a mason by the name of Ned Bright? Do you know him?"

It was slight, but Robert detected a cooling of her attitude as her eyes narrowed, and she turned her body slightly away from him. So Bright was known. And not well thought of, if her reaction was any indication. "Ned Bright? Yes, I know him. What there is to know anyway. What do you want with him?"

"It's a private matter, but as the rain seems to have let up, I think I'll walk over and see if I can find him before they end work for the day. Thank you for your help." Robert paid for his ale and information and headed out. A short walk, following the young lady's excellent directions, brought him to the abbey.

Much like the priory at Longleat, Lacock had been converted from a religious building to domestic use. It was still a work in progress but livable, as there had been no debilitating fire. Unlike Longleat, part of the old cloister had been left intact and was still recognizable. As he approached the building, his mason's eyes were drawn to the corner of the building. A large octagonal tower rose above the main structure. Despite being covered with scaffolding as masons continued to work on the top, Robert could see what it was going to look like upon completion. It was somewhat out of character with the rest of the square building, and yet at the same time it complemented the design. He wondered whose idea it had been.

Several masons were at work, and Robert began to relax. Masonry came much more naturally to him than did sleuthing, if that was what he was doing. He watched them work, unconsciously appraising their abilities and teamwork. This was the group that Maynard was supervising, although Maynard was apparently not here. Some of these men had previously worked at Longleat, he supposed, and wondered which ones. Remembering why he was here, he approached one of the workers and asked if he knew Ned Bright.

"Hey, Bright, someone here asking for you," the man called out.

Robert watched as a tall, heavy man squeezed his way out from behind the scaffolding and lumbered down the ladder. Everything about him seemed to droop. His shoulders slumped; his dark hair lay flat against his uncovered head. He seemed barely able to lift his eyes to see who wanted him. Robert stood dumbfounded. Could this be the man Mary Kington had been ready to run off with?

"Hullo? You wanted to see me?" Even his speech was slow and dull.

Robert shook himself awake and proceeded. "Ned Bright? I'm Robert Smythson, one of the new masons at Longleat."

"Longleat?" Bright blinked a few times. "Why? I already told Cavell I don't know where Spicer is."

"Relax. I'm not here about Spicer. I want to talk to you about Mary Kington. I believe you knew her?" The heavy lids flickered at the sound of Mary's name. "Is there somewhere we could go to talk?"

Bright looked around him in confusion and finally led Robert beyond the workshop where a table with stools was set up outside, clearly a place for the men to take a break, perhaps eat their midday meal. Ned gestured weakly toward a stool, then lowered himself down onto another. "Is Mary all right?"

"Have you not heard? I thought the news would have reached you here." Robert hesitated. Had Maynard not relayed the story? Surely, the husband of someone who liked to gossip as much as Betty Maynard did would have brought the news with him up to Lacock? Had he not been back to Lacock since her body was found, or had he purposely hidden the information?

"No, I've heard nothing. Is she sick? Married? What's this to do with me?" His words were slow and deliberate.

Robert wondered if he was being slow on purpose. "No, not sick or married. She's . . . I understand you loved Mary Kington." Bright nodded. "This news will probably come as a shock." *Or maybe not, if you did indeed have something to do with it,* Robert thought to himself. "We found Mary's body buried at Longleat, in one of the piles of rubble left over from the fire."

Bright's head jerked, the fastest move Robert had seen him make yet. "Her what?"

"Her body. Ned, I'm sorry. Mary's dead and has been for some time. It looks like her body has been there since the fire last spring."

"Last spring?" Ned slowly moved his head back and forth. There was a look of confusion, disbelief, and general lack of comprehension on his face. Robert put his hand on the man's shoulder to steady him. Robert repeated everything he had just said, slowly and deliberately, watching the man's reactions to his words. Ned's confusion slowly dissipated until he became as lifeless as a block of uncarved stone. Robert shouted for help and was joined by the man who had called Ned to talk to Robert.

"I've had some unpleasant news for Ned, and I'm afraid he's taken it rather badly." The two men watched as Ned now rocked back and forth, letting out a low moan.

"What did you say to him? He's been doing better recently. Last year, he was like this quite a bit, but over the winter he seemed to settle down, and this spring he's been almost back to normal."

"The body of the girl he was supposed to marry was just found. I came to tell him and see what he knew about it."

"God's breath! No wonder he's gone off like this. Get some ale from that bucket there, and let's see if we can get him back."

As the two men worked together to ply Ned with ale, Robert said, "I don't think I introduced myself to you. I'm Robert Smythson, new mason at Longleat."

"Lord, I'd be happy enough if I never heard that word again."

"Longleat?"

"Yes, I'm George Russell. I had the pleasure of working for Thynne there at one time. God's teeth, are you saying that a body was found at Longleat?" The sarcasm Russell had started with morphed into disbelief as he comprehended Robert's news.

Bright sputtered and swallowed as the ale revived him. He had clearly been shocked and shaken by the news, but whether it was Mary's death or news of the discovery that had shaken him, Robert did not know. Russell moved closer to Bright, taking a protective posture toward his fellow mason. The move seemed to work, as Bright now took deep gulps of air between equally deep swallows of ale.

"Ned," Robert asked. "When did you last see Mary?"

"Last spring. We were going to be married. She was supposed to meet me. I went to Longleat for her." Ned stared off into the distance, speaking with a slow, monotone voice.

"What happened then?" Robert prompted.

"She gave me a letter. Supposed to come with me. Gave me a letter."

"She was going to meet you but didn't come? Is that it? Instead, she gave you a letter?"

"Yeah, only I can't read well."

"Ned, this is important. Did Mary give you the letter herself?"

"No, Alan brought it."

"Alan? Alan Maynard? He brought you the letter?"

"Yeah, and he read it to me. 'Cause I don't read well."

"So you never actually saw Mary, is that right?"

"No. She didn't come. She just gave Alan the letter to give to me."

"Ned, what did the letter say?"

"She's not coming. Changed her mind. Couldn't hurt her father. Couldn't leave him."

"Instead of coming to meet you, she gave Maynard a letter that said she couldn't hurt her father and wasn't coming, is that right?"

"Uh-huh."

"Do you still, by any chance, have that letter?"

"Might have. I'd have to check my chest, but as far as I know it's still there. Last thing she gave me." They both sat in silence for a few minutes before Ned continued, "Sir, I'm sorry, I don't remember what you said your name was. What happened to Mary?"

"Robert Smythson. I don't know. I'm trying to find out."

"Did they . . . Was she . . . ? Did they hurt her?"

"Yes, I'm afraid so. It looks like she was killed by someone."

"Oh."

Robert was puzzled by Ned's lack of response. "Ned, I think I need to see the letter Maynard gave you. Could you look for it?"

"I suppose. Won't help tell you anything." He didn't move. Robert cleared his throat. "Oh," Bright said, "you meant now." Finally, Bright rose from his stool, took a few steps, then shook his head as if to clear his vision and began to walk slowly but purposefully toward the masons lodge.

Robert turned toward Russell, who had sat quietly while Robert had questioned Bright. "Do you have any idea where I might find Maynard?"

"No, he hasn't been here for several weeks. I assume he'd gone home or maybe off to London to bid his design work."

"I recently spoke to his wife, and he wasn't at home. I got the impression she thought he was here."

"We don't expect him back. He's not needed here. The work is straightforward enough even for Bright to manage, well, usually," he said. "What do you want Maynard for?"

"If he's the one who delivered Mary's letter to Ned, then I fear he's mixed up in Mary Kington's death somehow."

"Have you made any progress as to who killed her?"

"No. Every avenue seems to be blocked. No one wants to talk about it, and when they do, there's a lot of finger-pointing. The girl's father still insists Ned is responsible."

"Heavens. I can't imagine that. For one, he loved her. For two, despite his size, he's a gentle one, not someone to use violence."

"I admit I have a hard time picturing it as well. Do you mind if I ask you a few questions?"

"No, not at all, although I stay clear of anything to do with Longleat and have done for well over a year."

"At the time of the fire last April, where was Maynard? Was he working here?"

"In general, yes. He was supervising, if you could call it that, and working on a chimney piece for someone—I forget who. Sharington lets him do his own work here, which keeps him available in case one of us needs help. Sharington's relaxed, so completely unlike Sir John."

"I see," Robert said. "I wonder why Maynard doesn't have a workshop at East Woodlands? That way he could be close to Betty."

"Sir John wouldn't like it. He doesn't want any work done for others to be done on land he owns. Besides, sometimes I think it suits Maynard to spend time away from Betty."

"Oh dear. They seemed quite happy when I first met them together."

"I don't know. Sometimes I've wondered if he's got a roving eye. He certainly spends quite a bit of time away from home."

Their conversation was curtailed by the return of Ned Bright, a grubby, crumpled paper in his hand. "Sorry, it was buried at the bottom of my chest," he said, giving it to Robert.

Robert opened it and scanned the lines. As Ned had said, it was a short note simply stating that Mary had decided not to leave her father, so that he would not suffer disappointment, and giving instructions for Ned not to chase after her. Robert had a hard time picturing Ned chasing after anything. He folded the note and gave it back to Ned. At least Maynard had correctly told him what was in it. There was nothing in the note to signify any depth of feeling on her part and no mention of a baby.

Robert realized he hadn't revealed that piece and wondered if Ned had known. "Ned, did you know that Mary . . . Did she tell you she was with child?"

Again, the sharp lifting of the head. "What? With child?"

"Yes, did she not tell you that?"

"No. No idea. A child?" He looked off into the distance. Robert watched his reaction carefully. He was no expert, but the man's surprise seemed genuine enough.

There was activity nearby as two servants brought fresh jugs of ale, loaves of bread, some handheld pies, and cheese and set them on the table. Other craftsmen began to gather as well. Robert noticed that the sun was setting, and he should make his way back to the Sign of the Angel.

"Ned, I've brought you a lot of bad news. I'm staying in the village for a day or two at the Sign of the Angel. Why don't you rest tonight, and we'll talk some more tomorrow? Perhaps you'll remember some more details, or you can ask me some more questions. Does that sound all right?"

"A child? As in baby?"

"Yes, Ned. I'm going to go now, but I'll come back tomorrow, and we can talk some more then." Robert said goodbye to George Russell, leaving Bright in his care, and retraced his steps back to the inn and went straight to his bedchamber.

Robert stretched, turned, and pulled the blanket back over his head. Frankly, he hadn't been this comfortable in a while. The tester bed in his private room in the Sign of the Angel was far more comfortable than the thin mattress he slept on at Corsley Heath. Perhaps he should consider finding a better home. He dozed for a few more minutes, enjoying the need to not be anywhere at any particular time. Letting his thoughts wander, he imagined what it would be like to take over Maynard's house in East Woodlands, as Betty had suggested. He pictured Anne there as his wife. Then he groaned. It was a useless fantasy. Like Mary, Anne was reluctant to leave her father. Nor could he ask her to. He wasn't worthy of any of this. Not of the nice house or the wife. He could scarcely believe Sir John still tolerated him working at Longleat. Only because he didn't know what Robert had done. Robert's breath caught in his throat, and he forced himself to look for patterns in the room, to count cracks in the walls until he could breathe again.

Feeling lost, Robert wondered if he should just go back to Longleat. But he had already paid for another night at the inn, so he walked around the village of Lacock, taking in the scenery. The rain of the previous day had given way to sunshine, and he admired the buildings made with local stone, the same quality and source as Longleat's stone. Soon enough, he found his feet leading him toward the abbey, pausing to study the gateway that led from the main drive to the building. Reminiscent of the one at Corsley Manor, it was beautiful, a smooth gray stone, with lovely, even ridges rising to a point above his head. It gave the feeling of peace, balance, and purpose, all of which were missing in his life.

While he stood, running his fingers along the ridges, feeling for imperfections or rough patches, a man approached him. "Can I help you?"

"Oh, sorry, I was just admiring the workmanship. Do you know who's responsible?"

"That would be Alan Maynard's work," the man said, looking him up and down. "Are you a mason too?"

"Yes, does it show that readily?" Robert laughed. "I'm Robert Smythson, new mason for Sir John Thynne." His stomach lurched as he realized he had once again left off the master mason title.

"Then what are you doing up here? Did he send you to poach Maynard off me again?"

"No, nothing like that. Does that mean you're Sharington?"

"Yes, sorry. Henry Sharington of Lacock Abbey. If you're not here for Maynard, why are you here?" There was no animosity in his tone, merely curiosity.

"I had some questions for young Ned Bright, but I'm afraid I got no good answers."

"He's not much use to anyone these days, but he's a nice lad, and my wife likes his singing, so I keep him on."

"Tell me, have you known him to have a temper?"

"A temper? Why no, he's quite gentle, especially recently. I don't know the particulars, but I think he's been crossed in love recently. Been quite melancholy. I hope he recovers soon because my wife would like him to sing when she entertains. Enough about him. What do you think of Lacock and the work we have going on here?"

"I'm intrigued. This arch is magnificent. I can see the quality of Maynard's work. And I do like the look of the octagonal tower. Who designed that?"

"Ah yes. The tower. My brother added that just before he died. The work of John Chapman, I believe. We're still modifying the top, adding the dome."

"It's lovely and quite unusual."

"Would you like a closer look? I would be happy to show you."

Robert readily agreed and followed the man to the main building. Once inside, they walked up a narrow staircase. As they entered the first small octagonal room, Sharington described the meaning of the shape. "I particularly appreciate the interplay between heaven and earth symbolized by the octagon. Part circle, part square, a transition between earth below and heaven above. Quite appropriate for a building that used to be a nunnery and is now owned by a man."

"I believe the octagon is said to symbolize rebirth or transition or renewal. I understand that the number eight can symbolize immortality," Robert noted. The craftsmanship of the room was beautiful, and the shape appealed to his sense of proportion. He could feel his body relaxing just being in the space.

"Yes, also the four cardinal directions and their intermediate points. I also like how it rounds the corner without actually rounding it. It's just pleasing."

"I agree. The shape gives interest. It can be difficult to get the angles right, but it looks like your masons have done a good job."

"Yes, my brother was quite pleased."

Robert's attention then moved to a table set in the middle of the room, a beautifully carved ornate base covered with a marble top, echoing the octagonal shape. "This is magnificent. This table will be here for hundreds of years. Just imagine what it will see." Robert was taken with both the tower itself and the table within. They both represented quality work and the marriage of form and function.

Sharington then led Robert out of the tower and through the original cloisters, unchanged and beautiful. Robert spent many happy minutes admiring the ceiling arches that rose above him in harmony, creating a smooth pattern that appealed to his sense of aesthetics while also holding up the roof. There was something beautiful about the old church buildings. And that thought led Robert to the old church religion, which led to Henry Kington, and the tangle of Mary's death clouded his vision once again. Robert thanked Sharington for the tour and moved outside, walking toward the masons' workshop.

He found Ned easily. He was sitting in the masons' workshop at a bench, mallet and chisel in hand, doing nothing. Russell said he'd been like that all morning.

"Good morrow, Ned. It's Robert Smythson from Longleat. Do you remember what we talked about yesterday?" There was no response. "Can I ask you some more questions about Mary?" Mary's name brought Ned out of his trance, and he slowly turned his head toward Robert.

"One thing I'm wondering about: Why did you not try to go after Mary? I mean, after you got the letter from her, did you never go back down to Longleat or Corsley?"

"No, the letter said to leave her be. Not to come after her. So I didn't."

"So after you received this letter and Maynard told you its contents, you just forgot about her and never wondered how she was or tried to see her?"

"I was just doing what she asked me to. I didn't forget her, but I didn't want to trouble her. I just . . ." He trailed off again. Robert waited for a few moments, then realized he wasn't going to make much progress.

An hour later, Robert was sitting at a table in the Sign of the Angel finishing a delicious meal of roasted meat that had set him back almost a day's wages. He knew he should probably save his money for when Sir John fired him, but it had been worth every penny. He ordered some more wine while he ruminated over what he had learned in Lacock.

Henry Kington insisted that Ned Bright had killed Mary. But now that Robert had met Ned Bright, he had his doubts. Ned didn't seem capable of killing anyone. He just did not move fast enough. And George Russell and Sharington both agreed that Ned had been sunk in melancholy for months. Could it be guilt that had overwhelmed him instead of just loss? Possibly. But what would his motive have been?

And what was the Maynards' role in all of this? The question of the two letters troubled Robert. One sent to her father telling him she was running off to be with Ned. One sent to Ned telling him she wasn't coming because she couldn't leave her father. Could she, would she, have written both letters? Not unless she had chosen a third path and didn't want either one of the men looking for her. That seemed unlikely.

Henry Kington had said that Mary left him the letter. Assuming that letter was genuine, Mary had left Cley Hill Farm with the intention of meeting Ned. What, or who, had prevented her from meeting him. Where were they supposed to meet? Robert realized he didn't know that. Could Ned tell him? Kington's theory was that Ned had killed Mary, dumped her body next to a burning building, and retreated to Lacock. Had anyone seen Ned that night?

If Ned's letter was genuine, and Mary had decided not to meet him, had she met with Alan Maynard, given him a letter before attempting to return home, but been killed on the way? In that case, Henry Kington's letter was a fake. There didn't seem to be any scenario where both letters could be genuine. So whoever killed Mary had written at least one of the letters. Robert had seen both. Were they written by the same hand? He couldn't remember. If only they had come with mason's marks, signs specific to each individual mason to show who had worked a piece of stone.

Either way, Maynard, someone who regularly traveled back and forth between the Longleat area and Lacock, had to be involved. What motive would he have had? Did that mean that Maynard had been at Longleat the night of the fire when all reports had him at Lacock? And if not, where and when had Mary given him the letter? Or had someone else given it to him if she had not written it?

Another question bubbled up in his mind. If Mary knew that Ned couldn't read well, and one would think that would come up between two people ready to marry, would she have used a letter as a means of communicating something so personal? It was a pointless question. Were any of these questions getting him anywhere? He had risked his job with Sir John to go chasing ghosts. Nobody wanted this death investigated. Why did it matter who killed Mary? It couldn't bring her back. Longleat was going to be a beautiful house, and, as everyone kept telling him, being its master mason would be the making of him. Perhaps it was time to give up and go back to Longleat.

Chapter 13

THE NEXT MORNING ROBERT started back to Longleat. He rode west at first, toward the quarry. It might be possible to catch a load of stone coming south from the quarry and accompany it back to Longleat. If so, it would be easier to convince Sir John that had been his destination, if Sir John got word of his travels.

He was in luck and soon ran into the heavy load of carts carrying the precious Bath stone toward Longleat. The men were surprised to see him but accepted his presence without question. Robert's mood improved as he observed the quality of the stone. He was pleased to see Young Fred Horton accompanying the load back.

Fred glanced at the direction Robert had emerged from. Did he suspect Robert's previous whereabouts? Robert smiled at him to reassure him that all was well and turned to the head driver to discuss their progress. The road was thick with mud, the wheels getting stuck often with the heavy load. The driver was worried, anticipating the usual demands for haste. He seemed relieved when Robert expressed more concern about the stone not being damaged rather than speed.

They were just getting the carts back up to speed after removing some of the mud when they heard hooves pounding up behind them. It was not unusual for riders to rush past them, but this one slowed as he approached. Robert turned and almost fell out of his saddle as he recognized the rider. "Alan Maynard? Is that you?"

Maynard appeared to be as surprised to see Robert there. In fact, it took a few moments for him to recognize him. "Robert Smythson," the newcomer said as he pulled alongside. "Fancy running into you here. Is the great new mason of Longleat lowering himself to transport stone from the quarry?" he asked with a tone of condescension. "And who is this I see with you?" He looked toward Fred. "I remember you. Young Fred, is it? What are you doing leading the quarry stone? Have they let you off your bench?"

Young Fred turned bright red and shifted in his saddle. "I took him to the quarry," Robert interjected. "He actually has a good eye for stone. As for me, I'm just ensuring that we get the best quality stone for Sir John and that the transportation goes as quickly as possible. You remember his desire for haste, no doubt. But why are you traveling this way? Are you on your way home? Or perhaps back to Lacock? I stopped by your house last week and visited with Betty. She says you're expecting big news soon."

"Yes, I've been in the north bidding for my new job. Since I was passing through this way, I thought I'd check on the lads at Lacock before heading home tomorrow." Maynard drew his horse closer to Robert's. "I hear you've been keeping my wife company. How nice."

Robert found it was his turn to redden. "It's not like that. I mean, I had some questions . . ."

"What could you possibly ask my wife?"

"Have you not been home? I thought for sure you would have heard the news by now."

"What news?"

"Perhaps we should ride ahead of the others," Robert suggested, and he led Maynard a short distance away from the main group, where they would not be overheard. Robert then gave Maynard a brief description of finding Mary Kington's body in the rubble, trying not to reveal more than necessary or add conjecture. Maynard seemed shocked, but despite close observation, Robert couldn't tell if his surprise was genuine.

They rode on for a few minutes while Robert tried to decide if he should confide that he had been to Lacock to see Ned Bright. He concluded that getting information from Maynard was worth the risk. "I've spoken with Henry Kington, and he seemed convinced that Ned Bright killed Mary. I've just been to Lacock and met Bright. I don't think he's capable of killing anyone."

"No, he's been distraught since Mary didn't show up last year."

"He doesn't look like much. How could a girl fall for him?"

"Oh, well, you haven't heard him sing, have you? Come to think of it, no one has recently. Lord, can he sing!"

"He says you were the one who brought him the letter from Mary. Is that true?"

"Yes."

"Where did you get it? Did Mary give it to you? When did you see her?"

"Why are you asking these questions? Why were you even there? Did Sir John ask you to investigate? Why you?"

"No, I . . ." Robert fumbled, wondering how to answer.

Maynard started to laugh, a deep belly laugh, slapping his knee and almost losing his breath. "He doesn't know you were there, does he? Oh, he's going to be furious when he learns of this. Why, I might as well pack up right now and head back to Longleat to get your job. That is, if I wanted it back, which I don't. Oh, this is priceless. You just left and came up here, didn't you? Can't handle that a pretty young girl was left for dead."

"Can you? What if that had been Betty? Would you just have shrugged and gone back to work?"

Maynard studied Robert with an appraising look. "Well, now. You raise an interesting point. All right, calm down. I admit it is bad of Sir John to just ignore a girl's death. But what is she to him? There's no love lost between him and Kington."

"When I met you several weeks ago, back at Corsley Heath, we talked about the fire. Do you think Kington could have played a role in that?" Robert was still convinced that the timing of Mary's death and the fire had to be connected.

"Perhaps. I'd never thought of that. He resented Sir John's success, that's for sure. Don't know that he'd go so far as to start a fire, but who knows? Do you think he's involved in this?"

"No. Maybe. He would never hurt his own daughter, not the way he felt about her." There was a pause while both men rode in silence. Robert tried another tactic. "What do you think of Cavell? Is he a good man?"

"That mouse?" answered Maynard with a shrug. "I suppose he's all right. Not much of a spine, just carries out Sir John's orders. He's easy to manipulate, I'll say that. Not one to speak up for himself."

"What do you know about him and Mary Kington? I heard he wanted to marry her but her father would not give his consent."

"I vaguely remember hearing that, now that you mention it. Honestly, I do not pay much attention to the mice surrounding Sir John. One squeak sounds much like another, *n'est pas*?"

"So you wouldn't think he had anything to do with Mary's death?"

"I didn't say that. But no, I don't. Too weak. If you want my advice, leave it alone, Smythson. Focus on the building. Are you still Sir John's golden boy, or has he turned off from you yet? He will when he hears about this trip—if he hasn't already." There was another pause, followed by another bellow of laughter. "So that's why you're traveling with the stone. It's a ruse to cover where you really were. Clever, Smythson."

"Sir John's desire for progress means they are bringing a larger load than I would normally recommend. I just want to see that it arrives safely. No sense bringing damaged stone."

"Oh yes. I see, quite cautious of you." Maynard rode closer to Robert and lowered his voice. "As you're new to these parts, let me give you a word of warning. Be wary of crossing Sir John. Most who try do not succeed. If you keep a secret from him, he'll find it. He's succeeded this far in life by always being in control of everything and everyone around him. But don't worry on my account. He won't hear of your real destination from me."

Robert was flustered. Was his worry so transparent?

Maynard continued, "In case you are wondering, I am good at keeping secrets. I think I'll skip Lacock this time. Sounds like they've already met with one qualified mason this week." He moved away and spurred his horse on, calling in a loud voice, "My wife awaits. I will see you lads later." He sped off, his horse throwing thick mud toward Robert as he quickened his pace.

Robert watched as Maynard rode off toward his spacious home and warm-blooded wife. What had Maynard meant by all that talk of secrets? Could he possibly know about Winchester? Was he suggesting that Sir John would find out about it as well? Robert was so tired of death and secrets and mysteries. He allowed himself to envy Maynard's freedom and comfort as the miles trudged on slowly, the team stopping frequently to dig out the cartwheels from the thick mud. When the site of Longleat finally came into view, however, Robert was caught again by its beauty and potential. He had a secure future here if he could just hold on to it. It might be prosperous enough to provide for a wife and family, if she would have him. He gave his full attention to the safe delivery and unloading of the stone and tried to put all thoughts of buried bodies behind him.

Robert didn't sleep much that night. Instead, he turned over the things he had learned that day. Playing over his discussion with Maynard, he realized that Maynard had never answered the question of how he got Mary's letter. As soon as Robert had asked, Maynard had changed the subject to Sir John's reaction to finding out where Robert was. They had never returned to the subject of the letters.

Longleat demanded all of Robert's time and attention for the next week, and there was no time to think of anything else. As the days extended toward their peak length, Robert was physically exhausted as the men crammed in as much work as possible. Stacks of squared ashlar stone were moved into position, scaffolding and winches were constructed, and the mortar was given one last turn. It was time for the walls of Longleat to begin their climb toward heaven. The weather turned warmer, and the periods of rain mercifully shortened. Cavell had questioned him closely about his need to accompany the stone from the quarry, but he'd accepted Robert's explanation and was glad to report visible progress in his correspondence with Sir John.

Sunday came as a welcome relief, although Robert sensed Sir John would have the men work on the Sabbath if he thought he could get away with it. Robert and John Hills took a long stroll up to Cley Hill. They walked in companionable silence, enjoying the warmth of the sun as it soaked the hill. Passing Cley Hill Farm brought Henry and Mary Kington to mind, and Robert filled his friend in on what he had learned in Lacock.

"I don't see how Ned could have killed her. I don't think he has that kind of violence in him," Robert concluded.

"Then any idea who might have?" The climb had been a lot for Hills, whose limp slowed him down. He lowered himself to the ground, facing the sun.

Robert sat next to him, staring over the countryside before replying. "Not really. Maynard knows more than he's telling, but I can't see why he would have wanted to kill Mary."

"What do you mean?"

"He is the one who brought the letter from Mary to Ned. But he wouldn't tell me how he got it. Have you seen him recently?"

"No. I heard he spent a day with Betty, then left again. Still boasting about his new job."

"Do you think he's telling the truth about that?" Robert picked at a long blade of grass.

"I see no reason to lie about it. Although you and I know better than to brag about a position before one is certain of it." Hills stretched his long frame out on the grass and closed his eyes.

Robert watched his friend relax and wished he could feel calm. But being idle wasn't in his nature. He watched a group of young men practicing archery in the near distance and considered joining them. An hour spent with a bow and arrow on target practice might be just what he needed. He had asked for the responsibility of master mason, but the weight of the job was a heavy load. And part of that load meant not being able to join the lads who saw him as their boss. It would ruin their leisure.

"Have you told Kington about the baby yet?" Hills asked him.

"No, honestly I haven't had time. Longleat's been keeping me busy, as you know. Also, I don't think I can face being in that man's house again. You know how disorder affects me. And his odd ramblings about the old religion and the Queen unnerve me."

Robert heard a voice calling his name and turned to see Richard Cavell approaching up the hill.

"Cavell," Robert called in response. "Well met. Enjoying the beautiful day?"

"Is it? I suppose it is. I hadn't noticed. You and Hills seem to be comfortable. No, even on Sundays I am not at leisure." He paused and seemed to take in his surroundings for the first time. A deep sigh escaped him, and he threw his head back, closing his eyes as he lifted them toward the sun.

Robert rose to meet the steward. "Are you here with more instructions from Sir John?"

"None, other than for the usual haste. I was wondering if you've had any news about Maynard."

"Not recently. Just the usual story of his bidding on some big, important job. I don't think he's been home in a few weeks," Robert answered. "Could he be up at Lacock Abbey? I thought I heard that he sometimes worked there." He tried to drop the name Lacock casually, but he was watching Cavell closely for a reaction.

"Lacock? Why mention that place? I suppose Maynard could be there, but if he is, then everything's all right."

"Isn't Lacock the place Ned Bright is supposed to be? I think I remember you telling Sir John that. Isn't Bright the mason Kington thinks killed his daughter?"

"I've heard that."

"Cavell, how well do you know Bright? Have you seen him during the past year?"

"No," he replied, taking a step backward as John Hills also rose to his feet.

It was Cavell's turn to study Robert carefully. "Why all the questions? When you went up to the quarry, you didn't take a side trip to Lacock, did you?"

"No," Robert replied calmly. "When I went to the quarry, I did not go to Lacock."

Cavell ran his hand through his thinning hair and leveled a look at Robert that Robert had trouble interpreting. Was it a challenge or a warning? "Robert," Cavell said, "I hope not. Look, I like you, but you've got to start taking Sir John's warnings seriously." He stood staring at the two masons for another minute, then shook his head, turned, and walked away, pausing to speak to a few other people as he went.

"That was odd," Hills said, suppressing a laugh.

"What?" said Robert. "That wasn't a lie."

"No, but it wasn't the truth either. It's not like you to be dishonest."

"You're right, but this whole situation has me not feeling like myself. I just can't reconcile myself to letting Mary's death go unsolved. And I can't help but feel that Maynard is in some way involved."

"I don't like the way Maynard's name keeps popping up," Hills said, tearing the head off a piece of long grass and tossing it on the ground.

"I agree. And I don't like the way Cavell keeps cautioning me against investigating. The more I think about all of this, the more convinced I am that someone is trying to hide something. Whether it's about the fire or Mary's death, I don't know. But there are definitely secrets here people do not want uncovered."

"I agree. But you're not going to uncover them today. Come on, let's head back down. I'm hungry."

"John, you're like a young apprentice: always hungry." He clapped his friend on the back and followed him down the hill toward food and rest.

Chapter 14

ROBERT SAT IN THE tracing room at Corsley Heath, reviewing the available staff and materials that would be needed to complete the main exterior walls before turning his attention to the staircases that would lead up to the roof and the banqueting houses Sir John wanted to add. It all felt meaningless. Building a beautiful house for a man who callously refused to investigate the death of a young lady on his property, who fought with his neighbors and his employees, and who tried to take advantage of all he encountered.

Robert glared around the tracing room, frustrated with everything and everyone. Masonry would calm him down. Some time at the bench, just the stone and his tools. Some people said that stone was unpredictable, subject to random breaks and splits. On the contrary, Robert felt he was better able to predict how stone would behave than people.

Whenever things felt out of control, as they did now, he turned to his drawings. If they did not give relief, he would bury himself with a piece of carving. At times like this, he preferred the repetitive patterns of a piece of molding—the predictable ups and downs, repeating steps and turns, everything orderly and in place. Precision, proportion, and balance were his trademarks and his strengths. They were also his comforts.

At Longleat, there was little work like that to be done at present. He wanted to be helpful or useful. His thoughts turned to Kington and how un-useful he had been in solving the man's problems. He also had not yet told the man his daughter had been with child at the time of her death. Then he remembered the crumbling wall at the corner of Cley Hill farmhouse. There was a way he could help Master Kington. He gathered his tools and supplies, loaded them into his horse's saddlebags, and rode off.

No one was home when he arrived at Cley Hill Farm; the place had a forlorn feeling. No matter. The work was external and would not require Robert to enter the property. He tied up his horse and moved his stuff to the affected corner. Kneeling, he poked around, moving away pieces of crumbled stone, testing others. Robert was gathering some pieces together to refit them and realized what he needed was a bucket of mortar. The stones were all there; they just needed to be replaced and set. This too seemed like a wasted effort. He was beginning to pack up his tools when he heard a voice hail him from the road.

"Is that you, Smythson? I recognized your horse. What are you doing over there?" There was a hint of harshness in Kington's voice. Robert rose and waved, wiping his hands on his hose, and approached.

"I meant no harm, Master Kington. Nor did I mean to startle you. I was just thinking I could start to fix this corner for you since I had a bit of free time today."

Kington reached Robert and bent to examine what Robert had done. "Much obliged to you, Smythson, but I cannot trouble you on such a warm day. Come and drink some ale with me. I've had a fresh batch delivered this morning, and it's cooler in the house." With his arm, he guided Robert away and into the dark, dank house.

As usual, the clutter and dimness made Robert wish he could have remained outside, but he could hardly refuse the man's hospitality. He took the offered ale and quenched his thirst with the liquid, mercifully not stale this time, keeping his hands fixed on the tankard so he wouldn't have to touch anything else. The two men spoke for a few minutes about the unusually hot weather and what it was doing to the summer crops. Once pleasantries were over, Robert broached the subject he had come to tell. "Master Kington—Henry—I have some news about your daughter."

"Does Sir John know the whereabouts of Ned Bright, the man responsible for my angel's death? Have you located him?"

"No, that's not it. Well, actually, yes, it is." Robert felt he was making a mess of this.

"Thynne knows where he is and still won't do anything about it!" Kington railed.

"The news I have is not about that. Sir, what I need to tell you is about Mary. Did you know she was with child at the time of her death?" Robert kept his voice gentle and even, knowing that the words he spoke would likely shock.

Kington slumped over as the blood drained from his face. Robert rose to refill Kington's tankard with fresh ale, giving the older man a few minutes to compose himself. "I take it you did not know."

"No, I . . . A baby?"

"Yes," Robert replied softly.

"How? Who?"

"We're not sure if she even knew herself, but Williams, he's the surgeon from Warminster who examined Mary's body after we found her, was fairly certain."

"Must have been Bright. Maybe that's why he killed her." Kington got up from his chair and began to walk, going back and forth across the cramped space.

"I don't believe Ned Bright killed your daughter," Robert replied quietly. "I cannot give you the details, but I have met him, and he seems to be incapable of such an action against anyone, let alone your daughter."

"You can't be right. He tempted her, deceived her. Then got her with child and killed her." His voice broke.

Robert rose and stood near the man, placing his hand on Kington's back. "Master Kington, I do not believe it. I have heard he has a good singing voice, but other than that, I assure you he has few charms to tempt a young lady. Their attachment must have been sincere."

Kington shook off Robert's hand and returned to his pacing, now waving his arms about. "No, you are wrong! He killed my angel. You are not a father; you do not know how I know. Bah! I do not want to talk about him anymore. I know what I know, but I can see that no one will believe me."

Robert questioned what he was doing there, listening to the ravings of a grieving man. He had said what he had come to say, and now it was time to get back to work. "I must be going. Thank you for the ale. I will return soon with a bucket of mortar to get that corner repaired." Robert rose, hesitated for a moment, looking for a spare place to set his empty tankard before moving toward a table scattered with various writing materials, papers, ink pots, and quills.

Kington followed his gaze and watched as Robert set the vessel down on a spare inch of empty space. "I've been trying to get news of Mary Stuart, writing to some of my friends in the north. Tell me, have you heard from Sir Francis Knollys? You worked with him, yes? I've heard that he is with her."

"I have heard the same but know not if it is true. I know only that our Queen trusts Knollys to faithfully pursue her interests to the best of his ability. Now please excuse me. I must get back to Longleat."

"Yes, yes, of course. Before you go, have you considered . . . would you consider traveling north to meet with him, find out how Queen Mary is being treated, assure her of our support? I could give you letters of introduction, letters to deliver." Kington rose and began shuffling the various papers on the table.

"What are you suggesting, Master Kington? I am afraid I cannot travel north or be of any help with the Scots Queen."

Kington looked crestfallen. "I suppose you follow this new religion, stripped of all its beautiful symbols and meaning."

"I believe a man should worship God according to the law and what's in his heart. I don't judge. I'm not perfect. I've made mistakes, big ones. They've taught me not to judge others. I won't interfere with your private worship, but I will also not interfere with the rightful Queen. I am loyal to our own Queen Elizabeth, the true and just ruler of England, and the Church of England. To suggest otherwise is treason."

"Well, if you won't do it, perhaps Maynard will. He won't refuse me. And he's soon to have an even better connection than Knollys. Bah, you're no use to me." Kington turned his back on Robert and went back to his papers, muttering to himself.

Robert shook his head in confusion and, if he admitted it to himself, disgust. "Master Kington, I bid you good day." Robert strode to the door and left hurriedly, shaken by the man's ranting.

A distraught Robert pushed his horse quickly down Deep Lane trying to get away from Kington. He slowed to catch his breath, feeling rather foolish that he had allowed the man's words to shake him up that much. As he approached the small village green of Corsley Heath, Robert saw an unlikely pair bent close together in what appeared to be an intimate, private conversation. Richard Cavell was leaning over Betty Maynard, who was talking quickly, as usual. They didn't appear to notice Robert as he approached.

"Cavell, Mistress Maynard, well met." Did Robert imagine the startled and guilty looks on their faces as they turned to greet them?

Cavell was the first to recover. "I was just inquiring of Mistress Maynard if she knew the whereabouts of her husband."

Betty untangled her arm from that of Cavell. "And I was just telling Master Cavell that I expect him to return quite soon with triumphant news. Any day now, we'll be ready to make the announcement."

"So now he's . . . where exactly?" Robert dismounted and walked beside the two, holding his horse by its reins.

"Oh, now, Master Smythson, you saucy one. I can't tell you that. That would spoil the surprise. You'll have to wait along with everyone else."

"Tell me, Mistress Maynard," he started.

She interrupted. "Betty, please," and she moved to offer Robert her arm.

"Mistress Betty, then. How long has this job been in the works? Has he been working on it since he left Longleat? Since last summer, perhaps?"

"You know my Alan, always has a thumb in every pie. Tries to stay as connected as possible."

"That is interesting. I just came from a visit with Henry Kington. He seemed to know the identity of your husband's future employer. Suggested that it was someone with more influence over politics than my former employer, Sir Francis Knollys. Knollys, as you may know, is Treasurer of the Queen's Chamber, a position of some influence, and is deeply trusted by Her Majesty. There are not many men in the realm of higher status than he."

Betty turned bright red. "You don't think my Alan could attract the attention of someone of high status?"

"I didn't say that. I'm just thinking that perhaps with this information I can take a guess. There are two men close to the Queen who are involved in building projects on a grand scale: William Cecil, the Queen's closest adviser, and Robert Dudley, the Earl of Leicester."

"Well, you can't believe everything Kington says."

Cavell had been listening to this carefully. "Cecil and Leicester, huh? Interesting. I wonder if Sir John knows."

"Oh no, Richard. Don't you interfere. Leave Alan's future alone." Betty appeared to be distraught, as if the situation was getting out of her control. "Don't believe Kington. He knows nothing, has his head full of Catholic plots and intrigues."

"Yes, I know," said Robert. "He was saying some rather disturbing things about the Scots Queen. Rambling, to be sure, but some of it was alarming. That's how I heard that your husband's connection is with a man of influence. Kington wants him to use that influence to get to Mary Stuart. I think his ultimate aim is to be a part of getting Mary Stuart on the throne of England."

Richard sighed. "He's going to get himself into trouble one day if he keeps on this way."

"So you know about his Catholic leanings and his interest in overthrowing the Queen," Robert said in disbelief.

Cavell blanched. "This is all too much for me. You both need to stay away from Kington and his wild theories. That goes for Maynard as well, Betty. Don't get involved. The man is getting more unhinged."

"Oh yes, I know," Betty said. "Alan came home from visiting him last summer with the most outrageous story. I don't remember what, but something about building him a priest hole in the farmhouse for him to hide weapons for the plot."

"What? What plot?"

"I don't know. Alan didn't either."

This information was confusing, but within it was hidden a nugget that might prove useful. "Maynard was visiting Kington last summer? After the fire? I thought he was at Lacock most of last summer."

"Oh, well, yes, he was. At Lacock, I mean. But also meeting with Kington. I don't remember when exactly or why. I'm sure it was nothing. All he told me was about the priest hole. Well, it's been lovely to see you both, but I must head home. If I don't supervise my maids, they just laze about all day. Well met, gentlemen."

Robert watched as Betty Maynard tucked her head down and walked quickly toward home. "Very unusual."

Cavell shook his head. "You went to see Kington? Even after Sir John warned you to leave Kington and his daughter's death alone."

"You knew I hadn't told him about the baby. Besides, I was being neighborly and repairing a crumbling piece of wall on his house."

"Did Sir John hire you to do wall repairs on his neighbor's house?" The two men began walking toward the masons lodge.

"I suppose I feel sorry for him," Robert said. "All alone and clearly struggling. Is he all right, I mean, in his head? Surely, we must do something."

"I advise you to stay clear of him. Sir John would say that if you were alarmed, it is no more than you deserve for going where you do not belong."

"I feel sorry for him, and I thought you did too."

"I do, and part of that is knowing when to keep focused on what pertains to you and stay out of other people's business. I mean it, Smythson. Don't get involved. Focus on your job at Longleat. And speaking of that, I've received some new plans from Sir John today that he wants you to have."

Robert shook his head as if to clear his mind of everything that had just happened. "You said you had plans? Come into the lodge, and let's look at them." Robert tied his horse and led the steward into the masons lodge.

Cavell pulled out some papers from his satchel. "Here, these arrived yesterday from Sir John. Focus on these plans for the banqueting houses for the roof."

Robert moved to the large desk and laid the plans out. It was the first detailed look he'd had of them. Small square rooms would dot the roof line, allowing guests to wander the roof enjoying the views while sampling sweet treats served in the small rooms. They were a folly, a frivolous idea for the wealthy to enjoy, designed to provide a cozy, private space for couples or small groups to gather. Yet Robert wished he could walk along the roof line, wear fine clothes, and nibble the sweetmeats, especially if he could do it with Anne by his side. He stared at the plans, living the dream for just a moment in his head. Something wasn't right.

"Whose plans are these?"

"I believe Sir John drew them up himself. Why?"

"There's something about the design . . . I'm not sure. I think it could be improved."

"Don't let Sir John hear you say that. He's happy with them, and that's what matters. Your job is to execute the designs. He will be away for a few more weeks. Let's see what progress we can make before he returns. I see the scaffolding is up and the stairs will soon be underway." Cavell slumped in the chair, gesturing to the stack of papers. "Every day, a new missive arrives, demanding haste and updates. Here's one," he said, reading from a sheet filled with lines of notes. "*Corsley Manor is too cramped for my family. We need to get Longleat completed so we can move back there*. Clearly, he's anxious for progress. Do you need anything from me other than these plans?"

"No, I think we can manage the next few steps without too much trouble."

"Good. I understand you feel sorry for Henry, but if he's not pushing for Mary's death to be investigated, I think we should let it lie. Keep the men working hard, and no more visits to Kington, understood?"

Robert agreed. After today's odd interaction with Kington, it was an easy promise to make. He could always send another mason up to fix the crumbling corner on the farmhouse.

After Cavell left, Robert stepped out into the sunshine and took a deep breath. What an odd day it had been. Nothing was ever easy or simple here. He allowed his thoughts to drift to Anne once more, wondering what she was doing, if she was thinking of him.

From Anne to Mary to Henry Kington. Should Robert report Kington's unusual behavior to Sir John or not? Part of him still felt sorry for the old man who had lost his only daughter and might lose his farm as well. Telling Sir John would likely result in the speeding up of that action as Sir John would not hesitate to turn the situation to his own advantage. He decided to keep the news to himself for now. Kington had been through enough in the past year, and what harm could he do from this far away and with so few resources?

Robert's thoughts then turned to the meeting between Cavell and Betty Maynard and Betty's admission that Maynard had been meeting with Kington. Robert didn't think he was imagining that Betty had tried to gloss that over, to minimize the impact of what she had said. Did Betty, or even Cavell, know more than they were admitting to? Did they already know how and why Mary had been killed and were choosing to remain quiet?

Chapter 15

ROBERT KEPT HIS WORD to Cavell and stayed focused on Longleat for the next couple of weeks. He had now been at Longleat almost four months. In that time, he and his team had begun what would be one of the most attractive buildings in all of England. He had successfully integrated his team with the craftsmen already at Longleat and had attempted to stake his claim as master mason, both at the job site and at the quarry. He looked with pride as the walls and stairs took shape in the building.

People were anticipating Sir John's return because they felt even he had to be pleased with the progress they'd made. While his arrival did not bring joyous words of praise, there was grudging satisfaction. He called Robert and Cavell into his office at Corsley Manor. When Robert arrived, Sir John was already speaking to Cavell. "The information you sent about Maynard was most helpful. I think I've been able to arrange matters for the best for Longleat."

"Sir John, do you think that was necessary?" Cavell replied before noticing that Robert had entered. "Ah, Smythson, there you are."

Robert noticed that Cavell did not meet his gaze directly, suddenly finding the ledgers in his hands engrossing. "I was just telling Sir John that you're doing a good job here. Sir John, remember what it looked like last year at this time?"

"Burnt rubble, I remember," Sir John said.

"And now the outline of the house is there, the walls climbing toward the sky, the site teaming with life and activity. I tell you, Smythson has things well in hand." Sir John grunted in acknowledgment. Cavell continued, "And there are still many months of work left before the site will be shut down for the winter."

"I admit, not bad for the first year. And if the rest of my plans go as they should, next year will be even greater."

Robert wondered what these plans were. "Welcome back, Sir John. I trust your trip was good."

"Satisfactory. You received the plans for the banqueting houses?"

"Yes, Cavell gave them to me. I don't think we'll be ready this year, but I suppose we can start preparing the pieces over the winter. I do have some ideas about the design. They seem a bit simplistic to me. Perhaps we could change the shape to add a bit more interest?"

Sir John gave him a steely look. "Are you questioning my ideas? The design is fine. No need to change them. If I'm satisfied, you're satisfied. Understood? Make haste, Smythson."

"Yes, Sir John."

"Now, Cavell has shared with me the business ledgers. Are you sure your team is being as efficient as possible? No wasted time. We must take advantage of the fair weather while we have it. When is the next load of stone expected from the quarry?"

Sir John was back; the questions never ceased, and no time was given to reply.

Another week of hard work went by, with the team looking forward to celebrating the midsummer holiday. Saturday came, with just a half-day's work to complete before the celebration of the year's longest day began. It was also quarter pay day, and Robert spent the bulk of the morning huddled with Cavell and Sir John's money keeper going over accounts. Robert was astounded by the amount of pay he received. The amount was not a complete surprise, as he knew his salary, but it was more money than he had ever received before. His expenditures were so low, mostly because of his choice of housing, that there was more than enough money left over from his pay to indulge any number of fancies.

When work was done for the day, the celebrations began. Sir John had forbidden any fires to be lit near Longleat, and few people disagreed as long as they could have the bonfire somewhere. The small green in Corsley Heath near the Royal Oak was transformed into a feasting area with lanterns, a fire, and ale freely flowing. Some wooden boards were set down to make a dancing platform and anyone who could play a pipe and tabor, a fiddle, or a lute, was recruited for music. The older women of the community had been busy baking while the younger had provided banners, ribbons, and floral wreaths to decorate the area and themselves. Robert contributed some of his extra pay to a feast for his workers and sat nearby, enjoying the spectacle of dancing and singing. Girls wore wreaths of flowers around their heads and sent flirtatious looks toward the single craftsmen, including Robert.

As the evening wore on, more and more couples drifted away into the nearby fields and woodlands to find some privacy, but Robert remained where he was, gazing into the fire, his thoughts drifting. Just as he was thinking that he might leave the celebration and go to bed, a figure approached him. It took Robert several moments to recognize him, but eventually he realized it was Ned Bright. "Bright? What on earth are you doing here?"

"There you are, Master Smythson, sir. I was wondering if I could have a word with you about Mary."

"Of course, but first tell me, Ned, have you come all this way just to ask me a few questions?" Robert was wondering how he could have made the journey. Had he come by himself, or perhaps Maynard had a hand in this? Had someone suggested he come? Had he thought through the risk of returning to Longleat? "Perhaps we should move somewhere a bit more private." Robert went and got two tankards of ale, returned to Ned, and led the visitor away from the festivities to a quiet spot hidden in a copse of trees.

Once they were settled, Bright said, "I just wanted to know a bit more about how they found her, you know, how she died."

Robert quietly explained about clearing out the last of the burnt rubble and discovering Mary's body. "We think she'd been there since the fire."

"That was more than a year ago. How could you tell it was her? Are you sure?"

"She was wrapped in an oiled cloth, the kind we use to protect stone from damage. It worked to protect her body, although there was some deterioration, which is to be expected."

"How was she, I mean, how did she die?"

Robert paused, considering what to say. The last thing Ned needed was a graphic description. Besides, there was the issue of Mary's father accusing him of the killing. "Ned, I'm not sure I should tell you that. You are considered a suspect in her killing. I think you know that."

"Me? Never!" Ned rose to his feet, visibly upset. It was the most animated Robert had seen him yet. "I would never have hurt a hair on her head. I loved her. Her deciding not to come was the worst thing that has ever happened to me. I haven't been right since then—ask anyone."

Robert spoke softly to him. "I have, Ned. I have. Sit back down and calm yourself. Getting upset won't change anything. Tell me how you met."

Ned began to talk, at first slowly, then the words began to tumble out in a rush, as if they had been held inside him. "I was an apprentice at Longleat. Never very good, but my parents said I needed a skill. Said my singing wouldn't be enough since I didn't have the looks or the grace to go along with them. No, no, it's not as harsh as it sounds. They were right. All I've ever wanted to do was sing, but for the rich people to hire you, you need to look the part, and well, I've always been kind of clumsy. Masonry's not bad, really. I mean, I smash my thumb a lot, but I've gotten used to it.

"I was working there when Spicer got promoted to head mason. He and Sir John used to have some great arguments, real yelling matches. The rest of us used to keep our heads down and try to stay out of it. Sometimes we would sneak off and let them go at each other. It was on one of those days when some of us masons snuck off. They were arguing fierce, and it was near the end of the day. We headed out toward Corsley, and that's where I saw her. Usually, I walked toward Frome, where I was still living with my parents, but that day the others convinced me to go with them up to the alehouse. We were walking, and I was singing, like I do. I was singing 'Hey Ho to the Greenwood' with the boys. Do you know it? It's usually sung in a round. Anyway, when we crossed over the bridge, a young lady walked by going the other way. Well, she just starts singing right after me, matching my tone and beat. It shut the fellows up, it did. Everyone stopped right there on the bridge, and we joined our voices together. Stood on that bridge singing for a good ten minutes before she realized what was happening and hastened away. I didn't know who she was. Her voice, it was unlike anything I had ever heard, sweet, lyrical, melodious. I could listen to it forever. I knew right then that all I ever wanted to do in life was to join my voice with hers."

"That is a beautiful story, Ned. How did things progress from there?"

"Some of the other lads knew who she was, the ones that lived up in Corsley Heath, so they took me by her father's farm, showed me where it was. I started looking for her whenever I could. We would meet in the evenings, go off together and sing. Then we just started talking more and more." Ned began to get agitated, the most animated Robert had seen him. "I would never hurt her—you have to believe me. She's all I ever wanted in this world. Well, that and to sing. With her, I mean."

"Ned, I have heard that you sing well, but I haven't heard it yet. Do you think you could let me hear something?"

"I don't know, Master Smythson. I haven't sung much since she left me. I think she took my music with her."

"Please, try. Think of her, knowing now that she did not leave you by choice." Robert watched as Ned digested these words. He appeared to dig deep inside, trying to push beyond his pain and find his voice. He took a sip of ale, then stood. Robert listened as a rich, deep tenor voice poured forth from the awkward lad, bringing a song so full of longing and pain and beauty.

Flow my tears fall from your springs,
Exiled forever, let me mourn
Where nights black birds hear sad infamy sings
There let me live forlorn

The song continued to the last line, *Happy happy they that in hell feel not the world's despite.* The song transformed Ned, and Robert finally understood how a girl could have fallen for him.

Bright's song had attracted a few onlookers, although no one seemed to recognize him. When he had finished singing, he slumped back down in his seat, returning to the lumpish mason. "It's better with a lute," he said apologetically. The couples who had gathered hovered, but on realizing that no more music was forthcoming, they slipped away into the shadows.

"That was beautiful. If Mary's voice was a complement to that, I can see why you two were so anxious to be together. Look, Ned, I believe that you didn't have a part in her death. But her father seems to think you did. Can you think of any reason he could think that?"

"No."

"Tell me about the day she was supposed to meet you."

"I left about noon; one of the other masons was going to cover for me. Plus, Sharington's not that observant. He probably wouldn't notice one less man working. I borrowed a horse and started for Longleat. Unfortunately, partway there, the horse went lame. He was hurt quite badly. I should have noticed sooner and stopped him, but I was anxious and didn't pay attention. So I had to walk the rest of the way. I was scared that Mary would think I wasn't coming. It got later and later, and there was nothing I could do. It got dark, and I think I lost my way a bit. Eventually, I got as far as East Woodlands 'cause I went that way. Didn't want to risk running into Sir John."

"I understand," said Robert who had taken the same route himself for the same reason.

"Well, see, I got as far as Maynard's place. Do you know it?" Robert nodded. "Well, I know Mistress Maynard; we grew up together. Sometimes I sing at her place when she wants to impress the guests. She convinced me to spend the night. Said it was too late to go look for Mary. I was exhausted since I had been walking for several hours. When I woke up, Alan was there with a letter from Mary. He told me he had seen Mary and she had decided she wasn't coming with me. What else could I do?"

"What happened then? Where did you go after he showed you the letter?"

"I'm not really sure. I think I wandered about for a while. I never went to Longleat. Eventually, I made my way back up here. What else could I do? She had decided not to come. Every day, I thought about going after her, trying to get her to change her mind, looking for her, wishing and hoping she would change her mind and come to me. Finally, I just gave up."

"Surely, you heard about the fire? Did you ever connect the fire with the night you were supposed to meet Mary?"

"No, not really. I guess I didn't see what one had to do with the other. I still don't."

"That's one of the mysteries I'm trying to solve. My guess is that Mary did go to meet you and somehow got mixed up with the fire and was killed—purposely or accidentally—by whoever started the fire."

"I hate to think of that. It was sad enough knowing she had rejected me. I think this might be worse."

The two sat in silence, each feeling their emotions deeply. In the distance, they could still hear the musicians playing, the thunder of feet dancing. Shouts of merriment, hope, and joy. Robert couldn't help but feel the discrepancy between the celebration on the other side of the trees and the sadness near him. A couple stumbled out of the trees, and Robert rose so they would notice him before becoming overly intimate. He was surprised to find Alan and Betty Maynard.

"Maynard, what are you doing here?"

"Can't a man celebrate midsummer with his wife? We've come for the merriment, of course. Heard there was a song fellow over here. How are you, Smythson? Who's that with you? A lucky lady, no doubt?"

"Um, no . . ." Robert stumbled before Bright rose and stepped into the last of the daylight.

"Ned Bright? So that's who was singing, was it? Whatever are you doing here? You haven't come back to work at Longleat, have you?"

"No, no," Robert answered, stepping between Bright and Maynard. He wasn't sure why, but he felt the need to protect Bright.

"He just came down because he had some questions about Mary's death. There's no need for concern; he's not here to cause trouble."

Betty pushed Robert out of the way. "Of course he's not, are you, Ned? Good to see you." She approached Ned, who looked surprised, and wove her hand through his arm. He pulled away. "Oh, come now, don't be like that. We're old friends, aren't we, Ned?" He nodded slowly and let her take his arm. "Have you come to sing for us? I'm sure the Longleat community would love to hear you sing again; it's been a long time." She tried to move Ned back toward the main festivities, but he wasn't moving.

"Alan, won't you encourage Ned to sing for us?"

"I'm not sure Ned wants to sing for us, do you? What kinds of questions? Has Smythson given you the answers you were looking for? You're not still asking about Mary's death, are you, Smythson? I thought Sir John told you to leave that alone?"

"I can't see what concern that is of yours, Maynard. The business between Ned and myself is just that: not your concern. Have you come to make your big announcement? Sometimes I wish you would just make it and be done with it."

"Patience, lad, all in good time. No, I just came back to give the mistress a bit of a squeeze and enjoy the merriment of midsummer. Didn't expect to find Bright here, but the more the merrier. And Betty's right, his voice would liven the night. Unless he's still too melancholy."

Somehow a crowd had begun to gather, although whether it was to hear Bright sing or to witness any sparks between the former and current head masons, Robert didn't know. He tried to show a calm, accepting demeanor, hoping to dispel any excitement, but unfortunately another newcomer made that unlikely.

The smell of stale ale proceeded the man, but he soon became visible: Kington. "What's all the excitement? Can't a man enjoy a summer's night in peace without all this shouting?"

Robert's stomach lurched, and his chest tightened. He didn't know what was going to happen next and had no idea how to stop it. How could he bring peace back to this joyous night? Even now, as twilight deepened, the sky grew rosy, and the air cooled after the heat of the day. In this small clearing in the trees between Corsley Heath and Cley Hill Farm, the two men saw each other. Robert watched as the recognition dawned on Kington's face. He saw the man's face grow red with fury.

"I'll kill him, just like he killed my Mary." Kington lunged toward Bright while Maynard took a step backward and Betty screamed.

Robert rose and tried to block the younger mason. Bright rose slowly from the stump he had been resting on. "Kington," Bright said, "you never wanted my Mary to be with me." Bright took a step toward Kington.

"Your Mary, never. She was never yours." Kington moved to within inches of Robert's face. "Move aside, Smythson, so I can see justice done."

"I'm not going to do that, Master Kington. I've already told you Bright didn't kill Mary. He's just as lost without her as you are."

"No, he's not. He killed her." Kington pushed Robert out of the way and swung at Bright. Robert lost his balance and landed with a thud on the ground as Kington's fist landed with a thud in Bright's stomach. The younger mason absorbed the blow and then wrapped both arms around Kington, lifting him off the ground.

"I tell you I didn't kill her. I loved her. Why won't you believe me?"

Robert scrambled to his feet and yelled, "Maynard, help me. We've got to break this up. They'll hurt each other."

Maynard just laughed. "Always something entertaining here at Longleat. Glad I came in time for the show."

The two men continued to be locked in a huddle, with Kington trying to kick and punch Bright, who just held Kington several inches off the ground. More and more people wandered over, attracted by the shouts. Through the growing crowd, Robert saw Richard Cavell pushing his way through.

"What the hell's going on here?" the steward yelled, trying to make his voice heard over the crowd. "We can almost hear you up at the manor. Bright? God's breath, what are you doing here?" Cavell looked wildly around, taking in the group assembled, his eyes going from Bright to Kington to Maynard. "Maynard, why are you always where nobody wants you? Lord, preserve us when Sir John hears about this! Bright, put Kington down! Lord, have mercy."

Somehow Bright responded to Cavell's authority and did as he was told. Kington wasn't finished. "He killed my angel. He'll pay for this!" He lunged again for Bright. Robert stepped in between and this time managed to intercept the punch, unfortunately with his face. Reeling, Robert grabbed hold of Kington and pinned his arms down. "Stop! Before something happens we'll all regret."

Finally, everyone stood glaring at one another, Robert rubbing his cheek. "Sorry, Smythson," Kington murmured. "Didn't mean to hit you."

"I know you didn't, but please, no more fighting. Cavell, what are you going to do?"

Cavell looked from one man to another to another and sighed. "Look, this wouldn't be happening if you'd just left well enough alone, Smythson. Sir John tried to tell you that no good would come of this. None of this is going to bring Mary back, Master Kington." Kington shrugged, defeated. "The rest of you, go back to the bonfire, enjoy the rest of the night." He spoke with authority, and the crowd began to slowly disperse. "Well, that will feed the gossip mill for weeks to come," Cavell said.

"Bright, I don't know why you're here, but there's nothing for you at Longleat. If Sir John finds you here, he may question you about the money Spicer took. If I were you, I would head back to Lacock and forget about Mary Kington." Cavell's harsh words took the air out of Bright, who folded in on himself.

Cavell wasn't finished. "Maynard, I suppose you're here to see your wife. I can't stop you, but focus on her and don't get involved in what doesn't concern you. As for you, Kington, I suggest you go home."

Robert saw Cavell's words as a desperate attempt to pretend the events of the evening hadn't occurred, to sweep everything under the rug. Did Cavell know more about Mary's death than he was saying? Robert watched each person, as hard as it was to see their expressions in the darkening shadows. Betty Maynard was watching Cavell and Alan closely, her glance darting back from one to the other. Robert was still holding Kington, who looked like he might still lunge for Bright. Bright collapsed back on the stump, again the broken man Robert had seen at Lacock. No one was that good an actor.

Chapter 16

ROBERT, ALONG WITH MOST of Corsley Heath and the neighborhood, slept late on Sunday. More than one person was seen nodding during the church service only to revive later for more dancing and feasting. This time, Robert stayed on the outskirts, spending the evening with Dick and Charlotte Crispin and John Hills. As he explained to his friends, the previous night had held more than enough excitement for him, and he wanted a quiet evening playing his share of card and dice games and laughing at the antics of the others.

Yet he could not get Ned's haunting melody out of his head or erase the events of the previous evening. In the end, nothing had been accomplished or settled. Robert was left with more questions than answers. Cavell had somehow persuaded Kington to return home, and the Maynards had returned to their home in East Woodlands without further scandal or news. And Robert had persuaded Ned Bright to sleep in one of the masons' cottages before returning to Lacock this morning. Fortunately, there was no sign of any of them Sunday afternoon or evening, for which Robert was grateful.

The highlight of Robert's evening was the Crispins' revealing that they were expecting a baby sometime that winter. But for as many joys as there were to rejoice over, there were mysteries and conflicts lying just below the surface. Visions of Mary's decomposed body continued to come unbidden to Robert's mind. And the fight between Bright and Kington the previous night remained locked in his vision. How could these men have so much hatred for one another? Because they had both loved. Both Bright and Kington had loved Mary, and only with such depth of feeling could one have such passion.

He had wondered if perhaps the conflict of the previous evening might provide an opportunity for an actual investigation. If Kington officially accused Bright of the murder, could there be a trial in which Bright's innocence could be proven? And Robert was sick and tired of the push-pull drama of the Maynards. May Maynard get the job and be done with the neighborhood!

Like all longest days, this one ended, and Monday morning brought with it the aches of a night filled with too much ale, wine, and food. Those who weren't groggy were belligerent and testy. Workers were clumsy and slow, and Robert steered everyone to non-important tasks. It wasn't worth the risk of damaging something.

Toward the end of the day, Robert made his way to Corsley Manor to meet Sir John and Cavell. He was to make a full report, summing up the accounts of the past quarter and preparing for the next. As he made his way to Sir John's business chamber, the two men were in a heated discussion.

"I don't think he's going to leave it alone," Cavell said.

"He will if I tell him to," replied Sir John before noticing that Robert had come into the room. "Smythson, good, you're here. I'm hearing disturbing things about where you've been during my absence."

"Oh?" Robert looked from one man to another, watching as Richard gave the smallest shake of the head in warning.

"Went to Lacock without my permission, I hear." No one in the room was sitting, and suddenly Robert felt light-headed, as if all the air had been sucked out of the room. Despite the lack of protocol, he stumbled to the nearest stool and perched on it.

"I went to visit Ned Bright. Henry Kington seems convinced that Bright killed his daughter, so I went to see him for myself."

"After I specifically forbade you from investigating?"

"Yes, I thought it was important—"

"Do I pay you to think? To investigate? Did I appoint you sheriff? Or have I hired you to lead a crew of masons down at Longleat?"

"The latter, but—"

"Enough! If I believed that there was any truth to what Kington said, I would have Bright investigated and arrested. However, I do not give credence to the ramblings of a madman, and I suggest you do the same."

Robert could not believe Sir John's coldness. "Have some compassion, Sir John. He's lost his only daughter, the only family he had left. Here you are with a flourishing estate and a family growing by the day. Is it any wonder if he wants a little of what you have?"

"Bah! He only wants things handed to him without having to work for them. I have worked for all I have. Earned it with my hands and my wits."

"And as a man with wealth, status, and position, is it not your role to look out for those less fortunate than yourself? All I am asking is that we investigate the death of his daughter and the

Longleat fire and bring those responsible to justice. I would think as both sheriff and justice of the peace that you would be leading the charge."

"Smythson, you are walking dangerously close to the line of insubordination. I think you need to ask yourself how much you want to work here at Longleat."

"I have, Sir John, I have. I've been asking myself that exact question for the past few days."

"Sir John, Robert, consider what you are both saying," interrupted Cavell.

"Cavell, stay out of this!" Sir John bellowed to his steward. Turning back to Robert, he said, "And what have you come up with?"

Robert ran his fingers through his hair, staring at Sir John. How could the man be so self-absorbed? "Sir John, a girl's body lay in a pile of rubble left over from your house burning down. Do you not feel responsible? One of your masons' tools bashed her head in. How can you be so callous?" Robert was standing again, filled with rage at this man's apathy.

"It was not I who killed her, nor I who left my tools laying around to be used as a weapon." His words were clipped, his tone cold. "It was not my daughter who was so foolish to go wandering about where she had no right to be. Her death has been nothing but a nuisance to me and continues to be. She was a nuisance to me in life and in death. If anything, her death did me a favor. Since she's been gone, her father has not once come around begging me to marry my son to her."

"That sounds close to a motive. Perhaps we need look no further for her killer or for a reason you do not want this investigated."

"Enough!" Sir John bellowed. "How dare you come in here and accuse me of murder."

"I . . . No, I . . . didn't . . ." Robert stammered. Had he?

"It sounded like you came dangerously close to it. I'm done. Either you put away this fascination and obsession with solving irrelevant deaths or you leave Longleat. You choose. We're done. Do not think you are the only mason who can build my vision. You can be easily replaced, if that is the choice you make. You can see yourself out." With that, Sir John swept out of the room.

Robert was left in the room with Richard Cavell, who slumped and folded himself into a nearby chair. Stunned by what just happened, Robert stood, unable to move. Cavell was the first to recover. "What just happened?"

"God's breath, Richard, I don't know, but I think I just lost my job."

"No, please don't say that. He needs you, we need you, and Longleat needs you."

"You heard him. I can be replaced. He probably already made arrangements when he was at court."

"Don't do anything rash," Cavell said. "Tempers flared. It's probably just the lingering effects of last night's merriment. Sir John will calm down, you will apologize, and all will go back to as it was."

"How did Sir John hear I was at Lacock?"

"I don't know." Richard shuffled through some of the papers on Sir John's desk. "Oh dear. Here it is. A letter from Henry Sharington in response to an inquiry by Sir John. Apparently, someone told him you were seen at Lacock, and he wrote to Sharington to confirm. I assume you spoke to Sharington while you were there."

"Yes. The ironic thing is that because of that visit, I am now convinced, more than ever, that Ned Bright had nothing to do with Mary's death. All my effort has done has cleared him of any suspicion."

"Maybe that's what Sir John is mad about. If Bright didn't kill Mary, then someone closer to Longleat must have."

"So his plan is to scare me off so a killer can go free in the neighborhood? That makes no sense—unless he knows who it is and wants to protect them. Richard, how do you put up with it? I'm not sure I even want to work here anymore."

"Please don't say that. It's getting late. Go home, get some food and a good night's sleep. This will all look differently in the morning."

Robert shrugged, allowing the steward to guide him from Corsley Manor without running into Sir John again.

Later that evening, lying in bed, Robert replayed his confrontation with Sir John. He considered Sir John's words: you choose. What if he chose to leave Longleat permanently, to return to Reading and Anne as a failure? Sir Francis wasn't there and had made it clear that he was putting the work on hold while he attended to matters of national importance. London? Would Lovell have something for him? Probably, but could he go back to his old mentor and admit failure?

On the other hand, he could not be worthy of Anne knowing a girl had been killed and he had done nothing about it. He flipped onto his back and brooded. Give up the investigation or give up Longleat. That was the ultimatum Sir John had given him. No more delay, no more side trips, no more questioning or digging around. Just focus on the building. How could Robert just forget the initial feel of touching Mary's bony hand? How could he forget the broken-hearted song of Ned Bright or the sorrow-filled wailing of her father? Did a girl's life mean so little?

Perhaps more importantly, did Robert want to continue working for a man who could be so cold and callous, so self-centered?

He had understood that Sir John was a harsh man, but surely there were limits and basic human dignities at play. Robert honestly did not know what to do. He looked across the room and saw the drawings, the plans and sketches he had made for the building. It was lovely. But at what cost?

He thought about all the young people he had seen the night before, sneaking off in pairs for some midnight romance. He knew more than one young lady had tried to attract his attention, but he had not seen them, at least not in the way they wanted to be seen. A deep hunger gnawed at him, but he told himself that it would not have been satisfied by a few hours spent in the arms of a stranger. His lusts were for Anne and Anne alone. For her support, her embrace, her encouragement. Thinking back to Bright's singing, Robert's longing for her only intensified. Passion, warmth, comfort, she provided all of these. He finally fell asleep, certain of the knowledge that his life would not be complete without her.

Chapter 17

Robert rolled over and groaned. His bedchamber, if he could call it that, was warm. He threw off the wool blanket and stretched out his legs. Still warm. Then the acrid smoke penetrated his senses, and he realized he smelled fire. The room had an eerie glow, odd shadows cast on the walls, light coming from below. Something in him shuddered, memories lighting up and licking his nerves like flames. He was trapped in his home, fire consuming the timber walls of the upper story. His sister was trapped in her small bedchamber behind his. He froze, unable to move, staring as the flames grew higher, hotter, knowing he should move, he should try to get past the fire to where she was. He couldn't. Robert shook himself. This was not his childhood home. This was Longleat. The fire at Longleat? No, that was in the past. Corsley Heath. The masons lodge. His chamber on the upper level of the masons lodge was on fire.

Wide awake now, he swung his legs over the bed and gingerly put his feet to the floor. It was hot, but not actually burning. He groped around for his shoes and shoved his feet into them, wrapping himself in the blanket. Standing, he inhaled thick smoke and coughed. He bent and looked down the ladder. Intense heat blasted from below, pushing him back. The ground floor was lit with flames.

Smoke was filling the upper room quickly now. He grabbed his shirt and wrapped it around his nose and mouth to filter some of the smoke. Robert heard a shout from below. Then another. How was he going to get down and out of the lodge? The flames had not actually made it to the top level, so he was safe for a minute. If the roof caught on fire, he was probably dead. Looking down the ladder again, he realized there was no way down to safety. It would have to be one of the small windows. Making his way to a window cut into the thatch roof, he pulled away the wooden shutters, yanking them from their hinges, sparing a thought of gratitude for poor craftsmanship for once. It would be a tight squeeze but infinitely better than burning to death. He grabbed a roof rafter and pulled himself up, swung his feet out the window and then wiggled his way out. The thatch was hot and sharp, but it was dark below. There was no chance of falling into the fire. He slid down the roof line until he reached the edge, the rough thatch scraping his bare chest, then let go.

He landed with a thud; his legs crumpled beneath him. Groaning, he tried to get up. Pain seared through one of his ankles, and he fell back down to the ground, coughing. He could hear someone calling his name and tried to respond. Soon, strong arms were lifting him up. "Robert, man, are you all right?" Dick Crispin pulled him to his feet, with John Hills coming along. Between the two strong men, they carried Robert away from the burning lodge. To the side, other craftsmen and their families gathered, trying to organize a bucket line from the nearby stream to put out the fire.

"The plats!" Robert cried, trying to struggle free.

"They're gone," Crispin said. "And you're in no shape to help. Come, Charlotte's brought some ale. Your throat must be burning." The men led Robert over to a stump and lowered him down gingerly. Charlotte pushed a mug into his hand.

"God's teeth, I hurt." Robert's hands were rough with burns and scrapes, but he managed to hold the mug and drink, the cool ale soothing his throat. He looked up at his friends. "What happened?"

"You didn't leave the fire going again, did you?" Hills asked.

"John, no. I swear, I banked it."

"'Twas no fireplace fire that did this," Dick said. "I think something was thrown into the lodge. I reckon they were aiming for the ladder. This was deliberately set."

"Who?" Robert asked, passing his mug to Charlotte for a refill.

"No idea," Dick said. "By the time we saw it, whoever did this was gone. The way the fire was burning, it didn't start at the fireplace. I tried to get in to get to you, but . . ."

"No, it would have been too risky. But I think your yelling was enough to get me to wake up, so thank you for that." Robert's body was beginning to shake. The enormity of what could have happened began to dawn on him.

"Charlotte, can you get him to our cottage? Robert, do you think you could make it that far? Come on, John, let's see if we can help them put out the fire." He turned to Robert. "Everything on the ground floor will be gone, but perhaps with luck we can save your personal belongings." Dick left Robert with Charlotte and joined them, pulling Hills with him.

"Can you walk?" Charlotte asked.

"I think so." He tried to stand up, but only one leg worked.

"Then let's get away from here. There's nothing more you can do tonight. Get some rest, some fresh air, and tomorrow you can see what you can save." She let him lean on her as he limped and hopped toward the Crispins' cottage.

A short while later, she had built up the fire and made a bed on the floor for him, covering him with heavy blankets until he stopped trembling. "Thank you, Charlotte. That wasn't my first fire, or even my worst."

Charlotte handed him a new mug full of ale and sat down, waiting for him to continue. "Just before I began my apprenticeship, our home caught fire. My sister and I were inside. I tried to save her . . ." His voice trailed off, his thoughts trapped in memory.

Charlotte touched his arm, and they sat in silence for a moment. "You made it out, but she didn't?" she asked gently.

Robert nodded. "My father blamed me. For all of it. The fire, not saving her. I tried to tell him it wasn't my fault, but he never would believe me. Always blamed me, always criticized me. Nothing I did was ever good enough, and it all stemmed from that fire. That's why Hills and Lovell—do you know Humphrey Lovell? No, well, he's the Queen's master mason, friend of my father. Hills and Lovell were worried that I might have trouble here because of the fire and the association, but it didn't bother me. Unless you count my need to know who started the fire, what the cause was. And I think my concern about Mary Kington's death is somehow connected. I couldn't save my sister. She was younger than Mary, still just a child. So was I, if I'm honest. But I carry that failure with me and my father's judgment and blame. From then on, he always saw me as a failure. Sorry, I didn't mean to ramble on like that."

"You don't have any family left? I think I've heard that your father and brother were killed in an accident several years ago."

Robert hung his head. Did everyone know about the accident?

"Yes, another tragedy to lay at my feet. Or at least that's what my father would say if he had survived."

"Surely not," Charlotte protested. The conversation was not continued as Dick opened the cottage door and came in.

"It's out," Dick said. "It's a wet, soggy, smoky mess, but it's out. Every last ember. Let's get some sleep. The sun will be up soon enough."

The Crispins went to their bedchamber, and Robert watched as the last of the fire burned low, unable to rest until all that was left was a small glow. He tried to sleep, but images of flames flickered in his mind. Too many fires, his sister, the lodge, even Longleat, although he hadn't been there. He woke repeatedly, gasping for air, until finally lying awake, staring at the ceiling, playing the possibilities over in his mind. The fire had been deliberately set, intending him harm, perhaps even death. The community was full of possible suspects. Sir John, obviously, after what had transpired earlier that day. Maynard was back in town. Could he wish harm to Robert? Kington? Perhaps he was angry that Robert continued to defend Bright. Or perhaps it was someone else entirely. He coughed, his throat burning. Whoever it was, if driving Robert away from Longleat had been their goal, they'd succeeded.

The sunrise brought Cavell down to see what the rumors were about. Robert found him sticking his head in the masons lodge, surveying the mess. "Good morrow, Cavell," Robert greeted him, his voice rough from smoke damage. The rest had helped restore some function to his ankle, and he was able to put some weight on it.

"God's breath, what happened? Are you all right?"

"All right enough. Someone tried to burn down the lodge last night with me in it. You can thank the team of craftsmen for putting out the fire and Dick Crispin for helping me get out." Robert took a few steps inside, kicking away some of the soggy mud of stone chips and charred remains of the wooden benches. The ladder leading to the loft was completely burned, so there was no way to immediately assess the damage to his personal belongings.

"Are you sure it wasn't an accident?"

"Yes, see for yourself." The worst of the damage was in the center of the lodge, not near the fireplace. "It looks as if someone threw something inside. Someone doesn't want me at Longleat. Sir John, perhaps?"

"How can you say that?" Cavell's eyes narrowed.

"After yesterday? Maybe he thought I needed a shove. Or perhaps whoever killed Mary Kington thought I was getting too close. Or maybe Longleat's just cursed. I don't know. I'm done, Cavell. If Sir John wants to replace me, tell him to go ahead." Robert limped outside, headed toward the carpentry workshop, hoping to borrow a ladder so he could climb up and see what he could salvage.

Cavell was at his heels. "Don't be hasty, Robert, please. Let's talk this through." Before they got any farther, Hills walked toward them, carrying a ladder. Robert nodded to his old friend, and the two turned back to the masons lodge. Robert knew he shouldn't be ignoring Sir John's steward, but he was running out of patience, sympathy, and even manners. All he wanted to do was build a beautiful building that would survive well past his life. A legacy, something to be proud of, something to outlast him. Longleat was supposed to be the making of him, and now he was going to leave before he really got started.

The new ladder in place, Robert gingerly climbed up into the loft. He tested the floor carefully, unsure if it would hold his weight. Thankfully, it did. The upper space had been spared the worst of the damage. The air was still heavy with smoke, so Robert pushed open the remaining windows. The lodge was probably unusable now, so it didn't matter much if Robert broke open some of the thatch to get some additional air in. The chest with his clothes was intact, including the lengths of thread he had bought for Anne. The pile of plats, drawings, sketches and plans had sustained damage but wasn't completely lost. Overall, it could have been a lot worse. Had someone intended it to be a lot worse?

The masons had begun to gather for their normal workday. Robert tried to watch each one, measure their reaction. Many of them had been there last night, so it didn't come as a surprise. Hills took charge, setting the men to carrying out all the debris, trying to salvage any usable tools or stone. "I think we're going to have to transition to the Longleat lodge for the future," he said.

"Robert, we need to talk." Cavell had been quiet while Robert checked the loft and greeted the men. "Let's go somewhere a bit quieter to talk this through. Hills, come join us when you get these fellows organized."

"I'm not going back to Corsley Manor," Robert said. In truth, he still wasn't feeling well. His throat was sore and his body a bit roughed up from the scraping and fall.

"No, no, that's fine. Let's see if someone at the Royal Oak will give us some space and some ale. Sounds like your throat could use the liquid."

A short while later, the three men sat at a table outside the Royal Oak. "This wasn't an accident, Cavell," Hills said firmly.

"Could it have been some leftover merriment from midsummer's night?" Cavell asked.

"No," Robert said. "I don't believe this was mischief. It was a deliberate attempt to either hurt me or at least scare me away. Cavell, I haven't had a chance to tell Hills about my confrontation with Sir John." Robert proceeded to summarize the previous day's encounter.

Hills listened quietly, asking a few questions for clarification, letting his friend unburden himself. "That's a lot for a man like Sir

John to take. He would not like to be accused of murder, especially with his past history."

"What do you mean?"

"Only that he has twice been sent to the Tower of London on suspicion of crime. I would imagine he would be sensitive to accusations. I also think that if he had done it, he would react differently." Robert gave him a questioning look. "I'm not sure how exactly, but the whole thing would have happened differently, starting with the removal of the rubble. If he knew Mary's body was there, surely he wouldn't have let you dig."

"Unless he planned on blaming someone else."

"Perhaps. Right now, I'm more concerned with your relationship to Sir John and what happened last night," Hills said, draining his mug of ale.

"Are you suggesting Sir John set the fire?" Cavell asked.

"I don't know. He could have had someone else do it," Hills answered.

"All I know is that it worked," Robert said. "I can't remain here and let Mary Kington's death go unresolved and have people set fire to my lodge. God's breath, I could have been killed!"

Out of the corner of his eye, Robert spotted movement. A tow-headed boy was watching them from behind a tree. Robert reached down, grabbed a stone from the ground, and hurled it in the direction of the boy.

"Woah there, Smythson," said Cavell. "I know you're frustrated but taking it out on a tree won't help."

"Not the tree. You there, come here!" Robert yelled. The other two men turned in time to see the boy run off. "I've seen that boy before, near Maynard's place."

"Do you think Maynard sent him? Could he be responsible for the fire? Trying to scare you off to get his old job back?" Hills asked.

"Possibly. Although Betty still thinks they're leaving as soon as Maynard gets his new job. Is he one of yours?" Robert directed this question to Cavell.

"What?" Cavell asked.

"Just because I've seen him near Maynard's doesn't mean he's from there. We all know how Sir John gets his information somehow. Cavell, is this boy one of Sir John's spies, spying on Maynard, not sent by Maynard?"

At least Cavell had the decency to turn red and not deny it. "No, he's not one of ours," he replied sheepishly.

"Is this going to be another case of a fire that isn't investigated? Another crime ignored?"

Cavell stared off into the distance. "I don't know what to say, Robert. Honestly, I don't."

"Perhaps I should go away for a while and let Sir John experience Longleat without me."

"What do you mean?" Cavell rubbed his hands together, clearly uneasy.

"I get it," Hills said. "Let him think this fire drove you away. If he had a hand in it, meaning to frighten you, let him think it worked. I think he needs you more than he realizes. Without you, the work at Longleat will flounder, and he'll beg you to come back. On your terms this time."

"I see what you're thinking, Hills. But it's more than that. I honestly don't want to work here anymore under these circumstances. I'm done. Murders, fires, all uninvestigated. Now my life is threatened. No. I'm done. Finished. If Sir John needs me that badly, let him say so and start to listen to me."

What would Sir John do if Robert left? Hire Maynard to come and lead his men? That was obviously the question Maynard had wondered and tested. Sir John's response had been to replace Maynard with Robert. Would he now find another mason to replace Robert? If Robert chose to leave, what would that mean for his team? They had come here because of him. Would they stay without him? Could they? Or would Sir John fire them?

"My only concern is for my men. My issue is with Sir John. I don't want my team to lose their jobs because I leave. John, do you think you can supervise the men for a bit longer?" Robert asked Hills.

"Yes, of course. I'll try to keep things going smoothly but not too smoothly. The goal is to get Sir John to feel your absence and beg you to come back, right? I'll help Cavell in any way I can with that in mind."

"I don't know if that's the goal or not. There's some great potential here, and I would love to be a part of it, but not under the present circumstances. However, one thing has become clear to me since I've been here: I made a mistake not asking Anne to come with me when I came in March."

Hills grinned. "About time you came to your senses. Go to Reading, see if she'll have you. I'll do what I can here so we can have you come back with Anne by your side."

Now Cavell smiled. "Someone you left behind at Reading? Yes, that might work. Let Sir John think you've gone for good, and you go see your girl. You've got the money from last quarter. With the few expenses you've had here, there should be plenty left to support you for a few weeks' trip to Reading."

"No promises, Cavell. I'll be in touch with Humphrey Lovell as well. He may have a better opportunity for me. Feel free to tell that to Sir John."

Chapter 18

Robert's pulse quickened as the scenery became more familiar. He stopped his horse several times along the journey, questioning the wisdom of just showing up, heart in hand but otherwise empty-handed. What did he have to offer Anne? If he had been reluctant to ask her to come with him to Longleat when he had the job, what was he doing here now that he had lost it? An unemployed stonemason with a history of accidents and death. He hadn't quite believed it when Lovell had recommended him to Thynne despite his past at Winchester. Now he had blown that opportunity, there wasn't likely to be another one. Yet here he was, ready to ask Anne to share his future. There was no logic to love. The shattered, broken soul of Ned Bright had showed him that.

He arrived at Greys Court, looking around at familiar places and people, remembering simpler times without dead bodies and fires. Turning his horse over to one of the grooms, Robert inquired as to where he might find Edward Palmer. He shook with nerves. How much should he reveal about the truth of his past? He felt it only right that he officially seek permission to marry the man's daughter, yet who would approve of him?

"You won't, sir, I mean, that is, you can't," the young groom replied with confusion.

Robert turned away. Somehow Master Palmer had heard of his intentions and was turning him away already.

"No, don't go. What I mean, well, sir, I mean, he's dead. Died yesterday," the groom stammered.

"Oh dear. Yes, I see your confusion now. Well then, might I see his daughter, Anne?"

"I dunno, you can try. Go to the main house and ask. Don't think anything's happened to her."

Robert made his way anxiously to the main entrance of Greys Court. His insecurities rubbed against his desire to comfort and protect Anne. Would her father's death hurt or help his chances at winning her heart? Must he now seek Sir Francis's permission to marry Anne? Sir Francis liked him, but he also knew the truth about what happened in Winchester. He would not trust his friend's daughter to Robert. Before he could reconcile his doubts, a servant was inquiring as to his business. "I'm here to see Anne Palmer," he said.

"Can't think she'd want to see you. Hasn't left her father's chamber to eat or do anything since her father died."

"I understand. Could you please tell her that Robert Smythson is here to see her. Perhaps she'll see me. Please, I've come rather a long way."

The servant called to someone, who agreed to carry Robert's message up to Anne. Robert waited impatiently while the servant looked on with mild amusement. He didn't have to wait long. Several members of the household watched with surprise as Anne Palmer rushed down to meet the newcomer. Robert's heart lurched as Anne's hands trembled when she placed them in his. He searched her face and found traces of tears and sleepless nights. His desire to protect and cherish her exploded in his heart, and he knew he had made the right decision.

Then someone recognized him as the stonemason who had sometimes met with Knollys and pushed them out the door, suggesting that he take her for a walk in the woods to the east of the house. Robert guided her outside into the sunshine, knowing they were being watched and gossiped about behind them, but not caring. Tenderly, he led Anne toward the woods, walking slowly and not speaking. She held on to his arm and followed willingly.

They soon reached the comfort of the shade, and Anne appeared to breathe more deeply. She looked up at Robert, as if surprised to find herself alone with him in the woods. "You're here," she said, fresh tears coming to her eyes. "How did you know about my father? How did you get here so quickly or even know to come?"

"I didn't. Oh, Anne, I'm so sorry about your father. If I could take away your pain, I would." He wrapped his arm around her and drew her to him. She clung willingly, and they stood entwined among the trees for several moments, letting the woods breathe for them.

After a short while, Robert led Anne farther into the woods until they came to a bench that had been placed in a small clearing. "Anne, I came because I made a terrible mistake when I went to Longleat without asking you to accompany me there. I didn't think it was right to take you away from your father and all you have known. Just to be a mason's wife. But there's a woman there, married to a mason. She's loud and vulgar, and if she can live in a nice house and have nice things, then so can you."

Anne laughed awkwardly at this rambling profession of love. "Are you calling me loud and vulgar?" she said, drying her tears and smiling.

"No, but trust me, this woman is. She's married to Alan Maynard, the former head mason, and they live in a two-story house with glass windows and a maidservant. I only have a room above the workshop for now—well, not even that. But if I go back, I can get us at least a cottage or something else until we can find a real home."

"If? Robert, is something wrong?"

"No. Yes. I don't know. Everything. I had an argument with Sir John about something I was doing. He told me not to, but I had to continue. He told me to choose, and I left." Robert's head was spinning. He knew he was botching this, but his thoughts were all jumbled, his heart was racing, and he didn't know where to start.

"So you don't have a job?"

"I don't know. I know I'm not making any sense. And I just turn up with no notice, and now your father just died. I'm so sorry. But I do have one thing for you." Robert reached into his doublet pocket and pulled out the lengths of thread he had been holding for just this moment. "I bought these for you. As soon as I saw them, I saw your eyes. I've been carrying them around since, waiting for this moment. I almost lost them in the fire, but—"

"Fire? What happened? Robert, what aren't you telling me?" Anne looked at him.

He returned her gaze. There was no judgment, fear, or animosity in her face, just gentle concern. "Let me try to explain this from the beginning." Holding her hand, he told Anne all about the discovery of Mary's body and the investigation. How he didn't believe Ned could have killed the girl, but her father was insisting it was him. He told her all of it, leading up to and including the fire that had finally driven him from Longleat. When he got to the part of his own lodge being set on fire, he hesitated to tell her. How could he tell her that someone had tried to kill him and he didn't know who? Could he bring her back into such a situation? He told her the barest facts, emphasizing that no real damage had come to him.

Anne listened carefully, occasionally stopping him with a question. When he finished, she sat back and looked at him. "I know, I know. How could I possibly ask you to marry me and come with me to a place where women's bodies are dug up at the building site and no one wants to investigate?"

"Is that what you're doing?"

"What?"

"Asking me to marry you?"

Robert was so embarrassed to have gone about this in such a clumsy fashion. "Yes, if you'll have me. I don't have much to offer you. The only way I can return to Longleat is to promise Sir John that I will drop the investigation into the fire and Mary Kington's death. Do you think I am right to do so?"

"I can't answer that for you."

"But would you take me without a job? It is too much to ask of you."

"Robert, I would marry you with no riches or all the riches in the world. Comforts do not matter to me, just having you nearby. If you think that you cannot return to Longleat because of Sir John's demands to stop investigating, then we will move on somewhere else. From what Sir Francis says, there are many men ready to start ambitious building projects. Surely, with his connections you could find another post."

"Perhaps. Sir Francis has enough on his shoulders right now. I do not wish to burden him further. Besides, there is something of great promise in Longleat. I'm not sure I'm ready to give it up yet. You should see it, Anne. There's even a miniature version of it, a kind of model, made of wood to see what it will look like. I think Sir Francis was right about Sir John's vision."

"I can see you love the work," Anne said. "You would like to return?"

Robert hesitated before answering. His voice was quiet. "I would, but I do not know if I can let that girl's death go unanswered."

"Have you any idea who might have done it?"

"No. For all the time I spent there, I am at a loss. I find it hard to believe that Ned Bright, her lover, could have done it. Although I suppose his melancholy could just as easily have arrived from guilt as from grief. One can see clearly how much he loved her. He doesn't seem capable of harming her."

"So who else does that leave?"

"I keep coming back to the fire. If the fire was set deliberately, she may have seen who did it and was killed to keep her quiet."

"That makes sense. Who had motive to set the fire?"

"Countless people. The mason Maynard seems to be almost constantly feuding with Sir John. Another mason named William Spicer apparently stole money from Sir John and was angry at being pursued. Neither of them was working at Longleat at the time of the fire, but they could have been in the area, and both seem to have been angry enough at Sir John to want to sabotage the building. There's even a rumor that Sir John torched the place himself to have an excuse to start over."

"Do you think he's capable of murder?" Anne shivered.

Robert paused. He knew his answer, but could he say it aloud if there was a chance of their returning to Longleat? Was he seriously considering taking Anne back to a place with a murderer? Apparently, he was. "Yes," he said slowly, "I do. I think he would stop at very little for Longleat. Also, it would explain his reluctance to have the crimes investigated."

"Anyone else? What about Mary's father?"

"Kill his angel? I don't think so." Another pause while he stroked Anne's hand. "Maybe I'm looking at this backward. Maybe the fire was set to hide the killing, not the other way around."

"In that case, who had motive? You say she was probably killed with a mason's tool? Would that have been lying around for anyone to pick up, or do you think it was a mason?"

"Her father seems to think Ned killed her. She was planning to run off with him, but what if she changed her mind at the last minute? But then there's the issue of the letter Ned has. If she spoke to him and told her she changed her mind, why does he have a letter?"

"Do you think he wrote the letter to himself? To cover his tracks?"

"I don't know. Doesn't seem likely, since Maynard has admitted to delivering the letter. The best thing to do would be to get the two letters, one from her father and the other from Ned, and compare them. But to do that, I would have to be investigating, which I am prohibited from doing. I just don't know what to do."

"I have faith that you will do the right thing. If you want to return to Longleat, then it is to Longleat we go." Anne looked back in the direction of Greys Court. "There's nothing holding me here anymore. If you'll have me, I will come back to Longleat with you."

Robert could not believe her words. After all he had said about murder and fire and Sir John, Anne was willing to accompany him back to Longleat as his wife. He looked deep into her eyes but saw no doubt or question. There were only two more hurdles to get over. "Anne, there are other things I haven't told you. Things that you need to know before you make that decision."

Anne pulled back. "Tell me."

"The first is that you, um, you and Mary Kington, the girl whose body was found, you look a lot alike. You could be sisters."

"I don't see how that's a problem, but I suppose I can see why that makes it important for you to find out what happened to her. What's the second thing?"

Robert paused. If he and Anne were going to make a life together, then she needed to know about Winchester. But he was reluctant to say the words out loud, knowing that it could end everything. He took a deep breath. "Toward the end of my apprenticeship, I was working in Winchester with Humphrey Lovell, my father, my brother, and a large crew." Robert's heart raced as he got through the story of his past.

He started by telling her how he loved to get lost in a piece of stone. That moment when it was all possibility—a limitless number of shapes and forms. He would gently run his fingers over the surface, asking the stone to reveal itself to him. From a young age, he had always believed that the stones could talk to him, share their inner being with him.

There was a moment, a quiet spark, when the stone would whisper its secrets to Robert: a hidden fault, a blemish about to be revealed. He had to be still to sense it. He couldn't explain it but had come to trust it since a time early in his apprenticeship when he had passed over a piece of perfectly good stone in favor of another. Others had laughed at him, but when a more experienced mason had worked the stone, it had cracked along an unseen line and was ruined. All eyes had turned to Robert. He shrugged. He had just known it wasn't the right piece.

His rebellion had come when his fingers could not achieve what the stone had revealed. He knew his intensity had unsettled some. "You're just a craftsman" or "Who do you think you are listening to stone" or "Robin Smythson in love with a piece of stone." Even his own father and brother had joined in. All of which had made him turn toward the stone.

Gradually, as he learned his trade, as his hands and arms learned the correct pressures, grips, and angles, he had gotten better at revealing the truth within the stone. His work began to get noticed. He began to climb the ranks among the bench masons, trusted with more difficult carvings. His opinions about designs began to be sought.

As his father began to realize that his son would outshine him, there was no fatherly pride, only resentment. The criticism began in earnest. Robert had long borne the nickname "Statue" for his unnatural stillness and quietness, but now the name was used with derision and mockery. True to the name, Robert hadn't fully absorbed the ridicule because he was too enmeshed with the stone. The older masons shook their heads, accepting the talent as well as the temperament. The younger ones were resentful; those closest to him were the least accepting.

This was the situation Robert found himself in that fateful day in Winchester. A large window piece was due to be hoisted in place. The team of masons and setters were ready. The carpenters had already built the scaffolding, and the pulley system was installed. The team worked together to place the ropes around the heavy stone piece and attach it to the pulley. Robert, still one of the junior masons, helped to control the swinging as the piece was lifted up. Something about the stone seemed off, and Robert's attention became fixated on a particular spot near the center. He stopped focusing on his job and instead stood rigidly staring at the stone.

Suddenly, the rope snapped, the scaffolding came crashing down, and the window piece broke in two, just where Robert had been staring. Two large pieces of stone fell to the ground, landing on several of the masons who had been helping and watching. Three men were killed, and several others were injured.

"My father and brother were two of the men killed that day. I killed them. My friend John Hills, you may remember him, was one of the injured. He still walks with a limp. If I hadn't taken my eye off the pulley rope and the stone, if I had moved, the accident wouldn't have happened."

Anne had listened as Robert told the whole story. "Do you know it was your fault? How could you be responsible for the scaffolding falling?"

"I was the only person not doing their job, the only one distracted. It's my fault, and I live with it every day. It didn't help that my relationship with my father was so turbulent prior to his death. The more my father criticized me, the more I withdrew. I loved masonry, but I thought about walking away. I had no idea if I was any good at it. There was external praise and inner joy, but the man closest to me had nothing to offer except criticism. He said I brought down the Smythson name.

"After the . . . incident, I stopped working. For a full year, I did nothing. At first, no one expected much of me. I worked the small piece of land for my mother. Eventually, Lovell put plats and sketches in front of me, left me drawing materials. It was the love of the lines that brought me back. Drawing angles, space, height, proportion. Later, he admitted leaving plats drawn incorrectly to irritate me. He knew I would feel compelled to redraw them, and he was right. But it was many months before I went back to work. Hills and Lovell saved me.

"I still feel deep shame and panic when I think about it. I feel like I want to find a split or a crevice in the stone and sink into it. If you are going to marry me, I need you to know who it is you're joining your life to."

"Thank you for telling me. We all carry things from our past that shape our present and future. I do not think you were responsible for the accident, but I can understand and accept that you feel you were. It doesn't change who you are to me."

"You are better than I deserve, and if you'll still have me, I promise to make you happy and provide for you. No matter what it takes." She nodded, and Robert lowered his head and kissed her.

Chapter 19

ONCE IT WAS DECIDED between Robert and Anne, she said she felt it was her duty to get Lady Catherine's permission to leave the Knollys household for good. A few days after Robert's arrival, Lady Catherine returned for a quick visit to Reading. She attended the funeral service of Anne's father as the Knollys family representative and then met with the new couple.

"What are you plans, Anne? You know that you have a home with our family for as long as you like. Indeed, with your sweet temperament and skill with the needle, I have half a mind to take you back to court with me. There would be a demand for your skills. Such fine work is sure to be admired and sought after. You could mix with a greater society than you have been used to, and perhaps we might even look for a suitable husband for you."

"Lady Catherine, that is a generous offer indeed, and I am indebted to you and your family for all the care you have shown my father and me. But you know I am not fond of crowds or strangers. And I have no great desire for a high position. A comfortable home among those I love is enough for me. Robert has offered me a future, and it is my wish to marry him." Anne took Robert's hand in hers. He had been sitting awkwardly while Lady Catherine spoke about him.

"I had plans for you Anne, plans. I was going to take you to court, find you a position as a lady-in-waiting to myself or one of the ladies of the Presence Chamber. You may have even served the Queen." Lady Catherine finally turned her attention to Robert. "Sir Francis speaks highly of you and believes you have a good future. I know Anne well enough to know that she would not join herself to an immoral man. We will hope for the best."

"Lady Catherine, I am grateful for all you have done for my father and me. I will always be in your debt. But I love Robert and believe he will give me a good life. Although it may not be a life of luxury, I would prefer to live with the man I love in simplicity than alone in splendor," Anne replied with direct honesty.

"I hope you're stronger than you appear. Your life with this stonemason is not likely to be an easy one. The dust, Anne! How can you conceive of such a thing?" Lady Catherine sighed. "I could have done much for you, if you would only have allowed yourself to be guided by me. Now I suppose it is too late. Well, I should apprentice you to the housekeeper so you can learn a bit more about keeping your own home before you leave us."

No matter how much Lady Catherine might have disapproved of Anne's plans, she was too preoccupied with her own duties as lady of the bedchamber to the Queen and with her many children. She couldn't spare the time to interfere, so she reluctantly gave Anne her blessing to make her own way in the world. Her one generous parting gesture was to give Anne a fur cloak she no longer used, for she knew that Anne was of a delicate nature and frequently cold. She gave the cloak, along with a warm hug, and returned to Hampton Court.

The day before the wedding, Sir Francis's steward sought out Robert. "Sir Francis has sent orders that you are to be fitted out as a presentable husband for the daughter of his old friend Edward Palmer. I have a new suit of clothes for you, and you're to meet with the tailor and barber." Robert blushed. He was unaccustomed to such attention, but in truth he had been concerned about his appearance. He wanted to appear worthy of his lovely bride, at least on this one occasion. And now, thanks to his generous employer, it would be a well-dressed and fashionably groomed man who would meet Anne at the altar.

On a warm Sunday in early July 1568, Robert was united with Anne Palmer in holy matrimony. Anne looked beautiful. As he stood next to her, Robert inhaled the rose water she had used to bathe herself. Her hair shone with its golden threads. Robert, ever the close observer, noticed the new pair of beautiful sleeves, embroidered with flowers in colorful silk thread, slashed to show the color beneath. Later he would learn that they were a gift from ladies in the Knollys household, who had grown to love Anne. Surrounded by the Knollys household still present in Reading, the church was filled with music and smiles as they exchanged their vows. A simple wedding feast followed at Greys Court, and then the couple retired to their chamber.

They had been given permission to remain in Anne's father's bedchamber in Reading. It was a bit unusual for a mason to be staying in such exalted surroundings, but since it was known that they would be leaving soon for Longleat or somewhere else, it seemed simpler than finding them new lodgings. Their wedding night was tender and sweet. The hours they spent alone in their bedchamber, in comfort and comparable richness, at least from Robert's perspective, seemed like heaven. Hardships were likely to come quickly once they left Greys Court, no matter where they went.

The only thing to darken Robert's mood during the days surrounding his marriage was the knowledge that he had failed at Longleat. He spent hours playing over the decisions he had made, and he would not have changed any of them. He believed that the girl's death deserved to be investigated, as well as the cause of the fire. What was the point of rebuilding without knowing if there was someone intent upon destroying your work? Now he had the wife of his dreams and no way to support her.

He tried not to let these dark thoughts cloud the early days of his marriage. They lived in a kind of in-between time, with little to do except be together. Robert knew it could not last forever, but he enjoyed it for what it was. He told Anne stories of the good things that had happened at Longleat and caught her up with the news of the other masons, whom she knew a little about. He described the Crispins to her, telling her how much she would like Charlotte, and made her laugh with stories of the Maynards.

Robert described the quarry trip and how he had been tested by the quarry master. After he finished that story, he told her about the legend of how Bath stone was discovered. "Imagine throwing down a glove and knowing with absolute certainty that the spot contained great treasure. I wish I could get a signal or sign with that much clarity."

Anne laughed at his desire, then stood up and asked for one of his gloves. Receiving it, she walked a few yards away, closed her eyes, and spun around before dropping the glove. "There. There's our treasure."

Robert went to where she stood and wrapped his arms around her. "You are correct. You are my treasure. With you by my side,

I have no need of anything else." They kissed for a few moments before Robert pulled away. "Of course, having a job would be a good thing. I should write a letter to Humphrey Lovell explaining everything and see what he advises."

"That's a good idea. I do have another suggestion we could try. Instead of legends and luck, we could seek the Lord's guidance. Will you pray with me?"

"Of course. Come here." He pulled her over to a bench in the tree grove, and they joined hands and prayed together for wisdom, guidance, and provision. A few moments later, they were interrupted by Knollys's steward.

He called out to them, waving something as he made his way over. "A letter's come from Longleat. It's addressed to Sir Francis, but in his absence I opened it, thinking it might concern you."

"And does it?" Robert asked.

"It does. I'll read the relevant sections to you: *Send the fool back to me.* I suppose that's you. *I just meant to scare him, not scare him off. Between you and me, he's as talented as Lovell said he was, he just needs to focus on building and not investigating irrelevant nonsense. Tell him to leave that girl's death alone and get back here to work.*" The steward grinned. "Looks like you've got your job back if you want it. What girl's death is he talking about?"

"We were clearing out the last of the rubble from the fire and found a girl's body. The daughter of one of Sir John's neighbors. It seems she had been there for almost a year, since the time of the fire. I started asking questions, and Sir John took exception. He forbade me to investigate. It seems that no one wants to know how she died."

"That does seem strange. Where were your inquiries going? Was it getting a little too close to Thynne himself?"

"What are you suggesting? Do you know the man?"

"Only by reputation. But I do know he did some fairly unscrupulous things to get his hands on people's properties."

"I don't think this has anything to do with that. It seems to be a lover's quarrel or misunderstanding. More personal than property related. I don't want to think Sir John is involved, although he is adamant that we not investigate, which does make him look suspicious. I think he just doesn't want anything to delay the building."

"Scaring you off seems to have delayed things, doesn't it?" The steward laughed. "Well, he wants you back. Can you live with the conditions?"

"I don't know. Now there's more than just myself to consider." Robert wrapped his arm around Anne, as he continued. "I'll be bringing Anne into the neighborhood. And to complicate things, she bears more than a little resemblance to the girl who died."

"Oh, I see. That could be awkward, but it does explain why you were so eager to solve the crime."

"Yes, exactly. I suppose now that I have my Anne, I could try to let it go. Besides, I do want to be involved in the building of Longleat. It will be truly remarkable once we can get it done."

As Robert considered Sir John's letter, he wondered if Sir John's statement "I meant to scare him" was an admission that he had been behind the fire to the masons lodge. Robert found it hard to believe that Sir John would risk damaging his own property, but it was possible. With the lodge unusable, Robert would need a new place to live, and he certainly wasn't bringing Anne back to cramped quarters shared with a tracing room.

The letter he later wrote to Sir John was the hardest letter he had ever written. He pledged his loyalty and obedience to Sir John, promising to not investigate the death of Mary Kington or the cause of the fire in return for his job and the renting of a cottage in Corsley Heath. Richard Cavell wrote to assure Robert that a cottage would be found and made available to the mason and his new wife.

Robert drove the cart packed with Anne's belongings slowly and carefully down the muddy lane. The Knollys household had been generous to the girl they had watched grow up. Her father's bed was chief among their new possessions, and it was far better than Robert deserved. Everything that was happening to him was better than he deserved.

He turned to Anne and smiled. He remembered his previous journey along this path, his initial arrival at Longleat and the nervousness he had felt. Now he was returning as a married man with Anne at his side. This time, he knew everyone at Longleat, and anticipation built as he got closer to his team and Longleat. How much progress would have been made in the weeks he had been away?

The only pall to his happiness was facing Henry Kington. Showing up at Longleat with a wife who closely resembled the man's daughter and knowing he was forbidden to pursue anything related to Mary's death would not be easy for anyone. Robert knew he needed to focus on his own personal happiness and that of Anne. Getting her settled into her new life and focusing on making as much progress on Longleat as possible during the remaining summer months needed to be his priorities.

Still, questions remained. Why did Sir John insist on ignoring Mary's death and the cause of the fire? Why would he demand such a concession unless he himself had played a role? Could Robert live up to the terms he had agreed to? Was the price he had paid too high?

They entered Warminster, and Robert guided the cart to one of the shops. "I have a promise to keep, and I'm eager to do so." Robert found a boy to watch the cart, paid him a penny, and ushered Anne inside the haberdasher's. "This is the shop where I got your silk threads. At the time, I promised the shopkeeper that when you married me, I would bring you here and buy you a pair of gloves. Pick out any you like. Hello, sir," Robert called to the shopkeeper. "I am here to fulfill my promise."

"Well met, and congratulations. Allow me to assist you. Ah, I see that your lady's eyes are the exact color of the silk thread you bought. I remember telling you that such a gift could turn a hope into a marriage." A short while later, the promise was fulfilled and Anne had a new pair of plain but well-made gloves.

"I'm going to use the remainder of the silk thread you gave me to make these gloves my own. A small decoration near the wrist, I think. Delicately stitched, just to mark them as mine."

"Like a mason's mark? The kind we add to each piece we carve so we know which mason carved which piece?"

"Yes, like that, I suppose. But also to tie together the promise fulfilled. The gift of the threads and the gift of the gloves, united as we are."

Robert smiled at his wife and leaned over to kiss her. Then he asked Anne if she wanted to continue shopping in Warminster or go straight to Corsley Heath and their new home. After a quick discussion of the provisions available in the small hamlet, they decided to continue. "Let us get settled first and see what we need before we buy anything else," was Anne's practical answer.

As the miles passed, they both grew more excited to see their new home. Robert did not trust Sir John, but he did trust his steward. If Cavell had a hand in the choosing, it would be suitable, at least as a start. Later, they could scout out a better location. Who knows, perhaps Betty Maynard was right in her prognostication that the Maynards would leave the area and the Smythsons could take over their house. Robert liked the idea of moving farther away from Corsley and the memories there.

Chapter 20

THEY ARRIVED AT CORSLEY Heath in the middle of the afternoon, and the village seemed quiet. As Robert wondered aloud how to proceed, a woman came out of a cottage. "Robert," she called. "Welcome home. This must be your new wife."

"Charlotte! You are just the person to welcome Anne and help her get settled. Darling, this is Charlotte Crispin. Her husband, Dick, is one of the carpenters at Longleat, and they have become good friends. Charlotte, may I present Anne Smythson. I do so hope you two will be friends."

"I'm sure we will," Charlotte replied with a welcoming smile. "Come in, come in. For this is your new home! Cavell asked me to help set up your new home for you, and I'm pleased we were able to find this one so close to Richard and me."

"I am too. Thank you for all you have done. I hope it wasn't too much work for you," Robert added, taking in the sight of Charlotte's swollen midsection. "I see things are progressing with your new addition."

Charlotte laughed. "Is it that noticeable? Yes, you are correct. We expect a little one sometime in the early winter, I think. But come in. Mistress Smythson must be curious about her new home and anxious to see it."

"Please call me Anne," Anne replied.

"And you must call me Charlotte. I'll leave the two of you to get settled. I'm just over there." Charlotte pointed to a cottage not far down the lane. "If you need anything, please come by, but I don't want to hover. Don't worry about supper tonight. Mistress Mercer and I have prepared for a meal with the whole team."

The Smythsons watched as Charlotte walked away before going inside their new home. "You're right, I am going to like her," Anne said. "And I'm going to like this home!" Someone, probably Charlotte, had scrubbed the cottage clean before their arrival and spread fresh rushes on the floor, but it would be Anne's job to transform it into a home. The simple dwelling consisted of a large main chamber with cooking and eating facilities at one end and a seating area at the other with two fireplaces, one at either end. There were simple wooden benches, a large plank table, and a small fire burning in the kitchen fireplace. It looked sufficient but not grand. Windows opened up along the long wall with shutters but no glass. They let in little light, and the place felt low and dark. A narrow staircase led up an upper story with bedchambers.

Robert brought the last of the crates into the room, placing them on the table, where Anne could reach them easily. His eyes searched her face, anxious that she should approve of the place. "Oh, Robert, it's lovely. Small, but it's all ours. Yes, it's completely different from the opulent surroundings of the Knollys household, but here we'll have privacy and independence. We shall be happy here, I think."

Robert visibly relaxed and took her in his arms. "I was hoping you would agree. I think so too. There are two small chambers aloft. I'll place our bed along the wall with the kitchen chimney for warmth. The other one we'll decide on later. I hate to leave you so soon, but Sir John will want me to meet with the team as quickly as possible. Will you be all right?"

"Yes, I'm ready to start my new life as an independent wife and homemaker and don't mind exploring alone for a bit. I'll unpack what I can and leave the rest for us to do together later."

Robert's pace quickened as he approached the break in the path where he knew he would get his first glimpse of the building. He paused just before looking up, reminding himself of how it looked when he had left it and how it would look upon completion. He was able to hold both visions in his mind simultaneously, and now he added a third. He knew he had missed the longest days of summer, days of extended daylight when great progress was possible on assembling external structures. He lifted his head and saw walls which had not been there when he left a month ago. Were those the beginnings of the staircases? He hoped Hills had had the men triple measure before they leveled the stone into place. Generations of Thynnes would climb those stairs for years to come.

Turning away, he completed the rest of the trip with haste. The men were expecting him and were not surprised at his presence. As he approached what he still thought of as Maynard's lodge, the image of Mary Kington's body lying on the large table now covered with drawings surfaced in his mind, but he squashed it down and greeted his team. John Hills stepped out into the afternoon light, and the old friends greeted each other warmly.

"Welcome back! It's good to have you back. I'm no master mason, that's for sure. I'll be glad to turn everything back over to you."

"I'm sure you did better than you think you did." Robert looked meaningfully at his friend. "Thank you. For encouraging me to go, for keeping things going here. Can you believe she agreed to come?"

"Yes, of course. I had no doubt. And you're most welcome. I look forward to seeing her again."

They were prevented from continuing their reunion by the arrival of Richard Cavell. "Smythson, well met my friend."

"Richard. It is good to see you too," Robert replied.

"It is good to have you back where you belong. Have you been to the cottage yet? Does your wife like it? What do you make of the progress we've made in your absence?"

Robert laughed. "So many questions; I begin to think Sir John is standing in front of me instead of his trusted steward. Yes, Anne is up at the cottage now, and we both approve. You must come back with me so I can introduce you. Thank you for making my return possible." This last sentence was spoken with some emotion, and the two men's eyes met as they understood one another.

"For the cottage, thank the Crispins. They have both done the work to make it ready. I think they were quite determined to have you close to them. As for your return, my motives are not unselfish. What's good for Longleat is good for me. While you've been gone, Sir John has looked to me to do much of the organizing work on the building. Hills has been a great help, but neither of us is a match for you."

"It looks like you've all made excellent progress while I've been away. Let's walk over so I can get a closer look." The three men walked quietly around the building site. Robert ran his hands over the stone, testing for smoothness, and checked the joints with his fingertips while the other men watched his reactions. He paused now and then to greet one of the masons or laborers working, giving encouragement or feedback. How he had missed this. Already he was making mental plans for the continuation and calculating how much they could accomplish before bad weather halted their progress.

After a short while, Cavell interrupted the tour. "Seen enough? I need to take you back to Corsley Manor to meet with Sir John. He's as anxious as ever for progress and has some questions about supplies. I am glad you're back to handle that kind of thing."

"On the way, let's stop by the cottage for a quick visit. I'd like you to meet Anne and see if there's anything she needs soon."

Thirty minutes later, Robert opened the door to the cottage, calling, "Anne, I've brought you a visitor." Anne turned from the kitchen area, some cookware in her hands. She smiled at her husband and the tall man ducking his head as he entered. "This is Richard Cavell, Sir John's steward and the man responsible, along with the Crispins, for our new home. Richard, my wife, Anne."

Anne bobbed her head in greeting, then reached out to grab the man who had turned white and was rocking on his heels. "Please, sir, have a seat. You don't . . . Robert, is he all right?"

"Cavell, what's wrong? Are you unwell?"

"No, I . . . I . . ." the man stuttered as he lowered himself onto the bench, his eyes still fixed on Anne. "It's like seeing a ghost. She's just like . . . Mary."

"Oh dear. I see. I'm sorry, Anne. As I said, you look an awful lot like the girl we found. Richard knew her well. I have just seen one portrait of her. And of course . . ." There was no need to finish that sentence.

"Should I fetch some ale? I don't have any, and your friend looks like he could use some."

"I'm all right, Mistress Smythson. Please forgive me. I am not usually so rude. As Robert says, you closely resemble a young lady I had the pleasure of knowing once. Welcome to Corsley and Longleat. And may I congratulate you on your marriage? I look forward to getting better acquainted with you soon, but right now I'm afraid I need to take Robert up to meet with Sir John. He will be impatient."

"Yes, certainly you must go. Robert has told me of Sir John's desire for haste when it comes to Longleat." She smiled as she said this and ushered the two men out, one of whom seemed anxious to leave.

As the two rode up Deep Lane, Cavell began to regain his composure. "I am so glad that our gamble paid off, both for you and for Longleat. Anne seems both astute and good-natured. I wish you both happy." Passing the turn for Cley Hill Farm, Robert's thoughts naturally went to the Kingtons and the reason Robert had left Longleat. "Anne's resemblance to Mary is uncanny. I suppose it does explain in part why you were so insistent on finding out what happened. Are you going to be able to let the investigation drop? I do not think Sir John is going to back down on that condition."

Robert looked down the lane, remembering his first journey to Corsley Manor and all that had transpired since. "I am going to do my best to focus on the work of building Longleat."

"That does not sound like a commitment or promise."

"That is the best I can do for now. I will not actively seek answers, but if I learn something that leads me to the truth of what happened that night, I will not pretend I have not learned it." There was more silence as Robert wondered what the future held. He changed the subject. "Any word about Maynard?"

"No, just the same. We've seen little of him or Betty, but when we have, they've been full of the same bragging of a new position. As it always is with Maynard, big plans but few details."

That evening, the Smythsons enjoyed a meal prepared by Helen Mercer and Charlotte Crispin with the rest of the team. The meeting with Sir John had gone as expected. Sir John had been gruff and had not shown any pleasure at Robert's return. Robert had played his part as contrite employee, but both men had been more interested in discussing the future work than in rehashing old arguments. There seemed to be a silent agreement that each one realized their need for the other if their dream of Longleat was to be achieved. Robert had left the meeting feeling optimistic and anxious to get home to Anne. Just the words had made him tingle.

As Charlotte had promised, Robert's team ate as a group that night, with the addition of the Crispins. Anne was introduced, although many of the team remembered her from Greys Court. Once the meal was finished and the others had left to go to their respective dwellings, Robert and Anne returned to their home. Robert was pleased to see that Anne had gathered some wildflowers to add to the rushes already spread out on the floor and put some in a jug of water. He hugged her from behind, nuzzling his nose in her neck. "I'm glad to see you're taking steps to make this your home.

She had unpacked the things she had brought from Reading, the linens, crockery, and such. While Robert set up the bed in the upstairs bedchamber, she carried her clothes, needlework, books, and other personal items up the steps to the upper level. As Anne set down her Bible and some of her father's books that Sir Francis had insisted she keep, she said, "I wonder what my father would think of my new home. I hope he knows I'm happy."

Robert came and wrapped his arms around her. "I'm sure he does."

"I never told you about a conversation I had with my father about you, did I?"

"No." Robert pulled her down on the newly assembled bed so they were sitting side by side.

"It was after his health had taken a turn for the worse and he was confined to bed for great portions of time. I thought he was sleeping and was looking at one of the drawings you left me, one of the many versions of the fireplace you kept revising. I was tracing the lines with my fingers and missing you. Suddenly, he asked me if the drawing 'was something that mason of yours had drawn.' I showed the drawing to him, explaining the different parts. The details of the drawing were lost on him, but I think he understood the way I spoke about you meant something. I told him how you told me that you can see the beauty of God's creation in the way light plays with stone, reflecting, bouncing, always looking different as the light changes. He liked that. We talked about your being an artist with stone the way he was with words and thoughts and the way I try to be with my threads. I told him I thought he would like you."

"I'm so sorry I never got to know him well," Robert said. "Sir Francis introduced us once or twice, but that was before his daughter became so dear to me."

"You two would have liked each other. And I think he would have approved of our marriage. He often said he was a simple man doing God's work. Then he told me that he had spoken to Sir Francis about you. He told me that Sir Francis approved of the match. He said Sir Francis believes you have a good future and that it would make him happy to see the two of us settled together, regardless of our backgrounds."

Robert reflected on what Anne had said. If only he had been brave enough to speak up earlier. But no, he would not have wanted to take Anne from her father, especially as it turned out that he'd had so little time left. "I'm glad you told me. I feel like we have his blessing now. I hope you don't miss him too much."

"I do, of course, but it helps to know that he would be happy to see me settled with you. Now where is the fur cloak Lady Catherine gave me? I want to put it on the bed."

The first night in their new cottage close to Longleat was the beginning of their life together. They had been married for a few weeks, and it wasn't their first night together as husband and wife. But it was the first night in their new home. Anne changed into her nightdress, and Robert removed his outer garments. They climbed under the linens and Anne's fur cloak, and Robert took her into his arms.

"I love you, Mistress Smythson. I hope you will never regret moving away from all you have known and into this small cottage with me. I pledge to you that I will always do whatever I can to ensure your comfort and safety. I hope to never give you cause to wish you were elsewhere."

"Enough talk. If you want to increase my comfort, hold me tighter and kiss me." He did as she requested, and they joined together to celebrate their homecoming.

Chapter 21

THE NEXT FEW DAYS were busy and happy for the Smythsons. When Robert returned home from work, he noticed all the little changes Anne had made as she eagerly set to work creating her first real home and commented on them. He had a good eye for symmetry and beauty, and together they made an attractive little space. "I'm enjoying this," Anne said. "It might be hard work, but there's freedom in it. I can please myself, not consider her ladyship's pleasure. I'm creating a space that suits our taste, choosing whatever flowers or colors I want. Is it weird that I often find myself humming while I do the work?"

"As long as you don't start singing, I think it'll will be all right."

"What do you mean?"

"Just, with your similarity to Mary Kington, who was known for her singing, if you start, it might confuse the neighbors."

Anne laughed. "No fear on that account. No one has ever praised my singing."

The Crispins had relocated Robert's cat to the new cottage, and she and Anne soon became good companions. Asking Robert what the cat's name was, he had replied, "I just call her Cat," so the name stuck. Cat accompanied Anne in the garden, ate scraps of leftover dinner, and kept her company when she was alone in the cottage.

Robert officially presented Anne to Sir John and his family several days after her arrival. Almost immediately after the introduction, Sir John started laughing, much to Anne's discomfiture. She asked him what she had done to amuse him. He replied, "Kington's not going to like this. She does look like his daughter." Anne colored. "Now, Smythson, this is not some strange scheme to start investigating again, is it? I hope we settled that."

"No, Sir John. I too am aware of the resemblance of Mistress Smythson to the late Mary Kington, but I assure you, it is merely a coincidence."

"Good, good. Nothing more to delay us. You've got your woman here, so I expect no more running off, no more delays. Make haste, man, make haste."

"Yes, Sir John."

The Longleat community was eager to get to know the newcomer. Word quickly spread that Robert had returned and brought his new wife with him. It also became known that the new Mistress Smythson came from the exalted Knollys household. When she first arrived, they were curious to see how she would comport herself. Would she think she was too high up to rub alongside them?

Anne had no vaulted feelings about her position, and she went out and met other neighboring women and asked them for advice. The result was that she had help. Her cheerful disposition and smiling face made her welcome, and her small size made the other women take pity on her and think she might need help.

Rumors were spreading that the Queen of Scots had been moved from Carlisle Castle south to Bolton Castle, where Sir Francis Knollys continued to act as warden. Anne was asked lots of questions, and she answered them truthfully and openly. Yes, she had been in service to Lady Catherine Knollys, who was one of

Queen Elizabeth's ladies, but no she had never been presented to the Queen. Her father had been in Knollys's employ as a tutor and chaplain, and Anne had been a junior member of the household out of kindness to her father. She didn't know what was happening up north with the Queen of Scots and didn't correspond with Lady Catherine. In truth, Lady Catherine had been disappointed in Anne's marriage and wasn't likely to continue a relationship with a woman who had become a mason's wife. After presenting Anne with her wedding gifts and wishing her well, Lady Catherine had probably forgotten about her.

On Sunday, Robert moved aside to allow Anne to enter the pew before him. They settled and awaited the beginning of the service. People entered the church, nodded to one another, exchanging greetings, the usual Sunday morning activity. Suddenly, the pleasant hum was interrupted by a gasp.

"Mary? How?" Heads turned toward the audible gasp. Robert followed their gaze and saw Henry Kington on his feet, moving toward them. The crowd murmured, all eyes on Kington. There was even some muffled laughter.

Henry Kington reached the Smythsons, stepping into the empty pew in front of them. He reached out and grabbed Anne. "Mary, you've come back to me!" Anne pulled back while Robert reached forward and removed Kington's hands.

"Master Kington, may I introduce my new wife, Anne Smythson. Yes, she does resemble your late daughter. I remarked on that when you showed me her picture."

Kington shook his head in disbelief. "Not Mary? But it's her honey-colored curls and the same small features and graceful movements."

"I can assure you this is Mistress Anne, newly come from Reading and the household of Sir Francis and Lady Catherine Knollys."

Kington appeared to struggle to understand Robert. "Your wife? Knollys? What does Knollys have to do with this? What has he to do with Mary being back?"

"No, Sir Francis has nothing to do with your daughter. Mary is not back. This is Anne, who has been living with the Knollys family at Greys Court until her recent marriage to me."

"So you haven't spoken to him about Queen Mary."

"No. Nor do I plan on doing so. Sir Francis is still in the north, in service to Queen Elizabeth." Robert tried to emphasize the last word. "I heard from him regarding my marriage to Anne. That is all. I hope you will join the others in welcoming my wife to the neighborhood."

Kington seemed to get a hold on himself and come back to the present. "Certainly, certainly. Good day to you, Mistress Smythson. I am sorry for the abruptness of my greeting. As your husband says, you bear a remarkable resemblance to my daughter, Mary."

Anne bowed her head in acknowledgment. "So I have heard from others. I am pleased to make your acquaintance Master Kington, and I am sorry for your loss. My own dear father died recently, so I understand the pain of losing a beloved family member."

"My dear, I am most sorry to hear of your loss. You are indeed welcome to Corsley, and I wish you and Master Smythson much happiness."

"Thank you, now if you'll excuse me, I believe the service is about to begin." Although it wasn't much of a worship service since most of the attendees couldn't help but stare at Anne, then at Henry Kington, who seemed agitated and restless. At least Corsley would have a lot to gossip about for the rest of the day.

Later that evening, Robert pushed his empty trencher away after enjoying his share of the eggs poached in a syrup made of sugar and rose water and seasoned with a bit of cinnamon and looked around the room with contentment. He was happier than he had any right to be. Making a comfortable home with his beloved Anne, surrounded by his good friends, the Crispins and John Hills. Charlotte Crispin and Anne were quickly developing a close friendship, and Robert was delighted. He found Dick Crispin to be a sensible, steady figure and good with the other carpenters. Charlotte was lighthearted but also practical and a good person to show Anne the ropes of independent life, including how to make eggs in moonshine, the dish they had all just enjoyed.

Robert reached across the table, taking his wife's hand while Hills refilled everyone's cups. Although it was late, no one wanted the comfort and camaraderie of the evening to end. Conversation soon turned to Kington's reaction upon meeting Anne. "The resemblance must be strong to elicit such a reaction from the girl's own father," Dick mentioned.

"None of us ever knew Mary, but the picture I've seen did bear a strong resemblance to Anne," Robert said.

"Anne, were your frightened?" Charlotte asked as she scraped a heel of bread into what was left of her syrup.

"No. I've seen the reactions of others in the neighborhood, those who knew Mary. I suppose I was prepared for her own father to find it startling. I don't mind him. To have lost a daughter, his only remaining family, to learn that she had been killed, that must be difficult for him. My own father . . ."

Robert reached out and took her hand while the others bowed their heads quietly for a moment. "I'm sorry, sweetest."

Anne shook her head, dispelling her grief. "I feel sorry for him. If we can help him in any way, I think it's our Christian duty to do so."

"I suppose so. There is, however, one thing," Robert said. "I'm fairly sure that Kington still holds Catholic beliefs. I know we've seen him in church, but he only goes to avoid any fines or trouble. I've seen what looks like an altar in his house. Just be warned. With your family history, I don't want you to be caught off guard."

"I wish we didn't use faith as a means of dividing us," Anne said. Robert had previously told his friends a little of Anne's family background, how her uncle had been burned as a martyr for holding to his reformed faith under the reign of Catholic Queen Mary. "Henry Kington has experienced a great loss, and if his faith brings him comfort and doesn't hurt others, then I won't hold it against him."

"And the man could use some help," Robert added. "His farm isn't doing well, and his house, well, it probably hasn't seen basic care since Mary disappeared. You all know of my preference for orderliness. I had a hard time being in there because of the clutter and disorder."

"Perhaps I could lend him a hand once I've gotten my own routine established," Anne said. "Maybe my presence could help ease his grief, and perhaps mine too." The rest of the group murmured their approval of her generous heart, and the party soon broke up.

One night, Robert stroked Anne's hands, running his rough fingers along their surface. "I'm concerned that you've taken on too much physical work for yourself out in the garden."

"I haven't done it before, but I can learn," she replied gently. "I'm not afraid of physical work, although I may not be used to it." Anne's previous gardening experience had been clipping blooms for floral arrangements or cutting herbs for strewing or cooking. "I like digging up the roots of old vegetation, pulling out dried-up stalks, up to my wrists in rich, deep earth with the sun warming my back. When I rise to stretch my legs, I'm able to see what I've accomplished. The visible progress is motivating. And Cat keeps me company. I may have missed most of the planting season, but I'm determined to have a kitchen garden as soon as I'm able. You create the grand formal building, but I will make a small modest home full of love for you to come home to. The Lord will provide for us."

"As long as you do not wear yourself out too much," Robert agreed.

"And Henry Kington visits frequently. Today, he helped me pull out a particularly stubborn old root."

"Kington? I'm surprised he has the time. He's never spent much time away from the farm before, unless it was to complain to Sir John about something."

"He's all right," replied Anne. "I don't mind him. I think it's sad that his daughter died, and if spending time with me brings him comfort, then it is a small gift I can give him." Robert squeezed Anne's hand. He knew they were both thinking about Anne's father and the dead girl. Perhaps it did make sense for these two to spend time together. They both were missing someone they could not replace. Again, Robert felt the pang of guilt at being unable to ease the man's pain by finding the truth of his daughter's death. It was a continual source of regret among the many blessings of recent weeks.

At Longleat, it was a race against time, but even there Robert felt like they were winning. Since his return, nothing catastrophic had happened and the team had been able to make steady progress. All during the long days, masons, setters, and laborers worked to add the finished ashlar blocks to the walls. The carpenters rushed to stay ahead as the walls grew higher and the scaffolding had to be extended. Interior walls were going up as well as staircases. The framework was coming together. Robert spent his days coordinating, ensuring that each group had what they needed for maximum efficiency. As the walls rose higher and higher, it was easier to forget about the fire and focus on the future. Even Sir John was relatively quiet, seemingly satisfied with the progress, although he continued his demands for haste. Cavell also seemed pleased that Smythson was finally living up to the potential they had been promised. A successful master mason meant less pressure on the harried steward, who had enough on his hands.

The only negative during the summer months was the continuing disquiet Robert felt whenever he thought about Mary Kington. That no one was interested in solving her murder seemed impossible to believe. It was almost as if the woman had never existed. And yet she had, with her own dreams and plans and disappointments. Robert wondered how Ned Bright was doing up at Lacock, but he was too busy to make the trip or inquire. He often recalled the abbey with its octagonal tower, beautifully curved arches, and cozy feel. He sometimes wished Anne could hear Ned sing and dreamed of taking her up to the Sign of the Angel for a break.

Instead, Robert had encouraged and even joined Anne in efforts to help Henry Kington. They had visited Cley Hill Farm and helped Kington to do a thorough cleaning. Anne had seen Robert's discomfort and assured him they were doing the right thing. "He has no one. The community has turned their backs on him. His daughter's dead. He's trying to keep the farm going. If

I can help him with some basic housewifery, surely it's the right thing to do," she'd said.

"You're right, sweetest, of course. It's just the physical space that disturbs me, and that's my issue, not his or yours." Together, Anne and Robert had pulled out the old rush mats and replaced them with fresh ones. Anne had gathered wildflowers and herbs and strewed them on the rushes while keeping the windows and doors open. These actions had done a lot to combat the smell and dankness of the old farmhouse. She'd also taken his dirty linens and washed them. In the end, Robert was more comfortable, and Kington was appreciative.

Chapter 22

The first signs of autumn were in the air: apples ripening, leaves changing colors, animals busy thickening their coats and storing nuts. Sunday afternoon was cool and crisp, and Robert took Anne for an afternoon in the sunshine. A walk up Cley Hill arm in arm was what a day like this called for. They tried to cajole the Crispins to join them, but Charlotte said that at her size long walks were no longer comfortable. She preferred her seat by the fire while Richard put the finishing touches on the cradle which would soon be put to use.

The hill was dotted with people enjoying their well-earned Sabbath rest. Robert nodded to several acquaintances but was reluctant to stay chatting for long. He stiffened, then groaned quietly as a couple drew near to them. Anne raised her eyebrow, and he whispered, "It's the Maynards," as he prepared a hearty greeting he didn't quite feel.

"Mon Dieu!" cried Maynard from several yards away. "She is Mary Kington, *n'est pas*?"

"Maynard, Mistress Betty," Robert acknowledged. "Maynard, I do not believe you have met my wife, Anne Smythson." There was an unmistakable emphasis on *Anne*. "Darling, this is Alan Maynard, the mason, and his wife, Betty."

"Well met." Anne bowed her head in greeting.

Robert turned politely to Betty. "How are you, Mistress Maynard?"

"Please, you must call me Betty. I am quite well, thank you, Robert, quite well indeed. And I suppose you will be too when we tell you the news. Any day now, we will be making the announcement, and then the two of you can move into our house. If you like, I can speak to my maid to see if she wouldn't mind staying on for you. I know she has hopes of coming with us, but I'm sure we'll want to find new staff when we go to London, won't we Alan?"

Throughout his wife's speech, Maynard had been walking around Anne, blatantly staring at her. "Remarkable. She and Mary were certainly carved by the same sculptor from the same piece of stone. A bit taller, but otherwise so similar. Whatever did old Kington say when he saw her?"

"He was shocked at first, but now they have become good friends. Anne recently lost her father as well, so I suppose they are bonding over their mutual grief."

"Grief, yes . . ." Maynard paused, then pulled Robert away from the ladies for a more private conversation. "I wonder at you allowing your wife to spend so much time with Kington. It's . . . unseemly somehow."

"I see no harm in it," Robert said defensively. "I believe I have heard that you too have some connection to the Kingtons. It was you who took Mary's letter to Ned Bright the night of the fire, was it not? Perhaps there is more to your connection with the family than you would care to have known?"

Maynard laughed loudly. "You're not still poking around that old story, are you? I wonder what Sir John would think if he knew." He paused, looking closely at Robert. "I understand your team has taken over my old workshop, isn't that so?"

"Yes, as you seem to have no need for it and the one I was using burned. You wouldn't know anything about that, would you, Maynard?" Robert held his gaze, waiting for a reaction.

"Oh, that's right. I heard about that. No, nothing to do with me. As you know, I wasn't here when that occurred. You're quite right, no need for a workshop at Longleat. Although I believe we left it in quite a state. I've heard that you are organized in your work. No missing tools or things left lying about?"

"I find a well-organized and tidy workplace tends to increase overall productivity," Robert remarked, baffled as to where this conversation was coming from.

Maynard laughed again. "Fancy being so well organized that one can keep track of all one's tools. How dull! I'm afraid my genius has never run along those lines. But if it works for you . . ." Maynard turned as if to rejoin the ladies, then changed his mind. "I have also heard that you volunteered to fix the crumbling wall at Kington's house. Is that correct?"

Robert had completely forgotten about that. It seemed like ages ago. Why would Maynard know about that? And why would he bring it up now? "It seemed the neighborly thing to do. What business is that of yours anyway?" Robert was getting irritated. "For someone who has been away for so long, you seem remarkably well informed."

"Shall we rejoin our wives?" Maynard turned and walked back toward the ladies, linked one arm through each of theirs in an overly familiar gesture, especially considering he had just met Anne, and left Robert to follow awkwardly behind.

Betty stopped walking and turned to Robert. "I was just telling Anne here about the parties Alan and I used to have when he was master mason at Longleat. After a long week, all the craftsmen would gather at our home for a convivial evening. Alan, don't you think we should do that again? Would be a wonderful time to announce our news, wouldn't it? Say, at the end of this week?

One last party before we say goodbye. It's almost expected, I would think. And from what I've just heard, the Smythsons couldn't do it. Their cottage is much too small."

Robert bristled. The sooner the Maynards left the area, the better as far as he was concerned. He would happily go to a party at their house if it meant saying goodbye to them. "That's a lovely idea, Mistress Maynard. I'm sure Anne and I would be delighted to attend."

Betty extracted herself from her husband's arm and took Robert's. "Betty, please. I insist. It's settled, then. Next Saturday. One last gathering."

"Master Kington came to visit me today," Anne said the following evening after Robert came home from another long day at Longleat. Robert and Anne had dragged a bench outside to enjoy the last of the evening's light. "He caught me working in the garden and sounded like you, worried that I was working too hard. He said a woman of my delicate nature should be involved in more delicate pursuits."

"I can't argue with that," Robert agreed.

"Then things got a bit strange," Anne said and proceeded to relay the full conversation.

"I do not mind it," Anne had replied to Kington's comment. "There is satisfaction in knowing one has worked a piece of the land. You must understand that, with your farm."

"Working my farm has become nothing but the devil's work. It is more than I can do on my own, and Thynne has taken all the laborers for Longleat." Kington had made no effort to conceal his contempt.

"You will forgive me if I do not share your views, as it is because of Longleat that I am here."

"Yes, of course. But why must you work so hard? It is too much for you, my dear. I want to see you settled comfortably with an easy life. If that husband is as important and talented as they say, why do you not have a maidservant or boy to do that work for you?"

"Because I do not wish it. I've come from a large household where there was little for me to do except stitchery and errands for Lady Catherine. Here I feel useful, and I am greatly enjoying making my own home."

"Yes, yes, the Knollys household. That reminds me, I wanted to speak to you about Sir Francis. Have you heard from him? I asked your husband to get a message to him, but I do not think he was successful. He may not have tried. But you would, I'm sure of it. For your father, wouldn't you do that?"

"My father? Why would I contact Sir Francis for my father? I'm sorry, Master Kington, my father died a few months ago. I mentioned it when we first met."

"Oh yes, my dear, I forgot. I was confused for a moment. You know what it is to lose someone, how confused you can get. I am sure you've heard of my daughter's death. Well, so you have lost your father, and I have lost my daughter. You are such a comfort to me, and I hope I can be a comfort to you." Henry Kington had reached out and taken one of Anne's hands in his own. "Your hands are getting so rough and worn. Mary's hands were small and delicate as well. You know, she had some gloves, as well as other items. I haven't had the heart to get rid of them yet. Perhaps you would like to have them."

"Perhaps," Anne had replied cautiously, "although I have all I need."

"Please make an old many happy and let me see you enjoy Mary's things. Would you like to come by the farmhouse one day and look at them, see if there's anything you would like?"

"That is kind of you, Master Kington. Perhaps you could bring them here?"

"Oh, there are too many. She had quite a collection. It would be better for you to come and see them. That way you only have to carry what you like."

"That is very kind. Please let me check with my husband first."

"Surely, there can be no harm in visiting a man who is old enough to be your father and indeed looks upon you as his own daughter."

When she had finished relaying this conversation to Robert, Anne asked if there would be any harm in taking some of Mary's old things. "The weather is beginning to turn, and perhaps there are some warmer clothes, more suited to my life as a mason's wife rather than a scholar's daughter. Besides, I feel sorry for him. And I do miss my father terribly. Perhaps humoring Master Kington would heal both our wounds."

Robert considered Maynard's warnings about Kington. Then he considered the source of the warnings. Out of the two, he mistrusted Maynard more than Kington. There was still something suspicious about Maynard's role in Mary's death. Was Maynard warning him away from Kington as a means of protecting himself? Everything he had heard and experienced about Maynard indicated that the only one Maynard would look out for was himself. Robert sighed. He didn't care about Maynard. The sooner he made his big announcement and left, the better. There could be no harm in Anne taking some old used clothes, could there? People did it all the time. "As long as you feel comfortable visiting him, I see no trouble. We've certainly made the farmhouse more comfortable for him. I suppose sharing Mary's things is a suitable repayment for our generosity."

Anne reached over and kissed Robert. "Good, I'm glad you see things as I do. He's just a lonely old man who wants to pass on his daughter's clothes to someone who reminds him of her."

"I hope you're right. But he also has brought up trying to get Sir Francis's help in supporting Mary Stuart. I don't know why he would think Knollys would help her. Just be careful and try to keep the conversation away from religion."

"Because my Uncle Jocelyn was burned as a martyr? So much bloodshed and hatred over how we worship. There's no reason for Kington to know about my uncle, so it shouldn't matter."

Despite his assurances that there was no reason for Anne not to visit Cley Hill Farm, Robert found himself anxious to know how the visit went and rushed home at the end of the day. Anne was at home, brushing a woolen cloak, a pile of other garments folded on the table. Anne showed Robert the cloak, which was a quality piece. "I don't have anything quite like it, and the winter here may be colder than I'm used to, so I agreed to take it. My visit made him so happy. He had apparently emptied Mary's whole treasury and left it out for me to pick through. By the time I left, my basket was filled with pieces of clothing."

"Good. If it makes you happy, then I am content."

"Oh, and he showed me the picture of Mary. I don't know why he hadn't shown it to me earlier. We do look alike, do we not? And apparently the same size, for her clothes seem to fit as well. I selected several linen smocks that looked almost new, a gown of russet wool, and a few aprons and shawls. The rest I offered to help him sell, but he insisted he didn't want to profit from Mary's death. He said he would much rather I have them, that it would bring him joy to see me wear them. How could I refuse?"

Robert agreed that it would have been rude to do so. He had been going through the garments. "This cloak was made from a fine piece of wool. It will keep you quite warm this winter."

"On the way back home, I had an odd feeling of disquiet. Perhaps it was knowing the garments had belonged to a dead girl, although passing along used clothing of the deceased is a common and practical practice. Perhaps it was a lingering effect of the odd smell and cluttered environment of Kington's home. Or perhaps it was simply a longing for my own father. He seems harmless, just a lonely man who misses his daughter. It seems he has no family left, and people around here don't like him much, do they?"

"No, probably because of his pride. Tell me, did you see any indications of the old religion while you were there?"

"That's what that smell was! I couldn't place it until just now. I think he was burning incense. Is that even legal?"

"I don't know. But it is unwise, if not illegal. Still, I suppose if he does it in his own home, he's not hurting anyone. There do seem to be signs that he still worships in the Catholic fashion. Did he ask you about Sir Francis?"

"Yes, a bit. Just some questions about my life with the Knollyses, asking about my father. I didn't say much."

"Good. He seems too interested in the Scots Queen for me to feel completely at ease with him."

"He didn't mention anything about her. I don't want to talk about him anymore. I've taken a few of his daughter's things to make him happy, but now I want to focus on your happiness. Tell me about your day."

"My happiness? Well then, let's have no more talking at all." Robert grinned and pulled his wife upstairs. Neither one gave Henry Kington any thought after that.

Chapter 23

THE WEEK ENDED, AND the Smythsons prepared to go to the Maynards' along with the Crispins and most of the other upper-level craftsmen. They didn't necessarily want to go but knew it was expected of them by all the other craftsmen at Longleat. "I admit I'm looking forward to his announcement and departure. This party is worth it if it means they're actually leaving," Robert told Anne as they dressed.

"Where do you think he's going?" she replied as she pulled her gown over her kirtle.

"I don't know. He keeps harping on about the importance of his patron. Perhaps the Shrewsburys? Lovell says they are undertaking a big project at Chatsworth."

"Haven't they taken over custody of Mary Stuart? Perhaps Kington should be asking Maynard for influence, not you."

"That's quite insightful, but I don't know if it's them. Could be Cecil? Or someone completely different. As long as he leaves Longleat, I don't much care where he goes."

"Are you worried that if he came back, your position as master mason would be usurped? I think Sir John is smart enough to recognize your talent. And anyway, no use worrying about something before it happens. Come, help me with these ties and let us be on our way. Do you think I made the right decision not to wear my farthingale? We'll be riding in a cart with several other folks, and although the weather is dry, I think I made the right choice to opt for sensibility and comfort over fashion."

"Farthingdale or no, you'll be the prettiest and most graceful woman in the room."

Anne gave him a warm hug, and they prepared to leave.

The Smythsons, the Crispins, John Hills, and a few of the other masons crowded into a cart together to the Maynards' house. Robert had been by a few times, but it was the first time Anne had seen it. Robert watched for her reaction as she took in its relative grandness compared with their cottage. Two full stories sat comfortably under the roof line with the lower level having glass panes in the windows, although the upper levels were linen filled. The house held at least eight sizeable rooms as well as some attic space under the roof. Robert saw Anne's eyes widen with surprise when the door was opened by a young maid who ushered them into a large room filled with comfortable settles, plenty of cushions, and Maynard and Betty presiding over the gathering crowd.

"Ah, the Smythsons and the Crispins and the whole masonry team," Maynard's voice purred with pride as he greeted the newcomers. "Welcome, welcome. We're most happy to have you in our home, aren't we, Betty?"

"Certainly. Please come in where it's warm; the evenings are getting chilly out here in the country. Is that Mary Kington's old cloak? Why, I haven't seen it in a few years. It never was pretty, but I suppose it keeps a thin thing like you warm." This remark was directed at Anne as she untied the cloak and handed it to the waiting maidservant.

The spacious chamber was already quite full, everyone eager to partake in the hospitality and the gossip. Most came out of curiosity and for the fact that the ale and wine promised to be as plentiful as the conversation. Rumors were circling that Maynard had some kind of announcement to make.

As Robert entered the spacious room, he felt the tug of inadequacy and perhaps jealousy, if he would admit it. He should be providing a nicer home for Anne. Here was Betty, holding court over a large gathering, not nearly as worthy of it as his Anne. Now he saw the inside of the building through Anne's eyes, the fine furnishings, the maid to help Betty. He felt he had let Anne down. The self-doubt tore at his heart. During the ride to the Maynards', he had been quiet, not joining in the light conversation of the others. He was playing Anne's question over in his mind: What would happen if Maynard rejoined the Longleat workforce?

Robert was unsure of how to answer this, but the question gnawed at him. Robert had arrived at Longleat ready to prove himself not only as a master mason, but also as a designer. He was just at the right age to either soar or sink, to establish his reputation as a master craftsman and project leader or to settle for being just another competent mason. He brought with him a team of men and now a young wife, all of whom relied on his judgment in taking this job to provide for their livelihoods. He had traveled to Longleat full of idealism and ambition. But within a few months of working for Sir John, he was struggling to keep his optimism. Having to constantly justify his team's progress and the constant pressure and threat of replacement. He knew that Sir John saw it as a way to keep everyone at their best, driven by fear and competition. Sometimes Robert wished Maynard would rejoin the crew at Longleat just to be rid of the constant threat of him.

Putting aside his private thoughts in the crowded room, Robert turned to find Maynard, appearing to relish the role of generous host and letting the wine flow freely, holding out two goblets of wine for Anne and himself.

"Well, Smythson, how are you this fine evening? Have you got something to drink? It is my pleasure to welcome you into my home."

"Thank you, I am well. You have a lovely home." Robert kept his answers neutral. The caution he felt was beginning to wear on him, so he took a sip of wine, which was too heavily spiced by his standards. "I believe Richard Cavell said you rent this from Sir John? It's nice of him to allow you to maintain the lease even when you are absent from Longleat."

"Nice? Nothing nice about it. I pay him a fair price for this place either way. Betty tells me she thinks you and Anne should take over the lease when we're gone. All of this could be yours." Maynard gestured toward Anne.

"We're quite comfortably settled where we are at the moment," Anne replied, holding on to Robert's arm.

"In that tiny cottage? Nonsense! Betty," Maynard called to his wife. "Imagine, the Smythsons would rather stay in their little cottage than take over our spacious house."

Betty made her way to the group, linking her arm through her husband's possessively. "Perhaps, as a newly married couple, they find the cottage quaint and cozy. A small space makes so many more opportunities for intimacy, doesn't it? Of course, I do enjoy sitting in my upper parlor looking out my glass windows for Alan to come home. But I suppose wooden shutters are easier to keep clean."

"Really, Smythson," Maynard countered, "as head mason, you must use your choice of housing to make a statement about your position. To both your fellow craftsmen and to Sir John. If you show him you don't think you're worth more, he'll treat you that way."

A crowd had begun to gather around them. This was what they had come to see: the two competing masons. Robert saw the curiosity in their faces and saw that Maynard was not exactly sober.

Robert had colored at Betty's words, but now he grew angry at Maynard's. "As Anne said, we're well situated for now, thank you," he said. But he also remembered that Hills had said the same thing.

"How odd," Betty exclaimed. "Well, we cannot force him to take what the position is owed. He must come to know his own worth in his own time. Like you, my dearest, who will soon be named master mason for one of the largest and most exciting building endeavors in all of England. Such a gifted sculptor. Sir John was loath to part with him, but bigger and better things are calling him onward. It's such a relief to Alan to know that Longleat has found a new mason who will suffice for Sir John's purposes. I know Alan feels he's done all he can for Sir John, don't you, Alan?" Maynard dipped his head in agreement, and Betty continued, "Once he had drawn up the plans, he felt it did not require his exacting skills to execute. Another mason could be found for that mundane job."

Robert looked quizzically at Maynard. "I'm sure Sir John was quite adamant that he alone had drawn up the designs for Longleat."

"That is what he wants everyone to believe. But you must suspect that a man of his background lacks sufficient knowledge of masonry and other crafts to draw up plans as complex as those necessary for Longleat."

Robert watched Maynard for any embarrassment or signs of lying but didn't see any. And he himself had questioned Sir John's abilities. Perhaps Maynard was right.

Anne asked the question they were all there to ask, "And where will you be going?"

Betty clutched more tightly at her husband and gave Anne a coy look. "To London first, then somewhere . . . I'm not able to say at present, but I can tell you that Alan will be working for someone quite closely connected to the Queen herself." Betty looked around the crowd to ensure she had everyone's attention. "Now, Anne, I have heard that you were in service to Lady Catherine

Knollys. Imagine," Betty continued, "you'll still be here, way out of things, while I'll be living among the ladies of the court, hosting my intimate evenings and wearing such fine gowns. It's like we've changed places."

Robert could feel Anne stifle a laugh and gripped her arm in warning. He listened as Anne tried to gently warn Betty that a mason's wife would never be accepted or presented at court, but her words fell on deaf ears.

Maynard must have gotten tired of his wife taking all the attention, for he drew himself up and raised his voice. He was speaking to Robert, but the news was clearly for everyone to hear. "I've come back from presenting my plans for a new building, very impressive, for a client of the highest position. At present, he doesn't wish his name to be publicly mentioned, but rest assured that when it does become known, Sir John will be quite jealous." At the conclusion of this speech, he looked around as if to gauge people's reactions to it. Some were murmuring, but many were still silent, waiting for Robert's reaction.

"Congratulations," Robert replied sincerely. "I wish you success in this new venture. I would love to hear more about it."

"I am not at liberty to share details. It is all secrecy. But tell me, how is your work going for Sir John? Is he still pleased with his latest genius mason?"

Robert chose to ignore the smirk that accompanied Maynard's questions. "We are making progress, but as you know, Sir John isn't often satisfied. Please excuse me, I'm going to join the rest of my team." Robert walked away, his temper growing hotter than the crowded room. He joined John Hills standing in a corner. The older man cuffed him around the shoulder to steady him. "Still no specifics from Maynard, no confirmed date of departure. Just more empty promises," Robert complained to his friend. "I'm getting so frustrated with Maynard's innuendo, comparisons, bravado. Life at Longleat is complicated enough without his whispering doubts. I wish he would just hurry up and leave!"

"In time. Be patient. Can't be long now," Hills said.

Robert nodded, took a sip of wine, and then turned away disgusted, looking for a place to set the goblet down. The stuff was undrinkable. As he looked through the crowded room, he saw Anne take a seat next to Charlotte Crispin. At least Robert was more fortunate than Maynard when it came to his choice of wife. Whoever this special client was, would Robert even want to work for him? He had worked for someone important in Sir Francis Knollys. That job had gone well enough until court business had pulled Knollys's interest off his own building. Imagine if it was someone of even more import? No, Robert wasn't envious of Maynard. Just impatient for the man to leave. And he still wasn't convinced that Maynard hadn't been involved somehow in Mary Kington's death.

Just then, he saw Betty Maynard talking to a youth with light blond hair. She was leaning over him, chastising him for something. Robert recognized him as the same boy he had seen after his lodge had burned and as the one who had pointed out the Maynards' house on his first visit. The boy looked across the room and met his eye. The two looked at one another for a moment, and then the boy darted away, his face a deep crimson. Details began to click into place like perfectly fitted joints, where the angles all lined up in beautiful harmony. The fire in the masons lodge. Betty's reaction to the news of Mary's pregnancy. Ned's story of spending the night at the Maynards' house. It might not be Maynard who was involved, but Betty knew something about Mary's death. Robert crossed the room, grabbed Betty by the arm, and whispered into her ear, "I'd like a word with you, Mistress Maynard."

Betty yelped in surprise, then quickly covered it with a laugh. "Of course, Master Smythson. Let's go find you some fresh wine. Come this way." She led him into the kitchen, dismissing the maid.

Once they were alone, she gave Robert a flirtatious smile. "You're not going to get me to divulge the name of Alan's new patron, no matter how nicely you ask."

"I don't care about that. I know. It was you who burned down my lodge this summer. Or maybe not you, but that boy out there, at your request. You know something about Mary Kington's death, don't you? You're going to tell me what you know right now, or I'll tell everyone you're to blame."

"No, wait. You can't do that. Please, not now. Now when we're so close to getting everything." Betty's tone was cajoling, her eyes pleading. Robert was unmoved, his head tilted expectantly. "Yes, I admit, I had young George throw that lit torch into your lodge," Betty said defiantly. "I was just trying to scare you off. You weren't hurt. And because of that, you went and got Anne. So really, I did you a favor."

"God's breath! I could have been killed." Robert balled up his fists and slammed them down on the kitchen table while his mind sorted through details.

"But you weren't, were you? Just a bit of harmless foolery. And now you're married and living in a better place."

"Be quiet. We'll get back to that in a minute." Robert loomed over Betty. "But first, you know something about the night of the Longleat fire, the night Mary died. I remember. Ned Bright said he got as far as this house and then stayed the night. You knew he never met up with Mary. And then you knew that Mary was never seen again and that she never made it to Lacock. You've known all this time!"

"Hush! Someone will hear you. Yes, but I don't know any more than that. All I know is that Alan came back with the letter from Mary telling Ned she wasn't meeting him. It wasn't until later that we learned Mary was gone. I didn't know where. Maybe she ran off with someone else. Maybe she just left. I swear I didn't know she was buried at Longleat."

Robert had been listening and thinking. Betty might be telling the truth, or maybe there was another reason she had stayed quiet. Maynard. "Somehow Maynard is involved in this. How?"

"Please, I'm begging you. Be quiet. I've told you all I know." Betty's lips were trembling now. She appeared to be genuinely afraid. "There's no proof of anything. Please, we're leaving. What point does it make now if he was? It's not going to bring Mary back, and Sir John doesn't want to investigate. Can't you just leave it?"

"Robert?" Anne poked her head around the corner. "Oh, there you are. Charlotte's not feeling well, and I'd like to leave with her. Are you coming?"

Robert turned to his wife. "Yes, I think we're through here. Good evening, Mistress Maynard."

Dick Crispin was more than happy to leave with his wife, so the Smythsons and Crispins prepared to leave. John Hills offered to drive the cart back to Corsley Heath with the two couples riding in the back and then return to the Maynards' gathering to collect the rest of the team when they were ready to leave. Robert was quiet on the ride home, thinking about what Betty had said and listening to the two women discuss the party.

Anne and Charlotte had a good laugh at Betty's idea of associating with the ladies of Elizabeth's court. "I pity Betty when she learns the truth, but I can't help but be amused at the thought of what Lady Catherine Knollys would think of Betty if she met her. If Betty were to associate with such ladies, she would find her attempts at genteel airs and polished manners quite out of place. Surely, she doesn't really think she will be mingling with Maynard's patron's family? She couldn't possibly," Anne said.

"Oh, I do not know what she believes." Charlotte laughed. "She's too good for the likes of us." Charlotte held an imaginary cup and mimicked her. "I'm sure this cup of ale is suitable for a simple country mason's wife, but it would never do for the wife of the great Alan Maynard. The nerve of that woman! Part of me hopes she's telling the truth because I am sure this neighborhood would be better off without her, and I would love to see the reactions of these wealthy nobles when they see who they have invited into their world." Charlotte and Anne looked at one another and burst out laughing. "Oh, I feel better already," Charlotte said. "I think it was just the crowded room and stale air."

The rest of the ride home passed in companionable silence. After the Crispins had been dropped off, Hills drove to the Smythsons' cottage. As Anne went inside, Robert asked Hills to remain for a minute and told Hills about his interaction with Betty. "She admitted to having the boy set the masons lodge on fire. Should I tell Sir John? What do you advise?

Hills looked into the night sky, thinking. "Let's consider your options. You could tell Cavell and see what he makes of it."

"I'm not completely sure I trust him, especially where Betty Maynard is concerned. There's something between them, but I don't know what."

"What do you mean? I thought you said Cavell had been interested in Mary Kington, not Betty Maynard."

"I've seen them together, huddled as if sharing a secret. Maybe it's nothing more than Betty liking gossip and Cavell needing to be well informed, gossip or fact."

"But you think it might be something more? Well, another option is to go directly to Sir John. How do you think he would react?"

"Well, he might be angry at the destruction of property. But Betty admitted that it was to get me to stop investigating Mary's murder, so Sir John might agree with her motive. I don't know. I'm so frustrated with everyone named Maynard! I wish they would just hurry up and leave!"

"I'll go back and see if I can find any information about when they're leaving." Hills took his departure, and Robert went inside.

Once safely in bed, Robert told Anne about his confrontation with Betty. "Do you think she was telling the truth?" Anne asked.

"About not knowing how Maynard was involved? Yes, I think she's made it a point of not knowing for sure. That way she can pretend he wasn't involved. Her fear was genuine, though. She's afraid of something."

Anne shuddered, snuggling closer to Robert. "Do you think Maynard killed Mary? Is he capable of something like that?"

"I honestly don't know. But Betty admitted to being the one to set fire to my lodge. Should I report her for that? Would Sir John even care? I'll be glad when they finally do leave the area! And another thing—when they do leave, we are not taking over their house. I don't think I could stand living there after tonight."

"Agreed." They lay in silence for a few minutes. "What are you going to do about Maynard and his role in Mary's death?"

"I don't know. I suppose I could confront him. Or go back to Lacock and question Bright about it all again. Anything I do will only anger Sir John. And," Robert sighed, "Betty was right about one thing. None of this will bring Mary back. Is it worth stirring it all up again? Kington seems to be settling down; we're getting settled. I don't know."

"Let's talk about something else. Charlotte says the baby's active these days."

"Do you want one?"

"Perhaps. I certainly don't mind practicing to get one." And all thoughts of the Maynards were set aside for the night.

Chapter 24

THE FOLLOWING DAY WAS Sunday, and the Smythsons spent a quiet day avoiding other people and the conflict surrounding Longleat. A steady rain fell outside the shuttered windows, and Robert and Anne let it cocoon them in peace. Anne spent the afternoon stitching by dim candlelight as Robert went over the building accounts, preparing for his upcoming report to Sir John. Neither spoke of the Maynards.

Early Monday morning, the clouds parted, revealing a glimmer of rosy dawn. Robert walked through the growing walls of Longleat, amazed at how much had happened in the past three months. It was fast approaching the next quarter day, Michaelmas, and Robert was stunned at how things had changed. At midsummer, he had walked away from Longleat toward Anne. Now he was back, with Anne as his wife, firmly in the role of head mason of a house that was bounding upward with each passing week. Three months ago, he lived in a loft over a masons lodge, in a space that should have been a tracing room. Now he was comfortably dwelling in a cozy cottage, with perhaps another move to come.

Just because he had decided not to take over the Maynards' house once they were gone for good didn't mean he shouldn't find a similar house. The rent on a spacious house such as the one in the East Woodlands was sure to be much higher than their present rent. He could probably afford it, but did he want to owe Sir John such a large percentage of his salary? He would ask Anne what she thought later.

Movement caught his eye, and he turned to see someone else inspecting the stone. It was Sir John, running his hands along the stone. "Good morrow, Sir John," Robert said. "What brings you down to Longleat so early?"

"Just wondering when I'll be able to move back down here," Sir John grunted.

"Next summer, the summer after at the latest," Robert answered warily, watching as Sir John continued to run his hands against the smooth stone.

"Tolerable, decent, perhaps, but nothing special," Sir John said.

"I beg to differ, Sir John. This is basic masonry, but it's the stone that makes this part shine. Just watch as the sun comes out. You'll see it glint off the surface, revealing the true worth of the stone. Beautiful."

"The real test will come later, when you get to the decorative stuff."

"Yes, sir, and my team is more than up for the task."

"I hope so. You are aware of the skills Maynard has at decorative carving, are you not? Are your skills up to that level?"

So that's what this is about, Robert thought to himself. *Maynard must have gotten to him, or he's heard about Maynard's new job and is feeling troubled.*

"I assure you, my skills and those of my team are more than adequate for the work here at Longleat." Just then, the first rays of the sun crossed the horizon and found the stone's face. As Robert had predicted, the limestone glowed. It never failed to cause his heart to skip a beat, how beautiful the interplay of light and stone could be. Robert grinned and nodded toward the stone, drawing Sir John's attention. All he got for his trouble was a grunt.

"Humph, we'll see about that."

Robert watched as Sir John continued down the line, inspecting the stone as he made his way toward his horse. Robert considered calling out to Sir John, telling him about the Maynards and their role in the lodge fire and Mary's death, but decided against it. Sir John didn't seem to be in a receptive mood and would probably just take the opportunity to chastise Smythson for interfering. Let Maynard leave, taking his secrets with him. Then Robert could focus on Longleat.

After Sir John left, Robert made his way over to the masons lodge as the sun continued to light up the sky and stone. Something wasn't right. The normally organized tools were strewn all over the floor, some of the masons' benches were knocked over. Stress rising, Robert began to pick things up. Next to the bench closest to the entryway, a small chisel lay on the floor. Near the entryway was another chisel. Just outside, another one, slightly larger. As the light began to increase, Robert found himself following a path of chisels, laid out like a trail of breadcrumbs leading him around the back of the lodge.

This side of the lodge backed up to some trees and was still heavily in shadow, so much so that Robert tripped over the last chisel, falling to his knees near the rear wall. As he stumbled, one knee struck a large stone that was protruding from the wall. Righting himself, he touched the offending piece and found that it moved easily. In fact, he was able to pull it right out, leaving a hollowed-out compartment, which, as he felt around with his hands, was now empty.

It had been purposely built; that seemed clear enough. And someone had tried to lead him to it by leaving a trail toward it. But why lead him to an empty space? Unless someone had beat him to it and removed something from the clever hiding space. Robert picked up the stone that had been removed and carefully laid it back in place. To the casual observer, the wall was solid. Only when you knelt down could you tell there was no mortar holding this stone in place.

"Hallo? What's this? Robert, are you here?" the familiar voice of John Hills called.

"Round here, John," Robert answered, "at the back. What do you make of this?" he asked as Hills joined him.

"That's odd," Hills replied, removing the stone, feeling around, and then replacing it, just as Robert has done. "Someone was determined to stir up the hornet's nest in the workshop," Hills said. "Do you think they were looking for something or just making mischief?"

"I think they were trying to draw our attention to this compartment." Robert told his friend about the carefully laid trail of chisels as the two walked back to the front of the lodge. "I saw Sir John down here early this morning. Could this be his doing?"

"What? Why?"

"I have no idea. But Sir John was walking around Longleat before it was light out, and then I find this." Robert gestured to the mess in the lodge. "And it was raining so much yesterday; I don't think many people were out just to cause mischief."

"Did Sir John say why he was down here?"

"Something about checking the progress and then some threats about Maynard's skills versus ours. Apparently, he's concerned that our decorative carving skills will not be up to the task. I think he's heard about Maynard's new job and is getting nervous."

"None of which would explain why he would want to turn the masons lodge upside down. Do you suppose this has something to do with your finding out that Betty set fire to the other masons lodge? A warning or a threat of some kind?"

"By whom? Betty? I can't see her leaving her warm house on a wet day to throw some chisels around, can you?"

"No, you're right. Maynard? Would he be protecting his wife? I wonder if he's still here? And what does that empty compartment mean? Someone was clearly drawing our attention to it. No one could be that clumsy to leave such a well-marked trail accidentally."

One by one, the lads began arriving for the day's work and were astonished to see the lodge in such disarray. One of the masons who had worked for Maynard before Robert's arrival commented that the lodge looked more like its usual self. They were surprised at how easily they had adjusted to an organized workplace. With so many hands, the lodge quickly came to order, the tools lined up and inventoried. Nothing seemed to be missing. Robert felt himself relax. "All right, men. Thank you all for your efforts to get our workshop back in order. Get your materials and tools and go about your business," Robert directed.

Hills shooed them all back to their tasks while Robert returned to the back of the lodge and studied the hole now that there was more light. What had been hidden within the wall? Assuming something was there and had been removed, why had the remover not covered up the hole again—unless they wanted everyone to know something had been there and now was not? Another mystery. Robert ran his hands through his hair and immediately regretted it, having just transferred the dust from hand to hair. Sometimes he was tired of the mysteries and drama surrounding Longleat. As if the endless demands for speed weren't frustrating enough.

Later that day, Robert decided to tell Cavell everything that had transpired in the past few days. He found the steward holed up with Sir John's accounts manager, going over budgets and pay sheets for the quarter day. Cavell was happy for the break and sent the accounts manager away. Robert filled Cavell in on Maynard's party, his announcement that had been full of hot air and empty promises, and the state of the masons lodge on Monday morning.

"It's my understanding that Maynard has left again," Cavell said. "He stopped by on Sunday, refusing to pay rent for the next quarter on the house in East Woodlands. Says he and Betty will be leaving soon, so there's no point. Sir John wasn't happy. And Betty is still there, I believe, so someone should pay the rent."

"Do you think he's really going this time? For good? Permanently?"

"I don't know. I think he believes he is. Sir John has said something cryptic about it, so I don't know who to believe. Focus on yourself and your tasks, that's my advice."

"And it would be good advice, but I'm afraid I learned something over the weekend that might shed some different light on Maynard. Betty admitted to setting the fire on the Corsley Heath masons lodge."

"What?"

"I know."

"Whatever for?"

"She said it was to discourage me from investigating Mary's murder, to scare me off. Which, of course, makes me wonder if she played a role in Mary's death and why she is so afraid of my investigation."

Cavell sighed deeply, rubbing his hands along the arms of his chair. "Smythson, not again. We can't keep rehashing this same thing. Sir John isn't playing games, not with this. You need to leave Mary's death alone."

Robert stared at Cavell. "You realize I could have been killed. Not to mention the destruction nof property, loss of the plats, the time lost. Are you proposing that we do nothing?"

Cavell tilted his head back, staring at the ceiling. "I didn't say that. Let me think about it. In the end, you weren't seriously hurt. You might even say that you found the courage to marry Anne because of that fire."

"Cavell! Think about it. A fire! Are the memories of Longleat burning so faded that this doesn't fill you with dread? Now we know who set the fire and why. Surely, something must be done."

"You're right, I suppose. But what? Your ankle healed, and the work is going well. I hate to stir up more trouble for something in the past. Sir John wants to focus on the present and the future. If I bring this to him, we'll probably just be causing more trouble than its worth."

Robert shook his head in disbelief, remembering the flickering flames as they licked the stairs leading to the loft. If Crispin hadn't woken him up, Longleat would be without a head mason now. Unless such a move had been Betty's intent all along in order to keep Maynard at Longleat. He looked back at Cavell, who was leaning back in his chair. "You're not going to do anything about this, are you?"

Cavell leaned forward. "No, I'm not. And you're not going to either, understood?"

Robert left Corsley Manor feeling dejected and confused. Dead ends, road blocks at every turn. Confessed crimes just overlooked. He felt manipulated, ignored, and endangered. Why would Cavell protect the Maynards? Robert remembered seeing Betty with Cavell, heads bent together in an intimate conversation. Was there more to their connection? Was he protecting her for some reason? Had she acted on his instruction? What game were they playing?

Cavell and Betty. Cavell and Mary. Maynard and Kington. Were all of them involved in Mary's death? It was time to visit Henry Kington and get some answers.

Chapter 25

ROBERT MADE HIS WAY to Cley Hill Farm. It was now midafternoon, the late summer sun warming the fields after yesterday's rain. He paused to look over Kington's fields, ripe with grains. It seemed more than Longleat was flourishing this summer, and Robert was happy to see it. He felt oddly responsible for the old farmer. A pang of guilt pulled at him as it often did when he thought of the man's daughter. Despite everyone telling him to leave it alone, Robert felt responsible for not solving the mystery of Mary's death.

He pushed through the gate and approached the house. Kington was home, which seemed odd. Shouldn't he be out working the fields? Robert was no farmer, so perhaps he was wrong. Kington opened the door wide to let Robert in. Robert braced himself for the stench and clutter but found neither. Instead, light came through the open windows, fresh rushes lined the floors, and the air smelled fresh.

"Master Kington? Your home is so open and inviting."

Kington let out a big laugh. "'Tis the work of your wife, Smythson. Look how she cares for me!"

"I see! And I'm most pleased for you. Indeed, not just your house, but you look better." Kington did. His flesh had filled out, his cheeks not as sunken or sallow. He stood a little taller.

"'Tis all because of Anne." Kington blushed. "It is almost like having my own Mary back again." Kington poured two tankards of ale and handed one to Robert.

"I am glad to see it. And your farm? The crops look healthy, I think."

"Yes, yes, quite prosperous. Best year I've had in a few. More than I deserve, for sure. Now what brings you to see me? Surely, old Thynne didn't let you away from Longleat for a social call."

"No, of course not. It's about Alan Maynard. I've been wondering how well you know him. What is your connection with him?"

"Maynard? The French mason? Um, well I suppose we know one another. Not well."

"Did Mary know the Maynards? Either Betty or Alan? I believe Betty said she knew your daughter when they were both young, when your wife was alive, perhaps?"

Kington got up from his chair and began to pace a bit, turning his back to Robert so that he couldn't read his expression. "Not when my wife was alive, for she died when Mary was very young, during childbirth with our second child. They both died. Left me to raise Mary all on my own."

"I'm so sorry. Isn't that quite unusual? For a man to raise a daughter all on his own. You never thought to remarry? To give Mary a new mother?"

Kington's agitation grew. He walked to the back corner of the room where he had a small altar set up, where his picture of Mary was, picked up the picture, and brought it forward. "It's not so unusual. The same happened to your Anne, I believe, from what she's told me."

"Yes, although Anne was older, and they were established in a larger household where Anne had other mother figures. But that does not answer if you and the Maynards know one another."

"Yes, yes. Well, everyone knows Betty Maynard—she makes sure of that. Even before she married that Frenchman. But I did not encourage Mary to be overly friendly with her. Why are you asking these questions. Isn't Maynard gone?"

So Kington knew about Maynard's plans. "I believe so, although I am learning that it can be difficult to know Maynard's exact whereabouts. He seems to have a way of sneaking around the neighborhood, only being seen when he wants to be. It doesn't mean he's not here at other times."

"What are you saying, Smythson?"

"I think Maynard may have been involved in Mary's death. It was he that gave Mary's letter to Ned Bright, although I do not know how he got it. Bright says he got no farther than the Maynards' house the night he was supposed to meet Mary. Everyone believed that Maynard was not at Longleat during the time of Longleat's fire, but I do not think that's true. Do you?"

"Maynard and Mary? I know of no connection. Perhaps they met a few times, but he was nothing to her."

"I believe Betty Maynard doesn't agree with you. She was shaken when she learned of Mary's pregnancy. Why would that be?"

Kington had resumed his pacing, his hands pulling on his scraggly beard, his movements twitchy. Robert continued, "And I have reason to believe that Betty has tried to stop me investigating your daughter's death. Why would she do that unless she thought to protect her husband?"

"Or herself?" Kington countered.

"I suppose. Do you think Betty Maynard capable of murder?" Robert recalled the fire in the masons lodge. Betty had admitted to asking the boy to set the fire rather than do it herself. And throwing a lit torch required nothing like the strength it would have taken to bludgeon someone with a hammer or chisel.

"I don't know," Kington replied sharply. "Have you told any of these claims to Thynne? What does he say?"

"No, not yet. You know he is reluctant to discuss Mary's death. I have spoken to Richard Cavell about Betty Maynard's potential role."

"What did he say?"

"Nothing of note. And he is anxious to let it lie dormant, as Sir John wishes. Which is why I came to you."

"And Maynard has gone? Left the region for good?"

"That is what we believe, yes. He has been boasting of a new position away from here for a powerful client."

"Bah! So you think you know who killed my Mary, and now you've come to tell me he's gone, away from my reach! What good is this to me? How can I get justice now?" Kington slammed his tankard of ale down on the table so hard the contents sloshed and spilled. Kington didn't react, didn't seem to notice.

Robert looked around for a cloth to wipe up the spilled ale. The closest one he could find was near the back of the room. He picked it up and began to mop up the spilled ale.

"Stop! Not with that cloth. Are you mad, man? To use the sacred cloth of purification to mop up mere ale! Sacrilege! Madness! That cloth can only be used with the holy chalice." Kington grabbed the cloth from Robert's hands and tried to smooth it with his hands. He bent and almost cried over it.

"I'm sorry . . . I didn't . . . realize it was . . . special." Robert stammered.

"Special? It's more than special—it's holy! I received that cloth along with the chalice it protects from the priory at Longleat. It's all I have left of my inheritance, my promise, my land. I tell you Longleat should have been mine, but all I have is a few pieces from the altar. And you have the audacity to use one of them as a rag."

"I'm sorry, I didn't know." Robert was mystified over his reaction, but he could see it was sincere. Kington was shuffling around in his dark corner and turned to show Robert a silver-and-brass chalice with a highly decorated bowl, the surface of which was engraved with images of the apostles. The stem was sturdy, flowing down to an equally decorative base shaped in five petals.

"This came from Longleat?" Robert asked.

"Yes, when they closed the priory, it was given to me by my uncle, who was one of the canons there. The land should have come to me; my family had given it many years prior, but that was forgotten. This is all that remains of my true inheritance. This chalice and the cloth, which will now need to be sanctified by a priest, if I can find one willing to do it."

Robert was confused. He had come to question Kington about Maynard, but the man seemed more upset about a piece of cloth than in learning who may have killed his daughter. "Again, I am so sorry. I wanted to prevent the ale from reaching the rushes, now that Anne has helped you to clean the house."

"Only a true believer could be expected to recognize the value of this cloth. Now, like so much else, it has been ruined. I have seen all the old things ruined. At least I have this." Kington turned and placed the chalice back down on the altar and shook himself, as if to rid himself from an evil force. "So you believe Maynard played some role in Mary's death. What do you propose to do about it?"

"I don't know. I'm not sure, I just . . . It's a feeling I have. He knows more than he's admitting to, and Betty is frightened. I think that's one reason she's so anxious to get away."

Kington returned to his seat and slumped, once more the defeated man Robert recognized. "Master Kington, I'm sorry. I didn't come here to upset you. I've brought you upsetting news and managed to ruin something of importance to you. I think I should take my leave from you before I upset you further. Good day." Robert rose and went to the door.

"Do not think I am not grateful, for it is you who brought my Mary back to me."

Robert left, wondering if Kington's last comment referred to his discovery of Mary's body, and thus brought him closure as to what happened to her, or whether he meant something else altogether.

Robert stabled his horse and returned gratefully to his cottage. It had been a long and strange day, and he was anxious to see Anne. If she was surprised at the strength of his greeting, the tightness of the embrace, she showed no signs of it, just dished up the pottage she had been stirring and bade him tell her about his day.

"Let me start by saying how wonderful your care has been for Henry Kington. I almost didn't recognize his house; it was so clean and fresh. That is all your doing, isn't it?"

Anne blushed. "Mostly, yes, but I think his appreciation means he's diligent in trying to keep it looking that way. After Mary left—died—I think he just gave in to his melancholy and stopped trying. Now, whether it's my presence or not, he's come back to life."

"Does his Catholicism bother you?" He told Anne about what had happened to the altar cloth. "Such devotion to a piece of fabric. It's unseemly. God is no more in that cloth than he is in this spoon!" Robert dipped his spoon to scoop some pottage and pushed it into his mouth for emphasis. "Delicious, certainly. But not holy."

Anne laughed but then turned serious. "There are times when Henry tries to talk to me of spiritual matters, times when he thinks I agree with him. Perhaps he is confusing me with his daughter, or perhaps he is trying to convince me or just thinks our beliefs are the same. I just try to steer the conversation in a different direction. I miss my father dearly, but this is one way in which Henry Kington cannot compare."

Robert reached out and rubbed his wife's arm in sympathy. "Are there ever any times where you think Kington's beliefs stray into a dangerous area? I don't want to look into other men's souls too deeply, but if we think his beliefs will lead him to treason, then I think we must report him."

"To whom? Sir John isn't one to bestir himself enough to do something about Kington's Catholic ramblings. And what harm can Kington do here? He's not at court; he has little to no influence, no money to put toward any plots. As much as I think his ideas and beliefs are misguided, I don't think they're dangerous. Now can we please change the subject?"

Robert then told Anne about the rest of the events of the day, including his conversation with Cavell. "The sooner both of the Maynards are out of the area, the better!" Anne concluded. "Now help me tidy up so we can go up to bed." And all thoughts of the Kingtons and the Maynards were abandoned in favor of more intimate thoughts.

Chapter 26

Another week went by, and Michaelmas came. There was no work that day, but following the morning worship service in honor of the archangels, there was a meeting at Corsley Manor to settle accounts and go over the work planned for the next quarter. Robert joined the other head craftsmen in the great hall, where long tables had been set up. Plans lay spread out, and the model had been moved from Sir John's office. Cavell and the other members of Sir John's business team were there as well as Lewis, Gaunt, and several other lead craftsmen.

The next several hours were spent going over budgets, dispersing salaries, and collecting rents and other debts. Many of the junior craftsmen found that they owed almost as much money as they had earned, which was disheartening, especially as the lean months of winter were ahead of them. The fall was a busy time, a race against the weather to get external work completed, the mortar beds prepared for next spring, and the detailed work that would keep most of the masons busy over the winter. Once the foul weather hit and conditions prohibited outdoor work, many of the quarrymen and laborers found work sparse, and the short days could turn into hungry ones.

Sir John was impatient for the banqueting houses that would be placed along the roof next year. Some of the internal detail work would be done over the winter inside the masons lodge and then assembled next year. It was these plans that Robert was looking at. Four square buildings were dotted along the exterior roof surface. Simple enough to execute, but there was something missing in their design. There was no time to solve the puzzle that was working its way into his mind as his attention was demanded to estimate work hours for another section of work. Working for Sir John was like trying to find new ways of squeezing blood from a stone. All pressure and no release. No time to let creativity meander through his field of vision.

His attention was pulled away by Cavell wanting to go over the proposed schedule again. "Cavell," Robert said, "Sir John is demanding work be done under conditions the weather and number of craftsmen cannot supply. I've submitted a more pragmatic schedule, allowing for fallow time or indoor work on days when setting would not be possible due to wet or cold conditions." Robert was growing frustrated. It didn't seem to matter how many times he explained that unfavorable conditions would mean that the mortar wouldn't set correctly or that the carts would get stuck. Apparently, Sir John believed that Robert could or should control the weather. Robert felt that it was better to draw up a realistic plan rather than an optimal one which would be nullified with the first frost. He explained all of this again but ended up losing the argument.

Sir John had overheard part of the conversation and laughed. Robert looked at him, puzzled. Usually, these kinds of confrontations brought out Sir John's anger and impatience. He was taking this remarkably calmly. Why?

Robert gave Cavell a look that asked why Sir John was so unruffled. Cavell shrugged in response. Robert wandered back over to the designs for the banquet houses and studied them again.

Perhaps this was something he could control. "You don't like my designs?" Sir John asked, joining Robert in the study of the plans and indicating Robert's frown. "What's wrong with them?"

"These are yours?" Robert asked. "There's nothing wrong, per se. I just think they could be more interesting."

Sir John tilted his head, looking from the designs to Robert. "And you can do better? They're fine the way they are. Simple and quick to execute. Your team will follow my designs directly. Am I understood?"

"Yes, sir," Robert mumbled, thinking that design should not always be sacrificed in the interest of speed.

"You don't agree, do you?" again Sir John laughed. "Do not concern yourself, Smythson, all is well in hand. I know what I'm doing." Sir John turned to leave, then stopped. "Oh, there's one more thing," Sir John began sifting through some sheets of paper in the portfolio he carried. "I received a letter from your friend Knollys the other day. Seems he's been receiving letters from someone here at Longleat who claims a kinship with your wife. Any idea who that might be?"

"A kinship with Anne? No, there's no one," but even as he said this, the name popped into his mind. "Unless it's Kington."

"Yes! The one and same. Apparently, Kington has been badgering Knollys with letters on behalf of the Scots Queen." Sir John read from the letter. "Knollys says here that Kington stops short of saying that Anne is his daughter but claims to have a close and personal connection with her."

"But Knollys is keenly aware of who Anne's father was! Surely, Kington understands that Anne's father was a trusted friend of Sir Francis."

"Who knows what that buffoon understands. Knollys writes that Kington is asking, out of consideration for Anne's feelings, that Knollys do all he can to promote Mary Stuart's claim to the throne of England or at least be named Elizabeth's successor. Have you ever conceived such a thing?" Sir John gave one of his rare barking laughs and tossed the papers back into the portfolio.

"No, sir, I don't understand. Why would Anne be concerned with Mary Stuart, a Catholic, and why would anyone think that Sir Francis would favor a Catholic over Elizabeth? Anyone who knows Anne's family's history or the Knollys family would know that."

"Smythson, I've warned you before. That man is trouble. If you continue to encourage your wife to befriend him, you may come to regret it. As it is, I'm going to have to compel him to stop making a nuisance of himself with one of our country's top officials. The gall of the man. Well, I've told you. Now make haste, and no more mucking about with plans that do not concern you. I want progress on the staircases. Make haste."

Robert retreated from the great hall before any more instructions could follow and made his way back to Corsley Heath in deep thought. What could have possessed the man to write those letters, and how were they even delivered? Anne could not possibly be encouraging him, surely not. Robert sighed. Anne had been spending considerable time with Kington recently, helping him clean his house and handle weekly chores. Robert had seen for himself the results. She said it brought them both a sense of contentment, usefulness on her part and comfort on his part.

He would have to tell Anne of these letters and hope that Sir John would be successful in bringing such inappropriate interference to an end.

That evening, the Smythsons ate dinner with the team that Smythson had brought with him to Wiltshire. It was a joyous evening, with the men happy with their quarterly pay and their steady employment. They were looking forward to the winter's shorter hours of work.

Once they were home and in bed, Anne asked a lot of questions about what the winter would be like. Robert told her of the shorter workdays, long cozy evenings by the fire, and meals spent in the company of friends. "Sounds lovely," she said. "Snug evenings spent indoors, me with my threads and stitching, you with your drawings and plans." She snuggled into his arms. "I wish my father could see my current happiness. I think he would be pleased. I can't imagine my life any other way. The glitter of court holds no appeal to me compared with the current contentment I have."

"I'm happy, but I'm afraid I do need to bring up something less pleasing." He told Anne about the letter from Sir Francis and the letters Kington had been badgering him with.

"Oh dear. No," she answered his question, "of course I haven't been encouraging him. I would never, you know that. But maybe he doesn't. I suppose I have let my natural compassion for him, my understanding of his grief, soften my heart toward him. I don't want to hurt his feelings, but I certainly do not condone any activity that goes against our Queen. Should I say something?"

"I don't know. I don't like to think of you getting involved. How much of his religion does he share with you? You remember I told you about the altar cloth. Have you seen anything like that when you've visited him?"

Anne propped herself up on an elbow and looked at Robert. "There was one time. I was reluctant to tell you because I thought he was just a forgetful old man. I still do. But once when I was visiting him, I saw that the back area of his main room was strewn with candles, some surrounding what was unquestionably an altar. In the center was an icon of the Blessed Mary. That type of display is illegal. If someone were to own one, they would keep it hidden. Here, it was brazenly out in plain sight. I remember I said something like, 'I shouldn't be here. Your altar, it's not right.' And Henry said, 'Surely, you do not object to my style of worship. You are so like the Blessed Virgin herself, that is why we named you after her.' I don't think he even realized what he had said. I told him my name was Anne, not Mary, he apologized, and that was the end of it."

"Do you think he was confusing you with his daughter again?"

"I don't know. Obviously, yes, to some extent. I think he's just a sad and confused old man. As I was leaving, I noticed that the walls of his farmhouse are deteriorating. It looks like some of the stone has come loose. I asked him if he had spoken to you about it, but he just deflected, said that you were much too busy to see to it."

Robert flexed his forearms, squeezing his hands open and shut. "This is my fault. I noticed that earlier this year and told him I would fix it for him. I tried once, but he stopped me. Then I got busy with Longleat and with you," he said, wrapping his arms tightly around her. "I forgot all about it."

"Now that the days are getting shorter and the cold winter is coming, perhaps you can find the time to fix it. I'm sure the winter would be easier for him with a solid wall."

"I will. You're right. I need to get up there and see to it. I think with Sir John's stricture not to look into Mary Kington's death, it was easier for me not to be around her father. Every time I see him, I feel like I've failed him. Now I truly have. I promise you, I will see to his walls soon."

"Good, now that's settled, tell me about the banqueting houses. I don't want to talk about Kington anymore."

Robert told Anne about the new staircases leading up to the roofline where banqueting houses would eventually stand. The subject quickly turned to what Robert would do with Anne if they ever found themselves alone in one of the banqueting houses, and then conversation ended for the evening.

Chapter 27

A FEW MORE DAYS went by, with the usual demands for haste. As the temperatures began to cool, there was a sense of urgency to get as much setting work done as possible before they all retreated indoors. Robert was busy, coordinating the teams, making sure everyone had the materials they needed. It was the work he had been hired to do, and it was going well. But the design work still tugged at his heart.

Early one morning, Robert stood in the room next to his bedroom, which he and Anne had made into a small business chamber for him. Most of the room was taken up by a large table on which lay plans and drawings, some for Longleat, others that Robert worked on for his own enjoyment. Robert often woke early and crept into this space, lit a few candles, and worked quietly. Usually, it was a time of peace, but this morning Robert felt uneasy.

There had been something about Sir John on Michaelmas Day, an excitement that the situation didn't seem to warrant. An anticipation that did not match the downward trend of productivity. It was as if Sir John were anticipating something special to occur, but whatever it was escaped Robert. He played the conversation he'd had with Sir John previously about Maynard over in his mind, growing more and more frustrated. Why did he feel like he was competing with a mason who did not even work at Longleat? He had left competition behind in his apprentice years.

Jealousy. That's what he felt. It was jealousy, not frustration. Maynard had a confidence in his own ability that Robert lacked. Here in the dark and the quiet, Robert admitted that he was jealous. Why couldn't he own his position as master mason? Why couldn't he stand up for himself and his ideas?

Take these banqueting houses, for example. Robert looked at the plans. They were sufficient, but not brilliant. They lacked interest. They were square blobs stuck on top of a large square. They could be so much more. If they were more interesting, some special shape. Like the tiny jewels they were meant to be. He closed his eyes and looked at the space in his mind, waiting for the image to come. Outside, he heard the birds waking up. There was something familiar about the birdsong. Ned Bright's music. Lacock. The birds at Lacock Abbey, early in the morning when he'd walked around the tower. The octagonal tower. Octagon. A shape with interest, with meaning, difficult but achievable, signifying life and posterity. What if the banqueting houses were octagonal instead of square?

He fumbled around on his desk until he found what he needed to draw it out. Then he got to work. A short while later, he looked at his completed drawing of the new Longleat. Large, impressive, yes, but there on the top, it was now dotted with interest, with something unexpected. He smiled at the work of the morning and went to wake Anne.

Robert brought a new energy and vitality when he met with his team that morning. They seemed to notice his renewed energy almost immediately. As soon as the crew was settled with their projects for the day, Hills asked Robert what had gotten him so energized. "I know what this means! You have a new idea for a design. Only creativity brings you to life like this." Hills said with a smile.

"Is it that obvious? Look at this." Robert unrolled the drawing he had finished an hour earlier and showed his friend. "What's different?"

"You've changed the shape of the banqueting houses. What is that? An octagon?"

"Yes, what do you think? Do you like it?"

"I do. You've added depth and interest to something that was a predictable repeat of the overall structure. Well done."

"Do you think Sir John will like it?"

Hills laughed. "Only if you can convince him it was his idea. The man does not like to be shown up. I've got things under control here. Why don't you go to Corsley Manor and show him? If we're going to change the design, the sooner we know about it, the better. We've got that new load of stone arriving from the quarry this week. If we're going to change the angles, let's get started soon."

Two hours later, Robert was in Sir John's office showing his sketches to Sir John and Richard Cavell. Sir John's eyes narrowed as he alternated between staring at the drawings and at Robert. Richard was watching Sir John's face for his reaction. Robert was explaining that the octagon shape represented rebirth, renewal and immortality. "Given the history of Longleat, the fire and now rebuilding, I was thinking about changing the banqueting houses on the roof from their square shape to an octagon. The building is rising out of the ashes, being reborn, and I know that you are interested in the immortality of Longleat, of the legacy that it will provide."

"Where did you get this idea?" Sir John asked suspiciously. "Do you think I don't know where you found this? I've been to Lacock. Do you not remember that I am friends with Sharington? I helped him find the craftsmen. I helped him with the designs. It all came from me. I specifically told you—"

Sir John was interrupted by the door opening without warning. Maynard burst into the room, followed by a harassed servant who had been unable to stop him from entering Sir John's private business chamber. "I'm sorry, sir, I couldn't—"

"You! You did this! It's your fault," Maynard roared. He wasn't a small man. The years of his profession had made him strong, and now his face was red with fury and his eyes dilated with drink. "You're responsible," he continued. "You can't stand that I'm not here, and you're trying to get me back."

"Hello, Maynard," replied Sir John, remarkably calm considering the spectacle Maynard presented. He then addressed the servant who had accompanied Maynard: "You may go. I can handle things from here. But stay nearby in case Master Maynard needs assistance."

Sir John turned his attention back to the belligerent mason and continued with a smooth, lazy voice, "I take it things did not go well. Were your great plans not accepted, then?"

"No, they were not! Wait, how do you know already?" Maynard hesitated and stared at Sir John. "Yes, I see I'm right. You had a hand in this. Somehow. Leicester all but promised me the job. We had meetings, he approved the designs, he nodded and said they were good. In the end, he sends a man to say, 'The earl has decided to go with another set of plans. He has chosen another mason, so he won't need your services.' He didn't even pay for the time I took or expenses or anything. Just 'thank you for your interest.'"

Maynard had begun pacing back and forth the already crowded chamber, glaring at Sir John while he spoke, but now he glanced around and noticed Robert's presence for the first time. "Robert Smythson, still the chosen one of Longleat, I see? Why are you smiling? Are you happy I failed? So goddamned smug, you think you could have done better? No doubt you do, but Sir John wouldn't have allowed that either, would you?"

"I'm sorry that things didn't go as you expected, but—" Robert tried to soothe Maynard but was cut off as Maynard turned his attention back to Sir John.

"You must be desperate. You know he gave it to Spicer, don't you? He passed me over for that cheating upstart. The man who stole from you, ran out on you, took your money, and ran away. Now he's going to build Kenilworth—Spicer!" Maynard spat out the name. "He'll be the one to build the most impressive house in the country for the Queen's favorite."

"Enough!" barked Sir John as he rose from his chair and leaned toward Maynard.

"Oh, I finally got your attention, did I?"

"Tell me what right you have to stand in my chamber and accuse me." Sir John relaxed as he said this, as if he had decided on a tactic to turn this outburst to his advantage. "If your work was unacceptable to the Earl of Leicester and he found in favor of Spicer, it must have been inferior indeed. You've allowed your inflated self-image to run too far. Or perhaps Spicer learned from me and traded it in with Leicester."

"Or perhaps you wanted Leicester to hire Spicer so Kenilworth would be inferior. You were afraid he would use my designs, knowing that if he did, Kenilworth would be better than Longleat, and you couldn't handle that."

Sir John shrugged. "An interesting theory."

"I see you don't deny it," Maynard continued. "You have to have the best, can't stand to be outdone, so you couldn't have Leicester using my designs or skills, could you?"

Robert thought this had gone on too long and tried to intervene. "Maynard, you've been drinking too much. Stop, you're embarrassing yourself and, frankly, our profession. You know that the earl was under no obligation to you, that you were probably competing with several other masons. You know that's how the process works."

"Oh, is the great Smythson telling me how things are done? What do you know about it? I know things that you have no idea of. I know things about Longleat that no one else does, but you don't see me lecturing you on all the things I know."

"Careful, Maynard. I'm sure you don't want to allow your anger and drunkenness to get you to say things you would rather not," Sir John warned Maynard, who blinked and backed down for a second before starting again about the earl promising him the job.

"What are you saying, Maynard?" Robert asked. "You're drunk and rambling. You know that until a contract is signed, the owner can always change his mind."

"Thank you, Smythson," Sir John calmly replied. He had recovered from his outburst and now seemed to be almost enjoying Maynard's accusations. "I don't need you to protect me from Maynard." Turning his attention back to Maynard, he continued. "So you think I would interfere with the earl's plans, that I would manipulate who he hires? Do you have any evidence to back up this claim?"

"I know that my work was better than anything anyone else could have submitted. What I think happened was that somehow you got a look at my plans for Kenilworth and realized they were better than what you had planned for Longleat. You saw that Kenilworth would have been better than your building and that Leicester is favored above all other men by the Queen and would have had the best building, and you couldn't stand it. I hope you're satisfied now that you got what you wanted."

"So no proof. Just speculation and conceit."

"Maynard," Cavell tried to reason with Maynard, "I don't see that this is the time or place, and I'm sure you don't want to alienate Sir John. I think you've had too much to drink and should return home."

"That's right—push me out, all of you. You thought you could build Longleat without me. You thought Smythson here could replace me. Well, now you realize he can't. You've fixed things so I'll have to come crawling back. We'll see. We'll see if I come back." Cavell left the chamber during this last speech and returned with two servants.

Cavell exchanged a look with Sir John, who said, "Yes, yes. Remove the drunkard and his accusations. Take him back to his house." Cavell then assisted the two men to escort Maynard from the chamber despite his lingering protests.

After the men left, Sir John turned to his remaining mason. "So, Smythson, what about you? Do you believe what Maynard said? Do you think I arranged for someone else to work for Leicester so that Maynard would come back here?"

Robert met Sir John's gaze and answered carefully but directly. "Sir, I believe that you are passionate about the building of Longleat and only want the best craftsmen working here. I also know that you take an active interest in the work being done at other building sites around the country and that you are a man of some influence. However, I have also heard some of the history that exists between you and William Spicer, and I do not believe you would want to see him elevated in the world."

Sir John let out one of his loud barking laughs. "You're not going to take sides. Well done, Smythson. Very diplomatically said. Now let's say no more about it and get back to this redesign."

Cavell returned to the chamber, and the three men turned back to the drawings. Sir John said, "I'll consider this idea despite its origins. I agree the shape is interesting. I'm concerned that it will take longer to achieve the angles and thus slow our progress, but the idea has merit."

Robert's emotions were jumbled as he rode toward Longleat, guiding his horse down the familiar path. He had started the day on a high note, improving a design to his own satisfaction. His idea had received a lukewarm response, yet he knew it was good. Robert suspected that Sir John had grudgingly agreed, using the bluster of being angry about Lacock to cover his frustration at someone having a better idea than his own.

Maynard's interruption and the news it had brought were more of a conundrum. Essentially, Maynard had accused Sir John of interfering with Maynard's job prospects. Could Sir John exert that kind of influence over the Earl of Leicester? Even if he could, would he use it to advance the career of William Spicer, the one man who seemed to have cheated Sir John and gotten away with it? Or was this all a coincidence, another mystery surrounding Longleat and its builder?

When Robert reached the building site, the story had beaten him there. No one had seen Maynard that day, but some of the staff at Corsley Manor had come down to the work site and relayed what they knew of the altercation between Maynard and Sir John. Soon, someone else claimed to have seen two men deliver a stumbling and incoherent Maynard to his home and to have heard the shrieks and cries let out by Mistress Maynard. There were many questions about what happened, so Robert decided to dispel gossip by sharing the facts as he understood them. He explained that Maynard had submitted designs for the expansion of Kenilworth Castle for the Earl of Leicester. The building was to be designed and built for the Queen's pleasure, and the rich earl was sparing no expense on her pleasure.

"We've all witnessed Maynard's certainty that he would be selected for the job," Robert explained to the crew. "Instead, Leicester has hired William Spicer, and Maynard believes that Sir John had a hand in the earl's choice. He's accused Sir John of orchestrating the job to ensure that no one else will get Maynard's talents."

Since people never let facts get in the way of good gossip, Robert's retelling the story did little to quell the interest and murmurings that sped through the work site. He spent the rest of the day trying to refocus the men on the task at hand and not indulging in idle gossip. But everyone had questions, including Robert, who silently wondered what the day's news meant for Longleat and its master mason.

Later that afternoon, Robert took the opportunity to ask Richard Cavell. "Do you think Sir John was responsible for Maynard not getting that job?"

Cavell sighed. "Probably, although I do not know the details. Sir John has said little to me about this whole affair, but he has seemed satisfied with himself recently, and you saw him: he did not seem surprised when Maynard showed up. I do know he's been in touch with Leicester and knew of his plans. He corresponds frequently with many wealthy landowners who have active building projects, including your friend Sir Francis Knollys and the Earl and Countess of Shrewsbury. It's certainly not beneath him or not unlike some of the things he has done in the past. On the other hand, I can't see him doing anything to benefit William Spicer. We'll probably never know what truly happened."

Robert mustered the courage to ask the important question. "Do you think Maynard will rejoin the Longleat team?"

"I can't tell you. He hasn't said anything to me specifically. He's satisfied with your work here, but overall he's anxious to see progress speed up. It's quite likely that Maynard will be hired at some point, but Sir John hasn't said anything to me directly yet."

Robert sighed. Just when he thought things were smoothing out, drifting toward the quieter time of the year, more controversy and upheaval arrived. What would Maynard's presence mean for Robert's role at Longleat?

"I understand your hesitance," Cavell said. "I don't think this will change your role here, if that's what you're worried about. Have faith, Robert. Faith in your abilities. Your future is linked with that of Longleat."

Robert tried to let it go, to do what Cavell had suggested and have faith in his future at Longleat, but some of the things Maynard had said didn't sit well with him. Instead of riding home after his work at Longleat was done, he found himself heading to East Woodlands, to Maynard. Soon, he was pounding on the Maynards' door, demanding that Maynard answer.

The door opened, and the Frenchman stuck his head out. Still drunk, if the fumes Robert caught were any indication. "Oh, it's you. The golden mason. What do you want?"

"Answers. Is what you said to Sir John true? Did he really persuade Leicester to give the job to someone else?"

"What? You don't believe me? You don't think Sir John is capable of that kind of trickery? Then you haven't been paying attention, dear boy. Yes, Leicester promised me the job and then awarded it to Spicer instead. Someone got to him, and the most obvious person is Sir John. I guess you're not as good as you think you are, Smythson, if Sir John decided he can't do without me after all."

Robert stood still, digesting all of this, trying to connect it to everything else that had happened at Longleat. Yes, he could believe that Sir John could be that manipulative, but did he actually need Maynard back? Yes again, if it meant more haste in the completion of the building. But did it have to be Maynard?

"You know your wife tried to kill me," Robert snapped.

Maynard laughed, doubling over and nearly falling. "What? Are you delusional?"

"The fire in the masons lodge at Corsley Heath during the summer. You didn't know that she's the one who started it?"

"You can't be serious, Smythson. What on earth gave you that idea?"

"She admitted it to me. Ask her. She instructed that tow-headed boy to throw a lit torch into the lodge to scare me off. I think she thinks you were involved in Mary Kington's death, and she wanted me to stop asking questions because I was getting too close to you. What do you say to that?"

Maynard pulled himself up and gasped for air. Then he shook his head, either in disbelief or because he was trying to sober himself up. Robert couldn't tell which. There was a pause while both men looked at each other.

"You've got the wrong piece of stone, Statue," Maynard said quietly. "Yes, I know your nickname, your story, and your reputation."

Robert's head spun. After all this time, to hear that name again. He thought he had left it in the past. Was all of that now going to be dredged up and dragged out for all to see?

"I think we're done here." Maynard turned and went into the house, the door shutting behind him.

Robert stood staring at the closed door, wondering what had just happened. After several minutes, he got back on his horse and rode away, blinded by tears of frustration and anger. Again. How many times was he going to let Sir John and Maynard get to him? He was so tired of manipulation and subterfuge. And so angry with himself for letting them get to him, for falling victim to their machinations, for caring. Damn Longleat and its potential.

Chapter 28

THE SKY WAS DARKENING and evening setting in as Robert rode past Longleat on his way home. Despite his frustration, he had his usual reaction to seeing the building, one of promise. He completed the building in his mind, dotting the top with his revised banqueting houses and setting it in beautiful landscaping instead of a muddy building site. It would be lovely, and he did want to be a part of it.

His thoughts turned again to Maynard. Robert had been so upset by Maynard's use of his old nickname that he had missed the words that had come before. "You've got the wrong stone," Maynard had said. He wasn't talking about stone. Robert understood that. Was he referring to Betty's role in the lodge fire? No, Betty had admitted that. To his role in Mary's death? Was this a simple denial or one based on real information?

Did it matter? If no one else was concerned with Mary's death, why couldn't he let it go? The answer was obvious: Anne. The physical similarities between the two young women, the vulnerability that they shared, connected them in Robert's mind. He rubbed his face and urged his horse forward. This was getting him nowhere. Sir John wanted to see progress on the roof and banqueting houses. If he didn't deliver, he had a feeling he would find himself replaced by the newly available Maynard.

Arriving home, Robert wrapped Anne in a big hug. "What's wrong?" Anne asked, eventually untangling herself to set some food in front of Robert.

He told Anne about what had transpired in Sir John's office, through Maynard's confrontation and Cavell's confirmation that Sir John had probably played at least some role in Maynard's failure. Sipping some ale and stroking Cat with the other hand, Anne asked Robert how he would feel if Maynard joined the team at Longleat.

Robert ran his hands through his hair and sighed. "I don't know. Many of his men are already working for me, and I think they enjoy the structure I bring. On the other hand, with Sir John's demands, having another skilled mason would certainly help. I've seen some of his work; Maynard is a truly gifted craftsman. Better than I am at the detailed stuff. On the other hand, it feels like chaos follows him wherever he goes, and I don't think I could handle that. If he could manage his team and leave me with fewer men to oversee, I think we could make some significant progress. I just don't know if the productivity would offset the drama and upheaval."

"What do you think will happen with the Maynards?" Anne started to giggle. "I wonder how Betty will accept that she's not going to court to mingle with the Queen and her ladies?"

"Did she really say that?"

"Yes, I tried to gently tell her that was not what would happen. Goodness, she'll be hard to live with. Do you think they will stay in the area or leave?"

"Probably stay. I think if he was going to leave, he would have done it already. Perhaps, like me, he sees the promise of Longleat and wants to be a part of it. Well, it's not my decision to make, just to live with. Enough about Sir John and Maynard. What did you do today?"

"Laundry. You know Thursday is wash day." Robert lifted one of Anne's hands and kissed it, noting the vanishing softness.

"I wish I could ease some of the burden, maybe hire someone to help you."

"Oh, Robert, I'm fine. Helen, Charlotte, and I, along with some of the other women, all work together. It can be quite social and fun even."

"Washing? Fun? If you say so. I just don't like to see you wear yourself out."

"I didn't. When we were done, I went up to Cley Hill Farm and saw Henry. I even had enough energy to clean his house and bring him some food."

Robert was quiet. Over the past few weeks, several people in the neighborhood had cautioned him not to allow Anne to spend too much time at Cley Hill Farm. He had tried to pass their messages on to Anne, to suggest that she not get too involved, but she had responded that he was a harmless old man still reeling from the loss of his daughter and with no one else to care for him. Robert also understood that helping Kington was part of Anne's own grieving process for her own father. If her visiting him helped both of them over their losses, who was he to forbid it?

"I haven't forgotten about fixing his walls, but with Sir John wanting the schedule for the next quarter and now this Maynard affair, I haven't gotten to it, but I will. I promise. Now let's tidy up and go to bed. It's been a long day."

Despite the long day, Robert found he had trouble sleeping that night. His conversation with Maynard kept playing over in his mind. "Wrong stone, Statue." Everything Maynard had said repeated in a loop. Robert longed to sit quietly at a masonry bench with a block of stone, mallet, and chisel and to create. Robert understood that as master mason those opportunities were scarce. Instead, it was his job to manage the project, interact with the property owner, and supervise, motivate, and instruct the craftsmen. In general, he loved those roles. He spent his creative energies at the drawing table, but sometimes he wanted to get his hands, and his hair, dirty.

After a restless night, Robert sought out Hills. He found him in the masons lodge, setting up a piece of carving for what would be a decorative cap for one of the windows. Robert joined in, picking up a long piece of stone and tracing a Greek key pattern. The methodical up, turn, across, turn, down, turn pattern soothed his brain, leaving it free to wander to other problems. As the men worked, Robert filled his friend in on his frustration with Maynard. "The man was submitting plans for Leicester! Leicester, for God's sake, the Queen's favorite!"

"And," the older mason replied, "you were working for Knollys, one of her most trusted advisors. Stop selling yourself short! Your ideas are worth ten of Maynard's, for all he might be the superior carver. Anyone can follow a pattern. It takes vision to create the pattern. I know it, Lovell knows it—that's why he recommended you to Sir John. And Sir John knows it too—that's why he brought you back. He's all bluster and show, but he knows he needs you."

"I have wondered why he hasn't fired me yet. Perhaps he will now that Maynard is available again." Robert put aside the drawing tools and picked through the chisels, looking for the right size.

"I doubt it unless you do something stupid again. Sir John needs you to make Longleat as good as he wants it, though don't expect him to admit it."

Robert heard what Hills had said, but he just couldn't get his mind off Maynard. "I cannot not bring myself to like or trust Maynard, as much as I admire his work. I know he was somehow involved in Mary Kington's death." He picked up a hammer, wiped the surface of the stone, and prepared to carve. "What did Maynard mean when he told me on the way back from Lacock that he was good at keeping secrets? Or when he intimated that he had other information about Longleat that he was not sharing when he was accusing Sir John? Was that information about Mary's death or the fire?"

"Robert, you're letting them all get to you," Hills said.

"There's too much noise and conflict. I can't quiet the space or see the way forward clearly in my mind. There is too much chaos and too many demands."

"Focus on the work," Hills advised. "You always think better with a hammer and chisel in your hands."

Robert nodded, then bent and focused. He tapped with the hammer, turned, tapped, turned. *Find the rhythm, clink, listen to the stone, clink.* Letting his heart find the rhythm, the space where all else quieted, letting the connections loosen, drift, and reform. *How do the angles all fit together?* Betty's afraid of something. Despite her bravado, she was afraid enough to try to drive Robert away. It must have something to do with Maynard. *What's the connection between Maynard and Kington? Religion?* Mary Stuart spent most of her early life in France. Or something closer to home? Had Maynard been interested in Mary before he married Betty? Afterward?

He paused, looked into the distance, and readjusted the chisel again. Maynard had been the one to deliver Mary's note to Ned Bright. Where or how had he received the note? If Mary was the person who had given the note to Maynard, was he the last person to see her alive? Did he have some unknown motive for killing her? Was Betty capable of such a crime? Did she have the strength to wield a masonry tool? Robert didn't think so, but perhaps she had come looking for her husband and found him with Mary in an intimate pose. Why? None of this made any sense.

And then there was the other thing. How had Maynard found out about his nickname? And had he found out the details of Winchester? Robert looked down at his carving. The proportions were all off. It was useless. It would have to be broken up and used as rubble. What a waste. "Hills, walk with me."

"Where are we going?" Hills asked, putting away his tools. "Hopefully, somewhere you can't do any more damage to good stone."

"My mind isn't right today. Maynard said something to me last night. He's been snooping into my past. I think he found out about Winchester." Robert led Hills away from the lodge to a place they wouldn't be overheard.

"God's teeth, Robert. There is nothing to find out. It was an accident. I was there, remember? When are you going to stop blaming yourself?"

"Maynard called me Statue. I thought I had left that name behind for good. I can't let all that get dredged up again."

"Listen to me. There is nothing to get dredged up. You were a young mason then. You've more than atoned for that accident, which was not your fault. The only person holding on to that is you. So what if Maynard's heard the story? Sir John's known about it for years, and it hasn't affected how he sees you. Why do you keep letting it change how you see yourself?"

"All those deaths. I couldn't save my sister or the men at Winchester. But if I can get justice for Mary. I know it doesn't make sense to anyone but me. I need to right the wrong. It won't save her, but somehow it may save me."

"And you think Maynard is involved."

"I do," Robert agreed.

"Then why would he come back here? Why not uses this opportunity to get away, where no one can ask questions?"

"I don't know. That's a good point."

"Come on, Robert. Let's get back to work. Don't we have a building to build?"

Over the next few days, the Maynards stayed out of sight while the entire region talked about the fall of the proud mason, most concluding that he had gotten what he deserved. Many of Robert's team, including those who had previously worked for Maynard, agreed that he had become overly confident, puffing himself up with an overexaggeration of his talents. After months of listening to Maynard brag and crow of his fabulous future, there was not a lot of sympathy for him in the neighborhood. Now he was back, and everyone was curious to see what would happen next.

Down at Longleat, the day's work was going smoothly. In the crisp fall air, Robert made his rounds to each of the workstations, encouraging and instructing. Hopefully, winter would come late this year and his team could continue the external work for a couple more months at least before having to move inside. Somehow Robert didn't think that Sir John would consider work done at the bench to be progress. He wanted visual results, walls going up, completed pieces being moved into place. Sir John had not commented on his idea of octagonal buildings instead of square ones, so the men had gone forward with the square ones. Everything was neat and tidy and in order, just the way Robert liked it.

"I'm going to head over to the mortar pits and check on them," Robert told Hills as they broke for their midday meal.

"I'll go, or we could send Vincent," Hills countered.

"No, I don't mind. That will give me the chance to take some mortar over to Cley Hill Farm and take a look at that crumbling wall. Anne has asked me to fix it before the weather turns." This might be a good day for that kind of work. Help a neighbor and get a chance to do some basic masonry work for a change.

"Then go, man. Things will be all right here."

"Some basic masonry work would do me some good. Sir John would have a fit if he found out."

"Don't worry about him. He was snooping around yesterday. He'll probably not come down today. If he does, I'll make some excuse for you. Go."

"Thanks, John."

Arriving at Cley Hill Farm in midafternoon, Robert tied up his horse and looked around. The buildings and fields all looked quiet, and there was no answer when he knocked at the farmhouse door and yelled for Kington. Well, even if no one was home, he could get started on the exterior. He walked around to the back corner and surveyed the damage. It was a couple of months since he had last looked at it, and it had gotten worse during that time. It should have been repaired long before it had gotten this bad. It must have been made with faulty mortar. If done correctly, the wall would still be solid. Never mind, he had the mortar now. An hour or so of work would fix it, and it should harden sufficiently before winter set in.

Stones were dislodged, crumbled, and laying scattered nearby. Taking out his hammer, Robert gently tapped away at the pieces that remained, testing which were firmly in place and which were loose. With his fingers, he scraped out the crumbling mortar and shook his head. Properly done work would not respond like this. After a few minutes, he had cleared the space, leaving a hole large enough to look inside the house. A strange smell emanated from inside: a mixture of candles and spices and something else he couldn't identify. Everything seemed quiet. Perhaps Henry was still out working in his fields.

Robert filled the hole with stone and mortar, enjoying the simplicity of the work. It was a small project, but it would make a difference to a man who was having a difficult time. Sir John wouldn't like it, but Robert could withstand the heat of his displeasure. After an hour or so, he was satisfied with the job he had done. No one had come to disturb him as he worked, and Robert felt content. He looked at the position of the sun and realized he should be heading toward home.

Piling up some unused stone near the side of the house, leaving everything as neat and tidy as he could, he bent to gather his tools. Something just along the wall caught his eye. A stone jutted out farther than the rest. Was this another section of wall about to crumble? He tapped at the stones with his hammer, hearing a hollow sound behind the protruding stone. Putting the hammer down, Robert used his fingers to pull out the piece of rock.

Just like at the masons lodge, a hollow storage space had been created within the wall. Unlike the masons lodge, this one was not empty. Carefully putting his hand inside, Robert touched something metal. Twisting and turning, he managed to pull the thing out. In his hands, Robert held a mason's iron hammer, the kind used for finishing work on soft stone.

His heart stopped as he held the tool up in the remaining daylight. On the iron head, the end that normally hit or tapped the chisel, depending on the force required, was a dark red stain. Something else was stuck to it as well: a single strand of hair—long honey-colored hair. Robert held in his hand the masonry tool that had killed Mary Kington. What was it doing here, tucked away in a hidden crevice at Cley Hill Farm?

Chapter 29

ROBERT REMOVED THE CLOTH he always carried with him to clean his tools and wrapped it loosely around the hammer, tucking it into his satchel. Then he retrieved his horse and headed for home. His mind raced as his horse plodded down the familiar lane. Either Kington had killed his own daughter and stashed the weapon, or the real killer had hidden the sharp-edged hammer at Cley Hill Farm to make it look like Kington was guilty. Robert thought about the matching hidden compartment at Maynard's old masons lodge. What had Maynard said that day on Cley Hill? Nothing specific, yet he had mentioned Kington's wall and the masons lodge back-to-back. Was he trying to draw Robert's attention to a connection between the two? He had also cautioned Robert against allowing Anne to spend too much time with Kington.

Someone had purposely drawn Robert to the hidden compartment at the back of the masons lodge. Without the signs pointing to it, it could have gone unnoticed for years. Now Mary's murder weapon had been found in a similar compartment at Kington's farmhouse. That could not be a coincidence. Whoever had disrupted the masons lodge was trying to draw everyone's attention to the hiding location of the tool that had been used to kill Mary Kington. But who had done that, and why? Was it to throw suspicion off the real killer, or did someone know who had killed Mary? Too many questions, and Robert began to suspect he would not like the answers.

Robert spurred his horse on, anxious to see his wife as a sense of dread began to rise from his gut. Carrying his tools, he took a minute to remove his boots near the door before entering. "I'm home," he called. "I'm just going to set these tools down." The place seemed quiet and colder than usual. "Anne?" There was no response, no fire, and no dinner preparations. Trying to quell the rising fear he felt, he told himself that she was probably over at the Crispins' and had forgotten to tell him, or perhaps he had forgotten. He smiled at his own forgetfulness. Still, Dick had said nothing, and he usually remembered.

Returning outside, Robert put his boots back on, and as he did so he was greeted by the friendly cat who had made her home with the Smythsons. Cat rubbed herself around his legs, meowing. Clearly, Anne had not given her the expected treats that she usually shared while she cooked. Robert walked down the lane to their friends' house. "Hello?" he called when he reached the door. "Is Anne here?"

"What?" Charlotte replied, standing in front of the fire stirring the Crispins' dinner. "Oh, hello, Robert. No, Anne isn't here. I have not seen her today, which, now that you mention it, is odd. Is she not at home?"

"No, I've just come from there. The cottage is empty and cold. I don't think she's been there for some time. I thought perhaps you had invited us over and I had forgotten."

Charlotte laughed. "No, not tonight, although you are most welcome." She paused from the food preparation she had been focused on and looked at Robert. "Are you all right? You look worried. It's probably nothing. Have you checked with your team? Perhaps the Mercers had an emergency."

"I suppose that's possible. I think one of their children is sick." He paused, considering how to say the next part. "There's something else. I was up at Cley Hill Farm this afternoon, and I think I found the weapon used to kill Mary Kington."

"What?" Dick said from behind him, returning home from his day at Longleat.

Robert stepped aside to let his friend pass so he could greet his own wife. "And there was no sign of Kington at Cley Hill Farm, and now Anne's missing. Dick, I don't like how this looks."

"Nor I," replied his friend. "Do you think he killed his own daughter? Why? From everything I heard, he doted on her."

"I don't know. I think it's more likely someone else moved the hammer up to the farm to make it look like he did it."

"Why don't you go up to Corsley Manor and check in with Sir John? Perhaps a letter from Sir Francis came and Sir John sent for her. You go there, and I'll go check in with the Mercers. If she's there, I'll come find you." The carpenter began to tug his boots back on.

"Robert, please let us know when you find her." Charlotte laid her hand on his arm. "I don't want to worry for nothing."

"Certainly."

"Better get a torch; it's getting dark." Dick ducked back inside and quickly returned with two torches. The two craftsmen headed off in different directions.

Leaving his horse with a retainer in the yard, Robert pushed his way into Corsley Manor, demanding to see Sir John. Thrusting servants out of the way, the usually mild-mannered mason now on the verge of hysteria, made his way into the great hall. "Is she here?" he demanded when he found Sir John, sitting at the head of the main dining table enjoying his evening meal along with the rest of the household.

"Who? Smythson, what are you doing?" Sir John's expression was one of surprise mixed with patient humor.

"Anne. My wife. Did she come here? Has there been word from Knollys? Did you send for her?"

"One question at a time, man," said Sir John, rising from the table. "No, Mistress Smythson is not here. As you would see if you slowed down enough to look. There has been no word from Knollys, and no one that I know of has sent for your wife. Anyone seen this man's wife?" He asked the last question with a tone of mocking condescension while gesturing to his companions. There was mild laughter, and many shook their heads.

Robert began to leave, for if Anne was not there, he had no reason to be at Corsley Manor, but Sir John detained him. "Not so fast, Smythson. What is this about? Have you misplaced your wife?"

"She is not at home, and no one seems to know where she might be." He began to fumble in his bag. "And when I was at Cley Hill Farm, I found this hidden in a wall." Robert pulled out the hammer and began waiving it about.

"Put that thing away, Smythson. You're beginning to sound like a madman." Sir John nodded to some attendants, alerting them in case Robert's actions became dangerous.

"I think this is what was used to kill Mary Kington. Look, there's blood and some hair."

Richard Cavell had made his way from his seat and was now standing next to Robert. He took the hammer from Robert and held it up to the light. "Aye, that's blood and hair all right, although as to its being Mary's, who knows? Where did you say you got this?"

"At Cley Hill Farm!" Robert yelled, losing his patience. "If Anne isn't here, I must continue my search. I fear some harm or tragedy may have befallen her." He grabbed the hammer back from Cavell and stuffed it into his bag while turning for the door.

"Wait!" Sir John bellowed. "What were you doing at Cley Hill Farm? That place and Kington are nothing but trouble."

Robert turned back impatiently. "I don't have time to explain. I must find my wife. You might be right about Kington being trouble."

"What made you think Anne might be here?" Cavell asked.

"Crispin suggested it. He thought perhaps you had received some word about Sir Francis Knollys or Lady Catherine and had sent for her to tell her."

Sir John sat down again. "Isn't Sir Francis still up north tending to the Scots Queen? Why would I have news?"

"Because you often get letters from court," Robert said with exasperation. None of this helped him find Anne.

"No, all I hear about Knollys comes from that idiot Kington. Always running on about the unfair treatment Mary Stuart is receiving. As if its England's fault the Scots Queen couldn't control her own people and then ran away. Kington should know better! I could lock him up for some of the things he's said, the raving Catholic! If he wasn't still distraught over the loss of his daughter, I wouldn't tolerate it. I've granted him some leniency, but my patience is wearing thin."

Robert and Cavell both stared at Sir John during this speech and then looked at one another as the wheels turned in Robert's head. "Sir John, do you think Kington could turn violent?"

"I don't know. Probably. The man's a nuisance and a lunatic!"

Robert stared at Sir John, turning his words over in his mind, remembering the smell wafting from the inside of Kington's home.

He was so tired of the games, the threats, the manipulations. But now Anne was missing, possibly in danger, and Robert began to have an inkling of who might be responsible. He made a move for the door.

"Oh no, you don't." Sir John rose with fury, quickly crossing the room to where Robert stood. "You gave me your word that your investigating days were over." Sir John towered over him, but this time Robert held his gaze. Robert's muscles tightened; he felt his blood rushing to his face as his hand tightened its grip on the handle of the hammer. The two men stared at one another.

"If you go after them in any way, you are finished here, Smythson. Do you hear me? Finished!" Sir John said, his voice low and controlled.

Robert's voice held equal emotion. "And if something happens to Anne and I find out that you knew something about it, I swear I'll dismantle every piece of your precious Longleat."

At Cley Hill Farm, all was quiet, just as Robert had left it an hour or so earlier. He stormed to the door and found it yielded easily to his touch. "Kington!" he shouted. "Where are you? And where is my wife?" He paused, listening, but heard nothing and then began to search the rooms one by one. In the main room, he stopped short. The smell he had detected from the outside was still there. A candle still flickered in the corner, illuminating an elaborate altar.

Robert stopped and moved more slowly. He needed to study the space. Use his vision to search for clues. He looked around the room and found a torch propped up in the corner and lit it using the candle. With the additional light, he saw the icon resting on the altar, as Anne had described it to him days before. The rest of the room was in disarray, but that was nothing new for Kington. He closed his eyes and smelled. Could he detect Anne's rose water perfume? No, the fragrance of incense was too heavy. He tried to feel for her presence but felt nothing. He began to move about the room slowly. Had Anne been here?

Two goblets stood on the table; someone had been here with Kington. He picked up one and smelled the contents, then recoiled. Beneath the spiced wine lay another smell: valerian root. The powder Williams had given him to help him sleep. Something was not right. Moving toward the table, he saw writing materials pushed aside. A quill lay on the table, something scratched just below it. It looked like an *N*. What could that mean? Or was it significant at all? Oh, why couldn't his brain think! What had happened in this room?

He ran outside to look for additional signs. When he entered the stable, Kington's mules stamped and snorted at him, expecting their evening feed. Kington's horse and cart were missing. He had gone somewhere. Crouching down, Robert tried to look at the ground with his torch. It was hard to see as the evening gloom gathered, but it looked like something had been dragged along the ground, probably to where the cart had stood. There was something in the corner, near the door. Bending over, he realized it looked familiar. A glove. Robert touched it carefully, running his fingers over it until he felt what he was looking for. There, at the wrist, was the unmistakable stitching of *AS*. It was Anne's glove. One of the set they had purchased together when they had first come to Longleat after their marriage.

Robert stood while his brain worked through these images. The smell of the drink, the letter *N*, Anne's glove. The old legend came back to him. Drop a glove and where it lands, there is your treasure. His treasure had been here and had dropped her glove. He knew how much those gloves meant to both of them. She would not have dropped it casually. It added up. Kington had Anne, had drugged her, then dragged her to the cart. She had pulled the glove from its place tucked in her waist as a sign for him to find. Where had Kington taken her? The *N*. Had Anne scribbled the *N* as a clue, or was it random? *N* for Ned? Ned Bright? Could he have gone to Lacock? Or *N* for north? Could Kington have taken Anne north to where Mary Stuart was being held?

Robert thought about what Sir John had said about Kington, that he seemed to be losing his mind. Had he gone after Ned at Lacock or farther afield, thinking that he could somehow use Anne to get to Knollys and then to the Scots Queen? Both were north. He would head to Lacock, and then if there was no sign of Kington, he would move on.

Either way, he would start his search at Lacock. Mounting his horse, he flew back toward Corsley Heath. He would stop at the Crispins' and ask Dick to come with him.

He filled them in as quickly as he could. Dick was ready to saddle his horse and go with Robert, but Charlotte stopped him.

"Hold on just a minute. You two are not going without me. Think this through for a moment. Robert, you go on ahead on horseback, but let Dick and me follow you in the cart. Give us a few minutes to pack up some things. I'll grab what food I can and a blanket or two. We don't know what we'll find when we get there or how we're going to bring Anne home. I'll move as quickly as I can." She put her hand on her swollen belly. "Dick, hitch up some fresh horses to one of the carts while I gather supplies. We won't be but a few minutes behind you, Robert. Which way are you going to ride?"

A few minutes more discussion, and they were all going in different directions. Robert kicked his horse to speed him along and was soon swiftly riding toward Lacock, knowing that his rational and caring friends were right behind him.

Chapter 30

Heading west toward Frome, Robert prayed for Anne's protection and for swift travel. He went the way he had gone before, choosing familiarity since there wasn't much of a moon to light the way. Passing the turn for East Woodlands, he slowed. Somehow Maynard was mixed up in all of this. Robert turned his horse south and rode on. It would be out of his way, but he had to find out what Maynard knew or how he was involved.

A short while later, Robert was banging on the Maynards' door, demanding to know where Anne was. Betty opened the door a crack, and Robert pushed his way past her into a domestic scene quite different from the one he had seen on his last visit. Then, Maynard had been drunk, but Betty was still anticipating a move up to better things. Now their spacious home resembled Kington's old place. Mugs and dishes were strewn everywhere, remnants of meals littered about, pieces of cheese left to grow mold, the stench of stale ale mixed with sweat and spoiled meat. In the corner near the fireplace, Maynard was slumped in a chair, a goblet of wine at his elbow.

Robert strode over to him and repeated his question. Maynard raised his glassy eyes in confusion and muttered, "How should I know? Misplaced your new wife already?"

Robert loomed over Maynard, fists raised. "I swear, Maynard, if something happens to my wife and I find out you withheld information from me, I will not be responsible for what happens to you. Understand? I know you have some connection to Kington. I know you are the one who delivered Mary's letter to Ned after she disappeared. I don't know why or how exactly, but I know you are involved. Where is my wife?"

"Not here. Welcome to look around." Maynard's head dropped, and his speech deteriorated into a stream of indistinguishable French.

"Stop it. I'm warning you, Maynard, this is not a joke. Anne is gone, and I think Kington has her. If you know anything, you need to tell me now."

"Kington, huh? I tried to warn you."

Robert grabbed Maynard by the shirt, yanking him from his seat. "God's breath! You're drunk! I need answers! What do you mean, you tried to warn me?"

"Those compartments. I left a trail for you to find. Moved the hammer." Maynard's speech was so slurred with drink Robert had trouble understanding him.

"What are you saying?" Robert's voice was low, his tone menacing.

"The hammer that killed Mary. Kington. Moved it. Tried to tell you."

"You moved the hammer that killed Mary up to Cley Hill Farm? Why?"

Maynard was getting more agitated. He swayed toward Robert. "So you would find it and figure it out."

"Kington killed his own daughter?" Robert asked, not believing it.

"Didn't mean to. Wanted that Bright fellow but got Mary instead. Rather careless, if you ask me. Don't know how he confused the two of them. They're so different in size." Maynard started to giggle.

"Maynard!" Robert shoved him back into his seat. "So help me God, that man has my wife!"

Maynard stopped laughing. "Oh dear. And her looking so much like Mary. That cannot be good."

"Where would he take her? To Lacock?"

"I dunno. No idea. Haven't seen either of them for days. Could be anywhere." He slumped back into his chair, head rolling to one side. "I've had my own concerns to worry about."

Robert glared at Maynard, then turned and crossed to where Betty stood. She looked haggard, with dark circles under her eyes. She also appeared to be drunk, wearing a stained apron over a stained kirtle. Her hair was limp, her eyes missing their regular spark. "I know you're mixed up in this somehow, Betty. Why did you set fire to my lodge? Did you know Kington killed Mary?"

"Kington killed Mary?" There was genuine surprise in Betty's expression. She looked across to her husband. "You didn't do it?"

"You thought Maynard killed Mary? So when you set the fire to scare me off, you were trying to protect him?" Robert asked.

There was the slightest tilt of Betty's head, as if she thought about fighting back. "You wouldn't stop digging around. Alan had something to do with Mary's death. I thought maybe the two of them had had an affair and he killed her when he learned she was pregnant. You just needed to stop asking so many pesky questions. I was right too. Look what it's gotten you."

"Shut up, woman. Stop making it worse," Maynard barked from across the room.

Betty shrugged and sat down on a nearby stool, exhausted. Robert looked from one to the other, making no attempt to hide his contempt and disgust. Whatever problems the Maynards had wouldn't help Anne now. "Where would Kington take my wife?" Turning back to Maynard, Robert said, "You clearly have had dealings with him. What would he want with Anne? Where would he take her?"

"She's not here," Betty said flatly. "Alan's barely gone anywhere in days. Whatever has happened to Anne, he's not mixed up in it." There was defeat in her voice. Robert looked at Betty and around the room. All evidence backed up her claim. Together, the Maynards had the look of a couple who had given up. The pretense of wealth and success that usually surrounded them was gone. No swagger. Just defeat. He turned away and walked out.

Robert leaned over his horse, nudging a little more speed, while he replayed what Maynard had told him. Henry Kington was responsible for Mary's death. If Mary's death had been an accident, as Maynard had said, if Mary had intended to meet Ned that night and Kington had tried to stop her, what could possibly be his intentions now? Why Anne? Clearly, Kington had confused her with Mary again. Anne had been at Cley Hill Farm; her glove showed him that. What about the *N* written on the table? His gut told him Anne had written that and that it referred to Ned Bright.

The next two hours were some of the longest of Robert's life as he urged every ounce of speed from his horse. Robert continued toward Lacock under the assumption that Lacock Abbey and Ned Bright were Kington's target. He tried to calculate how much of an advance start Kington would have had on him. Surely, Anne had not gone willingly. He remembered the valerian root. Kington must have drugged her. Would Kington have driven during daylight, or would he have waited until nightfall? But Robert had been there, working on the exterior wall. If Kington were waiting until dark, Robert would have come across him. Robert's heart plunged as he realized they must be several hours' ahead.

He rode as quickly as he dared push his horse, passing through the village of Melksham and on toward Lacock. His only hope was that if Kington was using his cart, he wouldn't be able to go as fast as Robert could on horseback. It was now approaching the middle of the night, with only the slimmest of moon to light the way. It took all his concentration to stay on the road, pushing his horse farther into the darkness. Where would this journey end? Fear drove him on.

Once he reached the outskirts of Lacock, he wondered where he should go. Straight to Henry Sharington? Was there a sheriff or local official? He did not want to waste time. At least he knew where to find Ned, which was one advantage he had over Kington. He prayed his instincts were right and that he would reach them in time. He dared not think of what would happen if he was wrong.

Robert turned down High Street, trying to remember the layout of the town. His ears were alert, his eyes searching as he rode through the wooded area separating the village from the abbey. As he approached Lacock Abbey, all was quiet and still. He pulled his tired horse up at the masons lodge a short distance from the main building. Dismounting and running inside, Robert yelled Ned's name. He climbed the stairs and sensed the emptiness. He felt around the dark room until he found a bed. It still held a trace of heat. Someone, Ned, had been here but was here no longer. Robert ran back down, verified that the workshop was empty, and ran outside. Where could he be? His instinct told him that everyone was here, and he headed toward the abbey.

The grounds of the abbey were shrouded in darkness. Robert crept on the gravel path and almost stumbled into a cart, the snort of a horse alerting him just before he crashed into it. He went to the horse's head and felt the sweat. It was tired, much like Robert's own horse, as if it had had a hard trip in haste. Moving to the back of the cart, he tried to still himself, to focus on finding clues. The cart seemed to be empty except for an old blanket. He sniffed the blanket. Was that a whiff of Anne's rose water? He groped around some more until his hand felt another, smaller cloth item. He held it up toward the dim moonlight and ran his hands along the item carefully, feeling for the delicate stitching at the wrist. It was the other of Anne's gloves. She was here. *Dear God, please let me not be too late.*

Chapter 31

Robert sensed movement before he saw it. Then, through the shadows, he saw two figures stumble across the yard. Neither was Anne. Two men. Robert stood motionless, not wanting to startle them until he better understood what was happening. The smaller man appeared to be dragging a larger one.

"Master Kington? What are you doing?" The voice was Ned's, as Robert had suspected, and the man standing over him was Henry Kington. Robert looked wildly around, his eyes straining in the dark. There was no sign of Anne. Robert considered revealing himself, confronting Kington, but decided against it. Better to get more information on Anne's whereabouts before interfering.

"Mary. She's waiting for you. Come on, I'll take you to her." Robert could hear something odd in his voice, an almost seductive quality.

"Come on, man. Let's go," Kington continued, grabbing Ned's arm.

"But Mary . . . Mary's dead."

"No, she isn't. That's what they wanted you to believe, but she's not. She's here, waiting for you. In the tower. All you need to do is come with me."

Robert listened as Ned responded, "Mary's here? What? But that mason, what was his name? He said she was dead. Thought I had killed her."

"No, no, he just wanted her for himself. That's all. But I've fixed it. I've taken her and brought her to you. Now you come with me, and we'll get the two of you reunited."

They took a few steps toward the abbey. "Wait." Ned stopped. "Master Kington, that fellow Smythson, he said you thought I had killed Mary. How can you bring me to her when she's already dead? This doesn't make any sense."

"No, no. It's all right. She's here. Nobody killed her. They made a mistake. I have her, and I've brought her up here. She's right up in the tower waiting for you. Come on." Kington grabbed Ned's arm again and began pulling him along. "Quit wasting time. We only have a couple more hours before the sun comes up. I need to get the two of you together."

As the men moved farther away from him, Robert left the protective shadows of the cart and followed. The tower. Anne was in the tower. *Dear God, please let her be alive.* Making no sound, he crept in their footsteps until he lost them completely in the abbey's shadows. All was quiet except the sound of his own shallow breath. They must have gone inside.

Terror filled Robert's mind and soul, but he pushed it down. *Focus. Concentrate. Breathe.* Surveying the darkness, he saw something flicker in the distance. A light where everything else was dark. He ran toward it, trying to remember the floor plan from his previous visit. He reached the exterior door that led to the cloisters and carefully opened it. No light shone along the long passageway, but he could hear some grunting in the distance. He thought back to the tour Sharington had given him of the tower. Two levels, each a single room with a single door, no other way in or out. If the door was blocked from the outside and there was someone inside, they would be trapped.

Quickly, but as quietly as he could, Robert crept across the length of the cloisters, aiming for the tower door that led to narrow stairs up to each room. As he reached it, he could just make out a dim line of light coming from beyond the door. Praying he had reached her in time, Robert inched the door open. He could hear shouting as he carefully let the door close quietly behind him.

"There you go," Kington yelled. "Mary, where are you?" There was a thud as someone hit the floor hard.

Mary? Surely, Kington meant Anne. Was it possible that he now truly believed that Anne was his daughter come back to life? Robert began to creep up the stairs, not wanting to announce his presence until he understood the situation better.

"The lovers reunite. For one last night only, I'm afraid," Kington said. "Come here, my dear. I've brought you to your lover at last." Robert heard a scuffle, something that might have been a blow or kick of some kind, followed by Ned moaning.

At the top of the stairs, there was a small landing, just enough for one or two people to stand while the door was being opened. Kington hadn't closed the door all the way, and Robert squatted down, peering into the tower room through the narrow opening. What he saw made his heart stop.

On the far side of the room, huddled against the wall, something in her mouth and a look of absolute terror on her face, was Anne. She was wearing Mary's old cloak, her honey hair tumbling down in disarray. Next to her, Ned lay on his side, blood oozing from a wound on his back. And Henry Kington loomed over them with a large wooden mallet in his hand.

Robert froze. He wanted to rush in there and save Anne but found himself rooted to the floor, unable to move. He flashed back to Winchester, his mind analyzing the angles of the scaffolding and the winches, his vision locked on to the center of the cornice. His inaction then had caused the death of several men, including his father and brother. Now his inaction might cause the death of his beloved Anne. Or maybe his action would. Another quick glance into the room showed Kington standing over Ned Bright, the masonry mallet held aloft, ready to strike.

The tower was dark except for one small torch in a holder on the wall. Robert focused on the flickering light, and another image flashed through his mind. The fire where his sister had died. And his failure to save her. Would this be another failure? Another death, another life lost because of his inaction? He somehow willed himself to inch closer and peered into the small room. As he remembered, the beautiful octagonal table stood in the center, with its intricate stone carving and marble top. Behind the table, Ned and Anne were huddled against the wall, Kington standing over them.

Robert watched as Ned hoisted himself up to a sitting position and looked at Anne. "Mary!" Ned uttered before another blow of the mallet pushed him back to the ground. She shook her head furiously. Anne's arms were tied behind her, limiting her movements. All she could do was swerve as Kington lunged for her.

Ned raised himself again, this time clutching the girl and pulling her away from Kington. Wrapping his arms around her in a deep embrace, Ned struggled to remove the rag from her mouth as Kington swung the heavy mallet down toward him. The blow landed on his shoulder, knocking him down again, but not knocking him out. Kington raised his arm to strike again, but Ned rolled out of the way, dodging the blow, and pulling Anne farther out of Kington's reach.

"Kington, what the hell are you doing?"

"Finishing what I started last year. No daughter of mine is going to run off with a mere mason. I will stop you both this time."

"Mary! Are you all right?" Ned clambered to his feet and backed up to the wall. He moved so that the table stood between himself and Kington. "Hold on, I'm just going to . . ." He pulled her toward himself, fumbling with the gag. Once he had pulled it down around her neck, he bent to cover her mouth with his in a kiss. When she didn't respond, he pulled back and took a good look at her.

"My hands, quick," Anne said. He turned and began trying to free her arms from the rope while keeping an eye on Kington, who charged at them, mallet flailing. "I'm not Mary. I'm Anne Smythson, Robert's wife. Henry thinks I'm his daughter, and I can see that you did as well. I'm not. I swear. Watch out!"

Anne's words came too late. Kington had taken advantage of Ned's distraction and closed the gap between them. He struck another blow, knocking Ned to the ground again, while Anne retreated a few more feet away.

Ned's size worked in his favor, as the older man's blows could not knock him out. "You killed Mary?" Ned again tried to pull himself up, leaning against the wall for support. "You killed your own daughter?" he asked in disbelief.

"Yes, I did." Kington leaned against the table in the middle of the room, catching his breath. "I didn't mean to. I knew your plan to take my angel away, and I had to stop you. I gave her herbs to help her sleep and went out to meet you instead. And when you showed up, I killed you. I smashed your head in so you would never get your filthy hands on my daughter again."

"But it was Mary instead?" Ned asked.

"Yes, somehow she woke and came to meet you. I made a mistake. I'm going to correct that mistake now. You should have died last year, not Mary. This time, I'll get it right."

Robert had watched all this, frozen in place, the statue he was accused of being. The three others were all on the far side of the tower room, the octagonal table standing between Robert and them. If Robert did nothing, said nothing, everything he held dear would be lost. His beloved Anne would be gone. Robert understood that if he failed to save her, he would fail to save himself. He would not survive another death, another travesty of justice laid at the feet of his own inaction. Somewhere from deep inside of him came the will to move. He stepped fully into the room and yelled, "Kington! Stop!"

Kington turned and looked at the newcomer, apparently not recognizing him. "No! I will finish this. Just let the two lovers have a few more minutes together, and then I will finish what I started. Go on, Bright, aren't you happy to see Mary?"

"Kington, that's not Mary! That's my wife, Anne Smythson. Don't you remember? Mary's dead."

"Don't lie to me. I know my own daughter when I see her."

"Anne, quick, sing something. Ned, can you sing? I know it's a strange request, but we need to show Kington that Anne is not Mary."

"What?"

"Sing! Both of you. Quickly!"

Anne obeyed first, beginning to warble out a song. Anne's voice was weak, feeble, partly from the ordeal she had been through that night but also because her talents lay in other places. Robert was never so happy to hear her flat, out of melody voice as he was that night. Ned was slumped on the floor, but at the sound of Anne's voice, he understood what Robert wanted. He recognized the song Anne had chosen to sing and joined in, softly so that her voice would not be drowned out.

It had the desired effect. Kington took a step back, looked at the two singers, and shook his head. He leaned in closer to Anne and studied her face. "You're not Mary. You're not my angel. What have you done with my angel?"

"That's right, Master Kington. I'm not Mary, I'm Anne Smythson. We're friends. I've done nothing with Mary, but I think you know that already, don't you?" She paused and caught Robert's eye. "He killed her."

"I know," he answered softly.

"What's happening?" said Ned. He had pulled himself up and was slumped against the wall for support. Blood still flowed from the wound on his shoulder, and he cradled his abdomen, which had received several kicks from Kington. "I don't understand why Kington killed Mary."

"I'll tell you why!" Kington answered, looking wildly from one to the other. "To stop her from wasting her life on the likes of you. A no-talent mason from nowhere with no prospects. She should have been mistress of Longleat. She should have been Lady Mary of Longleat. She would have been if you hadn't come along."

"Calm down, Henry. Before someone else gets hurt," Robert said. "I understand that Mary's death was an accident, but how did her body come to be wrapped in a builder's tarp and placed next to Longleat's walls?"

"It should have been him! She was going to meet him, but I found out and stopped her. I drugged her, then went out to meet this maggot. I went there that night to kill him, but she got in the way." Henry began waving the hammer wildly again toward Ned. "It was supposed to be you, but you never came. Only her. Then it was too late, and she was gone, her body limp. There was fire everywhere. I had to get rid of the body. Maynard was there. He said—"

"Maynard? Alan Maynard? Why was he there that night?" Robert asked.

"I don't know. It doesn't matter." Kington was agitated and jerking around in the enclosed space. Robert took advantage of his distraction and moved closer to Anne, but Kington saw him.

"Oh no, you don't. Get away from my Mary! She's mine. She always was mine and always will be. No other man can have her."

Robert backed off but began to slowly lower and open his satchel that had been slung over his shoulder, resting on his back all this time. Carefully, he removed the hammer he still had, the one that had killed Mary. "It's all right, Kington, let these two go, and you and I can talk about it. No need to hurt anyone else."

"No! I will finish this. Once and for all. Mary, go to your lover, if you want him so badly." Anne took a step toward Robert, then back toward Ned, unsure what to do.

"Stay where you are, Anne. Ned, can you stand up?" Robert asked.

"I think so. I don't understand what's happening. Why does Kington keep calling your wife Mary?"

"He's suffering from a delusion, I think. It's my belief that he killed Mary, and that Anne's close resemblance to his daughter has confused him, as it did you, didn't it?"

"Yes, but I still don't understand. My shoulder hurts. I think I'm bleeding."

"We can talk about it later. Right now we need to get that mallet away from him and get him subdued. Anne, can you get closer to me so I can untangle those ropes?" She nodded and moved toward him.

"What's going on?" Kington yelled. "No one is going to touch Mary but me." He lunged across the marble table toward Anne, arm outstretched and ready to strike. She saw it coming and was able to twist out of the way so that the mallet struck with only a glancing blow.

"Here, Ned," Robert called and tossed the hammer toward Ned. Kington swung around to face Ned. Ned lunged to catch the hammer, allowing Kington time to raise the mallet up and lower it onto Ned's head. There was a thud and a clatter as both Ned's body and the metal hammer hit the floor.

Kington turned his attention to Robert, moving around the room to where Robert stood, blocking Kington's access to Anne. "You next, I think, and then Mary." Kington moved toward Robert, who ducked, avoiding the blow. Kington swore and raised the mallet again, his face red with fury. Robert faced him, empty-handed. Mallet in hand, Kington swung again. This time, Robert was ready and blocked the blow by grabbing both of Kington's forearms and pushing him back.

The two men were locked in battle, both strong and both determined. They spun, knocking against the walls and then the table in the small tower room. Kington flailed with the mallet, but youth won out. Robert gave a final push, and Kington fell back toward the center of the room, his head hitting the edge of the marble table. His body fell to the floor, and everything was still and quiet.

"Is he . . .?" Anne asked.

"I don't know." Robert tried to slow his racing heart and looked warily at Kington's slumped body.

A moan sounded from the floor, and someone moved. "Stay back," Robert said to Anne and made his way over to the two men on the floor. Kington was lying on his side, a pool of blood beginning to form under his head. Robert rolled him onto his back; a quick look at the man's face told Robert that he was dead. Turning his attention to Ned, he saw the young mason bleeding from several wounds around his head and shoulders and holding on to his right arm. He was groaning in pain, but he was alive.

Footsteps were heard coming along the passageway. "What the devil is going on here? Who are you?" Henry Sharington entered the small room, a torch lighting up the gruesome scene. Robert slumped against the wall, exhausted and relieved.

"Anne? Are you hurt? I think Kington's dead. Ned, are you still with us?"

"Who is Kington? Who is Anne? Who are you?" Sharington took some steps forward, shoving the torch in Robert's face. "Smythson? What are you doing here?"

Anne lowered herself down to the ground next to Robert, and began to laugh, which quickly turned into a cough. Ned's moaning intensified.

"We need to get him some help," Robert said to Sharington.

"Is that Ned Bright? Whatever happened here? Who is that?" he said, indicating Kington.

"That is Henry Kington," Robert answered. "Of Cley Hill Farm, or formerly of Cley Hill Farm. Last year, he killed his daughter and came here tonight to kill Ned. Nearly succeeded too."

"The girl whose body was found at Longleat? Killed by her own father?"

"Yes, apparently. Now could we please get my wife and Ned here some attention? I'm afraid it's been a rough night for both of them."

"Yes, yes, I'll summon help." Sharington left the way he had come, leaving Anne and Robert alone in the room with Kington and Ned Bright, who had gone quiet. Robert hoped he was still alive but was too preoccupied with Anne to check.

He took a minute to finally free her from all the ropes still tangled around her and felt her all over, looking for injuries. Other than a nasty bump on her head, she seemed to not be seriously hurt. She wrapped her arms around him and buried her head in his chest, letting the tears flow.

Robert held Anne, letting her cry and thanking God for the miracle of her safety. After a few minutes, Anne raised her head. "How did you know?" she asked.

"I found your gloves and followed my treasure here. What happened? Do you feel able to talk about it?"

"He drugged me. By the time I figured it out, I had already swallowed too much of it. I tried to leave what clues I could."

"The *N*? I hoped that meant Ned. The other option was north. I wasn't sure if he had taken you to find Mary Stuart."

"Robert, I tried to get him to stop. I woke up on the way up here, and I tried to convince him I wasn't Mary. Then I tried to convince him I was Mary and that this wasn't what Mary would have wanted. I tried everything I could think of, but finally he gagged me and threw me into this tower room, leaving me here in the dark. I tried to undo the ropes, but the craftsmanship was too good. Not a single rough edge."

"Anne, beloved, I'm sure you tried everything you could. Kington lost touch with the truth a long while ago, carrying around the guilt of killing his own daughter. I'm only sorry I didn't figure it out sooner."

Just then, Sharington returned with several people in tow. His steward, a few members of his staff, and Dick and Charlotte Crispin. The small octagonal banqueting room was filled with people, torches, and questions. Robert reluctantly relinquished Anne into the care of her friend and filled Dick and Sharington in on the details of what had taken place. Several of the men were carrying Ned out and down the narrow steps to comfort and medical attention. Someone handed Robert a beaker of strong ale, and he drank gratefully. It was over.

Chapter 32

ROBERT TUCKED THE BLANKETS carefully around Anne and waited until she fell asleep, praying that the Lord would give her rest and healing. *Please don't let her be scarred by this, please return her to my sweet, kind, and cheerful wife.* He wanted to see the twinkle in her eye and the gentle smile as they shared a laugh together when she woke up.

He was too restless to sleep. Uncertainty lay ahead. The last time he had seen Sir John, he had been yelling threats as Robert left the room. "Go after them and you're finished here." Well, he had, so he supposed he was. It wouldn't matter. Nothing mattered except that Anne was alive and safe and had been returned to him. Sir John be damned! Robert had uncovered a murderer and possibly saved the lives of several others. If Sir John chose to fire him for saving his own wife, then Robert would leave happily. Who would want to work for a man with those principles?

He left the cottage and stood in the sun, stretching. He looked up and down the road. It felt like months or at least weeks since he had last been here, but in truth it was only a day. Had he eaten or slept during that time? He ducked back in and grabbed a hunk of cheese that someone had brought them, taking it outside and biting into it. Just the taste of it felt like heaven compared with what they had been through. His stomach growled as the food hit it, thankful for nutrients. He supposed he should think of something else for Anne to eat when she awoke.

The aftermath of the scene in the Lacock tower had taken hours to sort out. Henry Sharington had insisted upon a full explanation of the events leading up to Kington's death, and each person had to give their side of the story. Eventually, when Sharington understood the details, he ruled Kington's death an accident and assured everyone else there would be no trouble from the law.

The Crispins had quickly taken charge of Anne, wrapping her in soft, warm blankets and giving her spiced ale. Robert had made sure Ned Bright was going to recover before joining his wife. Ned had received several direct blows and would not have the use of his arms for a few weeks, but Sharington assured Robert that he would be well cared for. Sharington had then supplied the Longleat folks with fresh horses and even lent them a larger, more comfortable cart for the ladies to ride back in. All in all, Robert felt indebted to the current owner of Lacock Abbey. Perhaps Robert could go work for him when Sir John threw him out. But no, Robert knew he could never be in that tower room again without reliving the terrible moments of the previous night. He would have to seek employment elsewhere.

As he was thinking, movement caught his eye, and he looked up to see Richard Cavell riding toward him. "Hello, Cavell," he called out, finishing the rest of the cheese and wiping his hands on his jerkin. Time to learn his fate. Even in this, Sir John sought haste.

"How are you?" Cavell called out, dismounting. "Is Anne all right? If even half of what I'm hearing is true, then you two have had quite an ordeal."

"Let's walk a bit. Anne is asleep, and I don't want to wake her. She's been through more than most could handle," Robert led Cavell away from the cottage, his voice low. "An ordeal is a mild way of putting it. Unfortunately, it did not end without more tragedy, but Anne and I are alive and, for the most part, unharmed. Not sure what you've heard, but Henry Kington is dead after trying to kill both Anne and Ned Bright. He also admitted to killing Mary."

"And you, from what I've heard."

"I suppose."

"To think he was living so close by for all this time, knowing he had killed his daughter and covering it up. It's unbelievable."

"Yes. Now I suppose you're here to tell me to pack my things and move on?"

"What?"

"Sir John was clear with me, before I left to find Anne, that if I went after Anne and investigated, it would be the end of my time here at Longleat. Hopefully, he'll give us time to recover before throwing us out. Let me know what rent is owed on the cottage, and I'll try to get it to him before we leave."

"Is that what he said? No, he's given me no such instructions. Merely told me to come down and check on you."

"You know, I don't even care what he thinks anymore. He can keep me here or fire me. It doesn't matter. What he's doing with Longleat is going to be something quite special, and I would like to be a part of it, but not with his threats and his bluster hanging over me. I'm not going to beg or grovel. I'm frankly just too tired."

"I can see that. Why don't you sleep and take care of Anne for the rest of today and come up to the manor tomorrow? I'll see that some food is sent to you."

Robert watched him ride off, then returned to the cottage. After trudging up the stairs, he climbed in bed next to Anne and soon fell fast asleep.

Hours later, they both awoke and looked at each other. Within moments, they were tangled in each other's arms, reaching, touching, needing. As they sought one another with their bodies, all thoughts of what they had just been through were put aside. Only later did the realization of what they had almost lost overpower them, and they lay tangled together, tears of relief, fear, and joy mingled between them. At last, they felt satisfied enough to leave bed and search for food. True to Cavell's word, just inside the cottage door was a basket heaped with food: cold chicken, an earthen pot full of soup, fresh bread and cheese, and a jug of good wine. Anne warmed the soup and piled plates with food, which they carried back upstairs to bed.

They filled themselves, then burrowed under the blankets and sipped the wine. Neither said anything for quite a while, both just enjoying the quiet safety. Anne lay with her head on Robert's chest, one finger tracing lines up and down his bare arm. "What's next for us?" she asked quietly.

"I don't know. While you were asleep, I spoke to Cavell. He said to come up to the manor in the morning. Do you think it's morning yet?"

"I have no idea. I don't think so. Seems dark out. I think we slept through most of the day and part of the night. What do you think Sir John will say?"

"I told Cavell the truth. I don't care what Sir John says. If we stay, we stay. If he asks me to leave, we'll leave. Suddenly, I don't care that much where I work as long as I'm with you and we're both safe."

"Hmm, me too," she replied, reaching up to kiss him.

Several hours later, dressed in fresh clothes, another meal's worth of food eaten, Robert walked slowly up to Corsley Manor, remembering his first trip up Deep Lane. How much had happened in the six or seven months since that first trip? Despite being midmorning, the sun seemed to struggle to rise in the sky, and the cold air rushed down the lane. Even the air seemed to listen to Sir John's urgency for haste.

News of the events at Lacock had already traveled south, and Robert could feel eyes watching him as he announced his arrival to Sir John's page. He was shown immediately into Sir John's chamber, where Sir John sat behind his desk, as usual, surrounded by stacks of ledgers and scrolls. Richard Cavell was present, and to Robert's surprise, Alan Maynard was also there, looking clean and sober. What could his presence possibly mean?

"Hello, Smythson, recovered?" asked Sir John, his eyes giving Robert an appraising look.

"Sufficiently, thank you. Good morning, Cavell, Maynard." He replied nodding to each man. "I understand you wanted to see me, Sir John?"

"Yes. We're going to implement a few changes here in the coming weeks. Maynard here is going to rejoin the workforce."

"Does this mean you will no longer be requiring my services? Have you brought me up here to fire me?" Robert decided the direct approach was the best one. He was too tired to play games. He wasn't afraid of Sir John's response, just resigned to it and wanted to get it over with.

"No." Sir John leaned back in his chair, surveying Robert. He seemed to reach a decision. "I suppose a few words ought to be said. Last time you were here, I know I told you that if you went after your wife or Kington that you would be finished here." Sir John paused, as if preparing himself for the next words. "I owe you an apology. It appears that your knowledge of the situation proved greater than mine, and you were indeed right that my neighbor meant harm to your wife. In light of recent events, we will put aside my previous words and ask you to remain on as master mason of Longleat."

Robert gasped, and his knees threatened to buckle. He glanced quickly from one man to the other. Had he heard correctly? Had Sir John just officially named him master mason of Longleat? Had he actually used the title? Judging by the shocked look on Maynard's face and the big grin on Cavell's, it seemed he had. Stunned and elated all at once, Robert realized that Sir John was expecting an answer. He composed himself, attempting a neutral countenance.

"Yes, sir. That seems reasonable. I agree." He understood that this was the closest he would get to a thank you or an apology from Sir John, but he also understood the price it had cost Sir John to go that far. "If I may ask, what will Maynard's role be?"

"Cavell thinks it best if we let Maynard run his own team, just a few men, and work on the interior details while you and the rest of the masons handle the exterior and major pieces. You will retain oversight of the whole project, and Maynard will report to you. I expect the two of you to work out any differences and work together quickly and efficiently. We've had enough turmoil at Longleat this year. Cavell, pour the wine and let's have a toast to the success of Longleat."

"To Longleat," they all echoed and drank. As the oaky claret slid down his throat, Robert reflected on all that had happened to make this moment. Humphrey Lovell's trust in him, his tolerance of Sir John's demands, and his commitment to finding the truth of Mary Kington's death, despite the personal costs. Now he was officially master mason of Longleat with his bride safe at home.

"Now that that's settled," Sir John continued, "I am making some changes to the design of the building, specifically to the banqueting houses on the roof. They will be an octagon shape. I've been thinking that, symbolically, the octagon is the correct shape to represent the eternal aspect of the rooftop of Longleat."

Robert smiled, remembering how Hills had suggested that Robert needed to get Sir John to think the change in shape was his own idea. Under different circumstances, he might have protested the commandeering of his idea, but he was too content to argue. There was only one remaining mystery surrounding Longleat: the fire.

"On another topic," Robert continued, trying his luck. "We know who killed poor Mary Kington, but we are no closer to solving the mystery of the fire."

Robert watched as Sir John's eyes flickered momentarily to Maynard, who was suddenly deeply interested in the plans unrolled on the table. Sir John then fixed his steady gaze back on Robert, appraising and challenging him. "We may never know. Are you going to be able to live with that?"

Robert paused, looking around the room at the group of men assembled there and the plans for the building, and came to a decision. "I think I will have to be."

"Good. Now let's get that building back on schedule. Make haste."

Robert and Maynard left Sir John's business chamber together, walking outside into the courtyard of Corsley Manor. "I think we have a bit of unfinished business we should discuss," Robert said quietly to Maynard.

"Perhaps."

"You knew her body was there, didn't you? That's why that section of wall had never been cleared." Maynard did not deny it. "That's also why you were reluctant to return to Longleat, although you couldn't bring yourself to leave either."

"It felt like a piece of unfinished business. But you have finished it for me."

"I have you to thank for some of the hints along the way, don't I?"

"Once I heard you were going to pull down the north range, I knew you'd discover her body. I may have given you a nudge or two, but you figured it out."

"What I don't quite understand is why you didn't report what you knew. Why did you not uncover the body yourself or tell Sir John what Kington had done? Why keep it a secret, unless . . ."

"Unless what?" Maynard watched Robert closely with an appraising look.

"Unless Kington also had something on you." Robert walked a few paces away while all the pieces fell into place. Turning back to Maynard, he continued, "Kington had some kind of secret about you, and he was willing to keep silent as long as you did the same. Am I right?"

"Perhaps," Maynard's reply was cautious, ambiguous.

"My guess is that it has something to do with the fire." Robert watched the other mason closely, trying to read an admission.

"Now, Smythson, did I not just hear you tell Sir John that you were willing to let the subject of the fire go? You wouldn't want to jeopardize your position here by digging around for more secrets after promising to let it go."

Robert stared at Maynard much like he had just stared at Sir John a few moments ago, weighing his choices. Continue to push for information that everyone seemed to want to remain buried, or let it go and continue as master mason of Longleat. Robert was not one to allow truths to go undiscovered, but there was more at stake here than his own happiness. There was Anne, his entire team, and there was Longleat. For the sake of the building that was to come, could he keep the truth of the fire from finding the air it needed to breathe? Could he live with himself if he did not pursue it? He had given his word to Sir John that he would stop asking questions, and yet within a few minutes he had discovered another piece of the mystery.

"There's one more thing, Maynard. Your wife. You know she tried to kill me by setting fire to my lodge." He paused, but Maynard didn't react. "You have to control her."

"To be fair, she just wanted you to stop asking questions. She won't be a problem, I promise."

Robert sighed. He remembered the last two days and what he had almost lost. He had uncovered the secret of what had happened to Mary Kington at the cost of almost losing Anne. Did he want to take such risks again? The fire and its mystery were in the past. That building was gone, never to return. In its place was the beginning of something wonderful, something that he was to play a major part in bringing into being. That would be enough.

"You win," he said to Maynard. "Your secrets, whatever they are, will remain your own. I will keep my word and not inquire about the fire or the other events of that night. We will let the secrets remain buried and hidden under the foundation of the new Longleat."

"Agreed. Now, do you not have a wife to go home to? I bid you adieu."

Robert watched as Maynard walked away. Maynard had recovered from his drunken stupor awfully quickly and somehow managed to patch things up with Sir John while Robert was chasing Kington and Anne. He shrugged. Everything he knew about Maynard pointed to someone who would always find a way to turn every situation into an advantage for himself. At this point, Robert was too overwhelmed with relief and happiness to care.

Robert went home so lost in thoughts of what had just happened that he didn't even notice the turn for Cley Hill Farm. One mystery solved; another would remain hidden. So be it. The future was ahead, just down Deep Lane and through Corsley Heath. At Longleat.

Running the last part of the way home, he almost felt like a child again. Anne was in the kitchen, kneading bread dough. He picked her up and spun her around in the air, knocking rye flour over and spilling it, laughing at the mess he made. He didn't care at all.

"We're staying. Maynard's coming back. He will be hell to live with, but I don't care. Sir John has officially and publicly named me master mason. I am master mason of Longleat, and I have the best wife in all the world."

Anne laughed, catching his enthusiasm. "Even if I am covered in flour?"

"Yes, flour and all. Now all we need is to work with Cavell to find us a proper house and we'll be all set. I can't wait to get started."

The end.

Author's Notes

This book has been a labor of love for me for many years, stemming from my love of British country homes. As I learned more about the origins of these homes, one name continued to crop up: Robert Smythson. In reading more about him, I was struck by the diverse challenges he faced in his choice of employers: the demanding, miserly Sir John Thynne, the paranoid Sir Francis Willoughby, and the fascinating and powerful Bess of Hardwick. Any man who could navigate these personalities and build some of the most beautiful houses of the Elizabethan period, deserved to have his story told. After many iterations, you hold the beginnings of Robert's story.

While the mystery element of the story is invented, the events surrounding the building of Longleat hold true to what is known. The majority of the male characters are real people, their names pulled from payment records and other documents. The women, alas, are fictional as their details are lost to history. For example, history records that Robert was married, but no details remain about his wife, not even her name. Anne Palmer is an invention of my imagination, although there was a Jocelyn Palmer who was martyred after serving in the Knollys household. I simply made him Anne's uncle.

I owe a huge debt of gratitude to Mark Girouard who clearly loved English country homes even more than I do. His many books, especially *Robert Smythson and the Elizabethan Country House*, deepened my knowledge of the period and the man. Other authors, including Malcolm Airs, Gervase Jackson-Stops, David Burnett, and David N. Durant, also contributed to my knowledge of Elizabethan architecture. And I must also thank Sir John Thynne, for leaving behind such a robust record of the building of Longleat.

This book would not exist without many people encouraging me not to give up. To the late Anna Castle, my many thanks for your no-nonsense advice that gave the book structure and taught me to always enjoy the journey. I wish you were here to read the final version. Many other talented writer offered critiques, advice, and encouragement, including Kate Robertson, Alyssa Colton, Anna Karras, Christine Trent, M.K. Tilghman, and Jennifer Sherman Roberts. Appreciation for my cover designer, Dee Dee Book Covers, for patience throughout the process. Deep gratitude to my editor, Jenny Quinlan of Historical Editorial, for guiding the journey and keeping my story and my commas straight.

And finally, deep love and appreciation for my friends and family. For Charlotte, who inspired Charlotte Crispin, for many years of friendship and for always believing in me, even when I didn't. May you all have a Charlotte in your life. For my beloved Santiago, who always supports me, encourages me, and listens to my victories and defeats. And for my kids, John Henry and Rebecca, who indulged their mother's traipsing them across England, and who cheered with enthusiasm as I touched the stone on Robert's buildings for the first time. I couldn't have done this without your love and support. Thank you.

About the Author

Katherine J. Scott is a writer and librarian living in Austin, Texas. Born in the US to English parents, she grew up with a blend of both cultures. Over the years, she developed a deep love for English country houses and the people who built them. Her debut novel, *From the Ground Up*, is the first installment of a mystery series featuring stonemason Robert Smythson and the houses he built in Elizabethan England.

Katherine holds two master's degrees: an MS in Biology and an MLIS. She has more than twenty years' experience in library and information settings including school, public, and medical libraries. Katherine spent twelve years doing information management in the field of space life sciences for NASA. She is the author and editor of various publications including bibliographies, newsletters, websites, and research and position papers.

She is an active member of the Writers League of Texas and the Historical Novel Society, for which she served as the HNSNA Conference Bookstore and Readers Festival Coordinator for both the 2023 and 2025 conferences. Katherine loves reading, talking about books, and helping kids find just the right book. Her favorite part of writing historical fiction is the deep dive into research and travelling to the places her characters walked. She lives with her husband and two rambunctious cats, while also trying to launch her two young adult kids into the world.

Coming Soon

Robert and Anne's story continues in ***Lying on Rocky Ground***, coming summer 2025.

The Smythsons have relocated to a nearby village, and Sir John Thynne has purchased another quarry. While Robert conducts the final purchase agreement at the new quarry, Anne befriends a neighbor with a mysterious past. When one of Robert's team of stonemasons is accused of murder, Robert must untangle a web of lies to discover the truth.

Printed in Dunstable, United Kingdom

64105006R00184